Finding treasure is easy. Keeping it, a deadly art.

FINDERS KEEPERS

Published by

Paperback ISBN: 978-1-0685199-0-1
eBook ISBN: 978-1-0685199-1-8

Finding treasure is easy. Keeping it, a deadly art.

FINDERS KEEPERS

SEAN KINGSLEY

A *DEEPSCAPE FILES* ADVENTURE

For Felix Sky
One time… then suddenly…

1

Straits of Florida, 5th September 1622

The gold bars crashed into the waves, pirouetting in the foam, and were gone. The hurricane continued its chaotic revelry, unsatisfied by the lavish offerings. The ravenous blue god astride ferocious white horses locked his jaw on easy prey.

Midway between Havana and the southern spear tip of Florida, the ship pitched helplessly. Sailors by the thousands had gambled with nature on this poker table of an ocean and lost. The snapped backs of wooden merchantmen, spilled cargoes and shattered dreams carpeted the keys. The Straits of Florida respect no man.

The portents had been dreadful from the start. In the backwaters of Rio de la Hacha, along Colombia's northern shores, the tapestry of the Souls of Purgatory, painted in Toledo and shipped from Seville to the kingdom of New Spain, reached journey's end. The retirement gift commissioned for the fort's governor ended in humiliation. Heavy-handed dockers, hasty to sign off duty and have some fun, by mistake ripped the canvas in half. The painting was furtively dumped overboard in the night's pitch darkness to hide their shame. As ill luck would have it, the tapestry washed up in front of the governor's villa the next morning. The *gato de nueve colas*, cat o' nine tails, was busy that day.

Three weeks later, at the gateway to the long haul home from the Caribbean, Havana was supposed to welcome the weary sailors with open arms, rum and good times. The garrison's cannon fire celebrating the merchantman's safe return from beyond the civilised world struck the jib clean off. The spar slammed into the ship's master, saluting resplendently on deck with drawn sword, shattering his leg. If only Spain could replicate this one-in-a-million shot in battle.

Just a day out of Havana, finally homeward bound to Seville, a savage hurricane swept in from nowhere, ensnaring its prey in mountainous waves. A final dance of death was playing out to an inescapable fate.

The hold was under three feet of water. Dozens of rats that plagued the 1622 Americas' fleet were desperately treading water. Bloated from a frenzy of feasting on cooped chickens, cheese and hard tack, the greedy red-eyed vermin sank into the dirty bilges.

Below deck, the treasure groaned, thrown from side to side with the rolling seas. Wooden chests splintered into matchsticks. The thin gold bars cast by Native American and African slaves worked to the bone in the Spanish mines of Nuevo Reino de Granada – colonial Colombia – clattered up and down the keelson. Silver pieces of eight struck in Mexico rolled around the bulkheads, bewitching the crew with their tinkling melody. Only the pearls wrapped in pigskin bags, hidden inside Venezuelan tobacco leaves, stayed pinned down under a pile of copper bars.

The entombed ship was a force of nature, no longer steering under the flag of Spain but at the gods will after the shattered mast whistled overboard. The galleon dragged the split rudder through the waves like a stubborn puppy. The crew, cooks and merchants cowering in the stern cabin were united in tragedy. The hurricane had no respect for prince or pauper. A tsunami of a wave smashed the galley door open and for Captain Juan Limbre it was time to meet his maker. Should he stick or twist? Stay put or risk the unknown? In a split second, Limbre chose to go out fighting, as he had always done in life.

The dream was dead. Time to let go. The rest of the fleet was long gone, turned back to Havana, stranded on the low-lying sandbanks of the Florida Keys or spiked on the sharp rocks ringing Tortugas Island. For good reason, this marine graveyard was known to sailors as the Bank of Madrid – only more treasure lay in its sunken vaults than was locked up in King Philip IV's war-drained coffers. The ship was alone in the dark abyss. No help would come.

In a rush of adrenalin, Limbre threw a salt-stained leather saddle bag over his shoulder and forced his way through the galley cabin's violently rocking wooden walls. "God save your souls," he roared at the crew, ripping a gold medallion of Stella Maris, the guiding star of the sea, off his neck and throwing it into the back of the cabin. By chance, it landed in a clay cooking pot stacked in the corner of the galley and sank into the turtle meat stew, the last supper slopping onto the pine-planked floor.

Now or never, Limbre lurched onto the deck and, with several harsh blows, kicked a wooden chest locked with an iron padlock the size of a man's fist into the steaming sea. Only one thing more precious than his life's belongings was left. The woman with eyes ablaze as the full moon smiled and grasped Limbre's arm. They had come this far after fate brought them together under the azure skies of Nueva Cadiz on the Pearl Coast. The future had seemed so perfect, so peaceful there. If she could not live out her days as a chief's daughter at home in Venezuela or make it to aristocratic Seville as Limbre's wife, she must share his fate. Savarna pulled her greenstone necklace over her head and, following her husband's lead, slung it through the cabin door slapping wildly in the whistling wind on the one remaining hinge. Her fate was fused with Limbre now and forever.

The unlikeliest of lovers smiled at the furious blue god and threw themselves into the mercy of the ocean.

Far in the distance, a lone man peered through the sea mist from shore at the silhouette of madness born to greed. The naked American Indian threw back his head and howled.

2

Route 1, South Florida, the Present Day

At the time it seemed a swell idea. The air was cooling and the first chill of autumn drawing in. The never-ending party that started in New York had drifted south to Miami on the Truthmobile. Seven crazy days shuttling between bars, bottomless rum, card games in Coconut Grove, tanning in South Beach and the university's labs had brought unimagined highs.

They thought the summer would last forever. They thought they were immortal. Fate would soon lay bare that what this carload of kids really knew about each other was skin deep. They barely knew themselves. The next few months would change the friends lives forever, forcing them to take a hard look at who they were, their very being.

Journey's end for Isak Fitzgrove was Key West where the New World plunges into the Caribbean. He'd started his journey relaxing in late-night New York, catching up with old college chums, flattering themselves that their Oxford degrees could pivot the unfairly stacked world balance in their favour. Intellectual skirmishes had played out, ruffled egos smoothed over and unequal pay packets levelled by buckets of alcohol.

With his doctorate in marine biology tucked into his back pocket and a fresh law conversion degree sticking out of his breast pocket (study once for love and once for money his grandfather had told him), aged twenty-nine the world lay at Zak's feet. The cover story of *New Scientist* six years earlier, and his first book done and dusted by the quarter-century mark, everyone was enamoured by this neatly turned out, ever so polite English gent.

To the gods peering down from on high, Zak was on the fast track to academic rock stardom. The problem was nobody had told him. The scholar's internal compass was a mass of insecurities. Studying had broken his bank balance and his endless travels in search of scientific truths crushed a string of blossoming relationships and, with it, his fragile self-esteem. Girls don't wait forever. Beneath a bold and bright smile, only Zak knew the truth. His life was on hold, his mind a pit of despair. On the inside, he felt like a loser. A doctor would have diagnosed depression. Zak was far too stiff upper-lipped to moan about emotions. Best bury them deep inside.

"Put your foot down, man, or you'll never see your fricking turtles." Mitch Hunter was drunk. Or rather, he was still steaming. He had hit the sauce in New York in early July and continued relentlessly in a private duel with his liver. The off-season for surfing's minor royalty was the time to let your hair down. Mitch had bought two new surfboards, a Thunderbolt and a Peacemaker, waxed them to perfection and headed out to do some waxing of his own.

In the early hours of a heavy New York Saturday night and Sunday morning, Zak and Mitch ran into each other in the Nomad Bar on 28th Street. The American's three-point shot with a green olive missed its intended beer glass and almost took out Zak's eye. God didn't intend vegetables to go into alcohol, Mitch had sworn as an obvious explanation. Over a make-up beer or five, the unlikely lads from different sides of the tracks found a shared passion for the ocean and Key West especially.

Mitch was slowly partying his way down the East Coast to the season's opening event off Hurricane Hole Marina in Key West. He'd won it two years in a row. Zak had read about a new fleet of monstrous fishing trawlers called canyon busters ripping up the ocean floor and bulldozing coral reefs, more Frankenstein than fishing boat. With the promise of a scoop in *The Times*, he was on the hunt for proof of their destructive paths. If these monsters could be stopped in their tracks at Key West, ground zero, just maybe the sea's delicate ecosystems had a chance. Zak and Mitch pledged to make the trip south together in the surfer's Volkswagen camper van.

"Turtles are just one part of the nightmare," Zak cursed, decelerating for the hundredth time along Route 1, halfway between Miami and Key West. "The poor beasts in these waters never got over Spanish colonialists' love of turtle stew. These bloody canyon busters are blitzing the reefs, strangling more turtles, but also dolphins, in nylon nets and ripping entire fish stocks out of the food chain. No more fish and chips. And you and your kids can forget about sushi too." Mitch grimaced at the thought of children. "It's a marine Armageddon down there that's spiking the fishing industry for generations to come and killing off stunning marine ecosystems. End of the line. Well, not on my watch."

Zak was grumpy and on edge. The realisation had dawned that Mitch's friendship came at a cost. One: Zak drives, Mitch gets tanked. Two: Zak plays nice with Alona, while Mitch flirts with Nic in the back seat. The scales were falling from the scholar's eyes faster than the bucketing rain. Zak was nobody's wingman. Hurricane season had come early, and the dreamland of Miami's beaches was turning into a swamp. The potholed road was hard to see through the downpour and blistered windscreen wipers rarely needed on the East Coast. The Truthmobile was aquaplaning towards world's end.

Alona Hancock, thin as a rake, was easily mistaken for a kid in desperate need of a juicy steak. Under her baggy white hoodie, though, emblazoned on the front 'Always In The Moment', she hid a triathlete's physique. Not an ounce of fat. For the last two years, she'd been Mitch's on-off lover.

They'd met jetlagged and freezing in the seventeenth-century Cove House Inn on Dorset's Chesil Beach two years ago after killer swells delayed the Confederation of World Surfing series meeting in England. The pair were both San Francisco State University dropouts, bored of lectures that had nothing to do with real life and had ridden the waves to the same crest of the sport. They saw equal star power in each other.

Neither was clueless. Unlike Zak, they just weren't into deep discussions about the state of the planet. Mitch's childhood of hard knocks had taught them life should be a smorgasbord of pleasure. Soak up the good times while you can. Nobody gives you shit in life, Mitch Hunter Senior used to holler at his son. Junior had twisted the mantra to himself: don't take shit from no-one.

To the romantic backdrop of Chesil Beach, shagging like rabbits for two days while the British weather did what the British weather always does, a knackered Mitch and Alona still had enough reserves of energy to win their events. They returned in triumph to Uncle Sam the sport's golden couple. Two years on, and a few losses and lost sponsorship deals later, the stardust was running thin. The relationship was cracking at the seams as the pair headed for the season opener at Key West, financially, reputationally and romantically a must-win competition.

Zak could always fall back on the law if all else failed and rely on his big brain. Surfing was the be-all and end-all obsession for Alona and Mitch. Without it they would be washed-up has-beens living in a caravan, living off cigarettes and McMeals. Do or die stress had left the pair raw and on edge, bickering day after day.

Asleep in the front of the camper van, her mouth gaping open and Ray-Ban's slipping down her right cheek, Alona hadn't noticed Mitch's hand massaging Nicola's left shoulder in the back seat. She wouldn't have been surprised, though. His behaviour was genetic. Mitch Snr, a mean son of a bitch of a former Marine Corps officer, never did anything heroic and took out his personal disappointment by clipping Junior round the ear whenever it suited, just like he'd reduced many a would-be marine to a nervous wreck. Today you'd call it abuse. Back then it was character building. Joline Hunter was little help to her son, scurrying into the kitchen with a 'Yes Dear' as soon as the red mist rose. Who could blame her?

From day one, Alona realised that taming her man was always going to be an uphill battle – maybe even mission impossible. Deep down he was worth it. Mitch may have been too emotionally scarred to make the link, but she'd seen enough of the mating game to know they were soul mates. Alona would give it more time. She had enough emotional wisdom for two, thanks to the divine faith her pastor father and good lady bred into her growing up in small-town Virginia.

The Hancocks had moved north to Ocean City when their daughter was fourteen to save souls. Life in rural Virginia was too easy, preaching to the converted. New Jersey was a challenge to spread the word of God. The family liked to think they had historic roots in American society. Great-uncle Noel even claimed their descendants were among the earliest overseas settlers to reach Jamestown in 1607, England's first village in the Americas. His niece reckoned it was bull crap.

Alona's rebellion from god and family came as a blindsiding shock. Exactly what had her mild-mannered parents done to send her haywire? East Coast girls like her from Ocean City, a quiet town of eleven thousand souls, towed the family line. And sure as eggs were eggs, this was a family town. Grace Kelly spent her summers there, and James Stewart kept a holiday home by the shore in smallsville to stay grounded. A swell day out for mothers and daughters was gawping at the collection of 1880s bridal gowns on show in the Sea Isle City Historical Museum. Father and son stopped outside, skimming pebbles off the North Atlantic waves.

Ocean City may have been a perfect coastal family town, but to its eternal regret nature blessed it with killer waves. Unlike in West Coast California, the rise of surfing out East was a slow burn. Body surfing was a small-time caper from 1906. Only in the 1920s did local townsman George Bert Cropper build the first surfboard. Into the late 1950s, just a small hardcore of crazies hit the waves. It really wasn't the respectable thing to do. Ocean City closed its shutters and pretended not to look.

All that changed when The Beach Boys' Surfin' USA cruised to the top of the Billboard chart in the summer of 1963. The next year, Ocean City's first surf shop, Eastern Surfer, opened its doors in the basement of the Sandy Hill Motel on 18th Street. Then, in

1964 *The Endless Summer* filmed two California dudes chasing waves from Australia to Hawaii and South Africa. Surfing was red hot.

Ocean City was hooked. The long-haired peaceniks who poured into the family town weren't to everyone's liking, including Pastor Hancock's. The locals didn't like hippies or parasites who didn't contribute to society. Much to her father's sorrow, Alona embraced the call of the sea and the unfettered beach life. It was a minor rebellion. The good pastor knew enough about teenagers not to push back and risk losing his beloved daughter. But he knew what he knew.

When Alona fell for the spiky-haired bad boy surf dude Mitch Hunter at San Francisco State University, where she'd earned a scholarship, the god fearer told his wife the union would end in tears. The self-fulfilling prophecy came to pass when the pair dropped out of school and travelled the world to pit their skills in international surfdom. Only it was Pastor Hunter and his wife who were crying.

Of all the friends now drifting down America's East Coast, Alona's head was screwed on the tightest. Down the years, God had flown from her wings for no good reason. She didn't hate religion, it just didn't float her boat. The stable family backbone travelled with her, however, and for that she'd always cherish her parents.

In typical English understatement, Nicola pretended not to notice Mitch Hunter's pathetic hungover attention in the back seat of the Truthmobile. Quite frankly, she was too tired to care. Polite to a fault, she still had no qualms about kicking the lad in the nuts if he crossed the line. The persuasive Israel Defence Force art of Krav Maga Nicola picked up in classes shared with best friend Lucy Freckles meant she was pretty tasty at fighting her corner should life ever turn sour. So far, it hadn't. Right now, all she wanted was to reach Key West, cheer up her spirits with a relaxing cup of tea, hit a soft duck-feathered pillow and tune out.

Somewhere in the distant past, Nicola Medici's ancestors, the papal succession of the Catholic Church that bankrolled

Europe, had ruled Italy. The House of Medici was stacked with an inescapable reputation. On the back of its name, Nicola coasted through life with silver spoons inserted into her perfect orifices. Privilege, her circle had sadly noticed, didn't bring fulfilment or happiness to the young Medici. Nobody could quite figure out why. The curse of the Medici was a heavy cross to bear.

Four years had sped by since she graduated with first-class honours in European languages from King's College London. The exams had been easy: French, German, Spanish and Portuguese all came naturally to a mind fed by a team of foreign nurses, butlers and chauffeurs, topped up by long summers in the family estates across Europe listening to foreign and soon familiar tongues.

Daddy sat in the House of Lords, orchestrating the Conservative's economic policy, advising a succession of rising and fallen Secretaries of State, and greatly swelling his wallet. Nicola was under no pressure to bring home the bacon. Quite the opposite. Her four-bedroom house in London's celebrity-lined Little Venice had been bought with her parent's cash. Her trust fund was more than generous.

All daddy dearest wanted was her happiness, wherever it took her. Mummy dearest was on the lookout for grandchildren and fast. How can I bring precious life into a world that is so messed up, Nic obsessed endlessly. She expected she must be a great disappointment to her parents. Being an only child felt like a double curse on top of the family name. Why couldn't someone else shoulder the weight of lineage?

After years of wearing out wardrobes of Manolo Blahniks on the social treadmill, Nicola was sick of playing the game, swanning around country houses and greeting grinning politicians dreaming of getting into her Bond Street lingerie. She'd guest-edited *Grove Magazine* and filled its pages with celebrity gossip, taken an internship at Sotheby's wine department, but failed to turn up for the second week.

Who was Nicola Medici continued to puzzle this English beauty. What was the point of her life? She had never rebelled. As a teenager she'd never pierced a crusty ring stud through her nose, dyed her hair blue or provoked her parents' anger by sleeping with a bit of rough and bringing him home for Sunday lunch. Good lord, no. Maybe Nicola was just a very late developer. Her not-insignificant intake of top-drawer herbal exotica didn't bring answers, but sure eased the pain in short bursts.

Behind leaden skies above her canal-side windows, yet another summer failed to live up to its promise. Nicola's mood had sunk in tune with the planet's spiralling chaos. The House of Commons seemed hell-bent on self-harming the United Kingdom to end its long friendship with Europe. Rain forests were burning across Brazil and Australia like biblical plagues and war waged across the Near East. Greenland's ice caps were melting fast. The sweet polar bears marooned on breakaway mini-islets, innocent casualties of man's folly, shattered her heart.

America was insanely prodding China into a suicidal trade war. The land of the dragon was in lockdown to contain a killer pandemic spread by bats. Russia's 'Emperor' Putin, Syria, Iran and Beijing were cosying up far too snugly in the Persian Gulf. The fear of whether democracy was dead and what evil lurked around the corner kept Nicola awake night after night.

The caged panther was left drained with no control over the mad political dervishes whirling around her. There was only one thing for it: hit the road and decamp to Uncle Lesley's beachfront condominium in Miami. The next day she was on a plane. Nicola kept her long limbs to herself, rising at midday, breakfasting on fresh fruit and relaxing her body and mind with Ashtanga yoga.

She chilled out the rest of the time, tanning topless on the waterside decking, chilling to classical music on her iPhone. Unaware of the curtain-twitching Floridian neighbours peeking at her – both straight and gay – Nicola tried her best not to think. Karma would rock up if she could just relax and switch off. August failed to heal her anguish.

Finding a dog-eared copy of *Florida Wired* stuffed down the back of Uncle Les's sofa, Nicola's body strangely tingled when she spotted an entry about the Boca Chica nudist beach just outside Key West. Clear blue water, white sands and sun-kissed bodily perfection sounded exactly like the tonic she craved. Surely it would de-clutter her twisted soul. The beach's location in the shadow of a US naval base, naughty and decidedly not nice, added to the thrill. Yes, she would consciously flee her comfort, shed her clothes in Key West and find a new purpose and fresh identity.

Pushing Mitch's hand away, Nicola raised her long neck towards the front seat. "Hey Zak, do we need to pull over? Please don't try the impossible, ok. If we're a few hours behind schedule, I'm sure Key West will wait for us."

Zak melted. Ever since Mitch and he spotted the siren eating salmon sashimi and Japanese salad doused with ginger dressing contentedly alone in Miami's Coconut Grove, reading John Kennedy Toole's *A Confederacy of Dunces*, his heart had been turning somersaults. In time-honoured surfer tradition, Mitch had marched straight over and asked what she was up to that night. It was mostly bravado, the booze talking – exactly the gung-ho spirit his father expected.

Mitch was an enigma, even to himself. Alona knew from experience it would have taken a crate of liquor and a pile of bad news for Mitch to stoop low enough to cheat on her. And if he did, it would be game over and sore balls. Slowly and by stealth, she was trying to help him see what it meant to be a man in the twenty-first century. Letting out your emotions didn't make you a loser. Hell, she'd even got him doing some cooking and ironing. Just maybe he wasn't a lost cause.

Interrupted from her reading in Coconut Grove, Nicola had cocked her graceful head to one side in amusement and answered Mitch's arrogance with silence and a raised eyebrow. Zak had peered shyly below his fringe from time to time, pretending to be absorbed chewing morsels of succulent Cuban fusion fare. Idiot boy. This was no time to stare at your feet. Carpe the bloody diem.

For once, Zak judged the situation spot on. At the end of her meal, he'd been beckoned over after sending Nicola the compliments of an English Rose cocktail – gin, strawberries, fresh lemon juice, homemade rhubarb and bitters. Mitch was baffled by his new pal's social graces, listening to Zak playing the game of letting his credentials spill out slowly over refined conversation. Nicola was clearly well-heeled but gave little away. Was he too coarse, too common to pique her interest, Zak fretted.

Over more cocktails in Uncle Les's pool and jacuzzi, the plan was hatched. Mitch and Zak would escort the as yet unnamed Miss Medici to Key West, so they understood for sightseeing. If only they knew her real idea, their own plans would have gone out the window. Everyone who met Nicola fell under her spell, much to her annoyance. Why doesn't anyone take the time to get to know the real me, she raged. I'm not a box of bloody Leonidas chocolates.

"Just six miles to go, Nic," Zak promised. "If we can keep our heads above water, we'll be sipping cool beer in twenty minutes."

"Bugger the beer. Give me some Earl Grey," Nicola replied. "After last night's open bar, I feel like death. An early night, bath, bed and book for me."

Silence engulfed the Truthmobile, so christened by Mitch one very late Saturday night when the friends realized each was on the hunt for their own personal answers. Giggling like kids, Mitch and Alona stencilled 'Truthmobile World Tour' onto the side of their van. The rain lashed the blue Volkswagen. Only the scraping of the worn-out windscreen wipers cut the air.

Out of the window the mangroves dripped with water as they always had. The timeless Keys rose silently out of the calm water like the ageless home of forgotten prehistoric monsters. The sheer scale of the open spaces humbled the travellers. To the south, America ended and echoes of the exotic Caribbean began.

Rolling down the end of Route 1, Zak flipped on the radio. Gone was the repetitive diet of endless country music and hip-hop, replaced by the crackling drumbeat of distant Havana, a haunting cry of enslavement and freedom. Key West not only lay at the end of the line, it looked and sounded like a completely different world.

The innocents aboard this ship of fools glowed excitedly at their hopes and dreams. Answers and truths surely lay just around the bend.

3

Key West, Southern Florida

"Pare el coche, para el coche!"

Feet up in the front seat of the van, Alona banged her head on the roof, rudely awoken by the booming voice of a demented Spaniard pounding the back of her seat with his fists.

"What the fuck, Rodi, chill your boots, hombre," she snapped.

Little chance of that. Rodriguez Saumerez, the fifth member of the soul-searching motley crew heading south, and to any eye the odd one out, was all Iberian hothead who didn't chill at the best of times. And especially not now. He'd just spotted his long-awaited El Dorado and was screaming at Zak, "Stop the van, stop the van. I have to get out – now!"

The Volkswagen gently braked to the curb, cascading rainwater over a cream picket wooden fence. Whitehead Street in the heart of Key West was deserted. Usually lined three deep with partygoers drawn from the rainbow of life – every summer day is Mardi Gras in Key West – the town had battened down its hatches to ride out the latest storm.

Rodi had begged and borrowed his way across the Atlantic Ocean, only to end up sleeping rough on a downtown Miami seafront lawn. Just the smell of the Caribbean and the promise of Key West kept him going. Better than wasting day upon day down and out in his father's flat in Cadiz. Spain was broke, with crippling debt and fourteen per cent unemployment. No jobs, no future, no anything.

The twenty-four-year-old was a computer whizz kid with an

MA in programming from the University of Huelva. Just what the world needed, another bloody web designer, he cursed every morning. In between selling hotdogs (to his eternal shame) on the seafront where Christopher Columbus set off from Spain for the New World, the broken Apple Macs he'd bought for a song, re-wired at night and flogged in his spare time had bought him a ship's passage to Fort Lauderdale. From there, he'd hitch-hiked down to Miami.

Zak had befriended the Spaniard as he stretched after an early morning jog in Bayside Park. He had been sweating buckets against the elegant backdrop of porcelain-perfect, Botoxed yummy mummies and frozen-faced young men overtaking him with effortless grace. In the end Zak had quit busting a gut keeping up and was bent double at the park gate gulping down salty air. There, cross-legged and motionless, deep in trance-like concentration on a park bench, a half-eaten cheese sandwich by his blackened bare feet, Rodi looked lost in time.

The pair hailed one another as fellow vampire-white Europeans with no perma-tans and grabbed coffee in the Bookstore in the Grove, where Zak had his ear bent listening to a forty-five-minute one-way lecture about the genius of Ernest Hemingway. The lad knew his beans, even if his energy verged on the aggressive. Rodi's high energy made Zak's passion for the sea look like the whispers of a wallflower. The Spaniard was on a pilgrimage to the source of his lifeblood's inspiration, the old man and the sea's house in Key West.

The last in a long list of Saumerez obsessions, this quest was different. It was intimate. Eighteen months ago, Rodi's dear mother, Benita, got taken by leukaemia, leaving her only son broken and emotionally frozen. In the first few weeks of mourning, his mind wandered back to happy times he hadn't thought about in decades. When he was a wild street urchin at twelve years old, his blessed mother bribed him with chocolate and cash if he'd sit still for half an hour a day to read a book, any book.

Even then he couldn't relate to modern writing. Not until his mother left a first-edition battered copy of Ernest Hemingway's *The Old Man and the Sea* on his pillow did an awakening dawn. Benita had been overjoyed little Rodi adored the book as much as her. A wormhole into her son's affection was a rare gift. They'd even chatted about taking a trip to Hemingway's old home in Florida, he remembered. For reasons he couldn't exactly put his finger on, one of the few things that soothed his demons after she left him was the thought of taking that trip to Key West. It would be a homage to his late mother. If he could just lay some flowers on Hemingway's lawn, the swirling confusion in his head would fly away, surely.

When Zak heard about Rodi's sadness, he knew there was nothing for it but to invite the intense melancholic, born with an old soul, to crash in the van for two nights and head south with the gang. And since Rodi was starting to pong, Zak was happy to risk offering Uncle Les's pool to clean the environment.

Immune to the weather conspiring against the drifting aristocrat, academic, sportsmen and dropouts, Rodi's antennae had been wired since the Volkswagen rolled into Key West. Fate had brought him straight to Hemingway's front door. Exhausted, hungry and penniless, he was beside himself. The lights and any sign of life may have been out in the famous author's museum home. Nevertheless, the hyperventilating Andalusian was rummaging in the back, grabbing his gear and preparing to meet his destiny. Tomorrow would be too late. A mighty rumble of thunder reverberated across the ocean and shook the ground.

Mitch sat back with his arms behind his head and, with a wry smile, watched Rodi rake up his worldly belongings. Clothes and beer cans flew around the cramped van. The surfer began to whistle The Doors' 1971 classic. Alona picked up the gamely tune:

Riders on the storm
Riders on the storm
Into this house we're born
Into this world we're thrown
Like a dog without a bone

An actor out alone
Riders on the storm

By the third bar, everyone had joined in on the joke. Only Rodi, busy throwing open the van's sliding door, failed to see the humour. This dog was determined to get his bone and munch it to the marrow. No matter his bag landed in a puddle. He'd made it.

"What's the plan, man? Relax. We get it. You've got a serious itch to scratch. How will you find us afterwards?" Mitch asked.

For an instant, Rodi stopped, frozen in his tracks, and blinked. He hadn't thought about practical trivia. This was not a moment to be dragged down by tedious questions of safety despite the hurricane sweeping across Florida. A trapdoor in his brain reminded him he didn't have a home or a mobile phone.

Zak stepped in with the obvious solution. "Rodi, good luck amigo. I hope you find what you're looking for. When you're done, come and find us on Schooner Wharf. If we're not there, we'll leave instructions behind the bar addressed to a red-haired romantic."

Rodi flicked the royal two-fingered salute and was gone with the wind.

*

The Schooner Wharf Bar, part oasis, part hippy hangout, looked like a castaway driftwood semi-ruin stacked with every type of rum known to man and a few cases of bootleg that isn't. Drinking rum in Key West went back hundreds of years by way of imports from slave plantations in Havana to mass smuggling in America's prohibition years.

Key West doesn't judge. The town is famous for its kaleidoscope of people from all walks of life. Bankers, lawyers, hipsters and dropouts visiting for a few days have been known to drop out after a single night on the wharf and never gone home. The town doesn't bat an eyelid. Key West, for many souls, is the ideal retreat where nobody cares if you're a millionaire or a minion. All the world could do with a sip of the Key West spirit.

For the drinking capital of Florida, Key West is the driest town in the Sunshine State. Every day Mallory Square Dock revels in the sunset celebration. Street performers and psychics meet at the water's edge to bid the day, never to grace this life again, farewell and melt away their troubles, soothed by the sun dropping into the warm embrace of the Gulf of Mexico. Key West cherishes every dawn and every dusk.

Today was not one of those sun-kissed days. The Truthmobile surfed through troughs of rainwater and pulled into a deserted dockside carpark. Through the downpour, only the colour of the old reddish-brown brick warehouses showed any life. True to form, though, the lights were on in the Schooner Wharf Bar. A sign nailed to the entrance, swinging in the wind like a one-legged drunken sailor, greeted the road-worn drifters. 'Open, Come Hell or High Water,' it promised.

The friends found enthusiasm hard to come by. The forsaken lanes looked more pirate's Port Royal than a sunshine paradise. A collective grumpiness fell across the van. "Holy cow, what a dump. Tell me this isn't it?" Nicola said, capturing the deflated mood. The friends slammed the van doors shut, bleary-eyed and dispirited, without bothering to lock them and sauntered towards the bar entrance. In such bleak expectations, adventures of a lifetime begin.

Zak pushed the double swing doors open and stepped back in time to an alien age. This was a long way from his local watering hole, Oxford's Eagle and Child pub peddling beer since 1684 to the likes of J.R.R. Tolkien and C.S. Lewis. Small groups of people huddled in chinos, shorts, faded floral shirts, and ragged t-shirts emblazoned 'Crazy Alligator Lady', 'Warning. I Do Dumb Things' and a bit of ocean humour, 'Even My Mullet Has Crabs'.

Under deep suntans, the good folk of Kew West muttered softly into their rum as if they didn't want to disturb the wrath of the Big Blue god pounding the Atlantic Ocean. A light, constant smell from the sawdust, freshly thrown down once a week and licked with saltwater, saturated the bar. The cosy drinking den had every diversion a drifter needed: a dartboard, two pool tables and a deeply stocked jukebox.

Hundreds of photos of drunken frolickers, their sun-bleached edges curling, were pinned to a long, smeared mirror running the length of the back of the bar. A green parrot with a red beak hopped across the bar to his own merriment. The wooden rafters were pinned with cheques signed in good faith by partygoers who had lost days and too many brain cells in the bar but whose cash had bounced. That's Key West. The barmen would shrug. They didn't take it personally or life too seriously. There's always tomorrow.

Nobody noticed when Zak walked through the door until Nicola's long legs touched the creaking floorboards. The room rubbernecked as one at a rare beauty in any land. Nicola approached the bar. The oxygen seemed to be sucked out of the room. Or maybe that was just how the besotted Zak remembered the moment. Already those unwelcome old feelings of jealousy were raising their ugly head. I'm losing the plot, Zak thought to himself. His feelings were typically still undeclared, but the mind games had long begun.

The exception to the bar's testosterone spike was an elderly man of uncertain age and an unusually long skull sporting a shock of anarchic grey hair that hadn't seen a brush for many long moons. Sitting on a stool and leaning on his right elbow, he just went on slowly stirring his rum glass with a shiny metal swizzle stick that glinted amidst the blended liquid. Zak and Nicola reached the bar together and rubbed their hands together. Time to quench their thirst.

Without looking up, the elderly man simply said, "You're late."

Mitch and Alona had joined the drifters dripping at the bar.

"Sorry friend, late for what?" smiled Mitch, the eternal optimist. "Looks like nothing has been going on here for a while, and nothing is likely for the foreseeable future."

"You're two types of late," the man replied without turning

his head, talking to his drink. The parrot cocked its head and squawked, "Late, late, very important date." The mildly sinister mood lifted. Everyone broke into laughter.

Only now did the old man turn to greet the visitors with a grin. "Damn that parrot. He always steals my best lines and clips my wings. Thought that was the wife's job."

"Anyhows, one: you're just late enough because the eye of the storm is going to pass overhead within the hour. Trust me, you don't want to be caught in that heap of trouble. And second, I was just about to head on home and you'd have been late for the chance of a lifetime."

"Oh goody, I love a night-time story," Nicola gushed. Grabbing her glass, she arrived at the end of the bar in three large strides, offered her hand, pulled up a chair and introduced herself. "Hi, I'm Nicola, Nicola Medici. A pleasure to meet you." A knowledgeable forehead furrowed. Pointing her thumb over her shoulder at the approaching pack, she introduced Isak Fitzgrove, Mitch Hunter and Alona Hancock. Handsome, young and full of energy, the friends made a striking impression, although little swayed laidback Key West.

"How you do, too. The name's Kurt Barracuda. People just call me the Barracuda. And today might just be your lucky day."

"Jesus, who is this guy, Forest Gump's big brother," Alona whispered.

The Barracuda signalled for more drinks all round, and the unlikely group, thrown together under the shadow of fortune and the storm, moved to the corner of the room. Niceties were shared and the broad strokes of the last month that threw the friends together shared with fond memories. All the time, Zak was transfixed by the gold swizzle stick with which the elderly man not so subtly stirred his rum, slowly, relentlessly. Gold does that to people.

'And what about you, Mr Barracuda?" Nicola enquired. "What line of business are you in?"

"Me, I'm in the business of dreams," he replied, a cheeky smile rising from the corner of his lips. "I chase storms and the ships they chew up and spit out at the bottom of the ocean. And in those wrecks are unimaginable treasures, the lost wealth of the Spanish empire. You hear the grind of the waves out there?" Barracuda asked, nodding out of the window. "Well, beneath their chaos is a carpet of gold. Round here, we call it the Bank of Madrid."

"So, you're a treasure hunter. Very cool," said Mitch.

"Some people don't trust that name, sends a shiver down their spine, but I'd say it just about sums up me and my team. Course, it's not all about treasure at the end of the rainbow. If you don't love the history – mighty galleons, Indian slaves and ancient sea dogs – you won't last long. Once you've got the bug though, it's in your blood for life, no escape, do or die. This is a calling, a way of life. Man against nature."

The group was hooked. Only something in Zak's scientific DNA was sceptical. He was cynical at the best of times, and this setup smelt like a historical honey trap.

"Come clean. Have you found much down here?" Alona pushed, finding it hard to contain her interest. "I mean isn't treasure up there with fairies and dreams?" The real words she wanted to throw out were fools and nutjobs. Her polite upbringing stopped those words from leaking out.

"Fair question, friend," replied the Barracuda, only now stopping dead still to stare the surfer in the eye. He slowly dragged the gold swizzle stick – as long as his hand – out of his glass tumbler and held it straight up in the air, two inches from her nose. An image of Jesus nailed to the Cross, his head down, appeared sculpted to its top. "Does this look like fool's gold, sugar plum?"

"This was pulled up inside wooden chests stuffed with one hundred and fifteen gold ingots and a thousand silver bars, 114,000 silver pieces of eight and three hundred and fifty uncut emeralds from the hull of one of the greatest treasure ships that ever took to the high seas, *Our Lady of Atocha*. Would have been used to prepare hot chocolate, we reckon. Spain stole the secret formula from the Aztecs who got it from the Maya. Madrid used to get through five tons of cacao beans a year. A heck of an addiction."

"The *Atocha* was chugging along nicely on the fourth of September 1622 from Havana to Seville when, out of nowhere – boom – a mega hurricane, a hundred times worse than today's blip, dropped out of the skies and swallowed eight of Spain's finest galleons. Her wreck gave and gave, thank you, Lord, but she's been dry these last few years. Mind you, I sure ain't grumbling."

"I wouldn't mind a bit of that," Mitch thought out loud, scratching his week-old stubble. "If you've got fame and fortune, why are you hanging around the local bar on a dead-end Sunday? Haven't you got air tanks to polish or something?" the surfer asked spikily.

"This is the calm before the storm, son. Tomorrow will be all sun and calm seas, the start of something big, something new, something special. Could be the *Atocha* was small fry compared to what's just around the corner." The Barracuda paused, started stirring his rum once more, withdrew the gold bar and sucked a waterworn Jesus. Through tight lips, he hissed, "Friends, this is the big one, the motherlode. And the hunt starts tomorrow. As I said, shame you're late."

Even Zak found himself with a hundred questions despite his gut feeling the friends were being scammed.

The questioning was left to Mitch, who took the hook. "Late, how? You said you start tomorrow. Spill the beans, old timer?"

The Barracuda's drinking was done. He pushed back his chair, stood to his full six-foot-four-inch frame and stretched his arms high above his head. The eight *reales* gold coin he'd worn around his neck for two decades, rescued from the depths of Matacumbe Key, dropped out of his shirt front and swung from side to side hypnotically and not by chance.

"Well, if you want in, pop by the museum at 10.30 tomorrow," the wreck hunter shrugged. "We'll show you around the conservation lab, fill you in on a new discovery and you can meet and greet the team. Some fishermen are coming in with freaky curiosities they just brought up in their nets from deep offshore. Then we'll plan the search."

The Barracuda drew a circle in the air at the watching barman and said, "Hey, Big Dave, these are on me. So long, folks." The old man of the sea vanished into the howling night.

For the next forty-five minutes, the friends chatted about the Barracuda's tall tale. Mitch and Alona were transfixed. Treasure hunting trumped making money from surfing every day of the week, especially with their careers plummeting into the twilight zone. Timing is everything. Even Zak was having a re-think. The unexpected news of sunken wonders in fishing nets sounded like the perfect ticket to sneak into the world of pink gold, as Key West's rich shrimp harvests were known. This could be a new angle to expose how fishing trawlers were decimating the northwest Atlantic.

Only Nicola was unmoved. Grimy dive boats, second-hand silver and the lure of riches weren't her cup of tea. Money didn't concern her and adventures were common on her yearly trips to Monaco's superyachts during the Cannes Film Festival. How many get-rich schemes pitched to her old man had she heard, from tax-free film investments to backing Chinese-built nuclear power stations? How many film stars had lost the plot under the spell of daddy's champagne and offered to massage her feet, for god's sake?

The detached Londoner still felt a more delicious thrill at the thought of the Boca Chica nudist beach. Secretly, she promised to slip off to her liberating shore tomorrow while the others played rotten old boats. No need to spoil the mood. Nicola composed her social mask and smiled at her friends.

Big Dave, the eternally happy bar owner, had rooms free on the first floor and agreed to let them all crash in a double. Just when they started to think about turning in, Rodriguez Saumerez burst through the doors like a hyperactive teenager. Soaked to the bare bones but happier than anyone had ever seen him, the Spaniard had enjoyed his own adventure. After banging on the front door of Hemingway's house, a light went on in the upper room of the museum, and a fashionably dressed middle-aged woman had welcomed him in, charmed by the tale of his pilgrimage. They took coffee and cake on the very same warped table where the writer had spilled ink. The woman was amazed by Rodi's knowledge and ability to quote from memory pages of *A Farewell To Arms*.

Maisie had hardly got a word in edgeways, apart from shaking his hand and telling him her first name. Eventually finding a moment's pause, she begged tiredness and showed Rodi the door. Not before handing him her card and the offer of company any time in the next few weeks before she headed back cross-country to her second home in Los Angeles.

All Rodi had wanted was for a few minutes to peak behind the curtain of Hemingway's life and soak up the refined air where dazzling literature was born. Maisie's fading beauty – was she late thirties or early forties? – had been an unexpected bonanza. The Spaniard then released his trump card. Only when resting between running through the rain at the side of a beached fishing boat had the Spaniard read her card, 'Maisie Hemingway, Actress' alongside her email and telephone numbers. *Ay caramba*, he had squealed. The pain of the last year drained away with the downpour into the sea.

While the friends had been chatting with treasure hunting nobility, Rodi had been drinking with Hemingway's own great-granddaughter – dynastic royalty. His mind was blown. No chance of sleep that night.

One by one, the friends tiptoed upstairs to shower and sleep. Rodi would try to settle down on the floor, as usual.

Only Nicola held back, eventually whispering to Big Dave to give her the cleanest room left and slipping him a $20 sweetener. Slumming it on the road was one thing, but the British ruling classes didn't do sweaty feet and scattered underwear. Appearances needed to be upheld.

4

Front Street, Key West

A grey and white pixilated photo, with a minuscule smudge at its centre, flashed up on the projector screen. To the uninitiated eye it looked like a television unable to tune into the right station. It reminded Alona of a blob of chewing gum. To those in the know, the image was gold dust.

"Ladies and gentlemen, four hundred metres deep and seventy kilometres from nowhere, it's my great pleasure to give you the first photo of the Tortugas shipwreck. Welcome to pay dirt," the suit announced.

All of the sixty or so people in Key West's Antiquarium Maritime Museum conference room had signed a non-disclosure agreement after their mobile phones were confiscated at the door. Two pit-bull security guards with short-cropped hair and bad intentions, prettied up in black suits, guarded the museum entrance. A large screen ran across the front of a stage. A bulky square object, hidden under a sheet of black silk, lurched awkwardly to the right.

Zak, Mitch, Alona and Rodi had woken up late with heavy heads. It was 10.25 am by the time they sprinted round the corner to the Barracuda's museum. In shorts and t-shirts, they didn't look out of place. Anything goes. Big Dave was dressed the same. Others in the crowd preferred jeans or crisp Armani suits, a thin-slice of Floridian society.

Only Nicola was truant. Her note tacked to the friends' bedroom door simply said, 'Gone Fishing, Back Tonight, N xx' in understated Medici fashion.

In front of the giant screen, the Barracuda stood in ancient jeans and a brown and white tiger print Hawaiian sleeveless shirt. His combed grey hair betrayed the only hint he'd made any effort for convention's sake that morning. He was yet to speak and stood tall and alert, his hands crossed behind his back. His hawk eyes scanned the crowd like a lighthouse's beam sweeping distant waters. The Barracuda knew the next few minutes had to play out perfectly. The venture's financial success or failure hinged on it. The seated faces looked friendly enough. Didn't mean they would part with their hard-earned cash.

To the Barracuda's left, a nervous man in his late thirties squirmed on the edge of a table. His faded blue jean cropped shorts were freshly cleaned but would forever be stained by years of ship's grease and grime. A diver holding a Spanish olive jar, oxygen bubbles floating upwards, and the logo 'Deep Down We Care' swam across the front of his white t-shirt. A name tag, pinned upside-down, identified the man as Rusty.

The clean-shaven gent speaking behind designer glasses sported cream chinos and a blue polo t-shirt, 'Tortugas Crew' printed on his right breast above a print of a silver coin stamped with a cross and the date 1622 on its top edge. His name tag read 'Al Nassau, Chief Operating Officer, Keys Exploration'.

The slide changed to a painting of the riverport of Seville. The accompanying text read 'The Americas Fleet, 1590 – Alonso Sanchez Coello'.

"Ladies and gentlemen, settle down, please," Al Nassau began. "From the heady days of Christopher Columbus to the end of Spain's golden age, thousands of merchant ships were sent to the Americas to mop up the natural wealth of the native lands. Colombian gold and emeralds, Peruvian silver and Venezuelan pearls – the real-world El Dorado – turned Spain into the superpower of the colonial age. For a short period of time, the streets of Seville were paved with gold, my friends."

The willing crowd murmured to each another in appreciation. Rodi's jugular vein started to throb. His chest, puffed up with pride, had expanded two inches. Zak had taken a front-row seat next to Rodi and leant forward in concentration with crossed arms and alert ears. Mitch and Alona sat three rows back sipping coffee, their legs perched on the seat in front and lying over one another in a jumble of limbs. In the fog of anticipation, even they'd forgotten to start quarrelling.

"Spain excelled in three things in the early seventeenth century, over-mining natural riches into extinction, wiping out enslaved American Indians and Africans and, finally, sinking its own ships." Al had the tittering crowd in the palm of his hand. Rodi's chest deflated.

A seventeenth-century map of the Straits of Florida clicked onto the screen alongside an image of a monstrous clawed fish with two heads and the Latin words *Non Plus Ultra, Hic Sunt Dracones*, 'Nothing Beyond, Here Be Monsters'.

"Fast forward to the year 1622, people," Al Nassau continued, peering upwards at the map. "Madrid was imploding under a heap of debt from endless wars with England and the Dutch, whose piratical ships were blitzing the sea lanes between Havana and Tobago. Not only was the enemy carting off the treasures of Spain's colonies from under their noses, but Spanish merchants had lost faith in the Crown and were siphoning off the king's own taxes. Merchantmen returning to Seville often smuggled an extra forty per cent above the manifest cargo value as contraband. Every man for himself."

"It's July 1622. Inflation has soared by three hundred per cent, plague has ravished town and countryside, the wheat fields and olive orchards of Andalusia are deserted. The people are on the verge of outright rebellion. King Philip IV has one throw of the dice left. The largest fleet assembled in two generations is sent to the Spanish Main, the Americas, accompanied by crack marines and four warships to get the king's gold back home in one piece and bail out the bank. It's now or never, the eleventh hour, guys."

"Mission desperado is a success – at first. Over sixty tons of gold and silver bars and seventy pounds of emeralds are hauled into the fleet's holds in the rendezvous port of Havana. This is when events turned nasty. From what we can glean from the historical chronicles, the two-million-*peso* fleet was ready to roll by early August but couldn't find a fair weather window to catch the trade winds home to Seville."

"In port, friendly fire from a cannon almost killed a ship's master. While the sailors spent their cash downtown on fast women and free-flowing booze, the town's rats raided the fleet's stores and took to its holds by the thousands, literally. A priest on the 1622 *flota* described how, after just two days at sea, the crew killed two thousand rats that plagued every part of his ship."

"All that was background noise compared to what came next. As the 23-ship convoy headed into the Straits of Florida, a killer hurricane swept in from the Caribbean. The fleet was caught in its vortex. Eight ships went down. Bottom line, the sinking broke the Bank of Madrid. The golden age of Spain tragically collapsed. Think Diego Velázquez and the nobleman writer Miguel de Cervantes' *Don Quixote* and you can understand why everyone from King Philip IV to the great unwashed were left tilting in fury, not at windmills but at waves."

The slide switched to a sun-bleached photograph of a fishing boat, on the deck an abandoned net. Peculiar objects lay strewn among a catch of pink shrimp. "Now, Spanish salvors sent to the Keys found four of the lost treasure ships grounded on the reefs and sweated hard to recover about eighty per cent of their cargoes before Dutch privateers chased them off. The Barracuda here has found another two, making us all tremendously… happy." Light applause from the audience. Kurt Barracuda bowed gently.

"That leaves two lost treasure ships missing in action. The old texts, including Native American folklore, tell us that while the hurricane swept most of the fleet onto the Cayos del Marques, the Marquesas Keys, two hulls stuffed to the gunwales and pitching heavily in the high seas were slowly left behind until they slipped into a watery grave almost beyond sight of land. They were never seen again – until now. At this point, I'd like to thank you all for listening and pass you over to the Barracuda. All yours, buddy."

Kurt strolled centre stage and continued scanning the crowd. Looked like they were suitably impressed and relaxed. Nassau had done a perfect job softening them up. Time to strike.

"Thanks, Al. Folks, two weeks ago, a shrimper working out of Key West made an astonishing catch. The beds were poor pickings, so he steered out into the Straits of Florida to a patch rarely trawled. Dragging his nets around four hundred and forty metres down, the boat snagged hard, stopping the motor in its tracks. After an hour and a half of fighting the obstacle, the motor billowing smoke, he pulled in the nets, mostly shredded and good for nothing other than the garbage heap. But when they finally dropped onto the deck, a cluster of silver coins fell on his head, underwater manna from heaven. And ensnared in the nets were these motley objects. From left to right, you're looking at a Spanish olive jar, a rare bronze astrolabe for navigating by the stars and a ceramic plate painted with crossed keys and a crown."

"We sent the research ship out to the general GPS fix where this stuff turned up at the end of last week," the Barracuda continued. "Rusty ran some lines with the side-scan sonar and, bingo, came up with the ship-shaped target we shared at the start of today's show. It may not look like much, granted, but I'd stake my house on the fact it's one of the two lost 1622 treasure ships, untouched at great depth, just waiting to change history. Who wants to go where no man or woman has boldly gone before?"

The Barracuda paused as the room hummed with excitement before inviting questions from the floor.

A dour-faced suit in the middle of the crowd stood and enquired, "How can we be sure this isn't just some old debris washed against the side of a twentieth-century steel hull, the likes of which litter the Keys by the dozen?"

"Well, Gerald," the Barracuda replied. "I must have looked at a few thousand side-scan hits in my time, and steel ships make sharp-edged, bean-shaped targets because they haven't broken up. Wooden hulls that have sprung open and flattened onto the seabed unzipped are a very different kettle of fish. They look fuzzy-edged with faint definition. That sucker on the screen is pre-steel for sure and from the great age of sail."

Gerald nodded, content with the answer, and a graceful

lady with a blue cashmere turtleneck jumper and a single string of pearls merely said, "Talk to me about the ship's dating possibilities?"

"Without having dived the site, Maisie, this much we know. The olive jar is in the range of 1575-1625. The astrolabe can't be dated any closer. But the blue-and-white plate was made in the Triana suburb of Seville by Arabs forcefully converted to Catholicism after 1600. No smoking gun yet, it's true. But we've seen, and may I add bought at great expense, the catches and GPS fixes of several hundred shrimp snags over three decades. I've never seen anything remotely so promising. All the signs point to one prospect… ladies and gentlemen, I give you the final resting place of the *Nuestra Señora de la Merced*."

Rodi's fast-spinning head realised the questioning speaker was no other than Miss Maisie Hemingway. The red-faced Spaniard waved coyly in the direction of yesterday's coffee pal.

The discussions with the crowd went back and forth for several minutes before a no-nonsense turkey farmer in faded dungarees and cowboy hat stood up and asked, "If you know it's down there, why haven't you dived the goddamn site yet? What are we waiting for?"

"I'm darn pleased you brought that one up, Buzz," the Barracuda replied before adding, "Rusty, why don't you come on over and close the show."

The nervous engineer with the facial tick walked centre stage with his head down, muttering to himself. Through many pauses he painfully teased out the right words to explain the state of play.

"The *Merced* lies at a depth of over 400 metres. That's enough pressure to crush a diver's skull. You can't work that far down with SCUBA, and saturation diving has a useless cost-benefit ratio. Plus, you lose technical control over what the divers are doing on the seabed. This is why we are proud to introduce… Boss, if you'd like to do the honours?"

The Barracuda pulled the edge off the large object whose shadow loomed over the front right of the room to reveal an eight-foot high bright yellow robot. Two shiny arms with claw hands slightly raised faced the crowd, ready to pounce. Well-ordered, multi-coloured wires and tools were neatly arranged around its sides. A blue logo painted across the top of both sides read Juno 1.

The treasure hunter announced with a beaming smile, "Boys and girls, welcome to the future. Fresh out of the box from the factory in Scotland, I give you Juno, mother of the gods. She may look like a menacing beast but don't be fooled. Trust me, underwater she dances like a prima ballerina. Juno is the most advanced archaeologically-tooled robot between here and Timbuktu. This is how we're gonna dive the *Merced*, dig out her secrets and pull up treasure. Rusty, why don't you fill us in on her vital statistics?"

Excited at the sight of his latest toy, which he'd been dreaming of getting his hands on for years, soothed much of the technician's hatred of public speaking. Rusty was a doer, not a talker. Only now had one of Keys Exploration's major funders dropped $2.5 million to custom design the robot, which would change the rules of marine exploration forever. The team could now dive to the bottom of the Atlantic, outside State waters, and see the invisible for the first time in history.

"Juno 1 is what's known in the marine ops business as a remotely-operated vehicle, or ROV for short, rated down to depths of 4,000 metres," Rusty explained. "She is buoyancy neutral, so underwater she can hover over the most delicate of timbers and work without having to touch down and crush anything. The ROV is tethered to the research ship above by miles of fibre-optic cable, which works its brains, all controlled by a pilot and directed by project managers watching her every movement live from a suite of TV plasma screens on the high seas. In theory, you could drive her remotely from anywhere, even live from the comfort of your sofa."

"The titanium manipulators up front can lift heavy objects up to two hundred and fifty kilograms and work on a master/slave principle. That means whatever movement the ROV pilot makes above the waves on his control console is replicated exactly a kilometre deep on the seabed by the bot's arms. Pretty neat. On the left side is what we affectionately call the Sucker, a silicon pad that attaches to artefacts and lifts them through the power of pressure suction. Again, the ROV pilot, which would mean me, draws just enough suction to lift the object without smashing it. Super smart. Finally, we have the dredge fixed to the left side, which sucks up sand and clears wreckage. The ROV can dig about a square metre of sand in twenty seconds if it needs to. That's Juno in a nutshell. The rise of the robots has arrived, folks."

The suit took to his feet again and congratulated the team on the discovery and technological progress before asking, "So where do we stand? What's the schedule and, to be blunt, boys, what's the size of investment needed to get from shore to site, recovery and monetisation?"

"The nitty gritty is pretty simple, Gerald," the Barracuda beamed. "The window of opportunity opens right now. A press release goes out across the wires at 23.30 hours tonight. That gives our friends here a full-day head's up. Bidding ends in forty-eight hours. We head to the site as soon as the first two million hit the account. Using Juno and the ship is a new dawn. But space age exploration sure don't come cheap. We're looking at $250,000 a week for a two-month operation, with total dive, recovery and conservation costs of $9.5 million. That's a big slice of pie, but peanuts to what's down there. We reckon the *Merced* sank with treasure worth at least $250 million in modern money. Ladies and gentlemen, I invite you to come and shake Juno's hand and take a project brochure. And remember, the clock is ticking. Let's dive."

5

Old Bond Street, London

Robert Brooker was engrossed in online porn of a very bad sort when the memo came through. Everyone else had gone home hours ago. The midnight shift was this lone wolf's choice domain. Nobody else wanted to man the offices of Jorvik & Silver in these ungodly hours, which suited Brooker just fine.

Brooker had been dishonourably discharged from the army in Iraq for peeping in on the women's showers through a hole in a creaking wooden partition wall. Just like in a bad teenage film, his enlarged pupil was spotted ogling through the steam. After receiving a royal beating from the squaddies, his own desert storm, with special attention paid to the nether regions, Brooker had been sent packing back to London. The incident was the last in a long line of indiscretions.

Because his father had walked out on the Brookers when little Bobby was a child, the ex-soldier was riddled with a feeling of injustice. Nothing was his fault. Now retreated to a one-bedroom studio flat above a Turkish kebab shop in Islington, the righteous man had a pathological failure to see both sides of an argument. As the months rolled by, and his blotted CV made jobs impossible to find, his feeling of being victimised grew. A fighting fit physique made way for a triple chin fed on a diet of doner kebabs and doughnuts. Brooker's eyes retreated ever deeper behind dark circles from staring at his computer screen, night after night. Bob was flat broke, had few prospects and little hope of a girlfriend, especially one who bothered to wash. This made the reject a dangerous loose cannon.

Jorvik & Silver specialized in maritime law from their well-appointed first-floor Georgian mansion at the Piccadilly end of London's Old Bond Street. With endless time on his hands and a big chip on his shoulder, Brooker had found a skill and passion for exposing what he saw as the unethical looting of World War I and II wrecked warships. Switching allegiance from the army to the naval world let him masquerade as a war-worn expert ex-veteran, scars and all.

When Dutch salvors started ransacking British battleships in the North Sea, a ballistic Brooker hit the alarm button. From his comfy leather chair, the ex-serviceman went over the top, as he put it, swapping bullets for ink to blow the whistle with pent-up rage. The campaigner wrote to his Member of Parliament, then to Phillip Hammond, the Minister of Defence, and gave an interview to the *Daily Mail* accusing Britain of destroying the maritime graves of 2,500 naval officers for the scrap value of a few steel hulls. A national disgrace, the newspaper called it.

At the time, Brooker was not wrong. For a few short weeks, he revelled in his fifteen minutes of fame, making the most of invites to talk to tiny historical societies about threats to the high seas. The fan mail quickly dried up. Yesterday's news turned into fish and chip wrapper. In his mind, Brooker still believed he had made it and that the doors to power were open to him. His four-page letters sent weekly to press and politicians were met with a wall of irritated silence. Short-lived fame rotted into infamy

Much to his surprise, his fawning letter to Jorvik & Silver pleading for a position met with a positive response. In this legal pairing, Brooker's venom found the perfect partner. James Jorvik and Dominic Silver came from old Suffolk money and, with their Cambridge educations, often took on contracts designed not to cash in but to climb Westminster's political greasy pole.

When a three-person Russian Mir submersible cracked the upper deck of the *Titanic* off Canada and pulled up a woman's leather boot and a doctor's Gladstone bag in its giant manipulator claw, Jorvik & Silver sued the Titanic 1912 Corp. on behalf of the International Council of Cultural Heritage – ICOCH – for damaging a global maritime monument and won. Just like Brooker, they got off on their minor celebrity status – big fish in a little pond – and felt one step closer to the knighthoods they dreamt about. Nothing more than what they deserved, so they often back-patted each other. Quite right.

Bob Brooker's physical disgrace revolted Jorvik & Silver's Savile Row snobbery. Yet the boy had the perfect radio face for manning the office in emergencies while Europe slept and their American cousins sweated. On paper, Brooker was responsible for compiling research files on live maritime scandals – sunken warships, fighter jets, submarines – and every low-life treasure hunter and salvor in the four corners of the world from the English Channel to Indonesia.

His Peeping Tom computer screens followed the movements of a who's who of wreck rogues across the high seas using state-of-the-art Automated Information Service satellite tracking software. This was curtain-twitching of the highest technological order. If an emergency needed fast action, all hands to the pump, Brooker was sanctioned to call either of his bosses on the red desk phone, a form of pomposity unique to this London firm.

At 4.37 am on a freezing early autumn morning down London's West End, just such an emergency kicked off. Only the delivery vans zooming down empty West End streets kept Brooker company. The light was still inky black outside the office windows. The email window on the left of Brooker's three screens popped up with an alarm tracking Keys Exploration's ship movements and online traffic. Faintly annoyed but with his curiosity aroused, Brooker opened the low-life Floridian's press release.

"Keys Exploration Announces Spanish Bounty, the Long-lost Wreck of the *Merced*. The World's Largest Treasure to be Salvaged," the opening lines of the press release read.

"Balls," Brooker screamed, falling head-first onto the plush cream carpet in his rush to reach the red phone. Decorum, Brooker, the warrior campaigner whispered. He tucked in his shirt, with regret closed the window to CountryFarmGirls.com, ran his fingers through his hair and pressed 1 on the telephone.

James Jorvik had already been awake for a quarter of an hour, waiting for the newspapers to arrive and sipping his first cup of tea. He picked up his phone and answered chipperly, "What can I do for you, Mr Brooker?"

Without bidding Jorvik a good morning, the great campaigner coughed and, barely concealing his excitement, announced, "News just in. Mr Barracuda of Keys Exploration has announced the discovery of the Spanish frigate *Merced* off the Florida Keys. They're planning to ransack it, Mr Jorvik."

"Oh goody," the lawyer replied, "we have the plundering weasel now. Prepare the *Merced* file for me. And let me know as soon as they land anything, be it a gold bar or a potsherd. Time to crush the Barracuda under the full weight of the law once and for all, me thinks. Good work Robert."

Brooker was indeed pleased with his night's work. Days of twenty-four-hour madness preparing for court would soon begin. May as well finish what I started, the sea warrior reasoned, flicking back to his favourite website. A little frolicking for Bobby, followed by a greasy spoon breakfast at Dom Vito's Café before battle commences. Surely Jorvik & Silver owed him that much for running their rapid response unit on a shoestring budget.

Bob Brooker dropped his trousers. Little did he know that the hidden camera in the corner of the office was capturing his every move. One day it might be his undoing when the old lawyers decided to upgrade him for a less monstrous sociopath. Only if a worse ending didn't catch up with the nasty piece of work first.

6

Key West Bight Marina, South Florida

The subscriptions didn't so much trickle as flood in. After thirty-six hours of pledges, the Barracuda closed the investment portfolio with a sufficient war chest to see the underwater dig through to January – a full three months at sea. Two days later, on a fine Friday morning, the *Golden Margaret* research ship, newly painted navy blue, was released from her dry dock and moored in Key West Bight Marina.

While Nicola enjoyed her beauty sleep, Rodi escorted Mitch and Alona down to the seashore to wave them off. The surfers grabbed the chance to sign on the dotted line to spend a month offshore helping tag, clean and document the finds. Mitch had already quipped that Alona would make a great pot scrubber, a term he picked up while drinking with Zak's English college pals. The pair were already arguing like cats and dogs at 5.30 am.

Alona had little confidence the madcap treasure hunt would turn up a lost golden galleon or any riches. Instinctively she felt the opportunity was a well-timed diversion, however. Mitch and Alona had been living on top of each other, worrying unhealthily about their future, rather than enjoying the here and now, for way too long. Their relationship was becoming as toxic as a diver's bends. Getting stuck in exploring and learning some new skills might freshen them up. A big distraction, not easy cash, was what persuaded Alona to sign up.

Mitch Hunter needed close managing for sure. What you saw was not what you got. He may have been deliciously easy on the eye with his spiky black hair, jet-blue eyes and dazzling white-toothed Tom Cruise smile, but Alona knew he was a serial responsibility side-stepper. At six-foot-two-inches, the all-American could have done anything. The Adonis with a killer six-pack could run four hundred metres in forty-six seconds flat off the plane in his first week at San Francisco State University. When he bothered to turn up and compete, he stole the show on the basketball court with a row of three-point baskets without breaking sweat.

A strict upbringing and regular roughing up at the hands of Hunter Senior, the former Marine Corps officer, shattered his son's dreams. Why bother reaching for the sky? He'd always be a loser in his dad's eyes. Nobody knew what was locked away between his ears because he never bothered taking risks. Mitch escaped responsibility at the bottom of beer cans. Only a fluke of genetics kept him trim.

Just one pastime centred the Californian: the sea. Mitch was brought up in Santa Cruz, the town of the Holy Cross, violent crime and terrible homelessness. Mitch never visited the downtrodden slums. Since he was out of nappies, he was only ever into surfing. It was in Santa Cruz that American surfing was born when three Hawaiian princes, David Kawananakoa, Edward Keliiahonui and Jonah Kuhio Kalaniana'ole – the so-called men who walked on water – rode redwood longboards in the town's waters in July 1885.

Dudes bitten by the bug went to crazy lengths to ride these seas. When the waves refused to roll in 1930, Claude Horan, a student from San Jose State and a pal, Wes Hammond, hired steamships to cruise around the bay to kick up the surf. Jack O'Neill invented the wet suit in Santa Cruz. The town had hosted international competitions like the O'Neill Cold Water Classic and International Longboard Association for ninety years.

Alona's armchair psychology diagnosed her man as too scared to commit. Mitch suffered from a fatal attraction: the crushing fear that crept into his bones in the night hours that one day he might hurt his wonderful girlfriend like Hunter Snr hurt him. Mitch was a project Alona wasn't ready to quit on quite yet.

Operation *Merced* would be an experimental gamble in romance.

Rodi had signed up to the wreck hunt as well but preferred to stay on solid ground to translate the 1622 fleet's outbound Spanish manifest copied from the Archivo General de Indias in Seville. Could any more historical nuggets about the *Merced*'s cargo and last voyage be teased out of the tricky words? The Barracuda expected Rodi would prove to be an uncontrollable, although useful, dogsbody and little more. When the finds landed, he could lend a helping hand in sorting and cataloguing. If he went loco, he'd be fired pronto. The unhinged Spaniard was one to keep a cautious eye on, the Barracuda warned his inner circle.

Rodi had another excellent reason to tie himself to Key West's sands. After the shipwreck project launch, Maisie Hemingway had invited him to spend Saturday with her and continue their meaningful conversation. For conversation, the Spaniard's spellbound heart skipped a beat, imagining hours of intimacy.

All three friends were giving their time for free in exchange for a small percentage of future profits, half a per cent per person of the total treasure recovered, a typical package in Key West's shipwreck salvage industry. Nothing ventured, nothing gained.

Nicola and Zak were conspicuous by their absence at the start of the great underwater game. Not just because of the ungodly hour, what Miss Medici called stupid o'clock. After the Barracuda's hook and bait circus at the Antiquarium, the friends met up in the Schooner Wharf Bar that evening to talk through the pros and cons of joining the treasure hunt. Booze failed to smooth out cracks in opinion. The honeymoon period shattered as the friends split into two warring camps.

From the start, the whiff of treasure bent Zak's nose firmly out of joint. His first undergraduate term studying in Wales preached a sacred truth. All cultural finds dug up from the earth are unique, whether they're Greek statues or smashed pots. All have crucial stories to tell, Professor Pasinski had made crystal clear, banging his hand on the desk. Zak had dropped into his course on the theory of archaeology just for kicks to top up his learning. The idea that the past is a sacred cow, never to be sold, was drummed into all students across the globe. It wasn't negotiable. Zak's moral code made the idea of joining the Barracuda unthinkable.

Zak had sat back, tight-lipped and cross-armed, fully expecting everyone to agree and do a Spartacus, rejecting the lure of treasure. He'd misread the mood. The unpleasant squabble reached the point of no return.

Rodi didn't get it. Computer scientists lived in the real world, not some artsy-fartsy castle in the air. In the creative economy, money talks, he'd explained. You want to go to Mars? That'll be four billion dollars. You want to map the world's seas like the Japanese Nippon Foundation? Two billion dollars. His metaphor about getting monkeys if you eat peanuts got lost in translation. The Keys Exploration galleon hunt wasn't about money, Rodi promised, his fist pumping and voice cracking. He was signing up for his country. Who knows, maybe some of his ancestors helped stock the *Merced* or even met their maker on its last voyage. He could give voice to the memory of the dead.

"At school, we all learnt about the Age of Discovery, Cristobal Colon, no?" Rodi justified. "Today is the Age of Rediscovery. Maybe I'm selfish. I don't care. When I go home, back to Espagne, I'll be a hero. I left a nobody. For my country, my family, it is destiny to save this lost secret. I'd do it for nothing. But Mr Barracuda has petrol to pay for, mouths to feed, conservators to hire. How can he do this for nothing? Wake up. What is it you clever Yankee smart arses say, quid pro quo?" Rodi's speech was by far the longest the friends had heard him spout.

Alona had listened without judging and found herself playing the devil's advocate. She saw both sides of the argument.

"This hits a sensitive nerve, I appreciate," she began carefully. "I'm sorry but I'm not sure I buy into your position, Zak. Didn't the Romans mint millions of coins every year? Are you telling me every single one is worth putting in a museum? I'm sure there's a legitimate antiquities trade worth billions of dollars every year. There are always pictures of Egyptian mummies and Roman statues in the *New York Times* being auctioned for megabucks by Sotheby's, Christies and Bonhams. Unknown Ming vases forgotten in sheds are always popping up in British houses and making fortunes. Better odds than winning the lottery."

Getting into her stride, Alona argued that "Society allows the sale of Fabergé eggs, Jurassic fossils, dinosaur bones and the works of every great master painting civilisation has ever known, right? What's so special about a bunch of cruddy old pots and silver coins rotting under the sea? The Metropolitan Museum of Art, British Museum and Louvre would all be stripped and become empty classrooms if you removed market forces. The stuff we're talking about has been bought and sold over and over again since the days of the Grand Tour. It seems to me the right to sell stuff is the cornerstone of an enlightened people."

Nicola was stuck between a rock and a hard place. Art worth millions was displayed in her family's homes. A pure white marble bust of some emperor or other was one of her grandfather's prize possessions. One day all those riches would be hers. Would she gift them to some museum or send them back to the places where they were ransacked ages ago? Hell no. Nicola knew. She was guilty of double standards.

"This furore isn't my field, but this I will say." After a lingering pause, she added, "The antiquities trade is pure evil. Remember when George Bush Senior invaded Saddam Hussein's Iraq in 1990 and the oilfields of Kuwait went up in flames? It took years to recover the loot pillaged by desperate peasants and organised crime. London and New York's dealers turned a blind eye to make quick millions. All the while, the Iraqi people's legacy was stolen."

The Greek's feeling of national loss at the British Museum's refusal to give back the Elgin Marbles was the topic of great debate in London's Sloane Square dinner parties. The antiquities trade wasn't some innocent recreation bringing culture to the masses, Nicola explained. It's a plague linked at the hip with gun running and drugs peddling. In simple terms, it's the third wickedest and most valuable illicit trade in the world.

Finishing her rambling thoughts, Nicola shrugged "you

have to be very careful what you buy. All that said, shipwrecked crockery and silver aren't the Elgin Marbles. If wreck hunting is legal, finders keepers, who am I to denounce it?"

The on-edge friends considered these tough words in silence. Eventually Alona summed up how Mitch, Rodi and she felt.

"Sounds like scaremongering bull crap to me. You trying to tell me the scale of the antiquities trade is the same as drugs and arms? Come on, sober up, princess. Moving drugs and flogging guns rip the beating heart out of families caught in the crossfire. And be careful what you attack, talking of clean and dirty money. I'll wager most of your precious Oxford and Cambridge colleges happily bowed when they took cash from dubious merchants down the decades. When they weren't banking dirty money from slave traders. What is the shell name arms dealers hide behind in the UK? They call themselves 'wine merchants', right? Do me a favour!"

The accusations continued to fly across the Schooner Wharf Bar, startling the gentle Southern folk trying to relax. When the words burned out, the drifters couldn't agree to disagree. Nicola and Zak walked out together, refusing to have anything more to do with the Barracuda's shipwrecked filthy lucre. They warned that going offshore was a total waste of time. Dreaming of sunken gold was the worst business in the world. May as well go and flush your life's earnings down the toilet.

Despite his posturing, some of it real, but some said to provoke, Zak was intrigued. He'd stick around and watch from the wings. Meanwhile, he planned to hunt down local fishermen, persuade them to share decades-old stories of raking the ocean floor and research Key West's fishing industry. The carnage created by today's canyon buster trawlers would still make a gritty news report.

Only Mitch had stayed out of the bickering. Balls to ethics. He wanted the cash. End of story.

*

Close to midday, the *Golden Margaret* slowed to a halt seventy kilometres out to sea, blew her ship's horn three times, revelling in the team's carnival mood, and deployed her DP. The old days of four-point mooring by slinging four anchors onto the seabed and landing on who knew what were long gone. Dynamic Positioning tapped into the boat's thrusters and gyrocompass to keep the ship sweetly hovering over a tiny patch of seabed hundreds of metres down. Through the hazy sunshine, the shore was invisible to none but the most calculating eye. Curious seagulls circled the intruders overhead.

Standing on the upper deck watching the grease monkeys readying equipment, Alona and Mitch – GoPro camera strapped to his head – were badly mistaken if they thought Juno was ready to power up and jump straight into action. Two hours later, the disappointed surfers gave up and went in search of a snack. No sooner were they seated than the ship pitched scarily to portside. Alona's coffee slopped over the rim of her 'Life Is Simple. Just Add Water' mug. The pair put their bickering to one side and raced onto the deck, half expecting a call to abandon ship.

Gleaming gold in the afternoon sun, the remotely-operated robot Juno was suspended in the air over the side, attached to a deck-mounted crane. Below the robot hung four-metre-long beacons, space-age exploration tracking and recording equipment that would calculate the robot's 3D position on the seabed after being set up on the sea floor.

Slowly Juno was lowered into the water and vanished under a spray of bubbling white froth. Rusty climbed down from the crane in a hard hat and cut-off jeans and waved his finger above his head in a circular motion. Matheus – called Bellhop by the team – pressed a bright red button and the winch slowly revolved. Next stop, the bottom of the Atlantic and all its treasures.

Rusty strolled over to Mitch and Alona, put his arms around their shoulders and, pointing at a silver shipping container bolted onto the upper deck in the stern, invited them to join him inside the tin can in forty-five minutes, where he'd drive Juno's every movement. The surfers shrugged in bewilderment – fake it till you make it, right? – and nodded in ignorance before starting a tour of the *Golden Margaret*'s innards.

The ship may have been a 1,600-ton, seventy-five-metre-long relic of the early 1970s that started out as a fishing trawler, but after being borrowed by the Royal Navy for minesweeping duties during England versus Argentina's Falklands War in 1982, she was sold off to Key West's fishing fleet. A few years later, the Barracuda won her in a high-stakes two-day drunken poker game. Out of a sense of honour and to keep the peace in small town Key West, he insisted on paying market value for the old girl. The respect he won that day made the gesture a fine investment. He'd been on the lookout for a new research ship anyway.

Since being refitted for high-tech marine exploration in 1993, the *Golden Margaret* had seen service across the seven seas. Narrow gangways led to two-person-wide corridors. Alona and Mitch toured the bowels of the hold, where three months of tinned food was stacked next to refrigerators, chugging generators and the boat's sweaty gym, rough, ready and more Rocky Balboa than chichi Miami. Alona winced at the centre page pull-outs of *Playboy*, and more graphic top-shelf magazine spreads pasted across the gym wall, before remembering with mild alarm that she was the only woman onboard.

By name, the *Golden Margaret* may have been a lady, but the ship's operations were old-school alpha male. Key West wasn't at all bigoted when it came to the fairer sex. It was just that the old ways changed achingly slowly. In pockets of the Deep South, a man was a man and a woman a woman. After a rash of bad behaviour the Barracuda realized that a horn-dog male crew couldn't be trusted, even far out to sea, and closed the door on female company with regret. He wasn't proud about being forced down that wormhole. Maybe the times would soon change, he hoped.

Alona and Mitch stuck their heads into the kitchen where three singing Filipino chefs rolled sushi and two other dinner options, none vegetarian. Three solid meals like this would be fine dining compared to the surfers' normal diet of fast food junk grabbed on the move. A room at the stern end of the mid-deck corridor was stuffed floor to ceiling with computers, high-definition screens and red, green and orange blinking LED lights. Thick plastic-coated cables snaked across the carpet. A world map was pinned to one wall, with pins labelling Keys Exploration's global wreck assets, and underwater photos of finds from past adventures on the opposite side of the room. Leaning over a large white map table, the Barracuda smiled at Alona and Mitch and beckoned them over.

"Welcome to my sanctuary," he roared, slapping Mitch on the back and in time-honoured southern gent style, being quite sure not to offer the same compliment to Alona. After shooting the breeze about how the pair were settling in, the Barracuda started explaining how the ops worked in his holy of holies.

"This room is the Arc Cave, it's where the archaeological magic happens. Be warned, this team is super tight and focused. Working twenty-four hours a day does strange stuff to your head wiring. So, don't expect brotherly love, ok. It's not personal. Time is money out here and the cash we're burning is others' hard earnings. Never forget it."

Authoritative, yet friendly as ever, the Barracuda introduced the team. Al Nassau, the business brains, always stayed on land to orchestrate the funding flow and all angles of the set-up, from legal hiccups to media contacts and safe storage of any shiny gold and silver if and when it surfaced. Sitting at the map table alongside the Barracuda was a thickly bespectacled sixty-year-old introduced as Brains, christened after the 1960s kid's TV programme *Thunderbirds*. The real-life veteran of Keys Exploration's adventures had served as the chief historian for twenty years.

Anything you want to know, from where the treasure might turn up to where the pottery came from or how the Spanish crew relieved themselves at sea, Brains is your go-to guy, the Barracuda advised. The mousy egghead blushed into his chin with mild embarrassment and smiled awkwardly. He wasn't in it for the glory.

A focused Ronald, hardly out of his teens, and zoned into his heavy-duty HP Omen X 2S laptop beneath headphones and a hoodie, was surrounded by a wall of seven plasma screens, four small ones above three large displays.

"This science suite is master control," waved the Barracuda. "From here Brains, the team and yours truly will track Juno live across the seabed and decide what we let her get away with. She's our eyes and hands in the deep. It looks tricky, but once you get your eye in, you'll quickly master the art of telepresence: projecting your mind and body onto the seabed from up here. It's rocket science, but ain't rocket science either if you catch my drift."

All Mitch could make out on the screens was the shadow of a looming yellow monster almost completely hidden in darkness.

"But I can't see crap. The water's pitch black," Alona exclaimed, thinking along similar lines. "How will Juno, and how will we, be able to see what's going on down there?"

"Patience, child," the Barracuda laughed. "You're right, it's a zero visibility of 100% blackness down there. Once Juno hits the sea bottom, we switch on the new girl's lights and she'll illuminate the wreck like a chandelier. Just wait and see. Get ready to gawp at stuff nobody has locked eyes on before."

Alona frowned, unconvinced. Having lived among the power of the cruel sea day in, day out since she was a kid, she knew Poseidon's limits. Were Keys Exploration heading not just into the unknown but into dreamland?

Completing the lab's day team – which would switch every twelve hours in precision planned twenty-four-hour round-the-clock shifts – Fritz, as he was affectionately known at sea, sat behind another bank of computer screens. His six-foot three-inch frame wedged into a tiny annexed cubicle, no more than two metres wide and five metres long, he was finalizing programming dive templates that needed to be religiously filled in every time Juno was recovered using Artefact Registration Sheet software or what the dry-humoured grandson of German immigrants preferred to call my sweet ARS. Fritz would manage all the scientific data. God forbid the man or woman who made an error. Ninety-nine per cent effort is shit, he liked to remind quivering new initiates. Nothing but perfection would do.

Tucked away in the next cabin along, still in the ship's bowels, without windows or fresh air, were three more twenty-somethings cracking jokes and waiting for the serious business to start. The Pap team, short for paparazzi, would run the live video and two still digital cameras fixed to Juno, following live instructions from the Arc Cave about what to photograph underwater.

Nothing was left to chance. Everything was recorded on Datalog software, designed especially for Keys Exploration, before the robot was allowed to touch any goodies: all vital dive stats from depth, area of wreck, Juno's actions, what was recovered and where it was put every second of every dive, the Barracuda explained.

"This is no lucky dip, guys. We may be easy-going and like to play hard, but there's painstaking discipline and slow science behind every coin or jar brought up. It's all been down there for centuries, and we have to respect the wreck and how it ended up there," the Barracuda said solemnly. "Only after meticulous study can we reconstruct an accurate snapshot of the *Merced*'s life and times. We owe it to the ancestors. Or run the risk of being haunted by them forever." At sea, even the most hard-nosed scientist was a prisoner of superstition.

Alona and Mitch were expected to keep out of the way and look and learn for the first two days before being thrown head-first into the deep end. For now, the Barracuda led them outside onto the middle deck into the finds shed, where they would be supervised by Mike the Mouse labelling all the finds brought up, photographing them and recording each artefact into Fritz's ARS. Mouse would teach them how to stabilize the finds by first-aid conservation before proper lab work started in the safety of the Antiquarium museum, where Rodi eagerly waited.

Alona wondered what a shrink would make of all the animal men. If you called a woman a Barracuda or a Mouse, not to mention the Whale running the on-shore conservation team, you'd get a down-dressing from Human Resources. Mitch started realizing this was no jolly but serious, focused grunt work. The surfers felt they would need to learn the equivalent of a new language or pass a Master's degree in the space of a few days.

A buzz of anticipation cut with nervous tension filled the ship. No drifting or escape in this tight-knit team. The surfers wondered whether they'd make fools of themselves and be outed as a liability. Brains, his reputation at stake, hoped his reckoning of what ought to turn up on the wreck, based on hundreds of hours of archival research in Seville, would prove correct. Fritz needed all his hardware and software systems to synchronize in perfect harmony. The Barracuda believed in the miracle of the *Merced* and its ability to change the course of history and, along the way, give up a king's ransom.

An exuberant Barracuda rubbed his hands together, flashed a smile and delivered his trademark line, "This is it. Finders keepers time."

7

Boca Chica Beach, Highway 1

In her mind's eye, getting to Boca Chica Beach would be a brief skip and a hop downtown in her flip-flops. Nicola had pulled on her Stella McCartney bikini, topped with a t-shirt she'd taken a fancy to at a Bellowhead concert many moons ago. The name of the band was intertwined with roots under a solid, trustworthy oak tree. Nicola loved oaks. Deep-rooted trees were something you could trust in life's bumpy ride. A bag containing pleasantries slung over her shoulder, she strode forth with excited purpose, humming quietly.

The old timer smoking and downing his first libation of the day outside the Cuban Coffee Queen brought deflating news. Boca Chica Beach was thirteen miles out of town, north of Key West in no man's land. Follow the sign for the US naval base, he advised. The minor irritation was quickly forgotten thanks to an elderly couple heading home to South Carolina up Route 1. Nicola hitched a ride, polite and eloquent despite her light clothing.

The mouldy sign and arrow pointing to Boca Chica, Geiger Key, was spotted, sure enough. Exchanging worried looks at Nicola's destination, Barb and Bryant offered the innocent abroad a quick lesson in self-preservation off the beaten track in Florida.

"Honey child," Bryant cautioned. "Just know that you'll find all sorts in these parts, the good, the bad and the downright dastardly. The highways and byways are mostly full of kind souls. Take the wrong turn and a den of old money, new money, drug money and no money is waiting to do bad things. The sun junkies are mainly harmless. Keep away from the cocaine cowboys, hard-on-heel bums and out-of-work dictators, you hear."

"Deep South Florida isn't just a pretty postcard, doll," Barb added. "Where you're heading are the dangers of the big swamp on top of the human trash. Have fun, but keep your eyes wide open. In the waters are jellyfish, Portuguese men-of-war and, sorry to say, a fifteen-foot great white shark was spotted in recent weeks. On the shore, avoid assassin bugs, tarantulas, scorpions, rattlesnakes and the nasty local alligators lurking in the shadows. Apart from that, knock yourself out."

Barb and Bryant welcomed Nicola to come visit any time she found herself in Charleston, safely dropped her off by the side of the highway and sped off. Strangely, they felt the more enriched by the charming encounter. What an exotic creature. She sounded just like that Kate Middleton girl, Barb had remarked.

Nicola, a little fearful, hopped over a rusty steel wire fence sagging from old age. The tarmac gave way to scrub. A gentle grass bank sloped towards the shore. More sensible footwear would have been smart. Still, there was no going back. The long-awaited nirvana was close. The bank levelled out to an isolated, washed-out track, once concreted over but never fixed after one of many hurricanes ripped through years ago.

The track petered out to nothing. Concrete gave way to a dusting and then piles of sun-bleached white sand, the edge of civilisation. This was more like it. Drooping trees hung over a winding path and hopefully hiding fate. Finally, there it was, miles of starkly marooned beach. A battered sign warned inadvertent trekkers, 'Clothing Optional Beyond This Point'.

Nicola kicked off her flip-flops and made straight for the water, still deliciously warm after the fading summer. To the south, the shore of Boca Chica, Spanish for the Small Mouth, turned into a rocky outcrop. Hermit crabs, sea cucumbers, starfish and urchins sunned in tidal pools. Further out to sea, uninhabited coral reef islands swept by the hundreds in all directions.

Where the mangroves guarded the foreshore, some wishful castaway had built a lean-to hut from old driftwood and stumps of coral. A Cuban chug boat abandoned near the tide line once brought runaway Cubans to the promise of an American dream back in the day. Where were they now? Did they find what they were looking for? To Nicola's great joy, the scene was one of utter solitude. This wild beach was the hidden gem she had dreamed about night after night.

Nicola was the sole occupant. Hallelujah, she sang, heading to the distant north end of the sands to undress as modestly as you can on a nudist beach. On top of her bag, she set down her t-shirt in case she needed to make a hasty escape and stuffed her phone under it, away from the scorching sun. She rolled out her wicker beach rug, rummaged in her bag for a dog-eared copy of *The Science of Yoga, The Risks and Rewards*, pushed her Ray-Ban's tight against her nose and prepared to do exactly nothing coated in factor sixty sunscreen for a slow burn.

The hours passed. Nicola read and swam to take the edge off the heat and repeated the exercise. She listened to Cuban jazz through her phone, breathed deeply and meditated in the lotus position. After three and a half hours, tentacles of unwelcome feelings started to resurface. Nicola found she was getting bored. She felt no different from the exotic holidays she'd enjoyed at hundreds of five-star beaches. Clothes on, clothes off – it didn't make a jot of difference. Nicola promptly fell asleep.

The sun was curving three-quarters down its arced migration to the far side of the globe when the crab twitching her foot rudely awakened her. As the British abroad manage so perfectly, Nicola was burned close to the colour of a London post box. Her head swam in delirium. She sat up, stiff and sore, took four deep gulps of bottled water and poured the rest over her head. Much better. The stupidity of crashing out under a desert-like sun for god knows how long, and the rooky error of forgetting to smear on more sunscreen after swimming, was clanging inside her head when Nicola realized she was miles from home without water or a ride. The grass was turning out not to be at all greener on the other side of the Atlantic.

Time for home and another philosophical re-think about

life, the universe, the bloody everything. Under a passing wispy white cloud, Nicola packed up her belongings and thought twice about a last dip in the Atlantic. Nature was calling. She decided polluting the ocean wouldn't do, even in the wild. Maybe the Russians were watching by satellite, she reasoned without reason. The privacy of the hidden interior, entangled in dense mangroves, would be far more modest.

The tangled and sharp mangrove was a far cry from the countryside around mama's Hampshire manor house in Beaulieu. In the New Forest, six hundred-year-old stiff-backed oaks ringed the rolling fields where Nicola used to hack out on horseback every Sunday morning after church as a kid. Her plan now was to swiftly cut through the swamp on foot, satisfy the call of nature, and stick out her thumb on Route 1. Then cocktails and a sleeping tablet in Key West to make her forget just how badly her skin was throbbing.

The interior was far wilder than she'd reckoned. Deeper and deeper Nicola roamed until she was satisfied that nobody would spot her from the beach. To the north, a short rivulet meandered through the undergrowth. Nicola unzipped her jeans shorts and squatted down behind an earthen mound. Mission complete, she kicked sand over her offering, hitting a sharp object with her ankle. Drops of blood seeped into the ground. Beneath a ray of light dappling through the shrubbery, Nicola knelt down and examined what had caused her pain. It was a light quartz-coloured triangular object about an inch long with a short shaft. Even to her untrained eye, she was sure the arrowhead sitting in the palm of her hand had to be ancient.

What luck. How on earth did such a thing of beauty with deadly intentions end up in the middle of nowhere? Nicola pocketed her find, threw her bag over her shoulder and lost herself scouting the ground. A side of the mound she'd found relief next to had recently collapsed. Worked stone, oyster shells and bones crumbled out of its side, scattered among the sand. Fascinated, Nicola circled the mound, wondering whether it was the work of man or mother nature, and ambled into the weeping mangroves.

A kaleidoscope of swallowtail butterflies, their brown and yellow wings flittering among the treetops, bewitchingly pulled her deeper into the undergrowth.

The soil started to become boggy and the trees thicker. Nicola's shoulders ached from staring downwards. A slow roll of her neck backwards and a three hundred and sixty degree look at her surroundings made it clear that her pathway had vanished. She frowned, angry at having been lured away with the fairies up the creek without a paddle. Suddenly a growling noise made her jump. Her pulse accelerated in fear. Images of snakes, alligators – and oddly cannibals – flashed through her mind. Was this how it would end? So much for spiritual awakenings. A bright green and orange iguana blinked at her and stared relentlessly. The Medicis were the endangered species around here.

For the first time in her life, Nicola felt a foreboding shadow of time past fill the air. The day had turned extremely queer. Had she time-travelled back into antiquity, she half-heartedly mused, to a time when Native Americans roamed Florida? Indians seemed so very un-Miami. The surreal noise in her head grew and grew until the most appalling sight appeared out of nowhere.

The growling sound turned into a low chugging. Through the twisting mangrove creek, a horrific hallucination came into sight, giving Nicola the shock of her life. A small boat gradually came into view. All along its sides, human skulls with gaping eye sockets grinned at her menacingly. Nicola Medici blacked out.

8

Boca Chica to Sugarloaf Key, Southern Florida

For a moment, Nicola thought she must have been in Amsterdam when she came around. The concerned face smiling back at her was straight out of a museum self-portrait of the Flemish painter Anthony van Dyck. Could the day get any weirder? The man scratched his chiselled white beard and slid off his cap. The voice that followed was all Southern gent.

"Well hello there, missy, pleased you're back with us. Looks like you've seen a bit too much sun."

"No, I can take the sun," Nicola replied, leaning on her left elbow, sand clogging her cheek. "It was a hallucination of being attacked by screaming skulls that freaked me out."

"Sorry about that, *Gollum*'s fault."

"What's Gollum got to do with anything," Nicola snapped, ill temper getting the better of her manners.

"She's my precious launch boat, little missy. I've been a swamp roaming on the good boat *Gollum.* We rarely see any mortals up here other than gators and racoons, certainly not lost Britons," the old man chuckled, pointing towards the creek.

Nicola's eyeline was confronted by a small white boat moored to a tree stump by a single rope line. The name *Gollum* was painted on the bows in black paint. All around the gunwales were nailed human skulls, their jaws wide open, empty eye sockets glaring outward in accusation of the modern world.

"Jesus, Mary and Joseph," Nicola exclaimed. "That's vile. Who the hell are your friends?"

"First things first, let's get you up and about." On spindly legs clad in tattered cream cotton chinos, held up by an old piece of twisted rope, frayed at the ends, into which was tucked a sleeveless blue shirt with one front pocket still fit for purpose, the other half ripped off, the old man tugged Nicola to her feet and brushed her down.

“There, no harm done. Apart from looking like a bowl of Polish borscht soup, you'll be right as rain. You need to squeeze some lemons onto those burns when you get home. And by the way, excuse my manners, my name is Grant Raven. Call me Skip.” The captain held out his right hand, which Nicola cordially shook, returning the favour of her own name.

The pair struck up a conversation about how Nicola ended up lost in time and place – the short, clean version. From time to time, Skip spat a black patch of chewing tobacco on the ground, unconcerned by Nicola's highborn ways. The sunburnt lady fired off a long list of questions about the captain, the time warp she found herself in and her discovery.

“Sorry, I can't help you before beating the dark and enjoying some fortification. How about we steam back to my place, throw back a cup of tea and then I'll drive you down to Key West. Sound good, little missy?”

The plan was a great relief and the pair were soon coasting north onboard the *Gollum* through the Atlantic shallows. Neither spoke. Nicola soaked in the setting sun. Despite her failure to achieve a Zen-like state, she felt unexpectedly content. Life twists in the most unexpected of ways. The yearning for solitude had turned into a private adventure, awakening her sleeping Agatha Christie.

After half an hour, *Gollum* peeled away shoreward towards the twinkling lights of Sugarloaf Key. White and blue colonial-style wooden houses, detached from each other, straddled a broad bay. Like all the keys, Sugarloaf – resembling an old-fashioned torpedo-shaped loaf of sugar – was low-lying and ringed by swamp. Sea grapes replaced the mangroves. Quail doves with purple-striped wings sat on the shade of round leaves, munching a free feast. Nicola deeply breathed in the stark beauty.

Skip steered the launch into a side creek and pointed out a dark brown shuttered wooden tower, its discoloured planks warped from years of punishing heat. The sun-bleached shack had been nailed up in 1911, Skip explained, to get a grip on the area's rampant malaria, dengue and yellow fever. Hundreds of thousands of mosquitoes used to drive the settlers insane and kill tourism. Bats, natural insect predators, were the answer to kicking the pests out of town, it turned out. At dinner time, an adult bat can eat six hundred mosquitoes an hour. The tower was their roost. They may have an evil image, but bats were the Floridians' friends around here. Nicola squirmed.

Gollum headed for a wooden pier at the very end of the key, a fifty-foot finger pointing seaward, perpendicular to the shore. A sign nailed to the landing stage at a rakish angle read Driftwood Rise. The end of the pier was hammered onto a reef bridging land and water. The island landscape was raw and wondrous. Between an unkempt morass of palm trees, Nicola spied a two-storey house, sneakily hidden, its horizontal shuttering painted mint green and capped with a white roof.

The odd couple grabbed their belongings and entered the double front doors standing wide open, just as Skip had left them, below a large bay window. The house had its own private beach and Nicola spotted a green hammock tied between two palm trees. Pinkish white conch shells lined the wooden steps creaking up to the front door. A wide deck surrounded two sides of the property. Definitely my kind of place, Nicola thought to herself. Old-time chic cool.

Inside, Skip started fussing, clicking on the kettle, and opening the fridge.

"First off, no disrespect, but I reckon you could do with a shower, little missy. Then lemons and tea."

Nicola was steered to a first-floor bathroom, where a wooden model of a two-foot iridescent blue Wahoo fish hung on the wall, complete with razor-sharp teeth and silver stripes, and was left to freshen up. The house was conservatively decorated compared to the wild exterior. White walls offset dark brown floorboards and ceiling beams.

After spritzing her sore body under a cold shower and feeling reborn, Nicola returned to the ground floor. Skip had laid out a spread of iced tea and homemade key lime pie. Both wiped off a double helping and, with a sugar rush kicking in, the captain started answering Nicola's long list of questions. All the while the Londoner dabbed her burnt bits with cotton wool saturated with lemon juice and water.

"When you met the *Gollum*, I was doing what I've been doing for five decades in my spare time," Skip started, "roaming the swamps searching for the Vanished People. And spare time is all that's left to me these days."

Nicola raised an eyebrow, perplexed.

"Ok, rewind. Cowboys and Indians, the Wild West, Buffalo Bill? Well, that's late history, nineteenth-century stories about how Western foreigners supposedly civilised America."

Nicola nodded, her mind funnelling down the right path.

"Many centuries before Billy the Kid, Butch Cassidy and Calamity Jane, native tribes were the original landowners of the East Coast. Down here in Florida we had the Chequesta. Not many people have heard of them, but when the Spanish started stealing the natural bounty of the New World and slaughtering the locals, the Chequesta, or Tequesta as they are better known, were big cheeses."

Nicola admitted she'd never heard of these noble Native Americans and wondered where and how they lived.

"Many different tribal kin roamed between their hometown at the mouth of the Miami River and the southern spear tip of Key West. The Tequesta owned La Florida for at least three hundred years before our good Lord was in diapers, but they are still a mystery. Stereotypes of man-eating and scalping die very slow, ya know."

Nicola sat back under the stars on the deck outside Driftwood Rise and chilled out, enchanted by Skip painting a picture of ages past. The captain got up and paced the floorboards in full flight. Over the next seventy minutes, Nicola learned how the Vanished People fished wearing deer hide loincloths for everything from sharks, whales and porpoises to stingrays, turtles and tiddlers. Sea-wolf, better known as monk seals, were set aside for the chief and his family.

The tribe snacked on clams and oysters. On land, the braves hunted for venison and deer. In the undergrowth, women clad in skirts made from moss and plant leaves gathered snails as well as fruit and roots from the local bounty. Kind of like in Key West, clothing wasn't a big deal. Nicola's sunburn saved the captain from seeing her blush.

Nicola next wanted to know where the Tequesta lived and what happened to them. Lineage was a big deal to Ms Medici's family.

"Well, you've hit the mystery button right on the head there," Skip pointed out. "Nobody can even say for sure how many Tequesta lived here. Some say just 800, other anthropologists reckon a tribe of ten thousand. Take your pick. Down the years I've mapped around sixty-five Indian sites between Miami and Key West. Now I was never good at maths, but say eighty people in every settlement gives a total population of around five thousand two hundred, right? That would be my best-educated guess. But they left no written records behind, so who knows? The meaning of just ten words from their language survives today. The depth of our understanding is prehistoric in its ignorance."

"As for their fate, that sadness accounts for why their story has never really been told. The Tequesta weren't hard-wired for agriculture. They were always roaming from camp to camp with the rhythm of the seasons. During the worst of the mosquito months, unlike today, the tribal folk from Miami came down to the keys for three months to escape the air riddled with what we now know was malaria. In their last one hundred and fifty years, the Tequesta spent much of their time side-stepping a far more deadly menace, the Spanish lords and missionaries arm twisting the natives to bow to Jesus and the Cross."

"The Jesuits set up a string of fortified missions between St Augustine and here in 1565, followed by the Franciscans, to save the Indians' souls. Anyways, after Britain finally pushed the old enemy over the edge and sent the Spanish back home with their tails between their legs, the king of England turned on the 'uncivilised' Tequesta. In 1763 they were herded like dumb cattle and sent on ships into exile in Cuba. Heart breaking. History is a set of ugly cycles. Britain did to the Native Americans exactly what the Spanish did to foreigners in Andalusia during the Inquisition. And so history turns, round and round, without the slightest lessons being learnt." Skip sighed, his eyes moist and vacant.

"So, what's Boca Chica got to do with the Tequesta?" Nicola asked a few minutes after the captain had ended his lecture and slumped onto a cushioned chair.

A weary Skip was visibly flagging but raised both hands towards the outside world and replied earnestly, "We have eyes, yet we see not. The Irish poet Jonathan Swift once said that true vision is the art of seeing the invisible. He's right. For me the invisible lies in the ground, and in the ground hides the secret of the Vanished People. Even here among our fake colonial houses, the past whispers through the wind. Right behind Driftwood Rise is a Native Indian mound of shell, pottery, flint and ancient drama. It lies bang north of the modern highway. Millions of people zoom past it every year. No one spends a second thinking what it means to humanity."

Nicola suddenly remembered her own date with the past that very afternoon and rummaged for her soil-caked arrowhead zipped into the front pocket of her backpack. Skip's face lit up at the sight of an old friend.

"That's a keeper, little missy," he advised. "Follow me."

The captain tore through a side door and thudded up the stairs like a teenager. Nicola followed in his wake. Upstairs she entered a room with no door packed full of folders, two walls of heaving bookshelves and posters of ancient cities and artefacts, one declaring 'Our Careers Lie in Ruins'. The musty scene was one of semi-bedlam. Skip had pulled a book off his shelf and mumbled to himself as he flicked through the pages. Nicola peered at its cover and read *Florida Arrowhead Typology* by Stephen and Claudia Granger.

"Here we are, got it," the captain confirmed, stabbing his finger at a photo and drawing. "You've got yourself a Type 35 stemmed Seminole arrowhead, used around 200 years before the present day. Not rare, but a pretty fine specimen."

"I love it. What would your pals, the Tequesta, have used this for?" Nicola asked, rolling her thumb over the flint to feel its ridged surfaces and tune into its ancient memory. Who was the last person who held it hundreds of years ago, and what were his fears and dreams?

"Anything, quite frankly," Skip replied. "Hunting animals or even humans." Nicola rubbed her skin, which had broken out into goosebumps. "There can be little doubt that the Tequesta could be savage when provoked. Some say they even practised human sacrifice, but the evidence is 50-50. What is sure is that Florida's Native Americans stripped the flesh from their own human dead, burned it and doled out some clean-picked bones to relatives as respectful keepsakes. The rest was reburied."

"The Tequesta thought three souls inhabited the human body," Skip explained, "one in the eyes, one in the reflection and one oddity skulking in the shadows."

"Very strange," Nicola recalled. "You'll think I'm crazy, but I couldn't help but feel something watching me from the shadows down in the mangroves of Boca Chica. Probably paranoia, I suppose."

The captain was gently reassuring. "The things I've seen and felt, nothing mad about that to me, little missy. The Vanished People live on in the landscape's spirit, watching and listening." Skip lost his thread for a moment before re-focusing. "Sorry, where precisely did you find your arrowhead?"

"Precisely, I have no idea," Nicola regretted. "I was hopelessly lost, but it can't have been more than half a mile from where *Gollum* gave me a heart attack."

Skip laughed and raised an arm in an apologetic salute.

"I found it on the edge of a dip in the ground, say eight

metres wide, next to some kind of earthen mound. The arrowhead sat next to a bunch of shells, pottery and bones sticking out of the sands. It all looked pretty old."

Skip stiffened. "My dear, you may just conceivably have stumbled upon an American holy grail." For whatever reason, Nicola's instincts told her Skip was not insane. Method underlay his life-long quest for the Tequesta past.

"For centuries, people in these parts have whispered about a great Spanish treasure buried in Indian lands. Nothing had ever turned up in any historical text. The few descendants of massacres, conversions and exiles, from St Augustine to Key West, told stories of a colossus of a white man who walked out of the sea, raised the dead, lived among them and died without giving up his secrets. Problem is nobody has ever found a morsel of Tequesta life near Key West. I've hunted high and low and like to think I have a good nose for Native camps. Still *nada* – until you came along."

"At times of famine and plague, the white man would disappear into Florida's deep south and return with food and medicine. Nobody knew where he got the money to buy it from the Spanish forts. For the Tequesta, it was a miracle. And people started talking. If he came from the sea, maybe he could breathe underwater and cart treasures off ill-fated sunken ships. Or so the old myth goes."

"You mean like the 1622 Tierra Firme fleet?" Nicola asked innocently.

Skip's eyes narrowed and he sat back in his chair. Crossing his arms, the captain replied, "What you know or think you know about the 1622 treasure ships isn't all it seems. I cannot confirm or deny if the story of the golden Spaniard is real or an old wife's tale."

Skip peered mischievously at Nicola before whispering into the night sky, "This much I am certain about, the treasure is very real. If only the good Lord grants me enough time to crack the codex."

Despite firing off a list of more demanding questions, Skip closed up like a clam. He shrugged that no doubt his thoughts were the ramblings of an old fool. "Ask me no more questions and I'll tell you no lies," he ended.

The captain was ageing as evening turned to late night. The mangrove hunter was worn out but insisted on driving Nicola home. She refused point blank. Telephone numbers and email addresses were exchanged and a taxi called. Skip presented his exotic new friend with a bag of lemons and a quarter of a key lime pie, and Nicola returned his kindness with a kiss and a hug. Bumping up and down the old trail leading away from the magic of Driftwood Rise and speeding south down Highway 1 back towards civilisation, Nicola struggled to make sense of the most peculiar day of her young life. Questions pressed her mind; unfamiliar emotions made her heart race.

In the end it had been the mantle of time that started to disrobe, uncovering a deep ignorance. The past was stirring the here and now. In the full sphere of the human experience I'm just a fly on the chronology of human existence, Nicola told herself. She hadn't needed to drop her pants on a nudist beach after all. What had she been thinking? At least she'd followed karma's path, throwing a pebble into the waters of her soul. The planet's rippling reward was a delicious mystery and a cluster of unsolved questions. Nicola ended the day feeling alive like never before. Now she had her own secret cause to chase.

Skip's sanity and depth of knowledge were undoubted. The idea of a golden Spaniard, supposedly remembered from centuries of idle chitchat, sounded like wishful thinking, though. Nicola was thankful eccentrics like Skip walked the earth, but she had never quite trusted things she couldn't see for herself. And a golden Spaniard who stepped out of the waves with bags of gold three or four hundred years ago was preposterous madness, a fun story but a fantasy not to be taken seriously.

The sharp arrowhead in her pocket, ancient and sticking into her thigh, spoke of very real possibilities. This weapon of destruction was authentic enough. Nicola pulled out her discovery and rubbed her thumb over its edge. What was real and fantasy started to blur.

Back at Schooner Wharf Bar, the sanctuary of a bath and cup of Earl Grey beckoned. Lost to her racing mind, she didn't hear Rodi welcome her from a dusty bench, downing an end-of-day libation. She was still shimmering in limbo between the veil of the present and the vanished world.

9

The Abyss, Straits of Florida

The drum of electric winches whirred relentlessly, day and night. The *Golden Margaret* was a hive of bright lights, glaring plasma screens, bustling bodies and sweat. An acrid stench of the burning diesel keeping the ship on station cut the air. Along the narrow tunnel warrens, scientists and technicians streamed up and down the heartbeat of the ship, dropping in and out of the cafeteria or Nosh Pit, as the team called it. Since smoking and boozing were strictly off limits, topping up cups of joe, sneaking a slice of cake or asking Angel and Benjie, the chefs, what was for lunch or dinner took on extra meaning to set your clock by. Life on a Keys Exploration's shipwreck project was shocking for the waistline.

Everyone except Alona and Mitch was unsurprised how quickly the surfers took to deep-sea exploration. Unlike many marine newbies, they were comfortable on the water, sleeping like old salts. The Barracuda had been spot on about what the deep looked like too. No sooner had Juno switched on her lights than the deep lit up like a chandelier, illuminating a playground of sights and colours, curious crabs and sharks disappointed that robots were far less tasty than divers.

Everyone had crowded around the lab's plasma screens broadcasting live from four hundred metres deep when Juno touched down eleven days ago. The robot had cautiously hovered around the site, flying foot by foot while the eagle-eyed engineers watched the seabed from all camera angles to make sure Juno didn't hit anything delicate or get snagged on a seabed surprise. The mysteries were starting to unravel. The *Merced*, if that really was the wrecked ship, had struck the flat seabed with an almighty crunch.

Few people have seen a shipwreck deeper than ninety metres down. Shallow-water paddlers convince themselves that anything deeper, beyond the limits of SCUBA, must look like something from a Disney cartoon: still standing proudly upright after all the years, the captain's fish-gnawed skeleton grasping the steering wheel. The Tortugas ship, so called because it sank a mile south of the Dry Tortugas islands, the nearest landmark, certainly wasn't intact. It was in far more impressive shape, though, than the rest of the hurricane-whipped 1622 fleet chased down by the Barracuda in the shallows closer to the Florida Keys. Parts of the *Atocha* and *Margarita* had turned up tens of kilometres apart, blitzed by waves, currents, hurricanes and trawlers in less than twenty metres of water.

The *Merced* was a very different beast. It settled into a low mound about a metre high. The Barracuda excitedly pointed out how she collided stern first, snapping off the rudder to starboard. Juno next lit up the kitchen stores, a blue painted plate, a bronze astrolabe for sailing by the stars, three anchors and large slabs of concreted iron containing who knew what goodies.

Ends of wooden hull ribs stuck out of the grey mud, their tips honeycombed with holes gnawed by ravenous shipworms, the silent assassins of the seas. Juno swept past piles of stones, the ballast needed to balance the ship to sail true. At both ends of the wreck, the robot spun around four bronze cannon, two on each side of the hull, its cameras zooming in to peer beneath centuries of marine crust in the hope of reading any inscriptions moulded onto them. No joy.

Brown ceramic jars were scattered by the hundreds around the edges of the ballast pile. These jars, the Barracuda pointed out, carried not just olive oil but anything from wine, vinegar, honey, figs and capers to gunpowder. Brains was almost hyper-ventilating as he pointed out a square wooden case, which Alona hoped might be a chest of riches but turned out to be the entrance to the hull pump, critical for baling out rising water when it leaked through plank seams. A respectful silence spread across the table when the wreck hunters realised the effects of this equipment's epic failure in the wild hurricane of September 1622.

The discovery on day one of the bell, the last sound to ring out before the crew met its maker, had been met with quiet respect as well. Frustratingly the ship's name wasn't inscribed on its corroded green surface, just the date, 1620. Good news, the Barracuda had grinned in delight. The wrecked ship once sailed the waves close to the year of the *Merced*'s last voyage. The boat's ruinous bones looked like a strong fit.

A stream of finds had started to surface. No sooner were they photographed and plotted on the seabed in 3D than Juno gently lifted them into DSF's, Deep-Sea Fridges, or what were really two square plastic crates. Each was numbered with a unique number and sub-divided with sponge padding into chambers to make sure every object, from a leather shoe to a cannon, was safely lifted to the surface. The surfers soon picked up the lingo, nodding respectfully when the scientists talked about context in almost religious terms. One thing they learnt swiftly, you didn't joke about context.

Over coffee in the Nosh Pit, Brains explained its sanctity. Just ripping stuff off the seabed kills identity, leaving a wreck without meaning. It wipes out the hard drive of history.

"Take the silver eight *reales* coin that turned up this morning," Brains pointed out. "On its own it's just a coin like thousands of others stored in museums or sold in antique shops. But in context, it becomes a fact. We found it inside a cooking pot, of all places. Fact 1: the coin is decorated with the Habsburg shield, the arms of King Phillip II, and the Mexico mint date of 1619. Bingo: the coin tells us the ship has to date after 1619 and is Spanish. Fact 2: pot and coin tell us that the space where they were found in the stern must be the ship's galley where cooking was done and personal wealth locked away. Not the bulky treasure, you understand, but the personal pocket cash of the merchant passengers. Except we haven't hit the actual cabin yet. We'll get there."

"Fact 3: and this is a weird one, the cooking pot, whose style we can now tightly date, is not Spanish but what potheads call colonoware, an ugly gritty vessel found in the Native American lands of Latin America. Only in 1622 the Spanish were so far along the way to wiping out the sorry Native Indians that enslaved Africans had to be shipped in from the Gold Coast *en masse* to replace them. The cooking pot's shape imitates West African village styles. This makes me start to wonder whether African slaves did the cooking on the 1622 Spanish fleet," Brains finished, looking very pleased with himself.

Alona nodded, deep in thought. Mitch's only question was "whose colon?" Brains patiently corrected the surfer that colonoware was a pretty dumb name for native cooking pots from the Americas. Mitch glazed over. If it didn't shine, he wasn't fussed.

The Barracuda, eavesdropping, was distracted. Something didn't stack up. If this really was the galley, where were the hundreds of red bricks and tiles that once insulated the ship's wooden floor from the fire? He kept the nagging thought to himself. And if the ship was truly Spanish, why had a Native Caribbean greenstone necklace been discovered in a cooking pot next to a gold medallion of the Virgin Mary?

Nothing much of any value had sparkled until Mitch and Alona went down for breakfast on day twelve. So far, they had brushed mud off thousands of potsherds and helped stage photos of each find with a funny little black-and-white scale divided into one-centimetre units. They'd dutifully bagged and labelled objects, more weird than wonderful, before delicately placing them in water baths to flush the salts out and stop the finds cracking in the open air.

Boredom was starting to seep into the surfers' bones. The couple started spending less time peering into the deep than watching the clock, eagerly waiting to return to dry land and cool beer. They agreed philosophically that the trip had been a good laugh, but that treasure wasn't all it was cracked up to be. Broken pots weren't going to send them into retirement.

All that changed on day twelve. At 8.15 am, the Nosh Pit was deserted to the surfers' surprise. What could be more important than waffles, eggs and syrup washed down with lashings of thick coffee to wake up to? Even the chefs had vanished. A puzzled Alona and Mitch shrugged and were happily laying into their eggs, sunny side up, when loud whooping boomed down the gangway. The pair locked eyes and ran. At the centre of a huddle of bent backs in the Arc Cave, the Barracuda beamed like a father to a newborn child. A white plastic tray dripped wet on a chair. Finally, the surfers understood what all the fuss was about.

Gold fever had struck. The whole ship's crew stared at a pile of two dozen silver coins and four eight-inch long golden bars, about half an inch wide, resembling bananas flattened by a truck. Each was stamped with indecipherable marks and notches. The whooping, high-fives and, in the case of Rusty and Brains, a strange jig from foot to foot continued for a few minutes before the Barracuda raised his open hand and invited everyone to calm down.

"Ok, boys and gals, listen up. First off, we've hit pay dirt," he started to a new outbreak of euphoria. When the revelry died down, the Barracuda explained what everyone was salivating over.

"This be gold, alright," the experienced wreck hunter confirmed, pretending to bite one of the bars. "This cluster turned up under fifteen centimetres of mud in the bows, so surely was once locked away in a side locker before nature did its thing. So, not the cargo motherlode, but a mighty fine start. Not very original, you'll agree, but we call these finger bars. Now then." The Barracuda bent down to pick up two bars, which he examined through a magnifying glass under a desk light.

"I reckon each bar weighs about eight hundred and fifty grams of twenty-one-karat gold. That's not me being a smart arse: each bar is stamped XXI five times," he told the crew. "The stamps are incredible, as fresh as the day some sorry miner cast them. I've never seen anything as mint fresh as these suckers. The mine names are super clear as well. See these three sets of words, SARGOSA PECARTA, SEBATN ESPANOL and PLENRADA?

They give us the whole back story."

The Barracuda explained how all the bars came from Colombia, christened Nueva Granada by the Spaniards. The Sargosa bar had been exported from the mining district of Zaragoza in the high hills of Antioquia. "If my memory serves me right, those mines were dug by two thousand West African slaves down by the beaches of the River Nechi," the boss continued. "The mine's shafts turned out about three hundred thousand *pesos* of gold dust every year. Zaragoza was the El Dorado for gold in the Americas, boys and lady." The old man bowed graciously towards Alona.

"As for Mr Sebatn Espanol here," the Barracuda pointed out, turning to the second finger bar, "this was manufactured in the mines of San Sebastian in Timana in the central area of western Colombia. All along the high basin of the River Magdalena, the rocks and streams are drenched in gold. The Spaniards from Bogota were forever brawling with the Timana Native people before the invaders built the city of San Sebastian de la Plata a kilometre inland around 1550 to work the mines."

"Finally, we come to the mystery of Plenrada," the Barracuda ended. "These boys could have been anyone. Plenrada was a family name, kinda the same as Smith or Jones back in seventeenth-century Spain. If I had to guess, dagger at my throat, I'd bet the Colombian mines were under the control of the Duque de Peñaranda de Duero, who also happened to be the President of the Counsels of Castille and the Indies. Together all this shiny goodness was stowed on the *Merced* in Cartagena, the main port in Colombia to and from Nueva Granada."

The Barracuda carefully returned the bars to their storage box and let the crew examine the fruits of their sweat. Only when Alona reached the centre of the huddle did she notice numerous panels of circular dots manically stamped on virtually every free surface of half the gold bars. The surfer put up her hand to catch the Barracuda's eye amidst the cacophony.

"Sorry, but what about these pretty circles," asked Alona. "Are they just decoration?"

The Barracuda composed his thoughts and scratched the back of his neck. The crowd fell silent. "I was kinda hoping nobody was gonna grill me on those," the boss admitted. "Those are *quintos*." The collective rabble shrugged and looked at one another.

"Back in the day, the king of Spain was master of everything and everyone. The government was a bunch of crawling courtiers who bowed, scraped and did whatever the monarch asked. The Crown hardly needed to lift a finger to rake in filthy cash. The *quinto* was the king's fifth, a twenty per cent tax for lazy royals lashed to all the riches imported from the Americas. These marks, Alona, tell us that the gold tax was pre-paid into the royal chest at the same moment when the bars were cast. So, they one hundred per cent belonged to merchants and not the Crown. The king sure ain't getting these suckers back," the Barracuda finished. The room went wild. Rusty threw his cap into the air.

Only Alona wondered what that made the other half of the gold bars not stamped with the king's sign of tax payment. After all these centuries, who would own those rogue ingots?

The Barracuda picked up the ship's satellite phone and called in the joyful news. Within minutes, Al Nassau, overwhelmed with relief, arranged for a five-seat Airbus Colibri chopper to head out from Key West's helipad to bring the booty home. Things were very much looking up. Nothing could stop Keys Exploration now.

10

Jorvik & Silver, Old Bond Street, London

By the time the red phone started ringing off the hook in the offices of the law firm Jorvik & Silver, down the south end of London's Old Bond Street, James Jorvik had nearly drowned in his Cornflakes. The Barracuda's gold was all over the idiot news, which couldn't tell real treasure from tin cans. After a not entirely unpleasant dawn chorus chat with Bob Brooker, at 6.00 am the law partner unfolded his freshly posted edition of *The Times*, popped a cup of tea with two sugars on the three-generation-old family oak table and savoured his breakfast ritual. The choking and spluttering brought about by the right-hand column of the front page even awoke Jorvik's wife, who didn't believe in rising before she heard the door slamming on James's back.

'Keys Exploration Strikes Spanish Gold', the article announced. Al Nassau had lost no time giving an exclusive to *The Times* with news of the Barracuda's exploits next to a money shot of the gold bars on a mound of silver coins, seashells and seaweed. By releasing the story the previous afternoon, Nassau planned to get the wires humming, pleading for more, before he saturated news outlets across the world. Jorvik scanned the column before being re-routed to the world news section. In thrilling technicolour, the paper showed an underwater photo of olive jars taken by Juno alongside a map marked with an 'X' where the wreck was discovered. A fuming Jorvik tore out his mobile phone, his hand shaking.

Bob Brooker was expecting the barrage. He imagined the vein on the side of Jorvik's neck pulsing as he hollered down the phone how Brooker was paid to keep the firm informed, two steps ahead of everyone else. Jorvik advised Brooker to pull his finger out and focus. Matters had moved far swifter than Jorvik and Brooker had expected. Bad mistake. They were spooked. Time to move up a gear. For a 4 pm board meeting, Jorvik expected a full briefing and battle strategy for putting an immediate halt to the treasure-hunting weasels – or Brooker could expect no tiffin and be out on his backside. The lawyer hung up.

The campaigner stretched out and groaned. Jorvik was too easily flustered. Only one thing for it: finally time for a bacon, sausage and egg sandwich with lashings of brown HP Sauce. Greasy food helped Brooker think. Munching down at Dom Vito's café around the corner from the office, he recapped where he stood. Call him what you want, a lazy sociopath, but when it came to dogmatic righteousness, he was king. When Keys Exploration's press release broke down the wire, early morning in London, Brooker had clicked into military overdrive, predicting the will of his paymasters, but mostly driven by personal loathing. Jorvik had been tipped off and, immediately afterwards, the campaigner had taken the unauthorized risk of spending some of the company's cash to steal a march on the day.

Where to start? First of all, Brooker had yanked out a dusty file on the 1622 Tierra Firme Spanish fleet to scan for clues to sink Kurt Barracuda, grand lord of the treasure hunters. The Barracuda had previous. In 1976 his team found the flagship of the 1622 fleet or rather its main hold. The State of Florida sued the Floridian, which menacingly demanded all the booty be turned over. Because the galleon sank inside territorial waters, it was government property, so they pleaded.

Keys Exploration countered that the State had no rights at all. The authorities had no clue where the wreck went down and had made no attempt to invest time, money or technology in recovering the heritage. They had consciously abandoned it. The Supreme Court upheld the Barracuda's rights, following the letter of the law, agreeing he was legally the old ship's salvor-in-possession. The little man beat the system. Finders keepers. The team pocketed tens of millions of dollars and destroyed one of history's most important shipwrecks ever discovered, Brooker told himself, spitting egg all over the table and down his shirt.

Jorvik & Silver's files listed the full vital statistics of all the 1622 fleet vessels – name, origin, size, tonnage, cargo, crew size, artillery – apart for two cases for which the cabinets were bare. All Brooker could learn about the missing ship came from a faded photocopy of the pamphlet *A True Relation of That Which Lately Hapned to the Great Spanish Fleet and Galleons of Terra Firma in America*, published in English by Nathaniel Butler of London in 1623. The report, copied from a first-hand Spanish account, claimed that after the sinking of the great treasure ships, the flagship *Atocha* and the *Margarita*, "in the same houre, with the same tempest, and almost at the same place, two Ships of the Fleete were swallowed in the deepest Sea, and perished before they could approach shore."

Damnation, Brooker seethed, realizing he didn't even have the name of the damned ship, let alone a list of what it was carrying home to king and country in Madrid. Until proven otherwise, Brooker would gamble that the Barracuda was right to pinpoint the wreck as the *Merced.* Still, the campaigner wouldn't put it past Keys Exploration to falsify the facts to scam their investors.

Brooker soon realised he was out of his depth and needed outside help. On this occasion, he'd risk not getting a budget signed off by Jorvik & Silver before firing the trigger. Timing was of the essence. America was out. His contacts on the East Coast would be snoring in their pillows. Best to wake up Spain, an early riser, and spread some Euros and love with his brothers in arms.

This could only mean Seville, where any self-respecting historian hoped to get to grips with Spain's voyages of discovery to the New World between the fifteenth and eighteenth centuries for one good reason. The port city was journey's start and end for all royal fleets. Here ships were commissioned, crews assembled, supplies bought and cargoes stowed.

More importantly, the king's royal warehouses stretched along the banks of the Guadalquivir River, making certain everyone and their pet monkey faithfully paid the royal *quinto real*, a tax on a fifth of all wealth, into Seville's Casa y Audiencia de Indias, the House of Trade of the Indies. Day and night dockers broke their backs dragging wagons of silver and gold between the riverbank, the royal treasury and, just around the corner, to the Casa de la Moneda, the royal mint.

Brooker flicked names through his mind. Who could work fast and accurately? Fuddy-duddy old school academics were out. Scholars needed at least three weeks to deliver and the firm would have to factor in another week to unpick their pompous language and turn it into human speak. No, someone young, fresh and hungry but with a decent publications record was the ticket.

Brooker scanned his bookshelves for inspiration and landed on an English translation of Dr G.A. 'Geronimo' Martinez's *La Conquista de Las Rutas Oceánicas Americanas*. Brooker grinned as he recalled two memorable evenings spent with good old Geronimo at the Amsterdam conference on Iberian Traders and the Atlantic two years ago. Brooker and Martinez had followed the crowd in the after-hours pleasures of Amsterdam but only kept one ear open to the dull conference gossip in forgettable bars. Both got far more pleasure discussing how to right the world of the pest of treasure hunters who dared turn a profit from the sanctity of the sunken past. Born to bitter old enemy nations, buckets of booze made the pair feel like blood brothers.

Time to call in a favour from his comrade. Brooker looked up Martinez's address at the Faculty of International Economics at the University of Seville, emailed a brief requesting data on the two missing deep-sea losses for the 1622 fleet sunk far from shore in the Straits of Florida and signed off 'Brookmeister, NYP' – Name Your Price. Pleased with his work, the disgraced serviceman had then decided it was nigh time to head out for that bacon, sausage and egg sandwich. Heck, maybe two were in order to celebrate his mounting excitement while he waited for Geronimo's news.

*

At 4 pm sharp, James Jorvik threw open the conference room doors on the second floor of Jorvik & Silver and was satisfied to see everyone present and correct. Dominic Silver didn't look up. He continued studying the crossword on the back page of *The Telegraph* perched on the knee of his impeccable Savile Row navy blue pinstriped suit. Two associate solicitors, booted, suited and closely shaved, stood backs erect on the far side of the room.

Brooker was busy triple-checking his notes. This was no time to cock up. His crusty beige safari jacket with four pockets on the front, polluted with a dark splodge of HP Sauce that got worse the more Brooker wiped it after breakfast, gave Jorvik little faith the meeting would be productive. He sighed and sat down wearily. The partner decided to place himself at the opposite head of the table to avoid the ripe odour wafting off Brooker, peering over half-moon glasses at his employee's stubble face and blood-shot eyes. God knows when the boy last slept or took a Vitamin C tablet.

Mr Jorvik, as all but Silver called their boss, started by summarising the state of play before confirming that the goal of today's meeting was to agree on the best legal way to force Keys Exploration to cease and desist from pillaging a Spanish wreck. Jorvik gestured to Brooker to take centre stage, reminding him to please focus on facts, not opinions.

Geronimo had turned up the goods, quickly mining his university archives for full details of the 1622 fleet. At some point, Brooker would need to bring up the rather painful matter of the £3,500 consultancy fee. Best to wait a few days.

"Good news all round I'm pleased to report," the campaigner began. Brooker had spent the last couple of hours throwing together a PowerPoint presentation of Martinez's results and flicked up the first slide, showing a Spanish merchant ship in profile and plan painted by the shipwright Manoel Fernandez for his masterly *Livro de Traças de Carpintaria* published in 1616.

"No visual images survive for any 1622 fleet ship shockingly, but this is the closest we can put our finger on the subject at hand. What does survive, though, are the outward-bound ships' registers and cargo manifests for the two deep-sea losses, which" – Brooker paused for dramatic effect – "I can reveal were called the *Nuestra Señora de la Merced* and the *Nuestra Señora de la Rosario*. I suggest we discount the *Rosario* from our investigation. Turns out she was a supply ship carrying food and no treasure. Of course, it's always possible that some merchants craftily smuggled contraband gold onboard with the intention of sneaking it off the ship at Cadiz before sailing on to fortress Seville, but I don't believe that fits our profile."

Brooker played the next slide, a high-resolution underwater photo of the Barracuda's deep-sea wreck in the Straits of Florida released on Keys Exploration's website for press use. Silver raised his head; Jorvik frowned. He didn't care to be reminded of the photo. Or, indeed, of any signs showing the damage those damn Yankees were doing to such noble history, left happily untouched for centuries. His blood pressure started to boil.

"Everything on this photo looks Spanish," Bob Brooker went on. "Andalusian olive jars. Check. Some kind of Seville blue-glazed maiolica plate that went out of use around 1700. Check. And in the left foreground, exactly the kind of bronze astrolabe you'd expect to see on a long-distance Iberian voyager before 1650. Check. So, the numbskulls at least seem to have got the boat's nationality right. Now look in the very shadows of the background. See it?"

Jorvik rolled his eyes and invited Brooker not to grandstand. "I am the senior partner in a law firm, Mr Brooker, not a grubby bottom feeder. Proceed," he cautioned.

"Lurking in the background, you can make out the outline of an iron concretion about two metres long," smiled Brooker.

"And what exactly has a pile of rusting metal got to do with treasure and entrapment?" Dominic Silver asked, awoken from his slumber by the thought that he might actually learn something new today.

Brooker turned to the next slide, a dark yellow document

covered with spidery black writing. Other than the date 1622 written in the right margin, nobody could make head or tail of the document. Brooker explained how the document was the original register for the *Nuestra Señora de la Merced* and moved to the next slide, which summarised its content:

- Owner: Juan de la Torre Ayala
- Captain: Juan Limbre
- Construction: Lisbon
- Length: 37 *codos* (21.5 metres)
- Tonnage: 125 and three-eighths ton
- Breadth: 11 *codos* (6.3 metres)
- Anchors: 4
- Crew: 10 sailors, pilot, 8 cabin boys, 3 pageboys
- Ordnance: 8 iron cannon, 12 muskets, balls, shot, lead bullets, powder
- Route: departed Guadalquivir River, fleet of General Juan de Lara Moran
- Destination: Cartagena by way of Nueva Cordoba

"Please note the *Merced* carried eight iron cannon for defence, while the *Rosario* needed none as a supply ship. The rusting metal highlighted in the explorers' photo is an iron gun. *Quod erat demonstrandum*: we may 100% categorically conclude that this vessel is indeed the long-lost Spanish frigate the *Merced*." A Cheshire cat grin lit up the campaigner's face at his eureka moment.

Jorvik & Silver overlooked Brooker's pomposity because Latin had been beaten into both of them at public school. They were happy to let the boy enjoy the moment for a first-class piece of detective work if it helped motivate him.

"Good show, Mr Brooker," Dominic Silver acknowledged, "yet I notice this ship seems very small. Are we seriously to believe such a jalopy could carry anything beyond its heritage value to make Kurt Barracuda sit up and take stock? Doesn't look like a gleaming treasure galleon to me."

"You are, of course, quite right, Mr Silver," Brooker agreed. "This worried me as well – at first. But I checked Chaunu's exhaustive catalogue, *Séville et l'Atlantique, 1504-1650*, and discovered that at one hundred and twenty-five tons the *Merced* was ten tons over the minimum threshold allowed for Spanish fleets. She was small but fast and effective. Plenty of room for cargo and treasure, trust me. Speaking of which…." Brooker moved to another impenetrable page of spider's writing and explained its content.

"On her outward-bound journey, the *Merced* was stuffed with the fruits of Andalusia, one thousand nine hundred pottery jars carrying wine, brandy and oil, plus sacks of quince meat, raisins, hazelnuts, chestnuts, capers and olives, as well as iron knives, fabric, women's shoes and hats. There was even a tapestry painting of the souls of purgatory. All were heading to the needy provinces of Nueva Cadiz in Venezuela and the Tierra Firme lands of Latin America, the home of Spain's gold and silver mines."

"Now the not-so-good news," Brooker continued as Jorvik winced – he didn't do bad news – "is that nobody, and I mean nobody, not even Kurt Barracuda, has the manifest from the homeward-bound voyage. The problem is not bad research. Turns out that the poor Spanish scribes and accountants of Cartagena and Havana took to their sick beds in the summer of 1622. Many never returned to their desks. What the overlords unfairly called the 'Indean Disease' had struck. Patients started bleeding from their lungs and turned yellow with liver failure. This wasn't some ancient Indian curse. Today we know these people, including huge numbers of Native Americans, died from Leptospirosis or rat catcher's yellows. Rats hitchhiking a ride on European ships made landfall and infected the freshwater supplies. These days we call it Weil's Disease. So, I'm afraid no accounts of ship cargoes or manifests were ever written for any treasure ships that left those shores in the deadly year of 1622. The only way anyone can prove for sure what went down on the *Merced* is by digging it up."

James Jorvik stood up and started pacing. "Yes, indeed, it does all sound extremely vile. What Mr Barracuda kids himself may or may not be on the *Merced* doesn't trouble me. Perhaps he got it right or maybe he's swindling America. Who cares. If his smart investors allow themselves to be defrauded, more fool them. I shall not weep for their pensions. Rather, I pray they all get rat catcher's disease." Bob Brooker nodded enthusiastically.

"Now, my boy, what can we nail them on? Looting culture in territorial waters is a matter for the State of Florida. Let's pay the Barracuda's lawyers the compliment of presuming they are fully aware of this fact and thus infer that the *Merced* went down in international seas, that is to say, outside the twelve nautical-mile limit under national control." Jorvik turned to face Silver, who confirmed this was the case. "Therefore, I repeat, what legal tripwire has Keys Exploration violated?"

Silence engulfed the room and everyone except a bulging-eyed James Jorvik chose to inspect their shoes. After two minutes of soul-searching, the partner made a decision.

"Cedric, get me Eva Clermont-Ganneau from ICOCH on the phone," Jorvik snapped at the shorter of the two silent senior associate lawyers listening in.

James Jorvik and Clermont-Ganneau, both respected lawyers, went way back, for fifteen years going to the same colloquiums on maritime law and, more recently, underwater heritage. Jorvik's career had been all about chasing money. His French counterpart was built differently. She'd followed her heart and liberal father's wishes to protect the past. In her role as the Director of the International Council of Cultural Heritage (ICOCH) in Marseille, Ms Clermont-Ganneau had roped Jorvik into helping her organisation draw up the Convention on the Defence of Underwater Culture and Heritage. The resolution went live in 2010, and so far Clermont-Ganneau had persuaded sixty-one countries to ratify its sacred rules.

The Gallic lawyer was preparing for a late night of dull paperwork when she happily took James Jorvik's call. He put her on speakerphone and explained his firm's position. "You see, we are ready to throw people and funds at this despicable predicament, Eva, but on which precise principle of law is my dilemma," he reported.

Clermont-Ganneau spoke slowly and clearly in Franco-Cambridge tones. "Bon, well it seems to me that we have two situations here," the director began. "Without doubt, based on their fundraising and press release, Keys Exploration is not taking this project for the good of humanity, n'est-ce pas? I do not need to remind you that they have already violated Rule 2 of our Convention."

Brooker nodded his head as he recited its pious wording under his breath: the commercial exploitation of underwater culture and heritage for sale or speculation by its irreversible dispersal is fundamentally incompatible with the protection of finite underwater remains. Maritime heritage may not be traded, sold or bought for the sake of commerce. Amen.

"All well and good," Dom Silver butted in, "but apart from using Rule 2 to publicise this evil deed, we need a smoking gun, not a wooden stick. The Convention is sadly only advisory and not law in America."

"Mais bien sûr," Clermont-Ganneau replied, "so we have to think more cleverly than the enemy, oui? Monsieur Brooker, am I to understand from your historical analysis that the *Merced* was a frigate?" Delighted to be the centre of attention once more, the ex-soldier repeated what the team had gleaned so far, paying close attention to the ship's eight cannon.

"Parfait, then the case is watertight," the director of ICOCH concluded. All four lawyers and Brooker held their breath, staring at the silent phone pregnant with pause. "If the ship was armed with guns, it was a warship. If a warship, the *Merced* is protected by the law of sovereign immunity. I remind you of Article 96 of the International Law of the Sea Convention. Ships owned or operated by a State and used exclusively on non-commercial government service, enjoy complete immunity from the jurisdiction of any country or person other than the original flag State. That sovereign ownership extends to lost ships, submarines, spaceships and planes of any era in any ocean. Where they sank, in or out of coastal waters, is of no consequence. Only last month, the English Ministry of Defence placed a parking ticket on a Dutch company trying to salvage bits and pieces from one of His Majesty's eighteenth-century ships in the middle of the English Channel. For this reason, alors, I suggest we talk to Spain, the true owner of the *Merced.* Let's pool our contacts to accuse Keys Exploration of defiling, with knowledge and intent, the property of the king and government of Spain. C'est ça, simplement," the French director confirmed.

The delighted lawyers chatted about timeframes and how to best share intelligence. James Jorvik promised to have a document ready to file on Key West in two days' time and privately wondered if this would be the ticket that would finally earn him a knighthood. Bob Brooker, meanwhile, was planning a different mischief. Finally, he would be back in the public eye and would turn this misadventure into the mother of all public scandals, strictly in the name of heritage and the benefit of mankind, of course. Dom Silver sighed and wondered how much this turkey shoot was going to cost him. He grimaced, as he always did, looking like he was suffering from painful trapped wind. It was just his face. He always looked that way.

11

Straits of Florida, Day 14

The Barracuda was legendary for working his body to the bone. On expeditions, he believed in setting the right example. Nobody out-sweated him, an ethic that was a matter of pig-headed pride, so his third wife liked to tell anyone who'd listen. Now the Barracuda was out cold. The underwater dig was moving along apace, the 24/7 rotating shift chugging at a relentless rhythm. Everyone knew their station and exact plans, where to excavate and why. Waking up the Barracuda other than for emergencies was taboo. Approach with extreme caution.

The nervous knock on the white cabin door had all the feel of just such fear. No reply. Rusty tried again, this time more forcefully. "Go away, nobody's home," came the tired drawl from the inner sanctum.

"Sorry, boss," the engineer replied, "but something's come up. We need you on deck pronto, I'm afraid."

"It better be important," the Barracuda hollered. "Put the coffee on or heads'll roll. Give me a few minutes."

The Barracuda struggled to open his tired eyes and sighed. Everything was going too smoothly. It didn't take great powers of deduction to guess what was afoot. The bloody Archaeofanatics sticking their beaks into other people's business. Those assassins of exploration who do nothing, know nothing and couldn't run an offshore project in a month of Sundays.

The captain's cabin was spartan. One bag of clothes, a rucksack holding his laptop, two portable hard drives to back up every day's data – belt and braces – just in case. Buried inside the bag were the essentials for when all else went south. The six bags of Riesen dark chocolate chewy toffees were his go-to luxury should he ever end up cast away on a desert island or, more likely, be taken into custody by Interpol. And at the bottom of the bag, a dog-eared, signed copy of John Goggin's *Spanish Majolica in the New World*, published by Yale University in 1968. The masterpiece was still the only top-drawer guide to identify the colourful glazed pots and pans that every self-respecting sea dog ate off to and from the Americas. These familiar comforts manufactured in Andalusia made Spain's sailors feel at home on the cruel sea.

The cabin wall was pierced with one brass porthole, always left open. On the opposite wall hung a large poster showing the captain and his team smiling ear to ear in front of goodies pulled up from the wreck of the *Atocha* in 1994: olive jars, sixty silver bars, an iron anchor and thousands of silver pieces of eight concreted into massive conglomerates of sand and rock. 'Deep Down We Care' was printed large above the treasure-drunk divers. No robots in those heady days of innocence, just face masks, lead belts, hernias and fond memories of brothers and sisters who'd long crossed over the bar.

What fun and mischief, the Barracuda reminisced. The sky was the limit before the heritage Nazis strangled the deep with political red tape and killed the fun. A young and bewildered Rusty stared out from the poster, his trusted partner always preferring to hang back in the shadows. If Rusty needed him right now, it must be serious. Forgot about yesterday; save tomorrow.

The Barracuda ran his fingers through his hair, pulled on a heavily faded red t-shirt imprinted over the pocket with a wave, lighthouse and the logo 'Fear the Sea' and quickly brushed his teeth. Sighing, he strode through the doorway in unlaced grey Converse basketball boots and yesterday's crumpled jeans, expecting the worst.

Rusty met his boss at the entrance to the Nosh Pit, a steaming hot cup of joe in his hands as a peace offering. The pair burrowed towards the Arc Cave and sat with their backs to the archaeology team. No need to share any headaches until absolutely essential.

"Ok, Rusty, spit it out. Who said what this time?" the Barracuda anticipated.

With one finger, the sheepish engineer slid over a sheet of paper without making eye contact.

"Just went live on the wire, 08:00 hrs GMT, so 03:00 am Eastern Time. Sorry boss, but I wanted you to hear it from me before the whispering starts," Rusty confirmed.

The *Golden Margaret* may have been an elderly lady, but she was fitted with internal Wifi. All she had to do was bounce a signal twenty-two thousand miles into space and wait for the satellite to send it back to Earth, still a slow, patchy process in the early twenty-first century. But it meant all the crew could stay in touch with loved ones in their downtime. Only outbound emails were read and signed off by Captain Jim to plug leaks before heading out across the ether. Light-handed censorship. Just in case.

Keys Exploration had made the front page of the *Daily Mail* of London this time. On the right-hand column, an article was headed 'Sunken Race For $200 Million Treasure. Spain Accuses Florida of Shipwreck Pillage.' The Barracuda read on.

"Spain is claiming a vast treasure as its sovereign property following Keys Exploration's announcement of a king's ransom in underwater gold," the article read. "The *Merced* was a Spanish galleon lost in a hurricane off the Florida Keys in 1622. When disaster struck, she was returning to Seville with the riches of the New World, Colombian gold and Mexican and Peruvian silver. Unlike the famous flagships of the fleet, the *Atocha* and *Margarita*, nothing of the *Merced* was ever seen again until now".

The article went on to quote Al Nassau, Chief Operating Officer for Keys Exploration: "Long lost and even longer sought, Keys Exploration is delighted to share with the world the discovery of the great galleon *Merced* somewhere off the Straits of Florida. The ship was found far from shore, hundreds of metres deep. The exact location is being withheld to protect the rare remains from being plundered. So far, gold, silver coins and cultural art typical of the 1622 Tierra Firme fleet have been landed. The confidence of bringing up more treasure is very high."

The Barracuda turned to page sixteen, world news, where Dorothy Kennedy's write-up continued over a full page beneath press images and an old 1990s photo of the boss, grinning broadly while he stacked silver bars from the *Atocha*. Does me justice, ageing well, he thought to himself.

"Europe's leading heritage groups are up in arms," the *Daily Mail* went on. "English, French and Spanish heritage watchdogs are united in stopping what they see as the illegal looting of their property. Dr Miguel Monteiro from Spain's Ministry of Culture said 'We have no intention of letting any foreign devils destroy our national patrimony representing the ancient splendour of our golden age of trade. Our message is simple: hands-off or we will cut them off'."

The Barracuda raised an eyebrow. This was fiery language, even for mad dog Spanish politicos. Looks like they're going for the jugular. The next sentence confirmed his growing unease.

"James Jorvik of Jorvik & Silver solicitors told this newspaper that 'These American treasure hunters have broken and entered into a world where they don't belong. Spain's patrimony is theirs alone. The *Merced* was a naval frigate and Spain, like all nations, has never abandoned the rights to its historic warships. Keys Exploration is not only violating these rules, they are pillaging unique remains on the seabed, smashing through an ancient graveyard. The International Council of Cultural Heritage Convention makes it absolutely clear underwater culture may not be sold, traded or monetised. The Americans will be brought to book – and fast'."

The Barracuda didn't need to carry on reading. He knew how this game played out. For a long minute, he put his head in his hands and processed the message behind the words. Clearly, that stuck-up horse's arse James Jorvik was stirring up big mischief. He'd already contacted Paris and Spain and put a plan in motion. It was only a matter of time before a deluge of lawyers' letters started flooding in. The sands of time were running out.

Thinking through the letter of the law to an obvious conclusion, the Barracuda cleared his mind and sprung up, almost knocking over a twitchy Rusty. While he was at sea nobody could file any court motion, and nobody was going to waste taxpayers' cash sending a military frigate to board the *Golden Margaret* over a bunch of rotten wood. All hell would let loose as soon as he docked, though.

"Gentleman, please give me the room," the Barracuda announced. "Rusty and Brains, stay behind. The rest. Go get some bacon and eggs and back in ten minutes, ready to roll up your sleeves." The Barracuda was pleased to see the surfers weren't up yet to ask any questions.

The crew scattered and the boss kicked the door closed.

"Ok guys, this is on a need-to-know basis and nobody else, and I mean nobody, needs to know. Nothing gets mentioned outside this room unless you're talking to Al. Keep it off the email." Rusty and Brains hadn't seen the Barracuda, the vein on his neck pumping fast, so exercised since the State of Florida accused him of smashing ancient ship hulls in the dark days of the 1980s before the courts came down on his side. Finders keepers, they had eventually judged.

"The heritage Nazis are coming," the captain explained. "They're going to make an example of us to scare the world's governments into signing that bullshit ICOCH Convention. I thought they'd been mighty quiet far too long. Looks like they plan to piggyback on our success to harvest free global publicity. Over the next few days, you're gonna read the worst. The kitchen sink is coming our way. They'll say we're smashing through ancient hulls, ripping apart unique history, all for the sake of gold fever and self-serving profit. They'll call you pirates of the high seas."

"But that's horse shit," Rusty spat. The mild-mannered engineer had fought hand over fist to persuade his company's money men to marry treasure hunting with good archaeology. Proper science was his personal crusade.

"Come on, we record every goddamn object on the seabed in

3D whether it's a gold coin or a bead. We can track any find from the deep blue to the lab better than most schmucks on shallow wrecks. If anyone on this project touched a wooden timber without my ok, they'd be walking the plank and back to the beach before they could say three sheets to the wind."

"You know it, I know it, that arse James Jorvik and his henchmen know it too. Make no bones about it. They've read our scientific reports cover to cover with curtain-twitching jealousy. Why do you reckon they never mention them? But don't expect any high-fives from that pack of jackals. They need us to be underwater devils and their tactic is to sling buckets of mud at us. Most mud just slides straight off the wall, right, but some will stick, even though it's total nonsense. You know how newspaper editors roll. Controversy sells, science is a snore."

"What you're saying is that we're royally stuffed, boss," piped up Brains.

The Barracuda thought quietly before replying mischievously, "Not necessarily."

After ten minutes the crew cautiously tiptoed back into the lab, where they were surprised to find their friends smiling merrily and busy documenting a pile of tobacco leaves just uncovered in the *Merced*'s hold. The ROV had been called back into action and was sucking sand in the stern, much faster than a few hours earlier.

The Barracuda stood up in the middle of the room and commanded the crew's attention.

"Ok compadres, change of plans," he opened. Pointing to a printout of a bird's eye view of the *Merced* stitched together from 4,612 photographs taken before any excavation was allowed to touch the wreckage, he picked up a red marker and drew eight rectangles across different parts of the remains.

"Starting now, we're moving into these trenches. No more touchy-feely exploring, time to get up close and personal with the hull – and what's inside it. I want these boxes dug out, done and dusted pronto. Rusty, dial up the dredge pressure to eighty per cent. This mud needs sucking fast."

Four hands shot up.

"Sorry team, no questions, you're just gonna have to trust me. The clock is ticking and the next few days are shit or bust. We still document everything, but if there are thirty iron nails on a wooden plank, don't measure every darned one, one in ten will do just fine. Let's get to work, folks. Peddle to the metal please."

The Barracuda calculated that he had seven days, tops, to get as much information and booty out of the *Merced* before the *Golden Margaret* ran dry of diesel and the heavies came knocking when they went to port for a top-up. The trenches he'd marked up on the photomosaic were far from random. They correlated with the hits seen in last week's non-disturbance MASH study (Metallic Archaeology Survey Hotspot) – mega spikes in buried metal detection and the most surefire targets where the *Merced*'s treasure was hiding.

Once he landed back in Key West, the team would have pulled up enough finds, added to the fruits of the last two weeks, to keep the lab busy for three months conserving and interpreting. That would buy enough time to pit his lawyers against Jorvik and sort out this dog's dinner of a mess.

Keys Exploration was nobody's fool. They challenged the deep in international waters exactly because this was the sunken realm of finders keepers. Tough luck if the law lagged years behind the limits of the latest technology. The genius of the robot Juno was allowing the Barracuda to jump the barbed wire fence that ICOCH had drawn up to legally catch anyone searching in territorial waters. The *Merced* went down in international waters, a no man's land governed by the freedom of the high seas.

The Barracuda would trust his crack team of lawyers who'd fought the law and won time after time. Unlike Jorvik & Silver's bubble-dwelling landlubbers, Keys Exploration's sharp legal eagles were tried and tested. They'd walked the walk and came out the other side unscathed and rich.

This time James Jorvik would be exposed once and for all for lying to the authorities and the masses. The arrogant upstart, a one-eyed king in the land of the blind, had missed the ace in the Barracuda's pack. The *Merced* was no warship, merely a lightly armed merchantman carrying no Crown cargo, but crammed with private property. By the letter of the law, Keys Exploration's prey was unquestionably not sailing on his majesty the king of Spain's exclusive military service. Nobody's fools had to triumph. The future democracy of the oceans was at stake.

The Barracuda turned back to the monitors, making notes about the wooden beams appearing below Juno as she sucked centuries of mud off the old merchantman. Catch me if you can, he muttered to himself.

12

Old Town, Key West

Compared to the long hours her friends were grinding out wreck hunting off Key West, to anyone watching Nicola looked like she was swanning about. Without advertising her movements, the Londoner had quietly jumped ship from the sticky floor-boarded Schooner Wharf Bar to settle into the luxury of the Pier House Spa licking Caribbean surf at the far end of Duval Street.

A pattern quickly emerged in Nicola's day. A late breakfast of coffee and whatever fruit the jovial, portly waitress Jean had on offer that morning. Next a dip in the outside pool, thirty minutes tops in the sauna and jacuzzi, shower and then on with her thinking hat – or at least a newly acquired Miami Marlins baseball cap.

Around 11.15 am Nicola would amble down to the Chart Room Café for her second coffee of the day and start dreaming, at least that's how the staff figured, gossiping behind closed doors. The indiscrete manager had googled her name and everyone from the pot washer to reception knew she should be treated as a VIP. A fine tipper and such marvellous manners. The Spa was a monied drifter's paradise.

For a change, Nicola wasn't drifting. Far from it. Night and day, her mind was possessed by the Vanished People. They haunted her sleep, leaving her frazzled and cranky. Either she'd be forced to re-bury her exotic arrowhead back where she found it at Boca Chica to get the Indian ghouls off her back or embrace the challenge that had landed on her big toe. What was it her yoga teacher in Primrose Hill, Maya, used to say? That's right, "You often meet your destiny on the road taken to avoid it."

Nicola wasn't a risk-taker. The romance of antiquity had bent her arm. Now she was all in. A plan whose ending she had no way of predicting was hatched. She would confront the Vanished People head on and give a voice to their memory.

To live up to her whirlwind adventure and the wicker chair Havana feel of the Chart Room Café, Nicola took to dressing in a white linen Ralph Lauren shirt and straight-legged army green cotton trousers. Though the slacks were Armani, not exactly crusty army issue. To outsiders, she looked as if she was lazing away the balmy late autumn hours, enjoying the life of Riley. Perhaps she spent all that time on her laptop checking her share prices, the staff imagined. Nicola wasn't dressed to play banking. A very different type of ancient auditing awaited, one that needed solitude and focused brain power.

Only a fool starts sleuthing like a headless chicken. Within a day of getting home after meeting Grant Raven, and a fretful night's sleep, an inspired Ms Medici had chosen her new path. Now Nicola needed to pull together some background research. She was on the hunt for the Vanished People of Florida, the Tequesta, so tantalisingly introduced to her by Skip.

First of all, she needed to draw up a list of books and articles in the British Library, a bastion of heavy-duty knowledge down London's Euston Road and the world's largest national library. Carefully stored along its six hundred and twenty-five kilometres of shelves were over one hundred and fifty million holdings from inscribed Chinese oracle bones inked up around 300 BC to original Beatle's lyrics. Much to her annoyance, only one title seemed to have ever been written about these Native Americans, *Ancient Miamians. The Tequesta of South Florida* by William E. McGoun. Skip was not wrong. Precious little was known about this mystery tribe.

Searching under 'Florida Indians' more widely generated a healthier three hundred and forty titles. Most turned out to be useless red herrings with little link to the Tequesta. A slither of the literature looked promising, particularly Jerald Milanich's *Florida*

Indians and the Invasion from Europe and John Hann's *Indians of Central and South Florida, 1513-1763.* Casting the net still wider, Nicola decided she better check out Clay MacCauley's *Seminole Indians of Florida* and Lucy Wenhold's translation of *A 17th Century Letter of Gabriel Diaz Vara Calderón, Bishop of Cuba, Describing the Indians and Indian Missions of Florida* as well.

In the next few days, apart from the odd jump into the sea to take the edge off the heat, a continuous drip of Havana rum mojitos and at least twice daily batting away the approaches of businessmen greaseballs, Nicola explored the minds of the Vanished People. For a woman who had always been easily distracted, often accused of having the attention span of a fly, Nicola found herself enjoying tunnel vision. The Londoner had disappeared under a rock and down a historical wormhole.

Courtesy of Zak's Oxford JSTOR and Internet Archive account passwords, Nicola could read any book or article ever published with a quick click of a button. If that failed, there were always dodgy Russian websites.

Hours of reading led in ever-decreasing circles to a few on-the-spot accounts of times past. *The Memoir of Hernando de Escalante Fontaneda Respecting Florida*, written in 1575 in the town of Espiritu Santo, Florida's modern sin city in Tampa Bay, was a gem. Nicola firmly got the bit between her teeth. Words transported her thousands of tides back to the shadowy glades of American Indian history once played out outside her very window.

The giddy sense of the past in the present was unlike any sensation she'd known. A romantic glow was tinged with an undercurrent of nostalgia and... something else. Like a ship watching out for a Cornish smuggler shining a lantern on a damp British clifftop to guide it home, Nicola's eyes were glued to a tiny fragment of light at the end of a long tunnel.

Fontaneda's memoir was a remarkable witness to late sixteenth-century Florida. This was a man who'd actually lived among the Tequesta, albeit captive, for seventeen long years after surviving a devastating shipwreck off Florida in 1549 when he was just thirteen years old. Fontaneda was a rare first-hand witness.

The youngster had been on his way from Colombia, where his father worked as a Spanish official, to get a gentleman's education in the colonial city of Salamanca.

Only a rude awakening replaced the thrill of the high seas. Shipwreck wasn't the worst horror. All the other crewmembers, including his brother, were sacrificed by Native Indian hands. Fontaneda survived by amusing the locals with his dancing and singing. After travelling far and wide across Florida from modern Key West to Tampa and learning several local languages, at the age of thirty the Spaniard was eventually bartered back to Spain thanks to the diplomatic skills of the first governor of St Augustine, Pedro Menéndez de Avilés.

Fontaneda's warts and all memoir left no doubt that the Florida Native Indians sacrificed people as gifts to their gods. Even their sons and daughters were killed when a tribal leader died to keep him company in the afterlife. The ritual slaying each year of a Christian captive to appease the Indians' divine idols, who they believed feasted on the eyes and heads of men, was even more grisly. At that time, so Fontaneda saw and wrote, "after the summer come, some sorcerers in the shape of the devil with horns on their heads, they come howling like wolves in the woods and these idols stay four months. They never rest night or day, running so much with great fury. What great bestiality that they do."

The idea of being a time-travelling fly on the wall to such a horrific spectacle intrigued Nicola, until she realised in all likelihood she would have been the one dumped in the cooking pot. Reading on, she fact-checked Skip's story that the Tequesta thought every man had three souls, one in the eye, another in a human's shadow and the third the image seen in a calm pool of water. This very unwestern theology was true. When a Tequesta brave died, two of the souls left the body. The third in the eye remained. This was why the Tequesta visited ancestral burial places to seek out the dead's wisdom. "And I believe that the devil speaks to them there because from what the deceased says they learn about many things that happen in other regions or that come to pass later," Escalante Fontaneda shared.

In early colonial times, the Spaniards knew Key West as Los Martyres, the memoir continued, because many sailors suffered like martyrs on the sharp rocks sticking out of the sea. Nicola ploughed on relentlessly, learning about lost villages called Guarugunve, the Town of Weeping, and Cuchiyaga, the Place of Suffering, where the men lived naked, and the women hid their modesty under a short cloak woven from weeds and palm leaves.

It didn't take long for the Tequesta to stumble onto the stage. "The Martyres end near a village of Indians called Tequesta," the 1575 memoir recorded, "on a bank of a river which comes from the interior of the country the distance of fifteen leagues and issues from another lake of fresh water. Around these waters are many towns, although not more than thirty or forty souls each." Nicola made a note to advise Skip to revise his calculations of the Tequesta's tribal size. As for food, the tribe feasted on river eels, each as big as a man. Alligators, snakes and tortoises the size of a warrior's shield were part of their daily diet.

Twenty-one pages deep into the memoir, Nicola took a sharp intake of breath, her eyes out on stalks. Shipwrecks and Indians fused. "The king of Tequesta is poor in respect of the nature of the earth and they are rich only by the sea," Fontaneda explained, "from the vessels that have been lost, well laden with silver and gold."

Towards the end of his book, Fontaneda reckoned the wrecked riches seized by the Tequesta in his day reached a million dollars or more. The booty came in all forms: bars of silver, gold, jewellery made by Mexican Indians and shiny baubles carried by passengers as family gifts. Other ships transporting vast wealth sank in search of the River Jordan, the book added mysteriously.

"With this, I will end and say no more," Fontaneda concluded, "for if the conquest of that country were about to be undertaken, I would give no further account of it than I have rendered. Its subjugation is befitting His Majesty in Madrid, for the security of his armadas that go to Peru, New Spain and other parts of the Indies, which pass, of necessity, along that shore and channel of the Bahama, where many vessels are wrecked, and many persons killed; for the Indians are powerful archers and oppose them."

The memoir advised Spain to build a small fort to protect the Florida channel. "I conclude so and, as this account may become important, I sign it. Hernando De Escalante Fontaneda, 9 July 1539."

*

Nicola pushed back her chair and stretched her arms towards the night sky. The Chart Room Café had filled up with bronzed Americans while she'd gone time travelling. White trousers, happy smiles and Panama hats patted each other's backs. The smell of piles of Florida crab dripping in garlic lingered under Nicola's nose. I wonder how many of these sun worshippers have ever heard of the plight of the Tequesta, she wondered.

Three days after disappearing down her literary hole, Nicola felt she understood the essence of the Vanished People. The Tequesta were Florida's original people, more rightful heirs to the East Coast than the immigrant Italians, Irish, Europeans, Jews and Latin Americans who sailed for the New World centuries later, dreaming of wealth and new beginnings. Where are the Tequesta now? Do any descendants even survive, she asked herself. Probably not. If the books she'd consulted were right, British muskets and disease drove them over the cliff to extinction in the early eighteenth century.

Precious few ancient sites had been discovered or dug up to make sense of the real faces of the Tequesta world. Villages had given up a few secrets here and there after being disturbed by building work in downtown Miami. Stains in the ground surrounded by abandoned conch shells, shark's teeth and remains of stingray spines, barracuda and whelk were all that were left behind, revealing the spots where round-houses once stood. Otherwise, the onslaught of 'progress' had wiped the Tequesta off the map. Burial mounds described in nineteenth-century travellers' diaries had been bulldozed and destroyed. The 1920s real estate boom across Florida finished the job, reducing the state's Native Indian heritage to dust.

Nicola's research had at least turned up images of what Tequesta life looked like thanks to a goldsmith, engraver and bookseller. Theodor de Bry never visited the Americas, truth be told. His illustrations were drawn on the run after the Spanish Inquisition exiled the Protestant from Holland in 1570. After his goods were seized, de Bry fled his homeland, now occupied by Spanish forces.

The artist found sanctuary in Antwerp, London and Frankfurt. De Bry gathered his impressions of the Americas by interviewing every adventurer he met. His 1594 publication, *Historia del Mondo Nuovo*, is a classic. Like the Tequesta, de Bry's displacement by the sword of Madrid brought great personal hardship and empathy with events on the other side of the invaded world.

Dozens of the Dutchman's images showed Spaniards setting up great wooden Catholic crosses on shores, and Indians offering friendship, gold and silver gifts to the newly landed overlords. In de Bry's version of Native American history, the local hand of friendship was cut off Tequesta torsos from the start. The conquistadors paid no respect to America's tribal rulers, kicked them off their thrones, tortured them mercilessly until the secrets of buried treasure were burned out of them and ransacked their ancestral tombs. The Native Indian and Spanish world views were a clash of civilisations.

The Tequesta didn't take their plight sitting down. A sequence of chilling engravings showed a novel reaction: conquistadors were pinned down by furious Native Indians and gold poured down their throats, forcing them to choke on the valuables they desired above all else. A strangely inventive and expensive death sentence.

A quick check helped Nicola realize that fact was again stranger than fiction. In the early decades of Aztec contact, Father Bernardino de Sahagun's *General History of the Things of New Spain* remembered how "The Spaniards seized upon the gold like monkeys, their faces flushed. For clearly their thirst for gold was insatiable; they starved for it; they lusted for it; they wanted to stuff themselves with it as if they were pigs." A Spanish governor paid the ultimate sacrifice for Madrid's greed in 1599 when the Jivaro people in Ecuador executed gold-hungry nobleman pigs by pouring molten gold down their throats until their bowels burst. What a shitty way to go, Nicola decided.

The Spanish attacks on the locals fascinated the English woman. Not the terrible scenes of rape and pillage but because the painted backdrops showed real Tequesta's villages. In some scenes, the tribe danced in tall feather hats, blowing long horns, bells jangling around their ankles. Nicola had always believed from the cinema that Native Americans lived in wigwams, but in de Bry's universe the Tequesta villages were built with dozens of oval wood, mud and straw huts arranged around a fire. Villages were protected by round enclosures made from wooden spikes several metres high. Wigwams were the stuff of Hollywood imagination.

Three days into her crash course into the Tequesta Vanished People, Nicola's head was spinning and her eyes sinking. But she now knew that Skip's version of events checked out. How did her arrowhead fit into a footnote of their world? Sure, it was a tiny cog in times past, but not an unimportant one, she vainly hoped. She scanned her notes for missed nuggets of knowledge and backtracked to Hernando de Escalante Fontaneda's mention of the lost villages of Guarugunve and Cuchiyaga. Neither had ever been found by modern explorers. Could the mound she tripped over on the call of nature somehow be related to the Town of Weeping or Place of Suffering? The thought of being the first person to find the physical past sent a tingle down Nicola's spine.

There was only one way to find out. Nicola pulled out her phone and from her contacts list hit 'Z'. "Hi you've reached Zak. I'm on assignment, so please leave a message," the answerphone said. Men, useless, Nicola muttered.

"Hi Zak, fancy a break from playing with fish and having a real adventure? Dinner tonight? Come and find me at the resort at 8 pm if so. Something rather splendid has come up," Nicola ended elusively. "Miss you," she blurted out mischievously before hanging up.

Remembering how starved she was of decent male company and attention, Ms Medici started to thaw recalling Zak's manners and smile.

Useless but still quite cute, she admitted.

The boy hadn't shown the remotest interest in the last few weeks. Was he blind or just far too into his science? Or maybe his smarts put him way outside her league?

13

Front Street, Key West

Zak was down his own hole chasing gold – pink gold – when his phone pinged. His body was wedged under a bush and his head staring into murky darkness below a white wood-framed house. One leg was raised awkwardly in the air. A stretched out arm swayed the arc of a torch light opened from his phone from side to side beneath the yard front. 'Nicola 4' the illuminated screen announced. Damnation. Of the several Nicolas Zak knew, number 4, Miss Medici, was his favourite. The present would have to wait.

While Nicola was pampering herself at the Pier House Spa, the casual observer assumed, Zak had gone to ground. After much cajoling, Mac Murphy, the fisherman who had stumbled upon the *Merced* after dragging up a net full of coins from the sea, had agreed to meet. That didn't mean the wily fisherman would talk.

Nicola and Zak had been keeping their cards close to their chests. Neither knew they had both been taking a crash course in history. While the Londoner burrowed into a forgotten tribe, the serious Oxford man had been peering into Key West's more recent times. Zak had quickly become an unwelcome face in town, harassing local fishermen to share their secrets and interviewing twitchy restaurant chefs about seafood stocks and sustainability. The word had spread. Doors were closing on his charming face and blunt tongue.

At least Mac Murphy, the hero who found the *Merced* and sold the Barracuda a legendary X marking a spot, agreed to talk. The news was a pleasant surprise: fishermen were notoriously secretive, jealously guarding their profitable trawling grounds. Today was a red letter day for Zak's hopes to blow the whistle on canyon buster trawlers blitzing the deep's delicate ecosystem.

The oldest fishing industry in all of America, it turned out, began life in Key West. The ebb and flow of its fortunes was terrific colour for Zak's newspaper scoop. Spanish fishermen salted and dried local fish in the eighteenth century to export them to Havana and Latin America. Until the Civil War years, Key West also supplied much of America's salt needed to preserve food in times before electricity and fridge freezers.

The town had earned its bucks in numerous ways. In the 1830s it was a famous centre of the cigar trade after the Cuban Revolution scared thousands of immigrant workers across the seas in rickety boats. Key West's population tripled. Many of the newcomers had sweated in tobacco factories back home and carried on under comfier conditions in Florida.

America's most southeasterly town next turned its hand to smuggling when prohibition showed its face in the 1920s. Smuggling contraband beer and rum from Cuba and whiskey and scotch from Britain by way of the Bahamas was easy money that made many Key West folk extremely wealthy thank you very much.

From earliest times, though, fishing was big business. Within a few years of being built, Key West was second only to New York as America's top fishing port. Boats sailed from St Augustine to work the local waters for eight months of the year.

The size of the marlins and tuna caught off Key West, snapped in harbour-side black and white photos of daily catches, often measured twice the height of a man. Zak had been amused to spot Ernest Hemingway, Rodi's old pal, smiling from a vintage postcard he found in a downtown antique shop. The famous writer, an eager fisherman in his own right, lovingly pitted his wits against raw nature. Hemingway was also an amateur preservationist who persuaded scientists from the Academy of Natural Sciences to look into ways to keep the local fisheries sustainable.

The black and white photo of a blissed-out Hemingway reminded Zak of the author's bleak writing in *To Have and Have Not* of what life was like for less fortunate Americans and fishermen in places like Key West during the Great Depression of 1929 to 1939 when business crashed. "Some made the long drop from the apartment or the office window; some took it quietly in two-car garages with the motor running," Hemingway graphically wrote. Others "used the native tradition of the Colt or Smith and Wesson; those well-constructed implements that end insomnia, terminate remorse, cure cancer, avoid bankruptcy, and blast an exit from intolerable positions by the pressure of a finger."

Those brutal jobless years must have been so painful for many, the opposite of England's soft snowflake generation today, Zak pondered. They'd never lived through extraordinary times or epoch-turning wars. Maybe that's why society's so unextraordinary and dull.

The absence of brilliance in his postgraduate years in Oxford had been a dreadful disappointment to Zak. When he took history and archaeology courses, most of the Institute's professors were socially awkward dropouts who hid their mediocrity behind ivory towers. Few reached the dizzy excellence of P.R.S. Moorey, Keeper of Antiquities at the Ashmolean Museum, or Bryan Ward-Perkins at Trinity College, the cream of the cream. Where were the J.R.R. Tolkien's and C.S. Lewis's, Zak had often wondered in his own day? Maybe you need to live a full life, turn grey and decrepit, before making sense of the whole cycle. Isn't that what history's all about?

Key West fishing, so the old newspapers said, had been pounded hard after the Great Depression. In the 1940s war years, the town looked dead on its legs. Then a miracle appeared out of nowhere when virgin shrimp beds, the richest in America, were found seventy miles off Key West in 1950. Salvation had lain right under Key West's nose all the time.

When news broke of the discovery off the East Coast of what locals liked to call pink gold – a century after the California Gold Rush was struck on the West Coast – there wasn't a single shrimp boat in Key West. In three weeks, every corner along the town's docks was choked with three hundred double-parked trawlers that ran in from Florida, North Carolina, Georgia, Mississippi, Louisiana and Texas to stake their claims. The new shrimp beds spanned a hundred square miles of seabed.

Sixty-ton engine-powered schooners with eleven-men crews widowed their families for a month stretch at a time. It was a bruising but lucrative job. Within a few months, five new fish-packing houses stood alongside the wharves. Fleets of ice trucks were brought in to drive the fresh shrimp north. So many trawlers sailed in from St Augustine that the old Spanish settlement in north Florida became known as Shrimp Boat City. In the very first season when pink gold was struck in 1950, fifteen million pounds' weight of shrimp was landed on Key West's quays. Boom time had arrived. The good times were rolling.

How could the eggheads, including those invited by Ernest Hemingway, have so spectacularly failed to notice these riches before the mid-twentieth century? The sneaky shrimp, it turned out, was a master of disguise. Shrimp are nocturnal animals. By day they bury themselves in grey mud and only come out to feed and play at night. Survival of the fittest at its best.

The Tortugas beds were first raked up by luck when a local fisherman broke his engine and, after working through the day to fix his boat, decided to make up for the lost hours by dragging his nets at night. Hallelujah. The after-hours lucky strike forced him to spend the next Sunday in church thanking the gods of the deep blue. The secret was out. And pink shrimp and the ocean deep were in big trouble.

*

Zak made the long trek to Key West to blow the whistle on canyon busters. The destruction caused by fishing boats dragging heavy nets to scoop up fish minding their own business had been on marine ecologists' furious agendas since the 1950s.

Canyon busters were underwater juggernauts that pulled steel nets over even the most challenging underwater terrains. And now the marine food chain was close to extinction. Zak's old friends, Professors Watling and Norse from the University of Hawaii, for ages had been lecturing anyone who'd listen, and many who wouldn't, that seabed fishing was like clearcutting forests, only underwater. With one huge difference. While a hundred thousand square kilometres of woodlands are wiped out worldwide every year, the area trawled underwater is one hundred and fifty times bigger. Each year, trawling rips up seabeds the size of Brazil, the Congo and India combined. Scientists started calling trawlers the bulldozers of the deep.

The politicians simply ignored the expert's doomsday opinions. At the National Geographic Society, Sylvia Earle summed up the problem. An appalled Zak had read how "In an action akin to bulldozing forests to catch songbirds and squirrels," she explained, "nets mounted on massive rollers are dragged across the seabed, strip-mining everything in their paths. Sometimes a single trawl tears away as much as 10,000 pounds of sponges, corals, fish and other life from the sea floor, leaving a stark, sterile undersea desert."

In *The End of the Line*, the British journalist Charles Clover angrily compared trawling to the brutal results of what would happen if a mile of net was strung out between two off-road vehicles and dragged at speed across the plains of Africa. In a horror story straight out of a *Mad Max* film, the nets would scoop everything in their way from lions and cheetahs to warthogs. "Left behind is a strangely bedraggled landscape resembling a harrowed field," Clover warned, calling deep-sea fishing the most destructive activity on earth. Brutal devastation on this scale would never be allowed on land. So why underwater?

Zak's deep dive in the libraries of Oxford and the Royal Society off Pall Mall in London confirmed a series of facts that kept him awake night after night. The impact of fishing on marine animals was one hundred thousand times more destructive than oil or gas exploration. Off Texas each year in Corpus Christi Bay, trawlers were scraping 2.1 million cubic metres off the seabed hunting for shrimp.

When he got in his stride, Zak's mind went into overdrive. Nothing in recent years had so seriously pissed him off as the rape of the world's seas. The usually calm and collected Englishman was possessed when it came to his pet topic. Now he was taking direct action in Key West and for two reasons.

First off, the shallows had been turned into dead zones stripped of sea life. So many young species had been pulled up in the trawl nets as bycatch that stocks had little chance of recovering. Most of what was caught was just thrown back into the water dead. And shrimpers in the Caribbean and Central America threw away eighty per cent of their catches as too small to eat.

So the trawlers were forced to move ever deeper and now ran their riotous nets down to depths of three thousand metres. Few people know what wonders are hidden down there and how the marine environment was coping or being wiped out. If the reality was anything like in the shallows, the deep was fast becoming a deadly marine holocaust. Out of sight and out of mind, politicians merrily ordered the best restaurant sea bass and put their kids' generation in environmental debt. Zak shook with rage.

The second headache was that scientists reckoned that by 2030 it would be game over, the end of the line for fish stocks. The effects weren't just collateral damage. No more sushi, no more fish and chips left to harvest. Jacques Cousteau and his love of the silent sea would be turning in his grave.

Before heading to southern Florida from his cosy Fellowship in Oxford, Zak had been alarmed by photos of a new breed of trawler, the canyon buster – twice as large as most boats and twice as heavy – being trialled in the Gulf of Mexico. He'd been spying on them using satellite surveillance. When he realized that the plumes of exhaust thrown up by their trawl nets could be seen from space, just like the Great Wall of China, Zak jumped into action. Now the canyon busters were heading for Key West's offshore shrimp fields, which were also rich feeding grounds for sea turtles. Not on my watch, Zak had pledged.

*

Meeting Mac Murphy, the skipper of the *Lazy Jane*, had been its own lucky strike. Zak had started the day early at the Antiquarium Museum where, with Rodi, Alona and Mitch, he first heard the crazy tale of the treasure of the *Merced* three weeks ago. The museum was stuffed full of finds the Barracuda had plucked from the waters the length and breadth of Florida and as far east as the Bahamas.

It was the junk that didn't make the cut, thrown into the museum's backyard, that interested Zak. From the research ship, Rusty had tipped him off by email that the odds and sods brought up in trawler nets since the 1950s were abandoned in the Antiquarium's back garden.

Zak's expectations were low when he rounded the corner of 200 Front Street, only to find himself staring dumbfounded at an ancient maritime junkyard. In one corner, rusting away, was a pile of busted old iron anchors snagged decades ago in fishermen's nets, now unwanted. There was no monetary or scientific reason for the Barracuda to have taken custody of this trash, but he always did so thankfully and with exaggerated enthusiasm. Sharing an object's cultural story with excited finders was crucial networking. The potluck discovery of the *Merced* just went to show that you never knew what a random fisherman might chance upon and drag into the museum. Protecting your million-to-one shot was power in the world of wreck hunting. Nobody spent more time at sea than hard-working fishermen.

Mac Murphy was a third-generation veteran trawlerman with forty-five years' experience under his souwester. He didn't need the cash especially but felt a kinship with the great blue and his ancestors to keep stirring the ocean like they had. These days he just dipped into the deep a few days a month to keep his hand in and show the boys he wasn't some stocks and shares-gazing yuppy. Walking up the steps of the all-white painted colonial-style house, Zak had no doubt the old fisherman had done remarkably well for himself. How much shrimp do you need to pay for a townhouse like this, he couldn't imagine.

Front Street looked like many upper-crust corners of the Caribbean. Lush green-leaved royal Poinciana trees, studded with bright red flowers bursting forth like tropical parrots, bent benevolently over the pavement. Elegant palm trees shimmered in the morning sea breeze.

The Murphy residency was unexpected. No sea shack here. A gabled gate gave way to a terracotta brick patio and a sizeable two-storey wooden home with elegant white shutters topped by a single-room attic. A stars and stripes flag flew to one side of the front door. In the window a faded election poster showed an orange-tanned Donald Trump promising to Make America Great Again.

On the opposite side to the flagpole, a bluish-green weatherworn bronze cannon pointing upward may have been designed to protect land and sea from unwanted guests but was now an antique intended to impress. Even to Zak's eye, it looked mighty old. The house wouldn't have been out of place among the mansions bought with cotton wealth in the mid-nineteenth century Deep South.

The Murphy residence was ridiculously well appointed. On the other side of the street, a sign for the Little White House steered tourists to President Harry Truman's summer retreat in the late 1940s. Like Mac's house, it was built in 1890, but as the officer's quarters for the town's submarine base. In those days the building was a waterfront property. Since then, silt and city had reclaimed tens of metres of Front Street, which was now pushed back three roads from shore. Mac Murphy could only hear the waves these days but had no sea view.

It was in the calm of Key West that General Dwight Eisenhower founded the US Department of Defence over the road in the Little White House in 1949. J.F. Kennedy and British Prime Minister Harold McMillan met in Front Street in 1961. Even in the Clinton administration, Bill and Hillary enjoyed long weekend escapes at this home away from Washington.

Mac's moody teenage kid, Donald, shouted for his father

when Zak tapped hard on the brass door knocker in the shape of a whale before heading back to his third hour of Saturday video games. Mac shrugged, reading the visitor's mind (it's a beautiful day, get outside, stop playing vampires) and led Zak to his man den. White floorboards gleamed beneath a quietly rotating wooden fan. In the hall stood a life-size sculpture of a peacock by Clarita Brinkerhoff. The living room was dominated by a calming visual sensation painted by the Russian artist Mike Cheval. Three angels, one topless, held and guided three wooden sailing ships across blue-green waves. "That's my pension," Mac volunteered, "and reminds me how lucky we've been and honoured by the protection of the sea gods." Jimmy Buffett's Son of a Son of a Sailor played softly from an invisible speaker.

Through the patio doors a swimming pool, just long enough to get in fifteen strokes, flanked by six wicker sun loungers, gave way to a cosy summer house. Zak could gladly have lived in a bolt-hole like that, backing onto a thicket of bushes and palm trees to give the Murphy's privacy from gawping eyes.

If Mac must have been in his early sixties, having started going to sea at fifteen, Mrs Murphy, tanning her legs by the pool, looked not a day over forty. The husband knocked on the patio door window and Jen, as she introduced herself after tying a beach scarf around her waist, joined them. Mango iced tea with a hint of lemon and a plate of watermelon were generously served. The mood mellowed from one of mutual distrust.

Mac, it turned out, had a loose tongue. Over drinks, he regaled his visitor with memories of how he started out as a deckhand on his grandfather's fishing boat. In those rough days, nets were still hauled in by hand before electric-powered drums made the heavy lifting child's play. In the 1970s, fish were abundant, but after stocks plummeted the Murphy family decided at a conference of war to move into shrimp and go nocturnal. Investing in new echo sounders and multibeam technology to track schools of fish on the move helped Mac skirt around the edges of the out-of-bounds Tortugas National Marine Park and pick up big catches without breaking the law. Pink gold seemed to have made the Murphys rich.

Zak had done his homework on the Tortugas reserve, one hundred square miles of seabed closed to motorboats and fishing, sixty miles off Key West. The reserve enclosed Fort Jefferson and the Dry Tortugas islands. The vast hexagonal stone fort was commissioned in 1847 to protect the trade routes running south to the Gulf of Mexico, north to New York and east to Latin America and the Caribbean. The old castle cost a king's ransom and soon became its own human folly, left unfinished, a white elephant in the sea.

The marine park's greatest contribution was to nature, Zak knew, since it protected the atoll string of eleven Tortugas islands, so named by Spanish explorers in 1513 because of the hundreds of turtles – *tortugas* – sunning themselves on its spiky outcrops before hungry conquistadors put the happy-go-lucky creatures in their Andalusian stew. Even Robert Louis Stevenson fell under the island's spell, writing in *Treasure Island* of people's fears of pirates there: "Dreadful stories they were – about hanging, and walking the plank, and storms at sea, and the Dry Tortugas." The island and its menacing low-lying coral reefs, surging tides, furious currents and autumn hurricanes had all the perfect makings for high-speed collisions between man and nature.

Mac and Jen were generous southern hosts. Zak, though, didn't want to get trapped talking niceties. Mrs Murphy mooched back into the sun glaze-eyed after the conversation turned to fishing and Zak started prodding her old man about the future of Key West's seas. Through a perma-smile, Murphy could talk the hind legs off a donkey, telling tale after tale about the good old days, huge catches, beer and parties at the same Schooner Wharf Bar where Zak and his pals first met the intoxicating Barracuda.

Forty minutes of dead time swept by, of polite nodding and failing to take a single note of interest. In the end, Zak changed tack when Murphy paused for air.

"Thanks Mac, it's truly wonderful to hear all about the tough realities of Key West fishing. What a rich life you've led." Zak looked around the den and continued, "And evidently a lucrative life."

Mac scratched his neck uncomfortably and mumbled something about how the big blue had blessed him and brought fortune.

"So, tell me, Mac, how did you manage to find one of the greatest treasure ships out there, the *Merced*?" Zak asked, hoping to drag a snippet of useful information out of the guarded fisherman.

Murphy's eyes lit up and he plunged into a tale he'd told dozens of times at dinner parties and in bars. For once, this was a story that didn't need embellishing.

"I remember it like it was yesterday. It was September the first, bang smack in the middle of hurricane season, but man must eat. Normally I would have pulled the *Lazy Jane* into dry-dock for the winter by then. You ever wined and dined at the Casablanca Bar and Grill in Miami, son?" Mac enquired.

Zak had not. He doubted it was anywhere near his budget.

"Well, you must. Find yourself a fine lady and treat yourselves on your way back home. Say Key West Mac sent you and they'll see you right. It sits on the Miami River, right next to those old warehouse conversions. Anyways, they've got this here motto, 'Fresh from our boats to your table' and had been let down by their regular supplier. They called this sucker here with an offer of big bucks to haul them a heavy catch for their autumn shrimp festival."

"Jen wasn't happy. The satellites showed a bad weather window closing in, but my bones told me otherwise. The sea was flat as a pancake. Only problem was haul net as fast as we could, nothing doing. Zip. It was as if the shrimp had packed up their suitcases and gone hibernate for winter."

"There was only one thing for it, steer out towards the Straits. Hell, I wouldn't have told Jen. Everyone knows it's a calamity out there, a graveyard of centuries of sunken boats and monsters but, if you get lucky, mighty rewarding. With the seas calm, we rolled the dice and steamed west for half a day."

"We mowed the seabed back and forth in around three hundred metres depth and saw nothing promising on the echo sounders. A few lucky dips brought up nothing but old beer bottles. Time and diesel were just about up when my deckhand, Chad, spotted a large school of fish zooming west. We rolled the dice again and dropped the nets in around four hundred and fifty metres, the limits of our cables," Mac explained.

Zak, now totally absorbed, leant forward to catch every word as the fisherman reached the juicy part of his tale.

"Nobody fishes out there, that place is full of scary stories, and we had no clue what to expect. But I had a funny feeling. Then dragging my nets at around four hundred and forty metres down, the *Lazy Jane* got caught on a snag. Damn. I was wrong, a pig-headed fool. We killed the engine and rocked back and forth for a while, gently trying to tease the nets free, brand new and costly, from what I guessed was some big rock. No luck, the son of a gun was stuck hard."

"The game went on for forty-five minutes. We changed the boat's direction. No luck. In the end, nothing for it but to give up and yank free whatever gear we could save by force. I pushed the *Lazy Jane* full throttle, the motor roared and smoke blew out of the ship's arse like a Wall Street banker's bull crap. I was just about to give up and cut the nets when the boat lurched to the side and, like a cork, bobbed free."

"We coiled in the nets as I cursed the Casablanca restaurant and myself for being such a greedy fool and taking that contract. This unwanted fishing trip was gonna cost me $15,000 in lost gear needing replacing for next season," Mac Murphy mused.

"I was distracted calculating my debt and how to tell Jen she could forget about Jimmy Choo's for Christmas when Chad hollered that something heavy was caught up in the ripped nets. I made my way to the deck, jacked open the trawl mouth suspended in the air and… holy crap, I was almost brained by a lump of concretion that rolled off my skull and landed at my feet."

"Inside the nets, only good for the garbage dump, was a bunch of pots and pans. Didn't mean anything to me. Around the edges of the concrete block though, the size of a car steering wheel, something grey with flat edges was blinking under the deck lights. Still dazed, I took a hammer, broke the stone open and almost fell over the side of the ship. It sure as heck was no rock, my friend, but a lump of silver coins concreted together for who knows how many years underwater. And there were hundreds and hundreds of the suckers."

"Chad grabbed some lemon – I don't drink joe no more due to my bowels, just honey, ginger and lemon, Jen's rules – and squeezed it over the coins, saying something about how it works like weak acid. Well, that sure as hell did nothing. But that boy sure perseveres. Next he ran off and emptied a can of Coke he'd been saving over a handful of coins. Hell's bells if the concoction didn't strip the coins clean like acid in minutes. Don't know what they put in that fizzy stuff, but I guess there's a good reason dentists warn us to steer clear of it. Now I know why: it even eats concrete."

"Anyways, these numbers '1621' slowly appeared alongside the bust of some big-nosed king and a couple of tall columns and I knew we had hit something mega. I carefully took the GPS position, scribbled it down on a piece of paper and folded and pocketed it. The fishing trip may have been a bust, but just maybe the Barracuda would bite. He was my only hope."

Everyone in Key West was on friendly first-hand terms with the crazy wreck hunter and, the next morning, the men shook hands on a deal that would turn very handsome if the hang could be ground-truthed as an ancient wreck. The Barracuda paid top dollar for the finds as well and exchanged the GPS coordinates for the promise of a slice of the pie of any shiny stuff dug up. Mac Murphy was in for two and a half per cent of whatever came up from the mystery shipwreck now strongly reckoned to be the final resting place of the *Merced*.

The tale of the treasure and what had been landed was by now familiar to Zak. Instead, he wanted to know just how often fishermen struck lucky. Murphy had shrugged his shoulders and played coy, vaguely admitting that from time to time stuff came up, the odd olive jar here, an anchor there, but never a lucky strike like he had made this September so far from shore.

Shaking hands in parting, Zak had thanked the Floridian for his time and hospitality and remembered to ask if Mac feared the new breed of canyon buster fishing trawlers about to steal the town's livelihood.

"Canyon busters? That's all hot air and too late. Best they stick to the Gulf of Mexico. Up here the pickings are slim, just enough to squeeze a living, but a catch wouldn't even cover the costs of a buster's fuel. That's a fool's economy, no doubt."

Zak, deflated and down in the dumps, finally had his truth and it wasn't going to make a splash, let alone land him a half-page scoop in *The Times*. Ecologists had been right to dread these marine Frankensteins. Away from the theory of the Ivory Tower, Key West's reefs and turtles were safe for now for one reason: their fate had already dropped over the cliff. There weren't enough fish to make it worthwhile for a Canyon Buster to work these waters. Looks like I'll have to head on down further south into the Gulf of Mexico to get up close and personal with a canyon buster, Zak realized. Was it worth chasing? The truth was everything. Then there was the emotional heartache of abandoning Nicola, too painful to consider.

*

Before heading back down Front Street to poke around the Antiquarium museum backyard some more, Zak decided to take a photo of the Murphy's stunning house for his files. The beautiful palms and Poinciana trees blocked his view. The Murphys surely wouldn't mind if he quickly shot the house from the inside yard, he felt sure.

Snooping a few phone camera photos took seconds. Zak was about to head off when something out of place caught his eye, sticking out under the house's wooden decking. It was at that exact moment that Nicola's phone caught him, beaming a torchlight under the house in too great wide-eyed shock to take her call.

The foundations of Mac Murphy's mansion, as far as the

eye and light could see, were covered with an Aladdin's Cave of years and years of old pottery, metal, busted anchors and smashed olive jars that looked identical to the backyard fishermen's cultural catches in the Barracuda's museum. Looks like old boy Mac hadn't been sharing all his discoveries with the world. The bones of a very different news story started to take shape in Zak's mind. Something important might still be salvaged from Key West.

Now Zak knew exactly how downtown boy Murphy could afford to live an uptown gent's life. He'd been raking up the Florida Keys' wrecked treasure for decades and flogging off the harvests.

14

The Antiquarium, Key West

The black suits were deep in a conference of war when the demented Spaniard started shrieking and banging on the Antiquarium's ground-floor glass office door. "Hoy es el día, hoy es el día," Rodi squealed, jumping up and down to catch the Barracuda's attention.

With the smooth glide of an Olympic synchronized swimming team, the four men and two women turned as one to peer at Rodi's manic dance. Al Nassau smoothed down his Hugo Boss jacket, crossed the office floor in three sharp steps and pulled the blinds shut. No more nonsense. His distracting madness could wait.

The team hadn't seen the Barracuda in so foul a mood in many moons. Hardly had he had time to decompress at home from the first phase of operation *Merced* when Nassau had summoned him to an urgent meeting. The wreck hunter was several days away from catching up with sleep and was more cobra than barracuda. Morning turned to lunchtime and his belly rumbled in anticipation of some fried alligator and swamp cabbage slaw, comfort food that reminded him of his hard-up childhood.

Usually, this room in the Antiquarium was the Barracuda's favourite honey trap. It sure beat sitting in bars swirling rum with gold swizzle sticks awaiting punters and the skies to clear. The sting was simple. The door of the glass-panelled office was always left ajar, deliberately. Visitors who had finished visiting the museum's splendours and dropped some cash in the shop found themselves funnelled into a direct view of a foot-long slab of silver shining on a Victorian wooden desk.

Curiosity lured them closer, like a thrill-seeking Icarus circling the sun. It was then that the Barracuda would pounce from the shadows, making the curious bystander jump with the well-polished decades-old promise that "If you can pick it up, you can have it."

Even for a Soviet athlete from the 1970s, pumped up to the gills on anabolic steroids, the game of one-handed grab was impossible. Boxers, basketball players and wrestlers had all tried and failed. Trying to grasp the perfect angle and all other sneaky methods were also useless. The Barracuda would carefully reel in the innocent, pointing out the Spanish marks on the bar, share the tale of where it was made, by whom, in what year and whether the owner had paid the Spanish king's tax or if it was contraband.

No, the wide-eyed amigo did not know that the officers and crews of Spanish ships illegally smuggled at least thirty per cent more treasure than was on official manifests to top up their pitiful wages. Ask no questions and I'll tell you no lies was an unspoken mantra among sailors voyaging between the Americas and Andalusia. Under the cloak of night, small merchant ships cruised off Cadiz and San Lucar stealthily offloading goods smuggled on fleet galleons and landing them far from the beady eyes of the king's spies who scoured the port of Seville for any sign of funny business like colonial-era CCTV. Scamming the monarch's greedy capitalist empire was a national pastime.

Lured into his trap, the Barracuda would regale the chosen one over rum or coffee with amazing anecdotes about his adventures chasing treasures across Florida. Many new friends failed to escape the Antiquarium's clutches without investing small sums in the latest underwater caper. From time to time a seriously big hitter was reeled in, addicted for life.

Al Nassau started out ensnared this way. Within a month he'd moved his dot.com business out of San Francisco and hauled his earthly belongings down to southern Florida. The financial cherry of treasure was pretty meaningless to billionaires like Nassau.

The thrill of the chase, mad capers and deep friendships were far more valued. Not for a day had he regretted the decision. The inspiring ocean even enlarged his bank balance once he joined the green economy. In the quiet season, Nassau hired the Barracuda's research ships and sent them offshore to rake up not gold but Florida's plastic waste, which he neatly recycled into Blue Ocean zero waste sandals and yoga mats.

Now the blinds were closed shut and the silver slab relegated to the floor. The directors of Keys Exploration, charged with overseeing the business of the wreck ventures, had been called to an emergency closed-door council.

Nobody was especially stunned by the turn of events, but the speed of Jorvik & Silver's legal attack had taken the wind out of the dig's momentum. Under the seal of the State of Florida, Keys Exploration had been served papers to cease and desist diving on the "said shipwreck purported to be the final resting place of the *Merced* and all related to her." Worse still, a consortium of the Kingdom of Spain and the International Council of Cultural Heritage, ICOCH, financed by Jorvik & Silver solicitors, were claiming the ship and its content as the exclusive patrimony of Madrid.

The Barracuda sat in stony silence, wearing a faded t-shirt, ancient jeans and flip-flops, while the hastily convened board of directors dissected Spain's claim.

"Now hang on a minute," Maisie Hemingway started, for twelve years a generally silent partner but now jabbing a burgundy-polished fingernail in the air. "The *Merced* went down outside State territorial waters. Surely Spain can't claim the treasure. Isn't this an open and shut case of finders keepers? Please tell me it is."

For longer than she cared to remember, Melissa Todd had sweated as head council for the Barracuda and was an expert in stripping back maritime case law to keep outsiders' greedy paws off her company's hard-gained bounty. Sporting a blond bob, grey trousers and a blue corporate cotton button-down shirt with Keys Exploration printed in gold over the left breast pocket, she may have looked to all intents and purposes the archetypal girl next door but in the dock Todd turned Rottweiler.

"Friends, let's backtrack to the beginning," Todd opened. Plugging her laptop into a USB socket, the office's end wall lit up with a projected document entitled United States District Court, Southern District of Florida in Admiralty, Miami. A header below read The Kingdom of Spain versus Keys Exploration, Key West.

The Barracuda scanned the introduction and knew he was in for a painstakingly dull few hours. "Comes now the Plaintiff, the Kingdom of Spain," he read, "and files this, its claim for the summary judgement of full sovereign possession of the vessel identified as the *Merced* and all that therein pertains." Lord give us mercy, the Barracuda swore, rolling his eyes and scratching his salt and pepper stubble. Apart from Melissa, he pretty much detested all lawyers, blood-sucking parasites who'd cost him millions in pensions. In his line of work, there was no doubt they were, unfortunately, a necessary evil.

"Let me break this down," Todd continued. "In short, whipped up by those reptiles at Jorvik & Silver, the Spanish Crown is laying claim to everything we found on the *Merced*, and I mean everything – the treasure, pots and pans, even the rotten wooden hull. They argue their rights are straightforward: 1. the wreck is unquestionably the remnants of the *Merced*; 2. Spain never abandoned its sovereign entitlement to the ship, particularly one of such historical significance; 3. under international treaties, Spain's warships must be given the same respect as those of the United States; and 4. the Court of Miami is legally bound to appoint Spanish jurisdiction over the wreckage under the Foreign Sovereign Immunities Act."

"Then follows several pages about the factual history of the *Merced*. Not bad at all. Either they stole our intel or they must have got some hotshot archivists in Seville onto the case pronto. Spain has poured over the PR photos we put out on the wires and reckon they can authenticate the wreck's ownership from the coins, astrolabe and pottery. No argument from me there, I'm afraid." The Board of Directors slumped in their plush black leather chairs.

"Fear not, however. In typical Jorvik & Silver obsessive fashion, they go way overboard," Todd cautioned, closely staring at page twelve and raising an eyebrow. "If this document wasn't so serious, their thoughts on the ship's cannon would be hilarious. They certainly seem extremely forced, special pleading, I'd say."

The legal filing hinged on the original manifest's listing of the *Merced* being armed with eight iron guns. The cannon uncovered underwater matched the size and style a Spanish frigate would have carried in the first half of the seventeenth century, Spain's ordnance experts claimed. Just by scrutinizing the widely publicized video and photographs released by the Key West team, Spain reckoned it could identify one specific lump of concretion as a swivel gun known as an *Asesino* or Murderer.

The Barracuda was in the right mood for doing some 'asesinoing' of his own.

"Ok, now we get to the nitty gritty," Todd continued. "Spain is insisting the wreck of the *Merced* cannot be owned by us under the centuries-old law of salvage and first finders rights, even though it sank outside US waters, because the Kingdom never abandoned its ownership of the *rem*, i.e. this 'warship'."

Spain's motion concluded that more than three hundred and ninety years had passed since the *Merced* sank sailing back to the Crown with the official Tierra Firme armed fleet of 1622. Her place of rest and all the brave men who perished on it that fateful day were left undisturbed down the centuries – until now. International law recognizes the solemnity of this national memorial and Spain's sovereign rights to preserve it however it wishes.

The Court of Miami is duty bound, Spain preached, to respect these principles for their nation's sea dead. It is this combination of self-serving interests among nations, Todd explained, that warranted granting Spain's motion to vacate the *Merced*'s arrest and dismiss Keys Exploration's claim to the wreckage.

The filing set out how the Kingdom of Spain expected the Court of Miami to order the Key West salvors to stop digging the

Merced with immediate effect. Keys Exploration was directed to return the finds to Spain within ten days.

The Barracuda had heard all this rot before, a confusing barbed wire fence of technical terms spun into legal speak that amounted to a steaming pile of horse crap, he shouted, pounding his fist on the table. A hushed silence fell across the conference of war. Todd sat upright awaiting questions. Al Nassau looked ready to bomb Spain. The Barracuda calmed down, lost in reverie. The bell tower clock struck high noon. The lunchtime promise of chicken fried in the First Flight Island restaurant wafted through the museum windows.

"Let me get this straight," Maisie Hemingway struggled to understand, starting to get hot under the collar and worried about her investment. "Spain claims they own the *Merced* even though they never made any effort to find it, save the crew or look for it in the three hundred and ninety-five years since the great hurricane of September 1622? Isn't this money for old rope, something for nothing? Surely the law protects the salvor's sweat in discovering the wreckage and returning its valuable cargo to the stream of commerce?"

"I hear you, Maisie," Melissa sympathised, raising both hands in submission. "Jorvik & Silver are sniping behind some very strong and politically sensitive law, the US Foreign Sovereign Immunities Act of 1976. This, in turn, is based on Articles 95 and 96 of the United Nations Law of the Sea Convention. It's the kind of complicated protocol that scares the crap out of governments and juries. But all's not lost if you read between the lines."

The lawyer grinned, glanced at her good friends, flipped through her file and added in slow clipped tones, "Listen very carefully. To remind ourselves, the precise letter of the law says that 'Warships on the high seas have complete immunity from the jurisdiction of any State other than the flag State. Ships owned or operated by a State and used only on government non-commercial service shall, on the high seas, have complete immunity from the jurisdiction of any State other than the flag State.'"

"And what the cotton-picking blazes does that mean in

normal speak? Even my grandpa wouldn't be able to decipher that drivel," Maisie exploded.

"To be honest, you're right. This has nothing to do with an ancient shipwreck or its precious custodianship," Todd surrendered. "Really it's all about protecting modern military secrets. Under the Clinton administration, this messed up law was powered up so that if, say, a modern American submarine armed with nukes sank in the South China Sea, no foreign power could touch the craft or the crew, no matter in whose waters it sank. It would categorically remain US property. The same would go for a Chinese warship grounded on a reef in the Straits of Florida. It all makes harmonious, mutually self-serving sense."

"The problem arises, Maisie, when you throw ancient ships into the mix. As far as I know, I've never seen any wooden wreck sunk with sensitive technologies, black boxes or state secrets. Yet some oily lawyer in Washington got the court to add to the sensible list of naval sovereign property. So, to the logical warships, submarines, fighter planes and even spaceships, some jackass got rotten historical wrecks added to the definitions of sovereign immunity. For this dumb ass reason, if the planks from a wooden warship once used in the third-century BC fleet of Alexander the Great turned up off Egypt, for instance, Greece or Macedonia could still claim them back. It's balls but heavy balls that are strongly upheld law just in case the you know what hits the fan in some distant wargame that nobody is supposed to know about."

Al Nassau chose this point to clarify the absurd. "Maisie, you have to suspend logic here. We find ourselves dragged into the world of geopolitical gamesmanship. Of course, it doesn't make a jot of sense. What if Israel started digging up the Roman military camps built in the Negev desert to starve the Jewish zealots of Masada into submission in the first century? Imagine if Roman armour, coins and the commander's gold turned up. Neither the pope nor the president of Italy would have any right to claim back finds lost on Israeli soil even if Rome, the imperial ancestor, built the fort and lived and died in it. But that's exactly what the law expects and is happening beneath the waves. It is, I'm afraid, the world gone nuts. The question is, Melissa, how the heck are we going to outsmart these Keystone Kops, stop the madness and keep dirty Spanish hands off our treasure?"

A pause in proceedings followed.

"If I may," the Barracuda offered, returning to the land of the living and picking his words with extreme care. "Our arrogant colleagues at Jorvik & Silver are creating a smokescreen here, it seems to me. Don't be fooled. Sure, I may think it's horse crap, but the Foreign Sovereign Immunities Act applies to ancient warships whether we like it or not. No contest. We have no choice but to live with it. However, suckers, there's one tiny problem with these great thinkers' strategy."

Sharp, hopeful intakes of breath sucked out the office's oxygen. The Barracuda kicked back his chair and stood tall, pointing at the legal writ projected onto the office wall.

"Guys, the *Merced* wasn't a warship. Period. They think we're hippy-dippy hicks who are easily steamrolled by tying us in legal red tape and so-called expert opinions. I say again, horse crap to that. Yes, the ship was in the State fleet of Spain and it's correct that she was carrying cannon. But I repeat, she was never a frigging frigate or a warship."

"Let's rewind and recap," the Barracuda suggested. "The outbound manifests from Seville show the *Merced* was the smallest class of merchantman allowed to sail with the Tierra Firme fleet. She was loaded with iron goods, shoes, clothes and jars of quince, olives and wine. And the guns weren't there to fight in battles, but as insurance should the captain end up chased down by Dutch pirates when his ship headed off-piste to the Pearl Coast in Venezuela. Remember, Holland was all over Venezuela's Araya Peninsula like a rash, hoovering up barrels of salt to keep their blessed pickled herring business going. I kid you not. King Philip IV had to build a garrison and fort at Santiago de Araya in 1622, manned by two hundred soldiers and armed with forty heavy guns, to defend the blessed salt beds."

"And, in fact, we only found four guns on the *Merced*. This could well be our ace. It looks like the other four were never installed, which is exactly what a merchant keen to fill his hold to the max with valuable cargo would do. Juan Limbre was a captain in a powerfully defended fleet. Maybe it wasn't such a big risk to dump some of the cannon in Havana and open up the deck space to boost profits. Basic economics, right?"

"How would you like us to officially respond to the Court then, Kurt?" Todd enquired.

The Barracuda thought for a while before his position became crystal clear.

"Nothing for it but to counter-sue and head to court. Our formal position must be that the *Merced* is a merchant ship, not a warship, and *ipso facto* does not enjoy the golden handcuff protection of sovereign immunity. Lost in international waters, the State of Florida can make no legal claim. We keep all rights as the finder and legal salvor-in-possession. And, finally, we demand $5 million from Spain in lost revenue for deliberately making a false claim and forcing the *Golden Margaret* to cease ops."

"I know what you're thinking, Al and Melissa. This stiff arming will surely bog down the project, but there's no alternative. We gotta hit back fast and furiously. The shift we put in on the wreck between the Jorvik & Silver *Daily Mail* statement and today's filing brought up more than enough booty to keep us busy cataloguing and conserving for a few months. Most importantly, we've already hit pay dirt: gold bars and silver coins. The investors will be beside themselves with excitement rather than put off. We spin positives out of this can of filthy politricks."

"We'll grease some scholars' hands and hire them to write expert opinions, leaving no shadow of a doubt what the *Merced* really was and was not. So, Ms Todd, if you will, notify Miami of our opinion. Put that poison in Jorvik & Silver's pipes and let them choke on a dose of their own toxic smoke. Folks, let's grab some lunch. I'm as hungry as a dentist-hating British sailor with toothache. Plus, I better check what the heck Rodi's going loopy about."

The dark cloud under which the meeting met lifted. The

Barracuda was back in his element, two steps over the horizon ahead of the enemy. Even Nassau, the hyper-realist prone to pessimism, bought into the strategy. Melissa Todd knew she could sell the logic to a judge. Maisie Hemingway was reassured. Keys Exploration, nobody's fool, was back in the hot seat.

15

The Antiquarium Fridge, Key West

In the end, the board of directors and the Barracuda batted away Rodi's barking on their way to lunch. They had far more serious fish to deep fry. A plate of his favourite fried alligator, fortified by a few tots of rum at the Schooner Wharf Bar while chatting about the Miami Dolphin's poor run of form with Big Dave, calmed the wreck hunter. Afterwards, he sauntered back to the museum basement to put the silver bar back on show. Time to reel in the next punter.

Back in his sanctuary, all hell had broken loose. The sound of smashed crockery clattered through the floorboards, accompanied by furious screaming. The Barracuda looked up and raced through the museum shop, scattering several startled Chinese visitors. The Antiquarium was a bastion of culture and contemplation about the beauty of the ocean and the sunken past. Fighting was a no-no. Leave it in the bar.

The Barracuda placed his thumb on the scanner reader that gave privileged access to the Fridge, the museum's conservation lab. Inside, the ambient room temperature dropped to ten degrees centigrade to protect the 175,000 archaeological finds stored there. The scene was one of total chaos. Whale, Alona, Mitch, Rusty and Brains cowered on one side of the workbench, hands raised to protect their faces. On the other side of the room, a red-headed demon, Rodi, eyes ablaze, screamed in Spanish and jabbed a scalpel towards his former friends. The black and white lino floor was strewn with a tapestry of jagged sherds, not ancient, thank heavens, but from any and every coffee cup Rodi could lay his hands on.

The Barracuda slid quietly into the Fridge, shivered at the drop in temperature and listened to Mitch trying to talk his pal down from the cliff edge.

"Boy, come on now, we're just guests here. Leave it to the professionals, ok?" the surfer suggested. The response was yet another flying coffee cup, engraved with the words 'Carpe Diem', whistling passed Mitch's right ear and even more frantic scalpel jabbing.

"Lo encontré, perras. Así que descubrí el rit. Esta es mi gloria," Rodi shouted back, reaching for another missile, this one red and white and decorated with the logo 'Keep Calm and Dig'. The furious argument clashed with the lab's chilled temperature.

"Rodi, my friend, decorum please," Whale pleaded, the eighteen-stone, triple-chinned master conservator loved by all who had been with Keys Exploration for a decade and was the best in the business this side of Paris. "No doubt the honour is all yours. You made the discovery and should be super proud. Bravo. That said, amigo, this is a matter of strict codes of practice. You just ain't qualified."

"I'm afraid Whale's right," Rusty added. "Anyone handling this stuff has to have an Institute for Conservation professional qualification for conservation. If not, you run the risk of damaging these delicate babies and that will cost us and you cash if their price crashes. And if you get acid burns on your skin or someone throws you out the window head-first, the insurance won't cough up. Right? You know it makes sense."

The threat of lost money for the impoverished Andalusian started to make the red mist clear. Rodi slowly put down the scalpel. The cowering friends breathed again.

"Can someone tell me what the heck is going on here? I'm trying to run a centre of cultural enlightenment," the Barracuda demanded, leaning against the entrance door, arms folded.

"Ah captain, welcome," started Whale. "I'm afraid you've stumbled on a misunderstanding and we're in the middle of delicate international relations."

"English boy, spit it out. Who's done the heck what to

whom?" repeated the boss.

Whale reddened various shades of beetroot and started to stammer. Rusty gently intervened. "Boss, we should be celebrating here, not starting a twenty-first-century War of the Spanish Succession."

From decades of watching people's reactions to his tales of the past and body language hinting whether an investment was on the cards or not from new-found buddies, the Barracuda noticed Rodi's neck vein starting to pulse rapidly. He crossed the room and put an arm around the Spaniard's shoulder. Even Alona started to think for the first time in twenty minutes she might get out of the lab in one piece.

"Whale had finished the first rough inventory of the *Merced*'s finds and allocated a workflow to everyone," Rusty explained. "I started cleaning the silver coins to prepare them for electrolysis. Mitch was in charge of emptying the olive jars of mud, and Alona with sieving the contents to see if we could find any seeds or the like to tell us what was transported or what the crew once ate. All top science. Now our good friend Rodi here was entrusted with the loose organic ecofacts, see."

At this, Rodi broke free of the Barracuda, jabbed his finger furiously at Whale and made his sorry fate clear. "They give me the crap, piles and piles of seaweed. Mush, nothing but mush. And now Rodi find *un secreto increíble*. Only Rodi, nobody else." The Andalusian really wasn't a team player.

"That you did, Rodi, and bravo. All power to you," Rusty tried to sympathize, throwing cold water over the crisis. The Spaniard started to calm down and beam with pride. "As I was trying to explain, boss, we were all getting on with business, when Rodi started screaming '*Eso es todo, eso es todo*', this is it, this is it." The engineer paused. "You know what boss, maybe best you just come and see for yourself what all the fuss is about," Rusty decided, winking at Alona and Mitch.

The Barracuda sighed impatiently. The day had been hugely trying already and he'd just about had enough amateur dramatics. Serious headaches needed sorting out pronto if he was to save the company. Rusty invited Rodi to lead the way and the motley crew processioned into the wet room in the back of the Fridge. The rubber-lined stainless steel work surface was carefully covered with the Spaniard's piles of mush. A metre away lay the fruit of Rodi's work, long greenish-brown leaves drying side by side.

The cleaned mush was immediately recognisable as tobacco leaves. Thousands of them. "Awesome, Rodi, fine job son. We've long suspected the 1622 fleet was loaded with puff," the Barracuda enthused. "Tobacco was worth a fortune in Europe and the man on the street was starting to get hooked. Seville even housed the West's largest baccy factory. We found tobacco merchant's lead seals on the *Margarita*, but this is something new, something terrific. We'll get a DNA sequence analysed to firm up where this stuff was grown. Maybe you'll even get your name on a scientific paper. How does that sound? We good?" he asked, patting the angry young man on the back.

The response was unexpected. "Atornillar el tabaco, screw the tobacco," Rodi exclaimed, banging his fist on the work surface. A few leaves jumped in the air in alarm. "You want treasure, I give you treasure."

Rodi grabbed the Barracuda's arm and led him to the end of the work surface where a plastic measuring jug stood three-quarters full of water. At first, the old sea dog could see nothing until an impatient Rodi peeled back two tobacco leaves nestled together. Taking a syringe, he spritzed deionised water over the mush. The mud lifted like Moses parting the Red Sea and the Barracuda whistled. A big grin spread across his creased face. Next, he grabbed Rodi and hugged him like a long-lost son. Maybe the day wasn't a bust after all.

"Well, blow me sideways; that's sure a game changer," whispered an amazed Barracuda. Rarely was he lost for words. This was one of those moments.

Rodi handed him the plastic jug. Peering closely inside, he spotted what all the fuss was about. A wave of joy swept his body at the sight of hundreds upon hundreds of tiny white pearls glistening like early morning dew drops. A more beautiful sight the wreck hunter couldn't remember for many a fine year.

The Barracuda carried the jug of pearls back into the main lab in two hands like a newborn child, followed by his disciples.

"Team, pull up a chair. Story time. Put the kettle on," he asked Whale. Rodi reddened as everyone realised no more cups had survived what became known in the years to come as the Battle of Tobacco Hill. Brains was dispatched downstairs for replacement 'Deep Down We Care' mugs from the museum shop and to invite Al Nassau and Melissa Todd to step into the Fridge. Rodi innocently proposed perhaps Maisie Hemingway would want to get in on the act. What a perfect moment for her to bask in his glory, and maybe afterwards? Well, a Rodi could dream.

16

Travels to the Pearl Coast

Fifteen minutes later the Fridge was full to bursting. Whale, assisted by a calmer Rodi, had laid out a pile of mush, cleaned leaves and tobacco folded open to reveal the wonders within. The mood had swung from war to peace. Even Rodi turned all light and sweet puppy dog when Maisie sauntered in. Alona and Mitch had felt the urge to slip out before Act 2 for a hit of vodka to settle their nerves after the Battle of Tobacco Hill. Now seated, they were suppressing a giggling fit at Rodi's theatrics.

Life was definitely looking up for the surfers. Once the mud sucking had shifted into full throttle far out to sea, every day brought enthralling gifts. The job felt more like Christmas day than work. Alona and Mitch had learnt how to x-ray concretions and pick out the undressed ghoulish shapes – here a cluster of silver coins, there a pistol trigger and, on one occasion, their star find, an emerald-encrusted gold cross. It was like airport security, Mitch felt, except that every scan turned up goodies. That night the couple hadn't slept, high on life rather than the booze that had patched them up in recent months.

Their so-called workload ran to washing mud off gold bars or rinsing blackened silver *reales* till they sparkled. Other days, they brushed with toothbrushes the ooze off Andalusian crockery imitating Chinese finery till the glazed patinas glowed once more. These were the best of days. When her mind wandered, Alona laughed that her relationship, cracking before the surfers hit Key West, was born again. Back on the beach, the peace was holding. Signing onto the *Merced*'s high jinks turned out to be cheaper and more effective than therapy. Hallelujah, as her good pastor father would have cried.

"Amigos, your attention please," the Barracuda began. "As we all know, the sea is the gift that keeps on giving. It's a bottomless blue hole of wonder. Just when you think you've seen it all, the deep smacks you over the head with a big wet tuna. And, as experience has also taught us, equally unexpected surprises can turn up on land in conservation or in the library. Today is one of those great days."

Whale, Mitch and Alona let out a series of tribal whoops, which the Barracuda humoured, his arms spread wide open in good grace.

Al Nassau's reality check settled the audience. "I don't need to remind everyone that what we are about to discuss is on a need-to-know basis and nobody outside this room needs to know. We are all under confidentiality agreements, ok?"

"Maisie and Al, our Spanish friend has darned well changed the complexion of the last twenty-four hours and tripled our profits," the Barracuda went on to explain. "So far Rodi has separated about two thousand five hundred pearls he spotted stuffed inside a consignment of what turned out to be tobacco leaves. Looks like some racketeering Spaniard went rogue and hid some pouches, probably once made of cloth, inside the tobacco as contraband. Down the centuries, the material rotted away and the pearls ended up caked in mush. Dear Rodi here has only processed about ten per cent of the organics. Just possibly, we could be talking about a hoard of twenty-five thousand shiny presents, boys and girls."

"Pearls weren't unexpected on the *Merced* – we knew she'd deliberately sneaked off to Nueva Cordobo in Venezuela, the Pearl Coast – but in this quantity. Holy smokes!" the Barracuda yelled, playing up to the crowd. "We've got ourselves the largest cache found on a wreck in any ocean. Pretty staggering, for sure. Now, since you looked into the pearl trade, Brains, before the dig began, it's only fair that you tell the story of how these suckers ended up lost at sea. The floor is yours."

A quiet man of few words who didn't care to be the centre of attention, Brains, the project chief historian, was nonetheless in his element among a small crowd of friendly faces. Away from the damp, he'd set up his laptop and clicked open a PowerPoint presentation named Costas de Perlas, part of a talk he'd given two years ago at the International Shipwreck Conference in Plymouth.

Brains drifted off for a moment at the fond memory of the best of pals cut from the same cloth, drawn from the four corners of the compass, who always came out to play in Plymouth every February. The real fun started off the clock down the Admiral Balchen pub when secret revelations about big finds squirrelled away from UK Heritage cascaded out of beer glasses and mutual trust. A few were made-up boasts – drunken exaggerations about the one that got away – but many were authentic. Phone photos backed up the claims.

Some old salts reckoned British law was so old school that under the Goodwin Sands less than five per cent of all shipwrecked finds were being declared to officials these days. Why bother? Threats and finger-wagging from the idiots at the Maritime Management Authority just made hardcore British divers do the opposite. The authorities weren't to be trusted. Without financial incentives nobody was going to declare even an anchor. They didn't get the ways of the sea.

Brains snapped back and popped the first slide. A map drawn by Peter van der Aa in 1706 showed a close-up of northeast Venezuela, where the island of Margarita nestled off the mainland of Cumana.

"Ok guys, here's the lowdown and I'm afraid it's a horror story," an always honest Brains explained. "These here pearls may look all shiny, pure and super valuable, but they are the Americas' version of blood diamonds. The death Spain was willing to inflict in the lure of pearls is one of colonial history's most despicable scandals."

"The *Merced*'s manifest written in Seville tells us that she was the only 1622 outbound fleet ship to swerve east towards Nueva Cordoba. Yes, Alona, I see you raising an eyebrow and rightly so. This confused us for a while until Professor Mike Schutz at the

University of South Florida confirmed this is just an antiquated name given by the native Indians to what was better known in the seventeenth century as Cumana along Venezuela's Pearl Coast."

Alona nodded in appreciation. Mitch whispered, "Swat" and pinched her gluteus maximus. Rodi diverted his gaze to another gluteus maximus of the female persuasion nearby. Maisie was oblivious to the bottom line.

"Cumana lay almost off the edge of the West's maps and here certainly lay monsters," Brains rattled on. "Why would our small merchant ship risk life and limb to head one thousand six hundred miles east from the recognised end of the Tierra Firme fleet at Cartagena in Colombia? What made such a huge peril worth rolling the dice? Well, the answer is staring us in the face – shiny gems."

Over the next twenty minutes, the chief historian preached an abbreviated MA course in Spain's colonial exploitation of Venezuela. Cumana, the team learnt, was first discovered by Christopher Columbus during his third voyage in 1498 after King Ferdinand and Queen Isabella sent him south in search of oro, plata, y perlas, gold, silver and pearls. After months at sea the natives surrounded his ship and bartered six marks of pearls with him, about one and a half kilograms. Far more importantly, though, the Indians tripped up badly by telling Columbus the secret where Venezuela's mysterious oyster beds could be found, a huge indiscretion which they paid for by extinction.

Alona was intrigued to learn how, in the early days, the great minds of the Enlightenment thought pearls grew on trees whose flowering dewdrops fell into the ocean as celestial sperm to impregnate the oysters. In his account of Columbus's third voyage, Bartolomé de las Casa described how in the Gulf of Paria off Venezuela, "Close to the sea there were countless oysters stuck to the branches of the trees which dip into the ocean, with their mouths open to receive the dew which falls from the leaves to form pearls."

Brains switched slides to reveal Johannes Vermeer's famous masterpiece, the Girl With a Pearl Earring, painted in 1665.

To its right he'd added the equally spectacular Armada portrait by George Gower presented to Queen Elizabeth I in 1588 after England chased off the failed invasion of Philip the Pious of Spain. Elizabeth was bejewelled with five heavy strings of pearls.

Brains pointed at the screen and delved back in time. "By the seventeenth century, mankind's love affair with pearls was millennia old. In the first century, Pliny the Elder's *Natural History* already knew that 'The richest merchandise of all, and the most soveraigne commoditie throughout the whole world, are these pearles'. The early inhabitants of Mesoamerica even believed men and women first emerged from the primeval ocean in a jar of pearls, which explains why the Aztecs called these gems heart stones."

The historian told his captivated friends the bitter truth of how Spain invaded the Costas de las Perlas, the Pearl Coast, in a frenzy of greed. At first, the humble Indians happily bartered their natural bounty for wine, linen shirts and firearms. Even better, Spanish conquistadors vowed to protect the Natives from marauding Carib tribes.

A pearl rush rampaged through the Caribbean and the new Spanish overlords built clay and straw hut ranches on the island of Cubagua. In 1504 the Crown gave the Spanish Governor of Hispaniola, Nicolas de Ovando, cash for a fort near Cumana to guard royal interests against rustlers illegally flogging contraband. Without any international laws to protect their interests, the pearl beds were seized as the sovereign property of the king of Spain. By the time Friar Antonio Vázquez de Espinosa visited Cumana in 1621, he counted two hundred Spaniards roaming the town, excluding Native and Black slaves. The settlement boasted a parish church and a Dominican convent under the patronage of Our Lady of Carmen that doubled up as a hospital for the sick.

The next slide grabbed from Google Earth showed a birds-eye view from the air of ruins scattered across the pearl market town of Cubagua Island. Flattened buildings and streets were piled high with smashed oyster shells. When the town was excavated in 1954, rectangular stone houses made from rough stones were picked out of the soil, their walls plastered with lime ground from coral.

Once the pearls were harvested down by the shores of Cubagua, Margarita and Cumana, they were locked away in strong boxes in warehouses. There, the royal *quinto* Crown tax was creamed off *in natura* as pearls, not cash, before the remainder was traded across the markets of Latin America and lands westward.

"But here's the odd thing," Brains cautioned. "Before Rodi's discovery today, the finest minds were convinced the age of the pearl trade was over before the *Merced* set sail for Seville in 1622. How do we know? Well, Vázquez de Espinosa told us in 1628 that 'The city of La Margarita used to be very wealthy, thanks to the pearl-fisheries... but nowadays it is poverty-stricken, for the pearls have given out... The opinion of most people in those regions is that the mouths of the Orinoco and other rivers along the coast as far as the Amazon expel and discharge a great mass of tainted water; its effect is like that of Greek fire or poison... and it killed the oysters from which they got the pearls. The great source of wealth is lost'."

Rodi smiled ear to ear and nudged Maisie with his elbow at being elevated to the status of one of Europe's greatest minds or so he fancied. Brains switched to a picture drawn by Theodor de Bry in 1594 of slaves diving from canoes for oysters off Cubagua. Spanish overlords supervised the work, peering into the ocean from the safe decks of heavily armed galleons.

To feed its unquenched thirst, after working all the local Guayqueri Indians to an early grave, in 1508 Spain invaded the Bahamas and enslaved its entire population of Lucayans. These islander Indians knew how to dive expertly to depths over thirty metres, skills they'd picked up collecting conch shells. The oysters scattered at fourteen metres off Cubagua were easy pickings. These gentle tribe's folk were enslaved and shipped like sardines to the Pearl Coast where they swiftly went the unceremonious way of the Venezuelan natives. In under three decades the whole population of the Bahamas, sixty thousand Lucayans, had been wiped out by 1527.

The colour in Brains' face drained. A horrific scene of blood and murder on the laptop screen showed Spanish soldiers collaring men, women and children in Angola along the shores of West Africa. The friends' mood matched the chilly temperature in the conservation lab. Alona shivered and nestled up to Mitch, who was surprised by the unusual lump in his throat and for a change not his pants. His soul really did seem to be saved.

"And now began an even greater terror of colonial history," Brains conceded. "It's a poorly known truth that the African slave trade started not in the Caribbean's sugar plantations, but here along the Pearl Coast. When the Indian population was all used up, and with pearl production on Cubagua at its peak, Madrid granted a slaving license monopoly to the German Welser merchant family. Thousands of West African slaves started to be exported to Venezuela. And life was cheap. As Friar Bartolome de Las Casas reported in the early 1520s in his *Brevissima Relation de la Destruction de las Indias*, for the oyster divers, 'there is no life as infernal and desperate that can be compared with it'. If being worked to the bone didn't kill the divers, the sharks attracted by their flapping legs got them."

"Before the great silver mines were opened at Potosi in Bolivia in 1545 and Zacatecas in Mexico in 1547, pearl exports were worth more than all other Spanish exports combined. But Spain went too far too quick. Between 1513 and 1540 the Pearl Coast's ranches sent 26,000 pounds' weight of pearls to the Crown in Seville every year. And that was just what the king took for tax, a mere fifth of all the industry. All in all, over these short twenty-seven years of hyper-exploitation 1.2 billion oysters – yes billion, friends – stuffed with forty million pearls were fished from the seas of Cubagua. The haul for the sixteenth century is reckoned to have been sold in Europe for two hundred million gold *ducados* coins."

"By the early 1530s, the oyster beds had reached the end of the line. Let me spell this out so everyone is crystal clear: the exhaustion of the beds along the Pearl Coast ended up going down in history as the earliest example of species collapse caused by a European power on the American continent. In terms of human suffering, it is also judged to have been the most appalling. These massive harvest overkills caused irreparable damage to people and species. The Caribbean pearl fisheries never recovered."

"By the time the *Merced* set off on what would be its last voyage in 1622," Brains ended, "as we now know stuffed with pearls alongside its other riches, the accounts tell us that just one hundred and thirty African divers were left working Margarita Island. And our Tortugas shipwreck, I am forced to conclude, is a sorry fossil and symbol of ecosystem extinction and the extermination of noble ancient populations and their ways of life. So it was written."

The audience whispered reverently among themselves. The Barracuda crossed himself and murmured "Amen". Rodi was no longer sure he wanted his name inked up in the annals of history for discovering the *Merced*'s pearls. He felt sick to the depths of his stomach at the horrors his forefathers perpetrated in the name of profit. Al Nassau was crunching numbers to work out what the shiny gems were all worth. Maisie reckoned the story would make a great film, with her in the title lead naturally. Mitch's rewired mind started drifting to the question of whether the Barracuda would give him one pearl to make into an engagement ring for his long-suffering dame. The timing felt just right.

"All those blood pearls ended up adorning the rich and famous of Madrid, Paris and London, then?" Alona asked.

"Mostly but not exclusively," Brains carefully articulated. "Yes, pearls were the ultimate fashion accessory, the Tiffany jewellery of their age. The fruits of the Pearl Coast travelled far and wide as objects of ultimate desire, sold worldwide to the Jews of Cairo, the Arabs in the Persian Gulf, Venetians and the Armenians of the Crimea."

"But there were less obvious uses. The Church revered pearls because they saw the pure white gem as a symbol of Christ's innocence. Beyond that, things got weird. The rich actually ate pearls," Brains added, warming to his theme and scrolling through his slides to a specific image of a gem-encrusted manuscript.

"What's that now?" a confused Mitch blurted out. The surfer had eaten almost anything everywhere in the world, even drank cat-shit coffee on the island of Sumatra, but pearls sounded like madness.

"Never judge the past, Mitch, they understood the best they could within their limits of knowledge. The scientific mind was yet unborn. This idea goes all the way back to the thirteenth century when a document called the *Lapidario* written for King Alfonso X the Wise of Castile made some crazy statements. Let me read what the book alleged. Here we go: 'The pearl is the most excellent in the medicinal art, for it is of great help in palpitation of the heart, and for those who are sad or timid, and in every sickness which is caused by melancholia, because it purifies the blood, clears it and removes all the impurities. They also make powders of them, which are applied to the eyes; because they clear the sight wonderfully, strengthen the nerves and dry up the moisture which enters the eyes'. The ancient Chinese, earth's oldest empire, held identical beliefs by the way."

Brains returned to tales of great splendour, such as how in the reign of Queen Elizabeth I the merchant prince Sir Thomas Gresham made a bet with the Spanish ambassador to London about who could host the most costly dinner. Gresham extravagantly won by buying a Venezuelan pearl for £15,000, which he reduced to powder and drank in a glass of wine to toast the health of the queen. An astonished ambassador bowed and admitted defeat.

Now that his moment of humiliation had passed, Rodi wanted full closure on the origin of his discovery. "You tell me the perlas from *La Merced* were smuggled cargo, eh? How el tabaco get onto the ship, too? Where was the magic hiding trick performed? And how come so many pearls if La Costas' oysters were *extinto* by 1622."

"All fair points," Brains conceded, mulling the question over and scrolling through his PowerPoint presentation until he landed on a letter of spidery words that even Rodi couldn't make head or tail of. "We have to start thinking that the *Merced* sailed to

Cumana speculatively. In 1622 the king of Spain was told that the fisheries were so badly drained that just one ship was needed to try and collect the royal pearl tax."

"Reading between the lines, we have to assume that a few Spanish entrepreneurs, probably specializing in tobacco, kept a dive team at Cumana and pushed them into ever deeper waters. Looks like they chanced on an undiscovered oyster bed in 1622," Brains argued.

"From there the pearls were secretly brought up and almost certainly not declared to the fort's governor. Maybe our man de la Torre Ayala, the main merchant who invested in the *Merced*, paid off the commander to look the other way. And the sleight of hand disappearing act was finished off using tobacco leaves."

"Caribbean Creole farmers started growing tobacco on a massive scale along the north coast of Venezuela in the late sixteenth century when Spanish Cumana became Europe's premier tobacco supplier. In 1605 a Spanish official called Andrés de Rojas described Venezuela's tobacco farmers as riff-raff who had no other source of income other than the tobacco crop that was highly esteemed in Flanders and England."

Once more in his stride, Brains told his friends how customhouse records showed that while no leaves were imported into England in 1558, by 1611 the country's tobacco use was valued at 100,000 pounds worth 400,000 gold ducats. The Netherlands, France and Germany bought up as much again. When the *Merced* sailed in 1622, tobacco was the most highly desired luxury shipped West.

In fact, Brains clarified, King James I was so furious at the devastating effects of the new addiction that in 1604 he published *A Counter-Blaste to Tobacco*, angrily condemning its use instead of medicine, complaining how it was taken "in place of a cure, a point of good fellowship, and he that will refuse to take a pipe of *Tobacco* among his fellowes... is accounted peevish and no good company." Peer pressure is nothing new, Maisie noticed.

"That's bang on right," the Barracuda added, bowing theatrically and thanking Brains for his lecture before taking centre stage. The natural order of life at Keys Exploration resumed.

"Manifests that do survive for cargoes, written up in the customs house of Cartagena in Colombia, leave no doubt that in 1622 the great galleons in the Marquis of Cadereita fleet were topped up with hills of tobacco. The fleet accountant, Martin de Urdaniz, calculated that 193,451 *pesos* of eight *reales* were paid by the Tierra Firme merchants at Cartagena to royal officials as Crown tax for 14,964 *arrobas* of tobacco. That's a whopping one hundred and seventy-two tons. Both the *Atocha* and the *Margarita* carried at least 3,772 official pouches of tobacco alongside their gold, silver and copper. Baccy was filthy lucre."

"I buy into all this historical backdrop, gents, fascinating," Al Nassau observed, before asking the million-dollar question on everyone's lips, most too polite to ask. "What's this haul going to bring us on the open market?"

When Brains started counting on his fingers, the Barracuda stepped forward, put his hand on his shoulder and said, "If I may. There are several reasons to be extremely optimistic. First off, these pearls come from a species which is now extinct, the Atlantic pearl oyster, *Pinctada imbricate.* As far as I can see, the shades of Rodi's pearls cover white to yellow and pink and the quality is outstanding. Second off, we've got the largest catch ever taken at sea. Fourth, boys and girls, I did a little checking of the markets while we waited for Al and Maisie to join us and am delighted to tell you that just one South Sea pearl could cost you $2,900."

Mitch wasn't sure his love for Alona could afford such a steep price tag.

The meandering history lesson sobered the friends like an ice bath. Who knew supposedly greedy treasure hunters cared so much about cultural backstories? Alona and Mitch whistled. Like everyone else, they still wanted to learn if they'd won the world's deepest lottery. The Barracuda scanned the audience, leaning forward like palms in the wind, and ended by very slowly and deliberately dropping his bombshell. "Let's be cautious here, but if the early estimates of a cargo of 25,000 pearls are correct… we're looking at a net value of $72.5 million."

As the value of Rodi's find hit home, nobody knew what to say or how to react. The sky-high figures were beyond everyone's dreams. And less than a quarter of the *Merced* had been dug up so far. Who knew what goodies awaited in the mud, guarded by sharks and conger eels?

"I hate to be a party pooper," Whale interjected to the ecstatic mood. "Just looking at these pearls, and without a meticulous count, it's clear that their sizes differ. So we should be wary. One size and sum may not fit all."

"Quite right, quite right. Thanks for reminding me," the Barracuda conceded, beaming from ear to ear. "My bad, I'm gonna have to drop that figure by twenty-five per cent to be cautious... But then I'm gonna add another forty per cent to cover the shipwreck effect – the unique historical story you just heard behind our discovery of the *Merced*, so splendidly narrated by Dr Brains."

"*Mea culpa*, team, my maths was bang out. Forget $72.5 million. Rodi's pearls are worth somewhere north of a cool $76 million. The Lord giveth and the Lord taketh away."

In the jubilant chaos that erupted, the shadow of a mega lawsuit with the Kingdom of Spain was pushed aside. The discovery of a motherlode of priceless gems on the *Merced* kicked off a killer celebration. Key West never needs an excuse to party, but even this was special. Only when the Schooner Wharf Bar ran dry twenty-four hours later did the woozy explorers drag themselves to bed with huge grins. Everyone thought they'd made enough to retire on.

17

The Interior, Boca Chica Beach

Nicola and Zak joined the party late and stayed dry. They felt in limbo, split from their friends' good fortune. The Barracuda knew nothing of the drifters' fallout. Anyway, the exotic out-of-towners came as a package in his head. An inclusive soul by nature, he happily let all the friends in on the discovery, pressing a sozzled finger to his lips. The English contingent couldn't help feeling sick to the pit of their stomachs at missing out on the once in a lifetime drama of the Battle of Tobacco Hill. The green-eyed monster haunts even the most stoic. An elated Rodi, plied with booze, didn't need an invitation to re-enact his heady discovery. Only when he crashed out on the floorboards, merrily dribbling into the Schooner Wharf Bar's sawdust, did his bragging cease.

The Barracuda's generosity of spirit didn't prevent Nicola and Zak from feeling disconnected from the fast-paced excitement swirling around the *Merced.* Partly because they weren't in at the deep end when the finds surfaced. Nicola had finished profiling the Tequesta people to her satisfaction. It wasn't treasure, but it was her own intoxicating secret adventure. She still had a nagging feeling her arrowhead unearthed at Boca Chica had more secrets to tell. Call it a sixth sense.

Zak had ended up precisely nowhere leveraging more information about how much treasures the local fishermen had hauled up off Key West down the decades. Every old salt had zipped up like a clam when the bombardment of questions started.

Nicola and Zak retreated to the corner of the bar, chatting

softly, catching up on each other's progress. That night a realisation started to dawn that team Keys Exploration didn't have the big picture about the old argosy's final voyage. Both were starting to believe, for different reasons, the story didn't end with the tragic sinking. They questioned whether the Barracuda's $250 million valuation of the treasure of the *Merced*, excluding the contraband of pearls, was fool's gold.

Mac Murphy's house and the wake-up call under his floorboards stuffed full of deep-sea cultural by-catch gave Zak good reason to fear the *Merced* had been targeted and roughly raked over by trawlers for over half a century. Was any sparkling booty left at all or had Mac and his pals ploughed it up long ago? If so, the Barracuda was being scammed, sold an 'X' marks the spot only after the wreck had been worked dry and had little shiny stuff left to give up. Only then did a savvy Murphy flog off the coordinates, leaving the junk behind – or so he imagined to be the case.

Zak desperately wanted to take a look at the photos and drawings of the old wreckage to make sense of the wreck's baggage. The Barracuda had agreed to mail him a copy as soon as the final versions were drafted. Was everything untouched as perfectly as the day the boat sank or were finds scattered all around the hull, a calling card typical of destructive shrimp trawlers bulldozing the seabed with heavy nets? Only in a week's time would Rusty have the results drawn up using laborious ArcGIS surveying software. Zak's itch would have to wait a little longer to be scratched.

Nicola was pretty content with life in Key West but bewildered. Something didn't add up for her either. Not at all. Ideas swirled through her mind. She couldn't let go of a few of old man Grant Raven's indiscrete comments. His voice played over and over in her head in a loop. He'd muttered something about a great Spanish treasure buried in Indian lands, a haunting white man who came from the sea, walked among the living and raised the dead. What experts thought they knew about the 1622 treasure ships wasn't all it seemed, he'd cautioned. Just when he started getting exhausted, Skip had spoken cryptically about needing enough time to crack some codex. This was a man who chose words carefully. They were no throw-away lines spoken to impress.

What struck Nicola right away was Skip's sincere reaction, not just to her arrowhead but to where she found it inland of the Boca Chica nudist beach. "My dear, you may just conceivably have stumbled upon an American holy grail," he'd let slip. Was the Indian mound somehow connected to any of these loose historical threads: the *Merced* and the Vanished People, not least the lost villages of Guarugunve and Cuchiyaga, the Town of Weeping or Place of Suffering?

Throughout the day Nicola had to work to keep calm in her eagerness to get going. Only now did she share her plan to return to Boca Chica. Zak felt the need for a cold shower at the very thought, mistakenly assuming she was inviting him to let it all hang out together on the beach. Sure, seeing Nicola as nature intended was a most pleasant prospect for the Oxford man, although he wasn't at all sure it made the perfect first date.

Zak's musings proved to be wishful thinking. Nicola's plan, hatched in greater detail the next mid-morning over iced tea at the Pier House Spa, was to hunt down the Indian mound again and search out more clues about its origin. Quality time with this perfect creature? A no-brainer. Zak was in.

That morning Nicola had a whale of a time shopping in Clinton Square Market, a shabby chic mall housed in a converted nineteenth-century US coal depot. The peeling white plaster veneer laid bare patches of the original red brick façade and inside a gem of independent gift and clothes shops. Nicola had picked out what she felt was the perfect style of khaki explorer's shorts, which she'd wear under one of her white Ralph Lauren linen shirts. The new uniform was finished off with a pair of brown Palladium canvas desert boots.

Marching home she felt providence tugging her sleeve when she chanced upon the AquaKeys Dive Shop and fell for an orange Garret Pro-Pointer metal detector known in the industry as a Carrot. At twenty-two centimetres long and seven ounces, it would comfortably fit in her backpack. Nicola snapped it up for $275 and, for good measure, bought a foldable Roughneck hand shovel. Success was guaranteed, she felt. Nothing could stop her.

*

Only the weather refused to play ball. The schemers lost another day to the heaviest downfall of the late autumn. Winter was on its way with a vengeance. November prepared to turn to December. Ripping winds whipped up monster waves. Nobody left home. As always in Key West the next day was all sunshine and steaming heat, unlike in London, where the monsoon downpour from battleship grey skies could happily continue for weeks on end.

When Zak saw Nicola in her smart new explorer's outfit, fusing sassy tough with cute, his heart melted. She played tough but a kind, sweet soul rattled around inside those fortifications. The big question was whether they could be breached. Truth be told, Zak didn't give a fig about Nicola's gilded pedigree. His rampant feelings weren't a matter of opposites attract. Neither did love rock up unexpectedly.

In her unsettled eyes, Zak sensed a fellow conflicted soul. He winced at the idea of dating a clone of himself. Thankfully the pair's politics and religious beliefs were poles apart. Setting all those distractions to the side, not to mention what her parents might make of his limited prospects, something elemental made Zak convinced they just might be soul mates. Maybe it was wishful thinking, a spell cast by this place's other-worldly charms?

Zak had thrown on a decade-old pair of lightweight black Carhartt trousers sporting a few hard-earned holes, his cloud-cushioned blue and white North Face Gore-Tex hiking boots and topped off his outfit with a plain American Apparel black t-shirt, a relic from before the no-brand brand went broke. The day, too, would surely be a bust but a deliciously fun bust. Anything beyond frolicking for a few hours in Nicola's blissful company would be a bonus.

Since Ms Medici didn't want anyone poking their noses into her business, she'd hired a black jeep. Zak marched up as instructed at exactly 8.30 am, was treated to the closest thing to an English breakfast at the Pier House Spa – why must the Floridians throw maple syrup on everything, including the bacon? – and then sped off north up Highway 1 in high spirits. The pair talked little, letting the invigorating smell of the sea and the view of the subtropical forest wash over them.

The wind caressed their hair and Nicola insisted on driving a little too fast. Zak tried to play it cool but couldn't help fearing at this rate they'd probably end up more tragic Romeo and Juliet than Indiana Jones. He put all his energy into grasping the door handle with white knuckles and praying for the best, rather than looking forward to time-travelling with the Vanished People. He wasn't sure he wanted to be impressed by the skills Nic picked up at an advanced driving course arranged by her father for her twenty-first birthday. That 'useful' present went down like a lead balloon in the Medici household.

Finding the overgrown side road leading to Boca Chica beach was the easy part. Nicola parked diagonally angle under a bald Cypress tree. Hopefully, its canopy would keep the car's heat down, unlike the scorching sun that had blasted her postbox red the week before.

The panorama greeting the friends after the previous day's storm was one of natural chaos. The sea had reclaimed its domain. No naked sun worshippers had come out to play today. Torn tree branches were strewn across the sands, tide-washed plastic had come home to roost and, at the waterline, the stripped-off sand laid the reef hardpan bare. Nothing looked familiar. Nicola searched her memory for some bearings. The place where she'd sunbathed and the path along which she'd retreated into the undergrowth for the call of nature were blown away. The only thing for it was to start poking about and hope to pick up the trail.

Zak preferred to weigh up lines of geographic plausibility. "Nicola, your wandering took you to a navigable stream, right?"

he nudged her. "May I suggest we work from the known to the unknown? Let's find the stream and eventually, hopefully, we should stumble across your Indian mound," the Englishman proposed.

Sitting on a large rock outcrop, Zak opened Google Earth on his iPhone and zoomed in on Boca Chica beach. Seconds later, Nicola pointed out a watercourse some six metres wide that ended at the shore but was barricaded by the late storm's flotsam and jetsam. The friends traced the meandering line of the stream snaking into the hinterland for two and a half miles, at which point it rose into the gentle foothills. About three miles west was a small secluded lake.

"Most of the terrain around here is flat with little relief," Zak noticed. "Look here, though. If you chase the stream about a mile inland, you can just about make out a series of what look like unnatural mounds due south of a sharp bend in the water course. I'm reckoning one of those is a fair bet."

Nicola agreed on the plan of action and the time travellers faded into the thick undergrowth of the Florida swamps. This wasn't the path she previously roamed by chance and the going was tough. The mile took forty-five minutes to hurdle thanks to the need to navigate a tricky obstacle course of fallen trees, diverting back on themselves to avoid impassable standing water, thick mud and sliding through narrow black mangroves. Both, nevertheless, enjoyed the spooky trek. The interior waited in foreboding silence. All of Nicola's heightened senses warned her she shouldn't be here. The truth, too strong for her curiosity to resist, was out there.

By the time the presumed mound area neared, Nicola's left cheek and white shirt were striped with mud and she felt utterly lost. Nothing looked familiar. Then again, she excused herself, she did have extreme sunstroke that day. Taking a pew on a tree stump, she swigged some water and caught her breath, scanning the landscape. Nope, nothing rang any bells.

Zak had checked Google Earth again and disappeared around a wall of dense macho ferns for three minutes when a voice boomed, "Nic, you might want to take a look at this."

Racing around the ferns, the familiar stream and thick branch where Grant Raven had moored the *Gollum*'s rope cable leered into focus. The only difference was that the mound was gone. So why was Zak grinning like a Cheshire cat? The day was a bust, as far as she could see. Back to the beginning.

"Is that a Hammer House of Horror smirk, Dr Fitzgrove, now that you've got me cornered in the back of beyond? And now that you've got me here, whatever are you going to do with me?" Nicola teased.

"Well, you've got two choices, Ms Medici," Zak joined in. "Take two steps forward." Nicola obliged with a frisson of anticipation. "Either I can tie you to that tree, cook you in my pot and eat you for supper." Nicola was rather disappointed by option one, while option two sounded equally disenchanting. "Or may I suggest you stop staring into my lovely eyes and focus on your feet."

Nicola looked confused, so Zak kindly gave her a clue, pointing his finger down towards the soil. The penny dropped. Adrenalin coursed through Nicola's veins at the sight of a carpet of man-made ancient objects scattered around her ruined Palladium boots. Flints, shattered pots, bones, coloured stone and slabs of masonry stretched as far as the eye could see.

Nicola squatted down and alongside Zak spent a glorious few minutes gently handling finds untouched by man for centuries: dozens of flint arrowheads, what seemed to be harpoon tips fashioned from animal bones and soft powdery stone – some kind of paint pigment – that crumbled when she picked it up and rubbed it between her fingers, staining her hands red and blue. And then she screamed. The gaping empty sockets of a half-buried face stared up at her.

Zak, equally shocked, was quick to comfort Nic with an arm around her shoulder while she acclimatized to what could only be the very face of the Vanished People. Up close and personal, Zak's heart beat reassuringly calmly. And he still smelt good. Was that the whisper of Paul Smith aftershave?

"Where did all this stuff come from? I don't understand. None of it was here two weeks ago. And the mound has completely disappeared," she exclaimed.

"The storm, Nicola. Don't you see? The stream burst its banks and, thanks to the wind and rain, swept away the upper part of the mound. Just the edges survive to the west. The elements must have been battering the remains here for centuries. By the time you picked up your arrowhead, it was just about ready to burst. We've lucked out. Right time, right place."

Nicola found the carpet of history littering the undergrowth overwhelming. Her hunch had proven spot on. Now she had no clue what to do. Zak, fortunately, had been here before or, rather, could draw on the memory of several archaeological digs where he'd assisted Professor Wolfgang Pasinski in deepest Wales as an undergraduate.

MP, the Mad Professor, so the students affectionately called him, was a polymath. He was the last of a dying breed and expert on all things prehistoric from Welsh megalithic tombs to the Native Indian camps he'd unearthed over a decade in the 1960s next to various sinkhole springs down America's East Coast. Too early for Zak's interests, but the Englishman had joined him in the hills around Lampeter in north Wales, recording second-millennium BC tombs and henges so rotted away that only the lightest of stains survived in the soil where wooden posts once supported roundhouse roofs. Wales's acidic soils had even eaten the pottery once used and abandoned. To most mortals, only the magic mushrooms growing wild in the local mountains, sought out with gusto by the local students, could bring the eroded past to life. If you can dig and make sense of the rotten remains of Wales, you can dig anything, Pasinski had instructed his clear-headed students.

From his black Barbour backpack, Zak pulled out a ball of orange plastic-coated string and six-inch iron nails. He didn't want to geek out Nicola, but with characteristic foresight, he'd come over prepared. Working knowledgeably, he set up a one-metre square grid of string wound around four nails. A GoPro camera and a twenty-centimetre plastic scale graded black and white next appeared from the bottom of his backpack.

Nicola watched enthralled as she learnt that before recovering anything, good science forced any self-respecting archaeologist to record the exact position where the artefacts lay in case their contexts proved meaningful. What underlay the finds, lightly buried, could end up being even more telling.

An impressed Nicola watched her partner in crime set about photographing the finds and counting how many artefacts and what types were scattered in each one-metre grid. Density and object form would tell the friends if the site was a settlement or cemetery. Although Zak already knew the answer – the skull fragments and absence of cooking pots made it obvious they were dealing with tombs. Zak sensed the shadow of his benevolent old professor looking over his shoulder, urging him to do the right thing and not let raw emotion, the thrill of discovery, turn him into a grubby tomb raider.

Nicola spent a jolly ten minutes videoing Zak photographing the finds before she remembered her Carrot. After waving the hand-held Garret Pro-Pointer metal detector in front of Zak until she got his attention, he reluctantly gave her the thumbs up to use it on the eroded edges of the mound. He handed her some lengths of white plastic, topped with red plastic mini-flags, to plunge into the soil where she registered any metallic pings. If anything turned up, they'd plot its position by GPS before trying a little light digging. Zak didn't want to crush Nicola's dreams, but the prehistoric Indians were Stone Age people who didn't use iron. His expectations of anything biting were so low as to be non-existent. What harm could her mini metal detector and spade do? Let her have some fun.

Nicola started scanning the low-lying mound, subconsciously humming the theme tune to *Mission Impossible.* Zak recorded the cluster of finds and then photographed the ancient site from all angles. His eye was now tuned into the subtle changes in the colour of the soil. A pattern started to emerge. Human teeth, parts of skulls and ribs were strewn between flint arrowheads, sherds of brown clay pots looking like urns and tiny beads. Something didn't stack up. The workmanship of the pottery and flints was pretty primitive. The sophisticated beads, a glorious riot of colours, ranged from cobalt blue to turquoise and white, the odd red example and an occasional striped stone. This really was most peculiar.

Twenty minutes passed, and Zak was forced to endure the tortured loop of the *Mission Impossible* soundtrack when the tune abruptly changed to high-pitched beeping. No doubt the Carrot had struck an old beer can. From the corner of his eye, Zak watched Nicola unfold her mini-shovel and with its edge, like a true pro, start gently shaving off the soil centimetre by centimetre.

The shriek that followed was neither the metal detector nor some old-school song dragged up from Nicola's memory but a cry of jubilation. No doubt she had turned up another skull, Zak chuckled. Peering sideways, the sceptic stopped laughing. In one hand, Nicola grasped the remnant of a wooden box and, in the other, a cluster of silver coins. Forgetting her airs and graces, Ms Medici's mouth was wide open in shock, her eyes out on stalks, wider than the eye sockets of the skull she'd spotted earlier.

Nicola was motionless, frozen. Nothing in life had prepared her for finding real treasure. And she was aware from the softness of the wood in her hand that the box's remains were incredibly delicate.

Zak told her not to move and yanked off his top. Nicola almost dropped the box, which her partner in crime carefully nestled on top of his shirt and set down on a square slab of worked masonry. The friends stared at each other and broke out in hysteric laughter, hugging and jumping up and down as if England's football team had finally ended decades of pain and humiliation by doing the impossible – winning the world cup.

"What do you make of it?" Nicola asked. "It's old, right? Let's clean it out."

"I'd love to," Zak replied. "But we'd run the serious risk of destroying this relic if we don't remove the soil crust in a lab before checking what's in its base. It's your find, your call, though."

Nicola considered the options while Zak rubbed the ancient soil from one of the loose coins. A cross appeared, dissecting two castles and two lions opposite each other. In its top quadrant, he could just make out the number ??22.

"Nic, honestly this find is massive. If I'm not mistaken you've come up with silver Spanish *reales* coins, pieces of eight. They could be seventeenth century or maybe even sixteenth. We need to get this hoard to a specialist before the evidence gets compromised."

Her gut reaction was to break through the soil crust coating the box to satisfy her curiosity, but Zak was right. And Nicola knew just the man for the job. Pulling her phone from her bag, she punched a few digits.

"Good day, this is Grant Raven. What can I do you for?" the melodious, reassuring voice enquired.

Nicola chose not to overcook her discovery in case she ended up with egg on her face. Zak could be utterly wrong. She briefly explained the situation and eroded Indian mound, now a forest of finds, and asked if she could show him something urgently.

Skip was a fine reader of people, alive and dead, and her fast-paced words sent his curious antennae sky high. The friends were warmly invited over to Sugarloaf Key. Grant promised them both a shower, lashings of iced tea and more key lime pie. Zak grinned and rubbed his stomach, too quickly to realize he was embarrassing himself in his eagerness to please.

Finishing up took another fifteen minutes. Zak guided Nic to place the box exactly where she'd unearthed it and took the liberty of theatrically laying the silver coins out on one of its broken edges. The photography finished, Zak slid the box into a zip bag he'd brought as part of his field kit and started bagging a selection of other random surface finds. To Nicola's disappointment he ended by brushing off and pulling back on his t-shirt.

In an act of sincere camaraderie, Nicola draped her arm around Zak's shoulder. The ecstatic adventurers headed back to the beach, this time along the path Nic originally followed what seemed an age ago. The camouflaged iguanas, bug hunting while effortlessly gripping Sabal palm tree trunks, blinked, unimpressed by the disruption. Nothing had changed. Everything had changed.

Just as they turned the corner, away from the small glade where the finds rested under dripping mangroves, Nicola turned her head back one last time and shouted out loud to nobody in particular, "the Vanished People are vanished no more."

18

Driftwood Rise, Sugarloaf Key

Time stood still, too, on Sugarloaf Key. An artificial marina and inland lagoon pacified the moody Atlantic. Waves broken by a short rock boulder breakwater licked the shore with a soothing swishing sound. The mangroves were less dense than at Boca Chica, as if retreating from civilisation. The mosquitoes still hunted in packs, chasing human and animal prey before night fell and the bats came out of their lairs, chasing them down the food chain.

For Nicola and Zak these were the best of times. The primeval landscape, the ancient and the modern, matched their dreamy mood. They drove north up Highway 1, the jeep bouncing across the stepping stones of Big Coppitt and Saddlebunch Key islands. Palm trees bobbed in the sea breeze. The flat azure blue ocean sympathized with their calm souls. Locals paddled across the shallows in slow motion, their kayaks looking like the alligators that were never too far away.

If the Keys weren't so perfectly appointed by the hand of god, so Nicola imagined, they'd be forbidding. She tried to conjure up an image of these lands four hundred years ago with no houses, fried chicken joints or shopping malls for sanctuary. Just camps of Indians moving to the rhythm of the seasons. How would the many sailors wrecked on these isolated shores have felt and coped? Nature they could have overcome: the landscape was rich in fresh fruit, wild animals and the bounty of the sea. When the Indians appeared, they would have been helpless, left to the goodwill of the natives and their old-world ways.

Nicola shivered, thanked her lucky stars she was born in the twenty-first century, and swung east at Turkey Basin, away from the white herons coasting across the wildlife sanctuary, and onto Upper Sugarloaf Key. Modern life was tough enough. Shipwrecked on Indian soil was a clash of cultures she didn't fancy. Pygmy blue and red admiral butterflies waved the jeep shoreward.

Sugarloaf Key was a mini Venice. Down the boulevard, a narrow water inlet cut into the shore divided each block of houses. The explorers drove slowly passed Captain Pete's Coconut Garden and Flying Fish Lane all the way to the Old State Road and veered back south. A shallow creek was forded with little fanfare and then the secluded Driftwood Rise beckoned. Nicola left the jeep in the care of a tall majestic palm tree.

A spellbound Zak felt he owed Nicola an apology, having assumed her description of her adventure with the skipper a couple of weeks ago was the stuff of rose-tinted romance. Asleep on the deck, swaying in his hammock without an apparent care in the world, was an old man with a grey van Dyck beard and cap, none other than the Vanished People hunter.

Nicola gently touched his shoulder. "Well, well, well," Skip said, wide-eyed and stretching. "Welcome back to the Rise, little missy. Hello sonny jim, my name's Grant Raven. Just call me Skip and we'll be right as rain."

Dr Isak Fitzgrove introduced himself and returned the compliment, inviting the old man to call him Zak. Skip took one look at Nicola's muddy face and legs and, feeling a sense of déjà vu, dispatched her forthwith to the shower. While Nicola freshened up, Skip busied himself preparing fresh iced tea and a whole key lime pie he'd rustled up that morning. Fussing over the hospitality, he fired off questions, asking Zak about his background, work and interests, listening intently.

Unusually, and against his normal ways, Zak opened up and told Skip all about his studies, publications, and how it grated that life was failing to deliver purpose and satisfaction. Skip advised him to live in the here and now and not sweat over what the future may or may not bring. What was it Seneca once wrote, "We suffer more often in imagination than in reality." Philosophically the pair were cut from the same cloth, even though the old man was far wiser.

Skip let slip he'd invested low in Keys Exploration's excavation of the *Merced*, more to get hold of up-to-date news of discoveries than for the lure of profit. Since he was also bound to secrecy by a non-disclosure agreement, Zak brought him up to speed on the finds and unexpected pile of pearls gleaming in the tobacco leaves.

Twenty minutes later, Nicola sauntered into the kitchen all sweetness and light. Zak realized the old man had hardly spoken a word about his own life or the Vanished People. Usually, Zak was the sympathetic listener.

"To business, friends," Skip began after generous double helpings of pie and cream were demolished. "What's all the fuss, rush and cloak and dagger secrecy about then? You've got me all on tenterhooks. Let me guess, you grabbed some pottery or maybe dare I wish for another arrowhead? Spill the beans."

Zak winked and carefully set down six bags of finds from Boca Chica. Nicola explained how the stream had burst its banks and washed away the mud supporting the mound, crediting Zak with recording the precise position of every find. Good lad, Skip remarked, turning the finds over in his leather-skinned workman's hands.

"Holy smokes," Skip observed, "I darn well wish I'd been there. I am humbled you'd entrust your goodies – a stunning revelation – with me. I think I can help."

Skip sped off up the stairs to his office, just like the week before, a man possessed, summoning the explorers to follow in hot pursuit. Zak agreed with Nicola. The old boy was incredibly spritely for an eighty-six-year-old. At this rate I'll be dribbling in a wheelchair by the time I reach the age of sixty, Zak cursed. Nicola hoped she wouldn't be on her third marriage by then like great-aunt Gertie.

The finds were removed and laid out on top of their numbered bags. Skip yanked a few books from the shelves. Zak scanned their front covers with much curiosity: *Distribution of Pottery Ware in the Glades Archaeological Area of South Florida* by John Goggin, Dorothy Downs's *Art of the Florida Seminole and Miccosukee Indians* and *Indians of Central and South Florida, 1513-1763* by John Hann.

"Hello old friend," Skip muttered, peering intently at a sherd. "The most obvious big-picture point to make is the lack of European pottery. No Spanish olive jar fragments, no white London tobacco pipe bowls. We truly are immersed among the indigenous Vanished People, alright. Good news."

Nicola beamed, crossed and rubbed her arms in satisfaction. She'd hoped as much but half expected her armchair sleuthing to be dashed to pieces.

"Now, see these here two linear cut striations under the rim of this ugly shell-tempered potsherd?" he went on. "That's from a Glades Gritty ware pot and I reckon we're bang smack in the middle of the Glades IIIc period, say 1513 to 1763. Pretty darn interesting."

"The who did what? Slow down," Nicola replied, not understanding a word Skip had spoken, even though she was skilled in many languages, several of them dead like Greek and Latin.

"My apologies. Let me back up. Into the 1930s, bits and pieces like these turned up the length and breadth of southeast America. It took a talent, no, a genius, called John Goggin to recognise similarities and differences across all the styles of the pottery and flints. In the Glades, Goggin was certain he was dealing with the garbage of just one tribe of American Indians, but at that point nobody knew who. He named the people behind the goodies the Glades Culture because the Florida Everglades sandwiched their camps and burial places. The name's pretty meaningless. Scholarship has to start somewhere."

"Got it. Like in Britain we call the folk who appeared out of nowhere in the Early Bronze Age with a new taste for continental pots, whose name prehistory doesn't record, the Beaker People after their crockery?" Zak clarified.

Nicola nodded. "And exactly the same as calling a villa in Pompeii something random when you have no idea who lived there? The House of the Lovers gets so called because of an inscription dug up reading, 'Lovers, like bees, wish life to be as sweet as honey', if I remember correctly."

"Bingo, little missy," Skip confirmed. "And then in 1947, after delving armpit-deep into colonial written texts, Goggin was able to sub-divide the cultures into the Calusa Indian lands of southwest Florida, the Tekesta ancestral home of the Florida Keys and the Okeechobee dotted around Lake Okeechobee. And guess what, no surprises. Your finds fit sweetly into the precise archaeological package of what we now call the Tequesta culture."

"What else have you fished up?" Skip bounced back and forth around the table, delicately handling the treasures. "See here, this is a shell pick used like an adze made from *Busycon perversa.*"

Nicola furrowed her brow again and sighed.

"In English speak that's a giant sea snail. I reckon the Tequesta ate its soft bits and then used the hard shell to dig, maybe even to make your burial mound. Maybe it broke in the act, unceremoniously dumped with the dead," Skip deliberated. "Curious. These two pierced stones are quite rare. Anybody want to guess?" the old man invited. Without waiting for an answer, Skip explained they were weights used to sink fishing nets.

"So far so good. This is where things turn whacko," Skip noticed. "Whoever ended up in this hole was extremely well connected. You've picked up about one hundred and twenty beads it looks like. Some are local, made of coral, but as for the rest..." The old man whistled. "You've got a bit of everything here: most are monochrome cream and orange beads from Europe, but there's also some small fragments of cut crystal from Holland and even what looks like an intact agate bead from Cambay in India. Very rare, exotic and not a little confusing."

"Now, these are useful." Skip turned over a couple of cobalt blue and amber beads. "These guys are best known as charlotte beads, fancy and expensive imports from Venice. The good news is they were so costly that after around 1630 Spain stopped buying them. And all this stuff reached La Florida on the back of Spanish hulls, either to barter with the natives or to flog at market. All your finds have to pre-date 1630."

"The collection, though, is starting to turn into a tale of the bizarre and unexpected. Something doesn't stack up," the old man noted, peering into the final plastic bag of finds. Skip picked up a dark brown pierced bead, about a centimetre in diameter, and laughed out loud. "Nicola, oh my. You know what this is?" Once more she shrugged in defeat.

To her shock, Skip bit the bead softly. "Well it wasn't for clothes or jewellery. If I'm not mistaken, this is made from African ebony and once upon a time was part of a Catholic rosary – a rosary belonging to a Spaniard." The same finds bag held what Zak learnt were three lead musket balls and a fragment of an iron flintlock pistol – again, all Spanish.

The reappearance of Spain brought Zak to his senses. Catching Nicola's eye, he pointed to her bag and raised his eyebrows in mock exclamation. The penny dropped as Ms Medici carefully drew out the treasure cocooned in a white towel.

"Skip, we forgot to show you our star find. This wooden box turned up near the mound surface and seems to contain something delicious." The find was honourably passed in two flat-palmed hands to Raven, who laid it gently on the table surface, rubbed his hands together, blew on them and unfolded the white towel.

"Holy cow," Skip exclaimed. "Are you sure this came from the mound, little missy, and you aren't hoaxing a gullible old fool?"

Nicola solemnly nodded her head. The old boy extracted a small brush and dental pick from his table's top drawer, pulled down a lamp to light up his work and started shaving off the soft soil coating the wooden box's eight by four-inch surface. The lid had long crumbled into dust. Almost immediately, more silver coins, their design crystal clear, emerged. Skip showed no emotion bending over the treasure. Nic and Zak lent in closer too, till their eyes were a few inches above the wooden chest.

After fifteen minutes of delicate teasing, sixteen pieces of eight (minus the three Nicola had secretly stashed in her backpack as a keepsake) lay side by side on the table. From the very bottom of the box Skip drew out a bronze medallion and an encrusted piece of brass looking like a modern belt buckle.

Several minutes passed before Raven sighed and confirmed what Nicola and Zak had guessed. The coins were Spanish silver sure enough. Beyond that, something was badly bothering Skip. He pointed out the common features on all the coins: a Catholic cross and the lions of Leon and castles of Castile, the crest of the Spanish crown. A few were engraved 'HISPANIARUM ET INDIARUM REX', standing for the king's rule over all the lands of Spain and the Indies.

Zak was impressed by the old man's skill at reading old coins like most people read books. Nicola expected nothing less. Her respect grew with every passing hour she spent in his company. Skip pointed at the letters 'OM' and 'P' engraved vertically on the coins, standing for the mints of Mexico City and Potosi in Bolivia where they were cast.

"What am I missing, come on. Something doesn't stack up. Ok, here we go," Raven observed. "The coin dates are all over the shop. Look here, we've got 1621 on one example, proving it was minted during the reign of King Philip II. On this piece, though, the letter L stands for the Potosi mint master Luis Rodriguez who was in office, if I'm not mistaken, from 1554-1569." A quick flick through Sewall Menzel's masterly *Cobs, Pieces of Eight and Treasure Coins* proved his hunch.

"Another weirdness, chaps," Skip added. "This sure as heck isn't new treasure freshly harvested from the mints for the king's benefit. If it were, I'd expect the hoard to be brand-spanking pieces of eight. But you've unearthed a mix of one, two and four *reales* as well, what I'd call loose change. Still, quite a hit – a master carpenter might earn just one *reale* a day, bear in mind – but nevertheless loose change for the Americas, an El Dorado overflowing with shiny stuff."

"Adding the other bits and pieces to your collection, well the story gets curiouser and curiouser." Skip brushed the dirt off a three-centimetre-long brass oval medallion and turned it round in his hands, pointing out the figure of Mary holding Jesus and on the flip side of the plaque, once fixed to a Catholic rosary, the carved body of the Virgin of Carmen, the Spanish patron saint of sailors and fishermen.

"As for this crusty piece of roached iron," Skip carried on, lightly dusting the pitted metal, "I reckon it's a buckle that once bolted together the shoulder strap from a bag, probably once some kind of leather. If I had to guess, and archaeology is forty per cent guesswork – don't tell anyone – perhaps your wooden box was kept hidden away in the bag. For some reason, Mr Big hid it in your ancient mound and over time the organics rotted away until the coins rolled out. Probably once owned by some Spanish merchant and, you have to guess, stolen by our not always friendly Tequesta. I cannot see how else the loot ended up in an Indian burial mound at Boca Chica."

Grant Raven was very pleased with his detective work. Nicola and Zak peered at him, incredulous at his powers of deduction. To finish off the forensic formalities, Skip brushed off the mud encrusted to the wooden box's sides. The colour faded from Raven's cheeks. Two crosses incised onto each flank of the base, and the extraordinary sight of two letters, the initials JL and the number 1622, appeared for the first time in centuries.

Skip's hands flew to his head in confusion. The old man fell back into his leather armchair, his brain short-circuited. His haunted eyes darted from side to side, processing a string of historical information. All the while, he muttered, "Impossible. This is simply not possible."

The old man started to speak very slowly and carefully, one finger suspended in the air. "Please, and this is crucial, tell me everything you can about the context of these finds. Leave nothing out. We've got the forensics. Now I need to understand the crime scene if we're going to crack this craziness."

Zak plunged his arm into the bag and explained he could do better than words. How would Skip like to fly over Boca Chica? He'd need twenty minutes. While Nicola and the old man retreated to the kitchen for more key lime pie and Earl Grey tea, nodding their heads in confusion and mulling over whether Zak had lost his marbles, the scholar clicked open the Agisoft Photoscan software installed on his silver MacBook Pro and downloaded the three hundred and twenty-eight images he'd taken of the Boca Chica Indian mound from all angles. With little fuss, the software digitally stitched the photos together until a single 3D image of the ancient remains was complete. Good enough, Zak declared and made his way downstairs.

The fruit of his industry was rough and ready, Zak warned. Skip whistled through his teeth. This time it was the youngster's time to play conductor as he flew the old man around the native Indian mound, tilting its 3D topography up and down, rotating the site three hundred and sixty degrees, and then zooming in to scrutinize the odd detail.

"Never could I imagine such a scientific marvel. The future really has arrived," Skip summed up, returning from his virtual voyage south to Boca Chica. "For sure I agree with your assessment. What you turned up is undoubtedly artificial and an unknown Tequesta burial mound built from black soil and shells. Way to go. The skull and dozen teeth you recovered all point to a human presence."

"Now, you see the six rectangular stone slabs scattered towards the stream? If I'm not mistaken, they were part of a crypt for ossuary burial boxes. The Tequesta would have left the remains of the fallen in shallow graves to decompose before reburying them with more dignity. I imagine this is one of their smaller tombs, say two metres high and fifteen metres in diameter, dedicated to VIPs who might still be buried bang in its centre. I reckon this tumulus has been eroding for decades under the forces of nature and water, which explains why nobody knew about it until today. Then you lucked out with the weather – typical Brits."

"The Tequesta buried their fallen away from villages in fear of the mischief the spirits might make in the afterlife. In their world view the dearly departed lived on in the hills, rivers and mountains. The tribe travelled to remote places like this making offerings of food, herbs and tobacco before consulting the ancestors to predict the future," Skip lectured.

"On its own, this is big news, front page stuff, sonny jim. But the story gets better and better," the friends learnt. "Modernization has destroyed most American Indian burial mounds in Florida and it's a miracle your Boca Chica relic has survived. Remember, this ancient folk were here for a very long time, more than two thousand years, and can lay claim to having been the Adams and Eves of Florida."

"This new sensation adds spice to the history of these noble ancestors. Your beads tell us they were far more sophisticated and connected than we ever imagined. They bartered with Europeans far and wide. This is all small fry compared to the big headline, though."

Skip was once more lost in thought, staring at the wooden box and muttering softly to himself whether the legend could truly be possible. Could this be the codex's missing link he asked out loud?

Raven showed every sign of exhaustion and losing his thread. Nicola and Zak had learnt bucket loads more than they had bargained for. They were starting to get the impression they'd overstayed their welcome. It was time to head home and, regrettably, to leave Skip to his private mumbling till another day.

Again, just like during Nicola's first visit, he chose not to elaborate on his rambling words and somewhat abruptly ushered the visitors away from Driftwood Rise with the excuse that he needed to think on his own and check his books. Something had seriously spooked the old timer.

The friends, explorers, future lovers – neither of them knew exactly what they meant to each other – drove away not completely satisfied. Skip promised to be in touch shortly. Neither knew what he was cooking up and whether shortly was southern gent speak for get lost. Foreigners in another's homeland, the pair wondered whether they'd overstepped the mark into a business that didn't concern them and they couldn't grasp.

19

ICOCH, Sunken Heritage Centre, Marseille

The Barracuda didn't approve. Fuck 'em and feed 'em fish had been his precise professional opinion. But Melissa Todd had demanded Keys Exploration reach out to Jorvik & Silver to at least try and break bread before the sky fell in. The lawyer had no patience for the eternal hours of dishonest billing much of the legal profession favoured, so the Barracuda always grumbled.

Since Todd was retained by the Florida shipwreck hunters and had a five per cent stake in the company, reaching a resolution without heading to the courts was in her own interest. Plus, they owed the call to the investors. Months and maybe years of legal wrangling would rapidly eat through Keys Exploration's cash and get the team no nearer finishing digging up the secrets of the *Merced*. Who knew what else was just waiting under all that crud?

Todd and Al Nassau had bitten the bullet. The team was dialled into a Zoom conference call with ICOCH, the International Council of Cultural Heritage in Marseille. Eva Clermont-Ganneau, its director, introduced her associates. On her left sat James Jorvik, suited, booted, freshly shaven and giving off his saintly butter wouldn't melt in my condescending mouth smile. And on her right – a little too close, she felt and smelt – Robert Brooker dressed for war in his assignment khakis (actually bought for little Bobby by his mother from Marks and Spencer's on Oxford Street nine years earlier).

Drawing on many years of studying kinesics picked up when he did a little hush-hush work for the CIA, Nassau realized from the hostile body language that ICOCH were putting all their eggs in one basket. They were playing a powerful game of go big or go home. Jorvik had paid to fly in the maritime historian Dr G.A. 'Geronimo' Martinez from Seville. Because Jorvik's knowledge of shipwrecks was technically zero, a truth he never admitted publicly, he also flew in first class the added ammunition of the Director of Maritime Affairs at UK Heritage, Marcus Pasterman, a flat-track bully, which was precisely why Jorvik held him in such high esteem. All Jorvik needed to do was wind him up and let Pasterman create unholy havoc, all the while keeping his own once-monthly manicured fingernails dirt-free.

Bob Brooker had hardly believed his luck when a Jorvik ticket sent him out to Marseille forty-eight hours before the main consortium reached town to smooth the groundwork. Clermont-Ganneau was less delighted and, being entirely au fait with the *Merced* case, had palmed off the ex-serviceman to one of her lowly interns, François. In turn, after an ugly hour in his company eating baked camembert in the unsavoury Brasserie Ok just east of the old port, François had decided to make her own French exit. If this was the job, ICOCH could stuff it. Excusing herself to powder her nose, the elegant Parisian exited through the greasy kitchen's back door and Brooker found himself double-dumped. Which suited him just fine.

Crawling from bar to bar along La Rue Curiol in the first arrondissement, and after four beers and a couple of shots of pastiche to make him feel more 'Frenchy' sophisticated, Brooker fell for the charms of the superbly overdressed Paulette. Only the next morning, under the haze of a throbbing hangover, did Brooker realize from an undressed vision reflected in the mirror that Paulette was a Paul. Something to add to the book of worldly experiences, the man on assignment shrugged. The knife Paulette pulled after Brooker refused to pay €150 for the night made him less philosophical.

The International Council of Cultural Heritage's Centre de Patrimonie Sous-Marines spread across the first floor of Fort Saint-Jean built in 1660 by King Louis XIV along the shore opposite Marseille's old port. From this piece of first-rate maritime real estate, the Military Order of the Knights Hospitaller of Saint John set out on the Crusades in the eleventh century to return as traumatized warlords. It was left to their wives and children to patch up their wounded bodies and condemned souls and coax them back to the land of the living. Too much idle time left the defeated infidels musing whether the years at sea, sickness and Saracen atrocities in the name of the Lord had been worth it.

Now it was ICOCH that invested war chests of European Union and African Confederation cash plotting world domination, once again interfering across the seas. A vast concrete monstrosity of a sign set up outside the entrance to ICOCH HQ read in Arabic, Hebrew, French, Chinese, Spanish, Hindi, Spanish and Greek, "Since war and brutality were born in the minds of men, it is in the minds of men that peace and civilisation should be built."

Next door, across a bridged water channel, the glass-fronted Museum of the Civilisations of Europe in the Mediterranean, MuCEM – or what Todd and the Barracuda preferred to call PuKEM over beers – welcomed the world. The museum promoted as built of stone, water and wind, so its architects waxed poetically, was a Turkish delight that had taken thirteen years, three French presidents and six culture ministers to get over the line. It ended up critically reviewed by the press as a glass box whose interior failed to live up to the drama of its façade. Just like the goings-on across the stream at ICOCH, the museum was said to have a sinister vibe.

In truth, behind closed doors Eva Clermont-Ganneau, the director of ICOCH's Sunken Heritage Centre, was a little tired of the Convention on the Defence of Underwater Culture and Heritage (CDUCH). The once zealous lawyer was passionate about diving and the sea's beauty, and many moons ago had mastered the art of breathing through mixed gases to stay in Poseidon's realm longer and deeper. The bewitching Mediterranean off southern France was festooned with Etruscan, Roman and medieval shipwrecks. Many a weekend Eva spent with fellow fish men and women immersed in the wonders of the sunken past. Those dreamy days were long gone.

Father always felt diving was a hobby, not a job, so she allowed family pressure to push her into the law. Long hours and a module in maritime legislation led her to the newly passed Convention, CDUCH, which she was charged with rolling out globally at any cost. Eva bought into the new cultural rules for exploring the oceans because she cared about protection and education. It took just two months for the scales to fall from her eyes. She realized she'd have been better equipped for the job if she'd studied politics and propaganda.

On the ground, the Convention turned out to be a delusion. ICOCH pretended to care about the purity of the deep blue's innocence, but early on it was highjacked by the elder fathers of marine archaeology to grab ever-greater power in the greedy hands of the few. Every propagandist needs a bogeyman and, in the swashbuckling devil take all and damn the consequences treasure hunter, the political Crusaders found a perfect enemy to go after, to spread malicious hate and whip up paranoia. The threat of modern pirates like the Barracuda smashing wooden hulls and destroying precious history was the perfect weapon of intimidation to dangle over heads of state. Under the banner of fear, ICOCH and its henchmen managed to get seventy-six countries to ratify the Convention. Clermont-Ganneau was the toast of France.

For seven years now, she'd been forced to bite her tongue when supposed expert lawyers and scholars told audiences the new Convention frowned on digging up wrecks. Leaving ships where they drowned, taking photos and leaving bubbles so future generations could enjoy them and use their superior technology to unlock the past's secrets became the mantra of the early twenty-first-century killjoys.

At first the French lawyer felt forced to stand up at conferences and political cabinet meetings to correct the elder fathers. The Convention didn't ban digging up old ships at all. All it asked was that an archaeologist weigh up whether the remains really needed to be disturbed or if they could be left untouched as the first option. If not, excavate carefully, minimally, record, preserve what's recovered and share discoveries responsibly with the public.

By now a jaded and disillusioned Clermont-Ganneau was searching for a way out. She'd stopped correcting her colleagues, who never listened to facts and were hell-bent on creating a mythological Utopia that her own early years diving off France told her was rubbish. Treasure hunters weren't the problem. They were an easy scapegoat to drum up free publicity. The real villains were trophy-hunting divers and fishing trawlers, not to mention the ferocity of nature's storms. Seeing her work highjacked by people like Jorvik and Brooker made Clermont-Ganneau's stomach wrench.

James Jorvik was a man of the worst intentions who'd never even put on a SCUBA tank or worked underwater. He couldn't tell the difference between a Greek amphora and a seventeenth-century Andalusian olive jar. Shipwrecks had become all about political power, fear and intimidation. Eva had also heard on good authority that Jorvik boasted indiscreetly about his real endgame: getting gonged by the king with a knighthood for services to the sea and strong-arming the UK to sign up to the Convention. The sunken past had turned into Frankenstein's monster in his grubby hands.

Eva never even got to dive these days. Instead, she found herself desk-bound paper pushing or roaming the world with secret envelopes, charged with negotiating – or bribing, she privately thought was a more appropriate term – undeveloped countries like Jordan, Palestine, Syria, Haiti and Nigeria to sign on the dotted line. And in return, ICOCH would help countries willing to play the game with social welfare reforms. Ninety-five per cent of the states that ratified the Convention on the Defence of Underwater Culture and Heritage did so through under the table back-scratching deals. The Convention was no honourable tool for saving the seas for the benefit of mankind. It was a protection racket.

*

"Thank you for reaching out to us," Clermont-Ganneau began by addressing Melissa Todd and Al Nassau. "As you know, ICOCH has felt duty bound as protector of our shared sunken past to intercede – through the concerns of Jorvik & Silver – in Keys Exploration's illicit intervention on the wreck thought to be the *Merced*. Your project is in violation of Rules 2 and Article 2.11 of the Convention. These forbid the commercial exploitation of underwater culture and heritage for sale or speculation and any organisation or state from interfering with sovereign immune property. The *Merced* was a Spanish warship, please remember."

"Yes indeed, accurately put Eva," James Jorvik cut in, much to Ms Clermont-Ganneau's annoyance. "This is very much a black and white issue and you have fallen very deeply into the dark. On behalf of the Kingdom of Spain, which has retained Jorvik & Silver to represent and defend its interests, our legal filing stands. You will cease and desist from destroying the *Merced* and you will return all materials recovered to Spain as its lawful property within ten days of the filing. I must warn you that the clock is ticking. Our patience is wearing thin."

Cool and collected, Todd replied by making the Barracuda's position crystal clear. "Be that as it may, your case hangs on questions of interpretation and precedent." Marcus Pasterman rolled his neck and tugged his white shirt collar to breathe more freely. A sure indication of lies and guilt, Nassau noted. "You will be aware that the *res* – for argument's sake, let's call it the wreck of the *Merced* – does not lie in US territorial waters and the US has not ratified the ICOCH Convention on the Defence of Underwater Culture and Heritage. You're totally outside your jurisdiction."

"You state the obvious, Ms Todd," Jorvik replied, overdramatically waving his left arm at an audience that wasn't there, "but you are spinning seaweed. Neither of these points specifically affect our position. Both are trumped by the Foreign Sovereign Immunities Act. The *Merced* was armed and sent to the Americas in 1622 under the protection of the Spanish Navy guarding the Tierra Firme fleet. It was naval and, by extension, Crown property. My client never abandoned its maritime property and now lays claim to what you have damaged. Hands off. You will be brought to book."

A furious Al Nassau found his head thumping listening to Jorvik's pompous drivel and returned unfriendly fire. He would not give that reptile the satisfaction of addressing him directly.

"Ms Clermont-Ganneau, if I may, Jorvik & Silver's complaint is malicious and knowingly bogus. You will have a hugely costly and lengthy time persuading any court of law the shipwreck found – not by Spain may I say, but by Keys Exploration – is either a warship or a frigate. What's more, by the very act of discovery we are the legal salvor-in-possession and owner, not Spain. To all practical intents and salvage law purposes, the *Merced* had been abandoned. You will also be aware that legal Florida precedent falls in our favour. The 1715 Spanish fleet scattered across southern Florida was approved by the court to be Keys Exploration property fifteen years ago, as was the content of the 1622 *flota*'s mighty flagship the *Atocha*. We have no doubt the modern legal system will follow suit. My recommendation, in summary, which I suggest you carefully consider and will find perfectly fair, is that we collaborate rather than fight each other. Melissa, if you will."

Todd flicked through her leather folder and picked up a single sheet of paper. "People, I think we can reach a Solomonic compromise here and save a huge chunk of time and cash. In return for dropping your case, at our own expense Keys Exploration is willing to invite two representatives, one from Spain and another from ICOCH, onto the *Merced* project to join the fieldwork and collaborate with the science. That's not all. We will gift to the Kingdom of Spain on a permanent basis a cut of all duplicate cultural artefacts for exhibition and the benefit of its people. Madrid will be offered first refusal to buy any unique cultural objects at market value."

James Jorvik kicked back his chair, hissing, stood up and

started jabbing wildly at the screen projecting the Americans and their backhanded insult of an offer to France. "Nonsense, you are forgetting the core rights here. You are in no position to negotiate gifting property which was never yours in the first place, let alone to commodify our past. Spain rejects this gamesmanship outright. Dr Martinez, Dr Pasterman, do you have anything to add? We're done here."

The well-rehearsed men stuck the knife into the Barracuda's offer.

"Our careful research, both historical and archaeological, leaves no doubt that the *Merced* was Spanish property," Geronimo Martinez confirmed. "Archival testimony backs up the discoveries as Crown patrimony. It will be a cut and dry case."

Marcus Pasterman hadn't pulled himself away from his desk not to join the lynch mob. UK Heritage had a vested interest in the case. If they could defeat Keys Exploration in America, they would have their own crucial precedent to see off more Yankee treasure hunters sniffing around the seas just outside English territorial waters. Rumour had it a US consortium had raised a king's ransom to go after the *Merchant Royal*, a Spanish ship loaded with jewels and 100,000 pounds of gold valued at $1.5 billion that sank off Cornwall in 1641 while sailing from Cadiz to London. It was the holy grail of shipwrecks in the British Isles. Pasterman wasn't about to allow the Yanks loose in his waters. Everything hung on the outcome of the *Merced*'s legal decision.

The heritage expert coughed in preparation. "The case over the *Atocha* and 1715 fleet is old news. The US court system based its decision on the finds' locations. Back then anything beyond State waters was finders keepers, it's true. That was then and this is now. Since those gullible times, the UN Law of the Sea Convention has been tested in court and upheld all rights of sovereign rule. In any matter, you must appreciate the despicable old days of ripping up hulls to seize treasure is dead and buried. Your business model and thinking are a fossil of a corrupt world order. Of course, UK Heritage would be happy to help you prepare plans that do fully comply with ICOCH rules.

That means no monetisation of any finds," Pasterman ended mischievously.

No way would the Barracuda bow to UK Heritage's colonial might is right arrogance.

"How very generous of you Dr Pasterman," Al Nassau snapped sarcastically. "Looks like we'll have to agree to disagree. See you in court."

Clermont-Ganneau sighed. This would be a lose-lose situation for everyone. The sunken blue everyone pretended to care about would be the biggest casualty.

James Jorvik smiled. Perfect. He had the American criminal scum exactly where he wanted them. Maximum publicity for the Convention and himself. Maybe he'd fly home by way of Rome and treat himself to a long weekend and a few new linen suits. By next summer he would have skewered the Barracuda once and for all.

Jorvik was salivating at the thought of the next card he was about to play, a special meeting in Seville that would stack the deck and win the war hands down once and for all. The lawyer almost felt sorry for the Barracuda and his pathetic, out-gunned little band of merry men. This was hardly a fair fight for such amateurs in his realm of heritage politricks.

20

Mallory Square Dock, Key West

The fiery stand-off, mostly between Mitch and Zak, was still crackling. Two months of living life to the max in edgy Key West had flown by. Torrents of water had flooded under the bridge since the drifters from such different paths of life landed in the southern tip of America to a backdrop of howling winds and lashing rain. In all honesty, the ex-pals hardly remembered what they'd fallen out over. Pig-headedness stopped either of them from making the first move to patch things up.

Nicola and Alona, caught in the friendly fire, had lost all patience. It was time to end this childish, macho Anglo-American standoff and put the special relationship back on track. The schemers bent over backwards to throw buckets of cold water over the impasse. Nothing doing. The chest beating showed little sign of tiring. The boys still refused to look each other in the eye. The girls had insisted, finally, on a long overdue night of drinks, fried chicken, cobb salads and revelry to mark the drifters' two-month anniversary in Key West in the hope one of the hotheads would be the bigger man and blink first. Both surly combative camps announced they were busy that night. And every other night.

The plotting's cunning was dialled up a few notches. A plan B on neutral ground was secretly planned. And so on a fine early evening Friday in December, an observant anthropologist would have spotted Alona, Mitch and Rodi strolling towards the centre of town from the north and Nicola and Zak striding forth from the south. Both parties were heading for Sunset Key in front of Mallory Square Dock. The tourists who flooded Key West in summer and Christmas time had thinned into a hard core. On sunny days like these, though, the locals still took to the shore to bid farewell to the plunging sun. See you at sunset was a year-round greeting in Key West.

The northerly posse crossed a narrow wooden walkway onto red stone paving fronting the ocean, lost among the boisterous sights and funky sounds. Bongo drummers of dubious ability, far-off stares engrained on zoned-out faces, competed with a lady north of the age of sixty hammering out Fleetwood Mac songs and hopping around to her own pleasure. In the shallows, millionaires' motor launches sprayed wooden boats powered by single sails. American, rainbow and pirate flags fluttered in the same Caribbean breeze.

All body shapes and sizes, ages, ethnicities and genders rubbed shoulders without the menace many Western cities attract. Grandads sucked on oversized cigars. Newborns carried by proud fathers ogled the curious scene. If you can be yourself anywhere on earth, this is the place.

You can never guess what you'll see in Key Weird. The eye jumps between celebrations of the senses. A magician with a London accent, jauntily clad in a floral red silk waistcoat – medieval jester style – topped off with a black bowler hat, was reeling in the punters. The white stubbled mischief maker plucked from the centre of an orange the ace of hearts selected from a pack of cards by an amazed school kid five minutes earlier.

All the time passers-by were assaulted with throwaway lines. "They don't believe I'm from England because I've got teeth," he told a chuckling grandma. A teenager was advised to "Get your hands out of your pockets, boy. That's a different game." When his gaze settled on the mirage of Alona slinking barefoot along the boardwalk in front of the crowd, he cheekily heckled "I know your socks match your underwear." Man, woman and child creased up and cheered. Alona was gracious enough to pretend to flash her thigh. Rodi was nowhere to be seen when the magic act ended. He'd performed his own vanishing trick, enchanted by a frozen margarita and chips, salsa, and crushed avocado dip he smelt wafting from the Holy Guacamole vendor's stand.

Unknown to anyone other than the mischievous girls, Mitch, Rodi and Zak's paths would soon innocently cross. For now, Nic and Zak soaked up some peaceful quality time, sauntering past a peroxide blonde psychic reading innocents' futures through the spiritual power of crystals. They silently decided not to tempt fate. Their future was unwritten but they were inching in the right direction. A man reading Tarot cards, sporting a sullen black undertaker's suit, was ignored as well.

To put some distance between thoughts of what might be and an awkward silence, the friends bought a basket of deep-fried lemon and lime conch fritters, diced jalapenos mildly burning the tongue. A happy-go-lucky beige Labrador, his tongue lolling uncontrollably around his salivating mouth, brushed Nicola's ankles. Looking down she shouldn't have been surprised to see he'd left the house sporting a pair of surf shorts. As you do in Key Weird.

Exotic entertainment was on show at the south end of the dock. Nic and Zak briefly enjoyed Dominique's black cat jumping through flames bursting out of a metal ring. The seventy-year-old French showman belly laughed at the crowd's uncomfortable reaction. Was it an amazing feat or abusive? The friends' arms brushed alluringly. Energy and expectation coursed through their neuron paths.

The early evening had the feel of all the fun of the fair fused with vaudeville. An elderly man, with his long white hair tied in a ponytail, juggled fire while perched three metres in the air on a silver unicycle. A four-deep crowd was digging a banjo player wearing his trademark hillbilly bucket hat. Morgan, his obedient brown cocker spaniel, stood to attention next to a heavyset twinkle-eyed twenty-something lad loudly and proudly showing off his navy blue 'Little Miss Sunset' t-shirt.

Pausing between songs, the street performer titillated the crowd by slinging out his own one-liners. "What's the difference between a straight man and a gay man in Key West?" he asked. "About seven shots of Jägermeister," came his reply. Even the bodybuilder posing in a light yellow sweatshirt with the sleeves cut off, and 'Suns Out, Guns Out. Muscles Not Missiles' emblazoned across his chest, roared in appreciation.

A graceful three-sheet sailing schooner flitted past Christmas Tree Island a kilometre offshore. Speed jets roared around its wake. At exactly 5.57 pm, the time-honoured moment when the upper orb of the sun dropped over the horizon, the throng raised its arms and cheered in ecstasy. It was during the crescendo of the sunset celebration that Mitch, Rodi and Zak turned towards their fellow man with deep-creased smiles, only to see the last people they wanted to clap eyes on. Sunset Key had turned into Standoff Key.

Alona and Nicola made a point of embracing like long-lost friends and started chatting merrily. The men, not quite rude enough to walk off in a huff, were trapped. The net was closing. Zak wouldn't admit it in the open, but he was quietly delighted to see his old chums. He couldn't remember what the silly fallout had been about. All so childish.

Rodi, grinning ear to ear, was on the same wavelength. Zak decided to be the bigger man, sauntered up to the Andalusian and offered to buy him a round. The kind-hearted Spaniard dropped his grudge on the spot. Zak addressed the faintest of nods to Mitch, who sniffed and turned the other surly cheek. Bridges still to repair there.

The first peace pipe was passed. Zak approached a throwback to nineteenth-century plantation days. Under a line of palm trees flanking Sunset Key, a wonky wooden wheelbarrow was piled high with fresh coconuts. A young man energetically lopped them open with a machete. His teenage apprentice added two shots of vodka to boost nature's goodness. Zak bought a round for all the crew. Mitch was forced to nod the faintest of appreciations, Alona was relieved to notice.

The slowly thawing group drifted inland, away from the water's edge. The girls sat down on a red brick plinth in the Memorial Sculpture Garden. In this peaceful haven, they could hear themselves talk. Unwilling to break bread yet, the boys dragged their tails between their legs, pretending to study the bronze busts of local celebrities who'd long passed over the bar. Harry Truman was rooted next to the Cuban plantation owner turned revolutionary Carlos Cespedes, famous for freeing his slaves and declaring Cuban independence in 1868. Key West became the capital of the Havana exiles. By the mid-1880s one-third of the town's population was born in Cuba. Cespedes also jumped ship, ending up being appointed the mayor of Key West.

Deeper into the garden a bust of Lena Johnson, a beloved local who sold cookies and candy to sugar-rushing Boy Scouts, spent the afterlife next to Sandy Cornish. The African American former slave saved enough money sweating to build the Florida Panhandle railroad to buy his freedom in 1839 and become a civic leader.

Zak was ashamed to realize he'd never even heard of another influential face, Ellen Russell Mallory, the First Lady of Key West. When she upped sticks from Carrick-on-Suir in Ireland in 1792, the orphan became the town's first white female settler. Her lodging house for sailors, the Cocoanut Grove, did well. A fine reputation for a caring character only increased when she nursed patients stricken by Yellow Fever.

With the proceeds from her boarding house, Ellen sent her son to be schooled at a Moravian academy in Nazareth, Pennsylvania. The investment was well spent. Stephen Mallory, honoured next to his mother in the memorial garden, rose to the rank of US Senator and Secretary of the Navy for the Confederate States. His lobbying for revolutionary iron cladding for wooden battleships in 1853 created a technological breakthrough in the war at sea.

Rodi was engrossed taking selfies alongside a bust of his hero, Ernest Hemingway, before sidling up to Zak. The friends stared at Tennessee Williams and clinked coconuts. Rodi shrugged when his drinking buddy remarked that Hemingway and Williams must have enjoyed the same sunset as the out of towners soaked up that very evening. He wasn't familiar with Williams.

Zak painted a cheery bio of one of America's greatest

playwrights, the author of the classic *Glass Menagerie*, a *Streetcar Named Desire* and *Cat on a Hot Tin Roof.* Tennessee Williams put down roots in Key West in 1941 until his death in 1983. Here he could be openly gay without feeling any shame, living however he liked and drinking to his liver's content in Captain Tony's Saloon. The salty fishermen living in the middle of an art colony that prided itself on a freewheeling bohemian lifestyle couldn't care less. A small part of Tennessee Williams's legacy, beyond the creative, was the gay-friendly atmosphere Key West earned in the 1940s. The playwright's don't give a damn spirit impressed Rodi, especially after he read online on his phone the writer's earliest memory of Key West, which was:

> the most fantastic place that I have been yet in America. It is even more colorful than Frisco, New Orleans or Santa Fe. There are comparatively few tourists and the town is the real stuff. It still belongs to the natives who are known as 'conks.' Sponge and deep sea fishing are the main occupations and the houses are mostly clapboard shanties which have weathered gray nets drying on the front porches and great flaming bushes of poinsettia in the yards… I am occupying the old servant's quarters in back of this 90-year old house… The rent is $7 a week. I shan't do anything the next few weeks but swim and lie on the beach until I feel human again. Then I shall learn how to fish. A good fisherman can thumb his nose at all commercial enterprise in the world.

*

While Mitch nursed his beer, sulking on the sidelines, Alona, Nicola, Rodi and Zak paid their respects to a colossal bronze sculpture towering above the park. Two muscle-bound salvors saving lives and dragging wooden barrels out of a shipwreck were the centrepiece of James Mastin's bronze tribute to Key West's finest, the wreckers who earned millions fishing the seas for old wrecks. Immersed among the great and good of the old town, Rodi, who had spent two months toiling all hours in Keys Exploration's conservation lab, felt the passing sands of time.

Against the grain, Rodi had knuckled down for the team. The Barracuda generously reckoned he'd picked up a Master of Arts' worth of knowledge already. By day Rodi lived the last voyage of the *Merced*'s tragedy through its finds. At night sleep often eluded him. The haunting of old Spain frayed his brain. Make no bones about it, the ancient ship's history was staggering, the stuff of dreams. It was the American ways that were starting to offend him. Overcooked Yankee burgers that tasted like charred shoes. The watery beer was far too weak for the Andalusian's tastes too. How Mitch chugged down that *orina* piss was beyond him.

The ill feeling Keys Exploration harboured towards Rodi's home grated the innocent whizz kid the most. The image of a devil-may-care Madrid despoiling the Americas, and modern Spain's vindictive obsession to bring to heel anyone ransacking its sunken property today, was a stereotypical whitewash. West is not always West. Huelva, like most cities, was home to ultra-conservatives and extreme lefties alike. How can you be so dumb as to tar a whole nation with the same brush?

In the shadow of the Antiquarium, home to dozens of lost naval tales, all Rodi could think about right now was a sloppy bowl of *pinga*, roast pork and chorizo melting off the fork. Mopped up with crusty bread baked that day. And washed down with a bottle of rioja, maybe a two-year-old Crianza matured in an oak barrel. As much as Rodi had been desperate to escape broken Spain, he now craved home comforts.

The trellis of pain that gnawed his grief when his mother, Benita, succumbed to leukaemia had withered into the soil. The pilgrimage to Ernest Hemingway's house had been a hit. Rodi was an expert royal pain, bloody-minded, no doubt about it. Knocking on the author's front door at the most ungodly of hours, morning and evening, was beyond exasperating. Clueless about social etiquette, Asperger-like emotional bewilderment did him no favours.

Rodi's progress, though, had exceeded the hopes of any downtrodden underdog. Top of his joyful list was open access to Maisie Hemingway and her grandfather's house and archives. Mostly to Maisie, in whose company he found he could control his temper and push away his anxiety about failing in life. If Maisie saw merit in him, it must be real.

In stories of Spain's glorious past and how they fitted in with the final voyage of the *Merced*, a tight bond was forged. The amigos – and amigos they would always stay, much to Rodi's disappointment – chatted about travelling together in the footsteps of the great merchantman. Maisie and Rodi shared a dream to check out Venezuela, Colombia and Havana, ending up flying down to Seville, which had always fascinated the actress. If Rodi could make her fall in love with his home, well...

Less mindless and more mindful, Maisie adored the red-haired rogue, though just not the way he wanted to be adored. She felt his pain. In the end, rather than letting him lay flowers on her father's lawn as a homage to his late mother, she'd arranged a short service with her artsy crowd. Rodi was taken aback when Maisie presented him with a Spanish lime sapling and invited him to plant the seedling in Hemingway's backyard. The tears the earnest son shed gave the tree a fine start on its future journey.

Alona watched the healing process unfold between the statues in Mallory Square's memorial garden. Only her boyfriend was moping, refusing to make peace. Mitch could be a total numbskull. Under the bewitching spell of Key West, the pair had missed the opening surf event of the season off Hurricane Hole Marina and not looked back. Pulling shifts on the *Golden Margaret* south of the Dry Tortugas islands turned out to be a stroke of emotional genius.

Neither missed competing. An inner calm had settled. Their bickering had ground to a halt, replaced by tenderness and thoughts of a shared future. It was time to move on from competition, leaving their indulgent youth behind, maybe open a surf shop, perhaps right here in Key West. Why not? The once chilling horror of wedding bells started to toll by day. By night they worked on cooking up a mini-Mitch. Alona's beguiling dark arts of persuasion, cast to cure Mitch's wanton ways, were paying off.

While Mitch huffed and puffed, Nicola was cheered to see Zak walking with his arm around Rodi's shoulder. That was more like it. Zak had made the long pilgrimage to Key West to investigate the destructive forces of a new generation of fishing trawlers, canyon busters threatening to rip up the deep and bulldoze coral reefs into oblivion. Perhaps more than anyone else, Zak's hunt for scientific truth mattered most to the world. It had not taken long for reality to crash down. He was too late. His assignment was crushed.

The sea's fate was sealed. Stocks were already decimated and species upon species of fish and marine habitats were on the edge of extinction. The plight of the deep sat in the lap of the gods. That didn't mean he was giving up. Zak was still hell-bent on furiously blowing the whistle on the damage man's greed had caused. Our botched custodianship of the environment was just another example of human folly. Maybe when he got home Zak would look into setting up an organisation with devastating bite to slam governments and hold them to account.

In the game of human chess unfolding among the friends, two queens, a knight, a knave and a joker negotiating life's complex board, the trap door to Nicola's soul had opened most unexpectedly. A calm had taken root, contentment that had nothing to do with dropping pants and everything to do with jettisoning the baggage of family expectations. London felt a world away.

Nicola didn't miss the daily ablutions and charms of fresh croissants at Gail's bakery, coffee from Raul's deli or even getting ripped off for the privilege of watching a film in the West End for £28 a pop. The clock she'd trusted to pace her days and weeks compulsively had been blown to smithereens. Tragic voices of native American Indians and a fragmentary archaeological puzzle possessed her. Dreams and reality merged. Making sense of the fate of Florida's forgotten people had become a personal crusade.

What was the connection between Boca Chica, Nicola's arrowhead and Juan Limbre's shipwrecked silver? The idea of rest was unthinkable until the mystery was solved.

*

The last glow of the blood-red sky reflected off the still waters. Human nature started to get the better of pig headedness. A man is not an island. The four jars of spiked coconut juice may have played a part. Booze vanquished September's fallout. An hour into the orchestrated rendezvous, the threads of the friends' voyages of personal exploration started to reconnect in this safe space. Nobody wanted to lose face by being the pig-headed odd one out.

Key West had turned out to be far more thrilling than the wildest imagination. Every day was a festival of astonishment. Deep into that Friday night by the side of Sunset Key, free-flowing beer, rum and coke added an intoxicating layer to the Caribbean warmth. Friendships were renewed with blissful satisfaction. The comrades rolled their eyes at the naivety of their former schemes hatched between New York and Miami. Despite their plans being rerouted by unexpected curveballs, nobody was grumbling.

Fragments of the big picture swirling around the good ship *Merced* started to snap into focus. To Rodi, the sunken remains signalled Spain's once glorious power, a porthole to peer into a golden, albeit ragged, past. Of course, he'd read all about Christopher Columbus, Las Americas and the king's gold at school. Feeling history in his hands was a transformative joy. The wreck's story, good and bad, made Rodi proud and solemn. It was a core part of his DNA, who he was. Memories of these months would be a terrific yarn to tell his grandkids one fine day.

A man of typically few words and even fewer polite ones, in Keys Exploration's lab he'd become a dab hand in the art of conservation and even sociable. Mending broken pots by matching thousands of shattered sherds was not that different to fixing computers, reconnecting frayed wires on circuit boards. The Barracuda entrusted Rodi with managing the digital finds records that tracked objects from the seabed to the lab. The Spaniard's professional resolve increased daily as he watched the story grow from small seeds, potsherds glued back together to form intact jars and glazed bowls fired in the kilns of Triana across the river in the Seville he knew so well. Rodi reasoned his work was fixing the hard drive of his country's history.

After subjecting Brains and Zak to a scientific inquisition, Rodi tweaked Keys Exploration's software to upload 3D photos of finds. The cool new technology let the team measure any part of an artefact to the nearest millimetre and create what the eggheads called pottery typologies. Thanks to a beaming Rodi's innovation, archaeologists from Florida to Barcelona could now date other seventeenth-century cities, villages or other drowned ships from similar finds to those they could see from the *Merced*. He had won his spurs to become a cherished member of the team. Discovering the *Merced*'s pearls, saving the project's coffers and the Barracuda's reputation earned the whizz kid a chapter in Key West folklore.

The work was therapeutic too. After the rest of the team went home to their families to wash away the day's toil, Rodi found his body aching from the physical evidence of the violence his forefathers unleashed across Las Americas. When he rinsed the cascade of pearls out of the shipwrecked tobacco leaves, his sensitive soul imagined them sailing to Spain on a waterfall of blood. Now he was the alien on a foreign shore. After the Battle of Tobacco Hill, when he'd furiously smashed every coffee cup in the Antiquarium, Rodi realized he needed to become an ambassador for the good in modern Spain. No more tantrums.

Keys Exploration's idea of Spain wasn't his. He needed to educate these damn Yankees to see his country in a more sympathetic light. Rodi's charm offensive was already two weeks old. Mitch, did you hear about the Robin Hood of Villarramiel, a do-gooder who anonymously slips €100 notes into the mailboxes of random houses? Only in Spain, eh. Mr Barracuda, Juno is beautiful technology. But did I ever tell you about one of my *compadres*, a kid called Aguilar, who was born without a right arm? Guess what? When he was nine years old, he built his first prosthetic arm out of Lego bricks. Amazing. Hand Solo, as he calls himself, is now studying bioengineering at the Universitat Internacional de Catalunya in Spain. Maybe he'll change the world.

Alona, you care about women's rights, yes? Just like my country. Come move to Espagne. In Bilbao, Oviedo and Cadiz we're renaming all those streets honouring that horse's arse General Franco and his henchmen in honour of talented women like Frida Kahlo, Rosa Parks and Jane Austen. What do you think of that? Brains, why do you fatties waste so much food? In the Basque town of Galdakao we have a Solidarity Fridge where the locals drop off leftover food for the poor and hungry. Florida should try it.

Rodi's sea change from hothead to scientist impressed Zak. The smart lad had little filter for keeping even the tiniest of secrets. Zak, by contrast, despite the melting international relations, wasn't quite ready to show his cards. His spirit of camaraderie didn't include sharing some deep concerns. The *Merced*'s pearls may have saved the Barracuda's bacon, but he questioned how Keys Exploration had failed so spectacularly to find the tons of gold bars and silver coins everyone was certain littered the old hull. Something odd was going on in the depths of the Dry Tortugas islands.

Zak had a strong hunch about where the gold was and was not. Brains had uploaded the finished photomosaic to let him work up a 3D graphic. Unlike the rough Boca Chica Indian mound photos, the quality of the data at his fingertips imported into Agisoft Photoscan software was top notch. A quick glance at the bird's-eye view of the wreck did little to shake off his worst fears. Only twelve per cent of the olive jars and finds, he calculated, lay on top of the wreck mound in their original positions when the ship sank centuries ago. The rest were scattered up to eighty metres away from the heart of the wreck. The cause of the destructive calling card was obvious. Mac Murphy and his pals had been ransacking the *Merced* with their fishing gear in a primitive game of lucky dip.

Keys Exploration would find nothing of value other than the odd morsel missed by the trawlermen or, by chance, snagged deep in the mud, like the tobacco leaves pinned under a pile of copper ingots. The treasure hunt would be a bust. The friends had been conned by an 'X' on a map into buying a fat slice of fool's gold. The trawlers were gone, the damage done and all the signs of the con – furrows cut into the soft sand by trawl nets – washed away. It was a perfect crime, like stabbing dead a victim with a spike sharpened from ice. Deadly yet invisible

How could Zak prove the invisible? There was still a winding road to trudge. In the here and now, Alona and Nicola's cunning scheme had played a blinder. The drifters' special relationship was back on track. Except for Mitch. That numbskull took grudges to distant places.

21

Museum of Fine Arts, Seville

James Jorvik couldn't contain his excitement. After a quick bloody steak in downtown Marseille, by the evening he was strolling along the banks of Seville's Guadalquivir River after a two hour and ten minutes flight west. The next morning he was up bright and early, dressed in a three piece suit and tie that clashed against the twenty-six degrees centigrade glaring winter sun. Standards had to be maintained and today like no other he needed to make a heavyweight impression.

At precisely 8.30 am a graceful Isabella López formally greeted Jorvik outside the five-star Mercer Sevilla Hotel, a swish of a matador's cape away from the cathedral. At €450 a night he'd slept wonderfully. Nothing could deflate his mood. On the one hand, Jorvik felt thousands of miles away from the drama he was orchestrating down in the Florida Keys, the heel of America. It was in the heart of Seville, though, where the modern fate of the *Merced* would be sealed. If he played his cards right today, power play would knock the Yanks off their smug perch for good. Jorvik almost felt sorry for their inferior wits and tingled at the idea of being two steps ahead of the enemy.

López frowned at Jorvik's outfit, the very apparition of a colonial Anglo-Saxon insisting on taking his ridiculous customs wherever he roamed and decided to keep quiet. If he roasted like roast beef, he roasted. Not my problem, she reasoned. López worked as a special advisor at the Ministry of Culture in Madrid. Today her remit was to babysit the lawyer on a short tour of Seville's highlights before delivering him in one piece at

10.30 hours sharp to the Minister, César Solano, and the US Ambassador to Spain, Edward Flanigan. Both would be waiting at the Museum of Fine Arts, which by government order would open two hours late that Thursday. The unlikely conspirators had a date with Camille Pissarro.

Before then Jorvik was steered through a crash course in the golden age of Spain. The broad Guadalquivir River linked the lush olive estates of the Sierra Nevada with the country's port at San Lucar, which led out to the Atlantic highway and endless promise beyond in the Americas. Seville had never bothered with flashy stone harbour works. The powers that be preferred environmental flexibility, piers and landing stages made of wood. Back in the day the Americas fleet just swayed in the middle of the river or were pulled onto the foreshore by musclebound slaves cranking capstans round and round.

The day trippers glided past the Torre del Ore, a gem of a twelve-sided watch tower defended by a couple of three-ton iron cannon. Here soldiers once peered day and night at the horizon, nervously awaiting the return of the king's treasure fleets or dreading the apparition of feared raiders. The Golden Tower was built in the early thirteenth century to guard the entrance to the city's docks,. When a naval threat to the city was spied, a heavy iron chain could be winched up from the riverbed between a matching crow's nest tower that once stood on the opposite shore. The twin sadly fell down during the earthquake of 1755. If the *Merced*'s shining booty had made it to southern Spain, it was at this very spot, Jorvik steamed in anger, that the Americas' treasure would have landed and been carted into town to be banked. The lawyer succumbed to a fit of furious coughing at the reminder of Keys Exploration's rape of the high seas.

The commanding front of the Casa de la Contraction, House of Trade, stood undamaged by earthquake tremors near the river, where the wealth of Colombia, Cuba, Mexico, Bolivia and Venezuela once poured into town to be counted and weighed by hawk-eyed royal bean counters. Back in the seventeenth century, the gold and silver didn't stay long in the stores but were soon taken a pebble throw away to the royal mint to be melted into pieces of eight. Only after Spain's golden age crumbled was the building turned into a cigar factory.

Before guiding Jorvik away from the river, Isabella pointed out the spot where a sixth-century Late Roman ship turned up in the mud. Jorvik remembered reading its hyped-up story in the international press. An *El Pais* journalist wrongly reported it as a Viking narrow boat after being fooled by an academic who'd drunk too many jars of the strong stuff.

Turning inland, a sharp-suited security guard stood beside a black Jaguar purring patiently opposite the University of Seville campus, seated his VIPs and sped off. Ten minutes of zig-zagging north through a labyrinth of narrow winding lanes and the Jaguar glided to a halt in the Plaza de la Encarnación. What Isabella advertised as Seville's best-hidden gem wasn't very subtle for a secret. Jorvik sneered at the futuristic wooden cream shade arching over a plaza known locally as the Mushroom. Isabella smiled proudly with the inside knowledge of the treat awaiting the poker-faced lawyer. They descended in darkness down a flight of steps into the mysteries of the Metropol Museum.

The mayor of Seville's commission to renew a shopping centre in 1990 was cheered by developers who soon cursed their bad luck when their bulldozers bit into a maze of Roman ruins swamped under the river ooze. The officials should have known better: their choice for the expanded underground station and a new shopping centre lay bang smack where Seville's ancient *cardo* and the *decumanus* main streets crossed at the height of the Roman Empire – the city of Hispalis built on wooden piers above the marshy lowlands.

In the Metropol Museum Isabella flashed her Ministry of Culture pass and was waved straight through like a sixteenth-century papal priest visiting the headquarters of the Inquisition across the river in Triana. The special advisor explained how the glass walkways, suspended a metre above the ruins, were designed to make you feel like you were walking on water. This trip to Seville wasn't the first or last time Jorvik was deluded by his messiah complex either.

Jorvik had the hots for the Greeks' sophisticated high culture and found the Romans a rather obnoxious, grubby bunch. Even he couldn't help but be impressed, though, by the virtues of this first-century AD villa. Beneath his eyeline survived mosaic floors bursting with scenes of kissing birds and the monster demon Medusa. The lawyer smirked. He couldn't wait for his next meeting at the Museum of Fine Arts to turn the Barracuda and Keys Exploration into stone too. What a superpower to have in your arsenal. Better than the law, which plodded along far too slowly for Jorvik's liking.

In the gardens, Seville's Roman entrepreneurs had bolted workshops onto the backs of the villa. Kilns once fired oil-lamps and glass bowls. Slaves ran between the river and the estate's fish factories with fresh sardines, mullet and mackerel to salt in large vats or boil into exotic sauces beloved by emperors and paupers from Palestine to Hadrian's Wall, the notorious border to Scotland. The villa managers stomached the pungent smell in return for the riches it brought their masters.

The day was turning out perfectly. Jorvik returned to the air-conditioned Jaguar and was whisked off. Out of the window, he spotted a poster for an upcoming play at the Metropol Museum, *Pontius Pilate*, performed by the Studio Theatre. It was time for the lawyer to rain down his own special justice on Key West – judge, jury and executioner. Jorvik clenched his fists. The signs were perfectly aligned.

*

The Museo de Bellas Artes de Sevilla was in lockdown. Nestled between the leafy Santa Catalina district and the river on the city's eastern banks, the old custodian sweeping leaves from the cobbled forecourt in the Plaza del Museo hardly blinked at the dozen black-clad suits talking into their wrists. He'd seen it all before and just hoped they didn't drop any litter.

From the TV news, he recognised his country's Culture

Minister, César Solano, and briefly wondered what he was doing away from Madrid. Maybe meeting a mistress, he chortled. Anyway, he'd check with his son's wife, Esther. She was smart, that girl.

Sebastian always swept in sequence from the front to the back of the museum. If he'd found himself in the rear forecourt, even he would have stopped to lean on his broom at the sight of a black bullet-proof Range Rover pulling up at the end of Calle Pedro del Torre. Its unsubtle stars and stripes flags waved in the air on each side of the steaming bonnet. The eighty-year-old probably wouldn't have recognised the US Ambassador to Spain, Edward Flanigan, but his curiosity certainly would have been raised.

Both the US embassy and the headquarters of Spain's Ministry of Culture were based in the political heart of Madrid. Why the two diplomats didn't simply walk the mile and a half between their offices for coffee weighed heavy in the winter air.

The American, flanked by two special service crewcut details, marched at pace along a narrow pathway made up of lines of black and white cobbles towards a perfectly manicured garden courtyard. Flanigan admired the silence disturbed only by his echoing leather shoe step. If only Madrid offered tranquil delights like these. Today would bring no peace, only headaches. The secrets he kept for president and country.

The former convent built in 1612 for the Order of the Blessed Virgin Mary of Mercy was designed for solitude. Voices only started ringing out of its hallowed halls in 1839 when the Museum of Fine Arts opened its doors to the good folk of Seville. The twitchy consortium hurried up to the museum's first floor.

Divine art stared at the visitors. The American passed a life-size sixteenth-century statue of a half-naked Saint Elmo grasping a cross. Nearby hung a painting of 1605 by Francisco Pacheco showing Saint Peter Nolasco embarking on a ship to save enslaved Christian captives from the African Moors in 1203. Flanigan found the painting far softer on the eye than the heavy pious art he was forced to put up with once a month at official events in Madrid's Prado Museum. Spain's artists getting high on the sacred, painted in thick oil, didn't do it for him. Flanigan preferred wicked profanity any day.

In passing, the ambassador scanned Francisco de Barrero's 1638 painting of Summer. A kitchen scene of ham, chicken and vino made him wonder whether he'd be wined and dined after the business was over as well. His desk in Madrid could hold out a few hours more. The joyful parrots, tree-hopping monkeys feasting on fruit and gentle deer in Jan Brueghel de Velours' *Landscape of Animals*, completed in 1620, brought a smile to Flanigan's lips. Nature's trusted cycle of life made existence so simple. Only man royally screws up the order of the universe.

All too quickly, the golden age of Spain – the genius of Alonso Vazquez and Francisco de Zurbaran – was left behind. At the entrance to the nineteenth and twentieth-century wing stood the Minister of Culture, César Solano, an old friend, hand raised in salutation. Next to him, an English dandy triggered an immediate feeling of distrust. The exaggerated smile was fake and the Bertie Wooster clothes surely a joke. Flanigan pigeon-holed the man as an oily snake and donned his own all business social mask.

Diplomacy in Spain was a tricky affair. The country still hadn't got over its hangover from the colonial past. Madrid's psychological scars at losing one of the world's greatest empires stretching to Venezuela, and then rolling over to let Franco tear the country apart a century later, left behind a gaping national wound, still to heal fully. To say Spain was sensitive, Flanigan learnt, was an understatement. Entitled snobbery and old school misplaced honour and justice were hard to navigate in the treacherous corridors of Madrid. The nation's sinking economy, the third worst in Europe, only increased the paranoia and political extremism swinging between the left and right wings. Spain's sanity hung on a thread the ambassador realised after four years of service.

Today's meeting was all diplomacy and politics, and in Flanigan's estimation a very bad idea. The president's office in Washington had sent down his marching orders, though, and march he must, to a tune he had a nagging feeling would come back to haunt the US. Oh well, need's must. The paymasters call.

The three men sauntered to the back of the gallery and stopped in front of the subject of their top-secret rendezvous. A few minutes idled by while they pretended to study Camille Pissarro's 1897 oil on canvas *Rue Saint-Honoré in the Afternoon. Effect of Rain.* All made appreciative noises and justly so. The eighty-one-centimetre-high work was one of the French impressionist's finest. Only Pissarro wasn't really French, as much as Paris had taken him to her bosom. The painter was born in 1830 in the old pirate's den on the Danish Virgin Island of St Thomas. For a couple of generations in the late seventeenth and early eighteenth century, this bolthole between the Caribbean and the Atlantic vexed the kings of England, Denmark, France and Spain like no other smuggler's lair. Its reputation was even worse than Port Royal in Jamaica.

Pissarro spent his early years sheltered in St Thomas's small Jewish community before a rude awakening. At age twelve, he was shipped off for his betterment and taming to the Savary Academy boarding school outside Paris. The rest was history. In his early twenties he travelled across Venezuela, sniffing out inspiration from Caracas to La Guiaira, the same coastal cities where the *Merced* stopped en route to the Pearl Coast in 1622.

Away from St Thomas, the citizen of the world was forced to move home as the turbulent winds of politics changed. The Franco-Prussian War of 1870 forced the artist to flee from gay Paris to the suburban drabness of Croydon and Norwood in southern England. His wife and mother's former maid and a vineyard grower's daughter, Julie Vellay, reluctantly joined him.

London was unready for Impressionism's revolutionary shakeup. Pissarro's work was rejected as vulgar. At the time critics rarely appreciated anything other than serious scenes of religious, historical and mythological life. By the time the terrible year-long war ended, Pissarro was distraught to hear that only forty of the one thousand five hundred canvases he'd painted over twenty years had survived back in Paris. The rest ended up destroyed by soldiers who used them as floor mats to keep their muddy boots clean.

Long after Pissarro's death, Hitler, who imagined he knew a thing or two about painting, seized many of his leftover masterpieces from private and public view. All Jewish property was judged fair game. *Rue Saint-Honoré in the Afternoon*, which Solano, Flanigan and Jorvik were gawping at in mid-morning Seville, was one such high-profile casualty of the Holocaust.

The scene had been painted in Paris during the winter of 1897 and 1898. At the age of sixty-eight, back in his beloved France and housebound with a wicked eye infection, the artist captured the view outside his hotel room in the Place du Théâtre Français. Day after day his brush dotted the canvas with obsessive craziness. It was little wonder Pissarro's poor eyes gave up early.

The painting had sold quickly. Lilly Cassirer Neubauer, born to a prominent Jewish publishing family in Germany, fell in love with the canvas. It ended up pride of place in the family's charming home in Berlin until the Nazis forced the Cassirer family to 'sell' the picture for a lowly 900 marks, around $360, in 1939. It wasn't a negotiation. Not agreeing would have meant a beating, imprisonment and most likely death. Nazi oppression of Germany's Jews was rising fast. The Cassirers fled the Third Reich without their art but lucky to be in one piece.

For decades after Hitler's fall from power, the family imagined the painting had been burnt during the atrocities of World War II. Low and behold the family heirloom surfaced in a New York gallery in 1976 when Baron Hans Heinrich Thyssen-Bornemisza acquired it under dubious circumstances. When the Baron died, the Spanish government purchased his collection for $350 million and hung *Rue Saint-Honoré in the Afternoon* on the wall of Seville's Museum of Fine Arts for everyone to enjoy. What was not to like?

The fact the painting was Nazi loot and never should have ended up in the hands of the Swiss industrialist and Nazi sympathiser Thyssen-Bornemisza or Spain in the first place was an inconvenient truth. Seville knew it, so did the USA. The Spanish government stuck out its jaw and refused to part with the masterpiece, arguing it was bought in good faith with taxpayer's cash. The bad publicity meant the painting had become a *cause célèbre*. Now the Cassirers wanted their loot back. After five years of quiet negotiations and working through diplomatic channels only got them patronizing smiles and sympathetic nods, they'd had enough. Neubauer's grandson, Claude Cassirer, filed a federal lawsuit in California against Spain to recover Pissarro's masterpiece, now valued at a cool $35 million.

The saga of the stolen Pissarro had been on James Jorvik's radar for years. Although he personally had little sympathy for the Cassirers claim, he appreciated the case was a public relations nightmare that had reached a dead-end stalemate. In Keys Exploration's discovery of the *Merced* off the Straits of Florida, he sniffed a sneaky opportunity.

Jorvik had contacted César Solano through colleagues at the Ministry of Culture he'd befriended at various international workshops on culture and heritage. For a modest fee he offered his services to represent the Kingdom of Spain to repatriate the treasure of the *Merced*. That's when the wily lawyer leant on a Washington stringer Jorvik & Silver occasionally retained to reach out to the American Foreign Service. Flanigan was pressured into taking his call.

In return for returning the shipwrecked treasure to Spain, where it was always destined, Jorvik proposed Seville might consider forfeiting its right to Pissarro's *Rue Saint-Honoré in the Afternoon*. The *Merced* gold and silver for the Pissarro. Compared to Cassirer's claim that was becoming increasingly hard to fend off, Spain realised it could be the political winner in this back-scratching deal. *Quid pro quo*. James Jorvik had played a blinder, a masterstroke of deceit.

Following legal etiquette, it was Jorvik who broke the silence while the three cynical men – a lawyer, politician and diplomat – surveyed the masterpiece and mulled over what it meant to so many interested parties.

"Gentleman, I shan't waste your precious time. Let's cut to the chase," Jorvik began. "It seems fate has rolled the dice of opportunity. Madrid demands the return of the cultural patrimony of the *Merced* and quite rightly say I. Yet the wheels of the law for shipwrecks in international waters are not unmuddied. Keys Exploration will tie us up in court for around three to five years in my opinion. We'll be obliged to carry out detailed research to prove the ship was a frigate, not armed for naval battle, not commercially inclined and sovereign immune. Between you and me, this is far from a clear-cut case, I must caution."

"Meanwhile, Mr Cassirer has deep family pockets, the sympathy of history on his side and the press and public are not going away. The question is this: can we reach a creative resolution to everyone's satisfaction? I suggest we can."

Not unexpectedly, César Solano began his side of the dance by making it crystal clear that "Spain's position is unchanged. Our government legitimately acquired the painting in 1993 along with the rest of the Thyssen-Bornemisza collection. Seville has been the peaceful owner of this prized possession ever since we acquired it and has exhibited it permanently. There can be no question of its ownership. Spanish courts are unlikely to force the museum to surrender, you understand."

Flanagan's position was simpler. With the Hispanic population of the United States soaring and Spanish America's second national language, the two countries were naturally drifting closer together.

"My country is sensitive to the Cassirer family's claim," the ambassador made clear. "We'd like to see this mess sorted out. It's a stinking bugbear for my office, to be blunt. The Keys Exploration and Cassirer claim, of course, are separate matters on different legal tracks. That said, we believe it is in both our governments' interests to avail ourselves of whatever margin for manoeuvre we can leverage. Both issues can be resolved in a way that will favour and continue to build our excellent relationship."

Jorvik beamed and nodded in his sycophantic way while Solano sweetened the deal.

"Spain is willing to sit down with the Cassirer family and sign over the painting, rest assured. This is, how do you say, small fry. The treasure of the *Merced* is a far bigger fish that can help us in our pressing war against treasure hunters raping our sunken past in the world's seas. We all appreciate the importance of this moment, yes?"

"More than this, my government would like to recognise Washington's brotherhood by funding cultural exchanges to promote mutual understanding and appreciation with Los Angeles' Hispanic community. Perhaps through an exhibition of 1970s and 1980s art held in our rich collections? In time, sponsoring a Museum of Latin Art in your City of Angels is not off the table. If we get the treasure back."

James Jorvik smacked his hands together and clapped both men on the back.

"Let it be so," the lawyer concluded. "May I propose that what we have discussed today stays between us and these four walls? No contracts, no written communications. Mr Flanigan, may we leave you to have a quiet word in your judiciary's ear? Agreed?" The deal makers looked around to make sure nobody was watching and each gave a single nod.

The diplomatic small talk that followed was of little consequence. A few minutes later the lawyer, ambassador and culture minister left by different doors. Fast cars whisked away the VIP's to their next back-to-back appointments. The meeting never happened.

Jorvik exited by a side gate. In high spirits, he promised himself an early evening royal stuff-up at Oriza on the Calle San Fernando before he caught the 19.20 flight to Rome, where a couple of fine new suits were awaiting him, and then back to London Heathrow.

Sebastian, still brushing leaves at the rear of the museum, was shocked this time to see the black Range Rover with stars and stripes flags on the side of the bonnet speed past him in the direction of the airport. Well, I'll be damned, he mused, taking a quick photo with his camera phone. Not that he was entirely sure how to get photos off telephones. He really would need to have a talk with Esther. What was going on? The long-time caretaker was befuddled.

22

Pier House Spa, Key West

November had turned to December and, as the Brits do, Nicola was desperate to soak up the last embers of the waning sun. She let the secrets of the sunken past tread water. For a change she embraced tourist distractions for five blissful days. Despite the unexpected oddness of this trip's escape from drudgery – was it even a holiday? – she'd found the ideal balance of body and mind craved back in rain-swept England after all.

The beaches, food, super jovial locals and Zak applying low-factor coconut sun cream on her back were perfection, even though she was starting to wonder whether the lad would ever make a move. Was there something wrong with the boy? Was he hiding some terrible secret, perhaps an embarrassing physical defect? Maybe he was born with just one ball? The mind of a Brit clocking in the hours on the beach needed to turn from ghoulish white to Florida brown wanders far and wide.

Another day in paradise was done and dusted when Marcel in reception waved to Nicola on her way from the pool to her room for a calming shower. She was surprised to be handed a cream envelope with her name scribbled on the front and 'By Hand' neatly written below. Probably another dinner invite from one of the whacky Keys Exploration team to be refused, she guessed.

The shower's spray soothing her body's excess sun knocked Nicola out for a couple of hours. The sun was setting and the clock read 7.50 pm by the time her brain unglued her eyelids from a deep slumber – the feeling of a hangover without drinking. Nic was late to catch up with Zak, Rodi and the team over dinner and hoped they'd left her some Atlantic crab.

Seven minutes later, she was ready to roll in a low maintenance white cotton shirt with a cut v-neck collar and red and blue embroidered flowers above the chest over Calvin Klein jeans. She'd spotted the shirt in the high-end Indigo Boutique along Duval Street. Ethnic Native American chic, its style was sold to her. Nicola slid on two vintage turquoise bead bracelets she'd also picked up in town and screwed her feet into a pair of white suede Superga shoes. Not too shabby, she thought, taking in her reflection in the mirror.

Only when she rummaged around for her Mastercard – the bare minimum, no bag needed – did she spot the cream envelope handed to her at reception. Best check its content before heading out. The hand-written lines were so unexpected and saddening that her legs turned to jelly and she dropped onto the bed. Hardly believing the words, she re-read the letter:

"Dear Nicola. A brief note to let you know that my grandfather, Grant Raven, has been taken ill in hospital. He's had some kind of seizure. He was rushed to Mount Sinai Medical Center in Miami last night. Nobody's saying what's going on. Gramps has lost his speech. We're waiting on tests. For now, we're asking friends to respect our privacy at this difficult time, but I wanted to contact you because, while drifting in and out of consciousness, Gramps has been growling and banging his fist. I gave him a pen and paper and he scribbled what reads like 'Nicola, Gollum's Head'."

The letter went on to explain that "Our family doesn't know a Gollum or a Nicola. A few weeks back, Gramps was telling us about a great time he enjoyed with a Nicola Medici down in the mangroves. I can only imagine he was thinking of you. I took the liberty of calling around a few hotels in Key West until I found a Nicola Medici at the Pier House Spa. I know this sounds crazy, but since Gramps was so agitated I promised I'd send you this cryptic message. So, 'Nicola, Gollum's Head' it is. Sorry if I'm wasting your time. Gramps is in a coma. My phone number is on the back of this envelope. Feel free to call me any time. Sincerely, Lauren Hoffman."

Nicola collapsed in tears. Pull yourself together, she scolded herself. You've only known the old man for five minutes. Nothing doing. Her head and heart were united in the kind of grief shown at a family bereavement. In just a couple of short meetings Skip had become one of her favourite people.

By the time Nicola hooked up with the team at the Thirsty Mermaid, midway between Hemingway's old house and the Key West Bight Marina, heartache had taken away her hunger. Alona and Mitch were necking beers and chomping on oven roasted chicken wings glazed with chilli pineapple, a local speciality. Between mouthfuls they noisily offered their own commentary on the football game on the big screen, the Miami Dolphins against the Dallas Cowboys. Rodi was focused on what looked like a chicken burger and chips oozing mayonnaise from all sides. Furious eyes had narrowed at the waitress's offer of a salad on the side. Lettuce is for rabbits, he'd growled at the scared girl just doing her job. Juice dropped down his napkin tucked into his collar.

Zak was patiently waiting for Nicola before starting dinner and was on edge. This evening he'd decided to ply her and, more crucially, himself with immense quantities of wine and see where they ended up. If he didn't make a move soon, the chance would be gone. He was running the risk of ending up castaway in the friend zone. Sitting on ice was a bottle of sparkling Gruet Brut Rosé wine made in Mexico. Nicola walked in the door, perfectly presented as ever. Zak's knee stopped jiggling. Immediately he felt something was wrong. Even the day's tanning couldn't mask the bloodless colour in Nicola's cheeks.

The team shared pleasantries and the usual jokes about the rain back home, the beauty of their expatriate paradise and toasted great riches from the sea. Rodi, too busy munching, raised his hand in salutation. Mitch still had the hump and blanked the British delegation. Nic was oblivious to his childish games. She gratefully grasped a tall glass of rosé, downed it in one and gestured for a refill and for Zak to join her on the garden decking. Words did not need to be exchanged. The English woman silently slipped over Lauren Hoffman's letter. Food and stilted conversation were the last thing Nicola needed. Being alone would be worse. Her whole being ached for one person, the ever-remote, yet reassuringly reliable, oddball Zak Fitzgrove.

"Skip was in such fine spirits and it was only a few days ago," Zak spluttered.

"Exactly, I'm stunned. I'm saddened, obviously. But I suppose he was – or is – eighty-six years old, no spring chicken," Nicola replied.

"What do you think happened? Should we go and visit him," Zak mused.

"We have to respect the family's wishes. We've only really known him for a few minutes, even though I feel a fierce bond from our shared adventures. At this point, we can only pray and hope for the best," Nicola ended.

The sun was dipping into the Atlantic on another day of who knew how many lost fortunes. A peaceful calm settled over the friends, who reflected on the twist fate had thrown them.

"But even in his deepest moment of suffering, Skip was trying to tell you something pressing. What do you make of this business about Gollum's Head? Was the old boy losing it, going gaga?" he asked.

"Far from it. I think he knew exactly what he was saying, crystal clear. Skip isn't, wasn't, a man to waste words," Nicola turned to Zak, a lump in her throat and a twinkle flickering in her eye. Watching her friends downing beer and cocktails in the Thirsty Mermaid, she sighed, faced Zak and put her hand on his cream shirt collar. "Humm, I wonder, are you up for another little trip, Dr Fitzgrove? If so, shut up and follow me." The drama wasn't necessary. He was in. Always in where Nicola was concerned.

Zak nodded like a gargling baby at the prospect of more quality time with Nicola. Any adventure would be a bonus. In classic Ms Medici style, the friends, couple, explorers – neither still knew exactly what they meant to each other – made their getaway through the exit and vanished into the night.

*

The decision to hold onto the rental jeep turned out to have been smart. Once more, Nicola sped north through the early evening dark night, her white shirt billowing ghoulishly in the wind rushing through the open window. The roads were empty and, despite the terrible news, both Nicola and Zak felt high. Most families were getting comfy at home, laughing around the dinner table, praising or scolding their kids for failing tests or forgetting to do their homework. Lovers and parents putting their children to bed turned their minds to settling down on the sofa after a hard day's work. The miracle of life, Zak felt, was the hope that despite all the hardship, pain and suffering in the world, everyone on Earth got up the next day and did exactly the same thing over and over again.

The white-knuckle ride to Sugarloaf Key was mercilessly short. Being a Friday evening, few police were parked up on the grass verges. Nicola dumped the jeep under the same tall palm tree as the week before and waved to Zak to hurry. The scientist was worried. This may be a bad idea. With the lights out in Grant Raven's house, the isolation of Driftwood Rise was Scooby Doo creepy. If it weren't for the half moon, the darkness would have been total. Zak gently laid a hand on Nicola's shoulder.

"Please, slow down a minute and tell me what the Dickens is going on. I can hardly see three steps in front of me. Do you have a plan or are you just trying to get me somewhere pitch black to take advantage of me?" he enquired, wondering if he'd overplayed his cards.

"Come on, old man, take my hand." Zak smiled and complied. "We're going to have a chat with Gollum."

Zak's disappointment at seeing a small torch pulled from Nic's bag in the jeep boot was short lived. Despite the enlightenment and fading fear, she squeezed his hand and showed no intention of withdrawing the warm bundle of joy.

"You wouldn't know, I never told you, but the crazy boat Skip steers through the mangrove streams is called the *Gollum*. I'm certain he was trying to tell me something important. He wanted to guide me to his madcap boat."

Zak almost had a heart attack when Nicola flicked on her torch, lighting up eight human skulls glaring into the night sky. Nic laughed wickedly and explained how Grant had found them down the years in Native American Indian mounds. In some eccentric pact with the dead, he'd nailed them to the boat's gunnels to guide him to their buried secrets. The weird factor had gone into overdrive.

In one graceful step, Nicola landed aboard the *Gollum*. Zak followed more gingerly. The boat was small and clean as a whistle. Not even a map could be spotted under the torch's beam.

"There's nothing here," Nicola cried. "Maybe Skip was delirious, sending us on another wild goose chase after all." The hasty Ms Medici looked ready to give up and head home.

"Hang on a moment. Remind me exactly what Lauren's letter said," Zak asked. Nicola repeated the short sentence, 'Gollum's Head. That's it', and shrugged.

"Well, there's two possibilities here, the obvious and the wild card. Nic, first off let's check around the skulls – the heads – for any clues."

Once more no notes or forensic clues came to light around the ancient human skulls. Standing hands on hips, Nicola asked about Plan B.

"Well, it's a stretch, but on historic ships the head was the name of the hold in the prow. When a ship like the *Titanic* sank bow first, she was said to have gone down by the head," Zak explained. "It's just possible Skip was talking about his motor launch's head." The scientist pulled off the front cushions covering four wooden seats to the sides of the steering wheel in the bows. At the far left a false floor with an inset brass ring appeared.

"And voila, we may have lift off," Zak said dramatically.

Much to his appreciation, Nicola rewarded him with a kiss on the lips, before turning to the ring. Abracadabra, she smiled. The floor opened up easily to reveal the inner bilge. With the torch in her teeth – not necessary, but she'd seen explorers do this on the

National Geographic channel – she bent over into the lower hull and invited Zak to hold her legs. The noble Englishman dutifully obliged, trying not to be distracted by the fine view.

The bilge looked empty other than a few leaves and a dead mouse. Nicola squealed and avoided its carcass. She delved deeper into the hold, forcing Zak to grasp her thighs and hold tight. Just when she was about to give up, Nicola turned away from the bilge and noticed a faint seam in the side of *Gollum*'s hold. She pushed it with one finger and a small hidden hatch popped open. Eureka, Zak heard her exclaim, asking him to pull her up.

First, Nic's well-appointed derrière, then her arms and finally head and hands grasping something bound in a dirty oil cloth emerged into the gloom. The friends fell in a heap in the middle of the *Gollum*, their hair tousled, and laughed hysterically. The embarrassing euphoria soon passed. Nicola began unravelling the object hidden inside like an Egyptian mummy and sighed, "Oh Skip, what have you been up to?"

Carefully nestled inside a second layer of clean cloth was an ancient leather-bound book in pretty fine condition. Zak and Nic's jaws fell open in ghoulish imitation of the skulls nailed to the boat's sides. Neither spoke. By the light of the torch they huddled together, cross-legged, taking in the sign of the cross stamped onto the tome's front cover. Both gasped at the letters incised beneath it, JL.

The same letters they'd found scratched onto the wooden box unearthed at the Boca Chica Indian burial mound. Surely this was no coincidence. Nicola closed her eyes and recalled Skip's rambling at the end of their first meeting. "What you know or think you know of the 1622 treasure ships isn't all it seems. I cannot confirm or deny if the story of the golden Spaniard is real or an old wife's tale or whether it started in 1622 or 1715."

"This much I am certain about," he'd whispered to her cryptically. "The treasure is very real. If only the good Lord lends me enough time to crack the codex."

Nicola's heartbeat skyrocketed. So, this is what finding real treasure feels like, she finally understood. Staring into Zak's eye with a sense of huge wonder, she slowly turned to the opening page of the codex.

"The Diary of Juan Limbre. St Augustine, Florida, 1 January 1623," the friends read.

The rest of the text looked all Greek to Zak, who shrugged his shoulders and expected the night's fun to end in failure. Nicola thought otherwise. Her years of studying Latin at school and European languages, including Spanish, at King's College London were about to pay dividends. Where Skip ended up flummoxed, out loud and much to Zak's amazement Nic gingerly started to trace the Castilian spidery letters in front of her and translate memories unspoken for centuries.

23

From the Diary of Juan Limbre,
St Augustine, Florida, 1 January 1623

To this day I do not recall the feeling of the water. Warm or cold I cannot say, for the ocean was a thing possessed. A furious spirit pinned my arms to my sides, scratched my legs, pounded my chest. The demons of the deep besieged my mortal soul.

This much I still see: Savarna's eyes, wide and wild, refusing to look anywhere beyond my own. The swirling monster had ripped off my Cadiz boots, but my leather bag stayed tight fixed across my shoulder. With great effort in the swirling maelstrom I tied my belt around Savarna's hand and held tight. Live or die, it would be as one.

We floated over the mountainous waves before plummeting far down into demonic valleys until a heavy object – my ship's main mast and shrouds washed overboard – struck Savarna unconscious. Delirious, we washed onto the mast and lay finished, our legs supported above the billowing sail, which once steered my fine ship across the seas. I lost all hope and fell lifeless. Through the thick spray I espied the *Merced*'s bows high in the air. My ship bowed farewell and started its final voyage into the abyss. All else blacked out.

*

These moments will never leave my memory, haunting my every sleep. The journey started with such promise. I now see the Lord had other plans. The heavens were making us pay for the terror my brothers and I shipped to *Mundus Novus*, the New World. For locking up the Indios in the dark recesses of our gold and silver mines, never to see the light of day, for working the braves to exhaustion diving in the Costa de las Perlas for the white shells at the bottom of the sea. That day the Lord cast our shame into the ocean. The king's hopes are dead. So fate has written.

Our own destiny began what seems a lifetime ago, in truth five months yore. As I give praise to the Lord for my life, these chronicles I commit to my log.

In this way it began. The 22 of August 1622. The whole fleet of Terra Firma, that is to say such ships of Spain and galleons belonging to his Majesty, came together in the port of Havana, a place appointed as a rendezvous, whither the navy was planned to repair to start the return home. Whereupon the Admiral, as you please, on the 23 of August, commanded every ship to register the gold, silver, bullion and merchandise into their books of account because they had a purpose to put to sea and set sail on the 28th day.

But our admirals cast many doubts of putting from the harbour until the new moon had passed, whose effects they expected the 5th of September. Whereupon the Governor of Havana called a Counsel, summoning all the officers, the general of the soldiers, the admiral of the armada, the captain general of the fleet, the treasurer, the captains and the pilots. With one voice we determined, aware of the new moon's mischief in September, to commonly bring tempests and turbulent winds, to respect the seasonable providence and remain quietly in harbour befitting the security of the armada until the change had passed.

We settled our affairs to await the time's appointment. But the evening promised such fair weather, and a serene element, with a pleasant and sociable gale of wind continuing two or three days together. We all repented and wishing to make good of the opportunity set forth. The general consented to these hopes, insomuch that after musters on Sunday the 4th September by break of day we weighed anchor and hoisted sails out of harbour. There were twenty-eight ships with their admiral, eight galleons, three *pinnaces* and other attendants upon the fleet with their consorts.

We sailed forward prosperously and had a time of fair expectations. Monday approached, the day of the new moon, and the weather flipped. The wind coming from the northeast raised a fear in the admiral. The galleons wound up their main sails, tied them fast to the yards and advanced with only their mizzens unfurled. We put in practice all the means which art and industry could afford to escape danger.

It seems tempests have their courses and are unbending. For the wind increased and whistled. The clouds thickened and blackened the horizon. The air was so dark and formidable we could not see one ship from another. By such disastrous misfortune, ere it was full noon, and with the winds continuing to perpetuate outrageousness, all the galleons heaved uncontrollably. The most part of the fleet went before the wind and took a course to save themselves as best they could. In which violence they were driven from one another and the wind continued so impetuous that it unloosened their tack and sails, broke asunder the foremasts and rent the main yards into splinters. The ships violently crossed the wind.

Wave rolled after wave and one mischief followed another. Presently the wind turned to the south. Although it gave us leave the better to manoeuvre, the tempest brought rain. The sea churned high. Then we feared another misfortune, to be thrust into some creek or bay on the coast of Florida, which we much suspected lay close by thanks to the great and wonderful haste made. Then there would be no hope but either splitting on the sands or perishing on the shore.

Many months later I pieced together from whispers, encounters and finally a news sheet from Madrid the desperate truth of what happened to my brothers that sorry day.

The fearful storm had continued with all rage until Tuesday following. Some ships still far off determined to return to Havana, in which course such as had masts and sails repaired.

For the great ships it was too late. The admiral ship heading the fleet ran herself aground in two fathoms water and a little more, where our *Lady of Atocha* broke in pieces on the coast of Matecumbe in La Florida with the loss of all her people except three men and two boys. The galleon *Santa Margarita*, the ship of the holy pearl, followed the same course and suffered the same misfortune, for she was lost coming to three fathoms of water. She was so violently thrust on a flat of sand that the keel sticking fast, and the billows extremely raging, her body shivered all to pieces. The passengers, when it was apparent they could not escape, saw as little mercy in the sea as they endured in the wind.

In the same hour, with the same tempest, almost at the same place, two ships of the fleet were swallowed by the sea and perished before they could approach the shore. Such was the destiny of my trusty boat and crew come from Cumana and Cartagena, all lost off Tortugas.

In the seven ships of my King Phillip's fleet lost, five hundred and fifty persons drowned off Matecumbe. I judge that one and a half million *pesos a ocho reales* went down in the two galleons. The sunken goods included 254,000 *pesos* for the account of the royal exchequer of your Majesty in gold, silver, tobacco and copper.

*

After how long – minutes or hours I cannot say – I came around to a new sensation. The ground beneath me was no longer churning and was becalmed. My left eye was coated in blood. Opening my crusted right eye, I espied white sands and light surf, trees and mangroves. By a miracle of the Lord's will we were castaway, saved. Savarna had awoken too, set my saddlebag under my neck and was softly caressing my forehead. An anguished look crossed her tight lips.

I propped myself up on an elbow and surveyed a scene of desolation. Morning had broken and beyond any chance we had beached. The shore was as God intended, untouched by man. Just now the white sands were stained with broken wreckage – here the capstan leaning sideways into the shore, there a broken parrot's cage, everywhere smashed timbers and burst barrels. I do not speak of the lifeless bodies that still haunt my tortured mind. My wooden travel chest, recklessly tipped overboard when we plunged into a wall of water, lay not fifteen *vara* from me, licked by the surf. Its lock was unbreached. The demons of the deep did not imprison everything.

As for my old ship, I can but imagine she broke into a thousand pieces of firewood under the violence of the weather. I tried to guess which of the beams blanketing the beach were the bones of my sweet *Merced.* No sign of my brave men. The crew was gone, I supposed swallowed by the blue monster, buried at sea, a fate all sailors dread. *Dios nuestra almas* – God save our souls.

I stood up on weak, trembling legs. Everything seemed in working order. Poor Savarna was less fortunate. The main mast had crushed her right arm. She wheezed, sucking in sharp pockets of breath. To my horror I espied a three-inch splinter of planking cast deep into her lung. In that instance I forgot my own pain, my travel bag and trunk. All that mattered was to save the one I cherished. My life's journey and dreams had turned halfway round the compass in the space of a few hours.

Where were we? How to escape this living hell?

*

My fear for Savarna proved just the beginning of dangers imminent. I espied a grove of trees at the rear of the shore and, with midday approaching by my reckoning of the height of the sun, I made a fire and shelter from a few bushes. The cover kept but a little of the falling rain from us. I lay Savarna to rest under the branches, our clothing very wet and cold.

Then a fear worse than the waves gripped the shore. About the third hour since I had awoken came two Indian men, naked except for a piece of platted silk-grass hiding their loins and fastened behind with a horse-tail. Their hair was tied in a roll in which was stuck two bones like arrows. The natives' countenance was furious and bloody. They were running from the south fiercely, holding knives and foaming at the mouth. The younger Indian violently seized Savarna by the neck, trying to cut off her hair, a demon possessed.

In fear he designed to end her, I seized my saddlebag and pulled out my pistol, in truth unloaded and wet to the bone, and put my trust in the Lord. The Indians must have seen gunpowder and shot before. Both froze in primitive thought. Slowly I pulled some tobacco and a pipe from my bag and held out my hand as if to becalm a wild horse. They greedily snatched the gifts and retreated into the trees.

I knew little of these barbarous people, but enough to fear they were generally accounted to be man eaters. Assuming they had run off to alarm their people, we sat down in each other's arms expecting cruelty and a hard death. The while we entreated the Almighty to work wonderfully for our deliverance.

Several hours later the Indians returned with a very great number all running and shouting. The storm had much abated, the rain ceased and the sun appeared. The natives sped up and down the sands, collecting whatever they could lay their hands on, opening all the trunks and chests on the shore. It pleased me to have taken precautions with my belongings, secured deep within the mangroves.

Their Casseekey, what they call their native king, with about twenty fearsome braves, came down upon me in a furious manner foaming at the mouth, large knives outstretched. These bloody-minded creatures kicked down the light canvas cover I'd hastily set up. They went to pulling off all our clothes, leaving Savarna with only a linen shirt. Ready to execute their bloody designs, Savarna put her head in her hands waiting for the men to begin their evil, high on words we did not understand. They rushed upon us and cried, Nickaleer, Nickaleer. We understood them not, though they repeated the shout. To my great surprise the Caseekey added, "English son of a bitch." We took Nickaleer to mean English. I looked up, pointed to my heart and cried "Espania."

Of a sudden it pleased the Lord to work wonderfully for

our preservation. Instantly these savages were struck dumb. The Spanish had influence on these brutish Indians. I started to realise we must have landed on the shore of La Florida and were once more in the land of my fellow man. Somewhere nearby must be a fort, a garrison or holy mission.

The skimmers and pelicans along the shore kept a good distance from the Indians, while the turtles pulled their heads inside their shell fortifications. We observed the Casseekey chief's heart tender towards us, as he now kept his petty robbers at arm's length and helped us build a new shelter. Along the shore the natives shouted and made great noises in their plunder, hundreds of them revelling around the wreckage. The Casseekey went down to the waterside among his people and returned with two dead men's coats, wet and torn, for Savarna and I. We offered gratitude, more tobacco and a pipe to the chief. A great fire was lit and once more I lay my woman down with fortune lightened.

The hideous noises continued down by the waves, to whence I walked along the beach, bare foot. In a heap of metal and wood of no meaning to the natives, I picked up an astrolabe, took an observation and found ourselves to be in latitude of twenty-four degrees and five minutes. My ship had come to grief in the southern spear tip of La Florida of which I knew little other than what idle tongues spoke. Searching my tired mind, I remembered the frontier was ruled from a strong fort to the north. I began to enquire about the town called St Augustine.

The Casseekey nodded but his winged babble meant nothing to me. All I could do was shrug. I revealed Savarna's wound and in tears and meaninglessness besought to explain that without medicine she was finished. What could I do but hope. The Indians killed a hog found on the shore, carried by the flag galleon to feed the crew. The smell and succulent meat heated our bones. I hoped of living another day.

The morning of the 6th September broke with much noise and excitement. The Indians had seized Savarna, as I soon appraised not for harm but care. She lay on a palm leaf and wooden stretcher, a haggard old Indian woman rubbing green cream into her wound. The last part of my ship that had so violated Savarna's lung was removed from her side. Much blood seeped from her side and fear seized my soul. The scene was not one of fortune. The medicine woman's face was a cloud of dread. She nodded her head in a sign of loss. Savarna had fallen unconscious.

*

Some time later, how long I cannot say, the Casseekey chief kicked sand over the fire, cried out an order, and four braves took up the two poles and sail canvas where Savarna lay. I followed behind, useless. The trees and mangroves pulled us into the interior. The sun had come extremely hot and after a little time we came to a thin winding stream. On the other side stood a marvellous sight, the Indian's village, being little round huts, about a man's height, made of small poles stuck in the ground, which they bended to make an arch and covered with thatch of palmetto leaves.

The Casseekey drew back the side of the largest hut, his very abode, and settled Savarna to one side, sat down cross-legged and started eating berries greedily from a basket. I too partook. Other Indians brought in oysters. The water passed around in a palm leaf was salty and I swallowed hard to keep it down. The chief passed some time opening my fleet's chests and boxes with his wife, taking out all they wanted. The rest was thrown outside where the braves jumped on the treasured morsels with unfettered excitement.

The evening drew in and tall fires were lit from the wooden wreckage hauled inland. The natives danced, looking full at the moon and making hideous noises like the howling of a wolf. The women joined the cries. Providence had embraced us by a truly remarkable deliverance, yet a stranger future awaited.

The morning dawned with great dew and extreme cold. Savarna had not moved all night. Her head was clammy and cold. We set her down under a grape bush, her faint lifeless body at death's door. The Casseekey, dressed in raw deer skins, looked upon us with a mild aspect and sent his son with a sharply pointed staff to the inlet to strike fish.

We devoured the grilled sea beasts kindly caught. Taking a drink made from casseena leaves, a deep brown liquid handed round in a conch shell, a great noise broke out to the north. A multitude of Indians crossed the water waving their spears and bows and arrows. In the midst, a head taller than the highest braves, marched a man with a grey flowing beard dressed in brown woollen cloth grasping a tall walking pole. A wooden cross fastened around his neck swung across his chest. Salvation came too late.

The priest introduced himself as Francisco Villareal, hugged me warmly and gave the sign of the cross. The padre lived in a small Spanish mission of twenty-eight houses, a chapel and stockade next to an Indian settlement at the mouth of the Myaamiaki river. He was six days abroad seeking repentance among the Wild People. Father Villareal explained that we were cast ashore on the key of Matecumbe in La Florida in the land of the Tequesta, a savage people living for many a hundred year along the eastern seaboard. These Indians did not till the soil, neither sow nor reap, but speared for fish in the daytime and with torches at night searched for oysters, clams, crabs and crewfish. The Tequesta had some loyalty to the Spanish from fear alone, and like the king took the British Nickaleer as detested enemies.

I explained a need to hasten to St Augustine to seek medicine for poor Savarana. Father Villareal spoke without false words. At our pace the Spanish frontier town stood twelve days walk to the north. Savarna would not survive and nor would we in all chance.

If we were caught treading the sacred land of the ancestors, the Casseekey told the padre, who spoke the savage tongue, our throats would be sliced, our scalps cut and our bodies burnt and eaten. Just last month a crew of Dutchmen, their ship stranded on the Bahama shoals, was devoured by cannibals. Last year six merchants from Bristol were put to death in the next town of Jece as Nickaleer. Eleven Indian places stood between here and St Augustine.

What Francisco Villareal spoke next I will never forget, though I swore never to share its wonder. Our surest defence was to hasten with all speed not over land but by water with him back to Myaamiaki and there offer Savarna up to the lord of the circle. In this desperate instance, and my woman being native herself, Christ would forgive the pagan's faith, the padre promised. The plan was agreed. What more could I do?

The Casseekey had sent his men to shore and soon after they returned with one of the fleet longboats, at the sight of which we rejoiced. At high noon we left the Indian town to set sail in our little vessel, a little leaky but secure. The Casseekey's kindness extended to recovering from the wrecks for our journey what Indians did not care for: butter, some balls of chocolate, a hogshead of sugar, ginger and a keg of wine. From her own kitchen, the chief's wife delivered broiled fish, two parcels of clams, berries, coco plums and sea grapes wrapped in grass. The children had made platted balls stuffed with moss for pillows on which Savarna's fading body lay pale and motionless.

Wreckage coated the shore a mile long. A burnt hull smouldered on the sands. Time was of the essence and to travel as swiftly as we may I set up a small makeshift sail. Father Villareal's native servants, Solomon and Caesar, manned the oars with the good padre. The countenance of the weather was unkind. No sooner had we taken to the sea than all wind ceased. We were left to power through the waves by oar far more slowly than needed.

Thanks to the lost breeze my spirits faded. The air was thick with sand flies and mosquitoes. Eight miles to the north we veered sharply out to sea to flee the flying arrows and designs of a wickedly bent Indian town, whose men rushed into sea shouting Nickaleer, Nickaleer. Further ashore we espied an old man, with staff painted red and white like a barber's pole, dancing in ceremony with six rattles. A second man howled. All around him Indians painted black with red, carrying sheaves of arrows on their backs, bowed back and forth around the pole like furies, stamping on the ground. I fired my dried out gun in the air and the Indians fled like dogs. The noise was terrible to the braves.

My new crew rowed hard for Savarna's soul. We passed league after league of parcels of marshy land separated by creeks and twisting mangrove creeks. Dark tunnels burrowed into the interior, bordered by gnarled trees on spidery roots, reaching the bright light of the beach. All around us was the eternal rustle of shells chewed by surf and sand fleas digging frantically into the receding surge. We travelled all night, muscles aching, flanked by a boggy marsh, and I admired god's greatness in preserving us.

By morning all our hopes lay in dust. The boat had sprung a leak and water was fast wrecking us anew. The Lord, though, had other plans. We had landed and my bare feet burnt on the sands while I weighed our fate. Indians from a nearby town had fastened to the scene. Only by waving my empty gun did the braves run away. It was but a matter of time before the tribe fell on us. Father Villareal cautioned again, these were unfriendly shores.

Our destiny looked sealed when a multitude of Indians, howling like savage dogs, appeared from the north. I loaded my gun with the idea of shooting Savarna to spare her their depravities. Solomon and Caesar were cowering under the overturned boat. The padre was ashore on his knees, holding his cross and praying aloud. Just as the end seemed nigh an explosion ripped through the air. A ball of iron flew over our heads and we turned as one to the sight of a *patache* scouting boat heading directly for us, skippered, as he later introduced himself, by the Commander of the Northern Coast, Luis de Salinas.

The Indians fled for good. De Salinas greeted us as *comerradoes* and quickly appraised the grave scene. He was on his way to Matecumbe to register the Crown's losses from the Tierra Firme fleet, but swore to divert a ship for Myaamiaki. Father Villareal spoke nothing of the lord of the circle, just of urgent medical help needed from the town. De Salinas listened for a while, for this was his first hearing of the great storm and lost fleet. His head sunk low for he knew he would be forced to report the gravest of news to the governor of St Augustine.

Espagne's golden days and the desperate expectation of king's treasure were finished. The commander switched ships to continue to the wrecked shores of Matecumbe. We waved him off. Aboard the departing boat, blacks formerly enslaved to dive on oyster beds jabbered in a distant tongue. Now they would turn their rakes and equipment invented to chase pearls to salve the lost hulls.

The air was full of flies and creeping things, but we were saved. Thirsting after an extreme manner, my kindly brother, amazed at our resurrection from the deep, fed us a meal of chocolatta drink, bread, corn, strung beef and boiled pumpion leaves. Both Savarna and I were clothed in fresh linen shirts.

On the second day at sea since departing the blessed grand Tequesta Casseekey of Matecumbe, the Myaamiaki River of happy countenance appeared. Our *patache* sailed directly into the town. Mud huts gave way to white stone houses plastered with lime. Savarna was carried to an abode where she was undressed, washed and put in a fresh white linen robe, her breath barely heard. Father Villareal handed me a cup of Spanish wine and sent me to the kitchen with Solomon and Caesar to warm our feet. Another new shirt, hat and a pair of woollen stockings arrived with great kindness. My journey was over. Once more I was returned to the denomination of Spain and the Roman faith.

For Savarna her journey was just beginning. A low chanting reached my ears and the Myaamiaki Indians surrounded the house, stamping each foot and pointing greenstone axe heads to the ground. Father Villareal approached, put his hand firmly on my shoulder and told me it was time. I should say farewell to Savarna, whose mortal spirit must now pass over to the Wild People, their gods and fate. I reached for my saddlebag, but the padre held me back. No, he explained, we were not permitted to follow to the sacred soil of the ancestors, where one world ended and another began. Savarna's soul lay in the hands of the Tequesta, a faith of which we knew nothing.

Beyond the windows my wife, wearing a shark's teeth necklace, was carefully set down by the native women on a wooden cart strewn with white lilies. It took all my power not to rush out and embrace her. I had promised to follow her to the end of the world. We had travelled so far hand in hand. Now I had to break the pledge to my eternal love and my oath to her father so far away. I watched the procession wind its way past ordered houses, a friar gawping unhappily outside the worshipping house, towards the ocean. Tears streamed down my cheeks. The hogs and fowl knew nothing of the great miracle about to unfold. We swore never to speak of this day.

Our hard passage hither was complete, wherein God's mercy and wonderful loving kindness delivered and preserved us to this day and time. I hope that I, with all those of us that have been spared hitherto, shall never be forgetful, nor unmindful, of the low estate we were brought forth from. That we may double our diligence in serving you, Lord God, is the breathing and earnest desire of my soul.

Thanks be to God and the many mysteries of which we understand nothing.

Thanks be to the Great Deliver in the Fountain for our encircled mercy.

24

Key West to Deepest Wales

"Well screw me sideways," Nicola ended, blowing the air out of her cheeks and sucking in the cool night air to refresh her lungs. Her head throbbed and eyes felt fuzzy from concentrating so hard in the darkness by the narrow light of her phone torch 'candle'.

A fitful clarity broke over the night-time travellers. The discovery of the diary in *Gollum*'s head was an unimaginable gift. Whether minutes or hours had passed, neither had a clue. Time seemed to have stood still. The focus of translating and absorbing Juan Limbre's diary had dragged Nicola down another wormhole, miles out of her comfort zone. Her dilated eyes darted from side to side, her brain trying to compute the meaning behind a long departed Spanish captain's last words. Nicola found herself petrified by a cast of ghoulish forces. She had come face to face with aliens. Only these aliens lived hundreds of years ago. Whatever was going on was far greater than her small worldly experience. Nicola felt tiny, insignificant.

"Zak, I don't understand. How can a diary be so well preserved for, what, 390 years? Who is Juan Limbre? There are so many loose ends trapped in this time tunnel. What on earth is going on? Is the Barracuda's shipwreck, my Indian mound and this diary somehow tied together? And where the heck do we go from here?"

Zak had closed his eyes and seemed not to be breathing. Nicola allowed him a moment to process the unprocessable. After a few minutes, Zak returned to the land of the living, slowly opened his wide eyes and smiled in the darkness. He took Nicola by the hand, without speaking, walked along the wooden jetty, stopped under the tiniest slither of the moon, took the enigmatic English girl in his arms and kissed her tenderly.

Only then did he reply, "I haven't got a clue. But I know a man who does."

*

Wolfgang Mordechai Pasinski paid little attention to the clock. At Lampeter University in the wilds of northern Wales, a landlocked town hidden among forests and rolling hills midway between Bangor and Carmarthen, MP as his students lovingly called him – Mordechai Pasinski or the Mad Professor, depending on who they were addressing – was married to the past. Wolf was something of an institution. His twenty-four books on subjects as varied as *The Road to Eldorado* (Cambridge University Press, 1968) and *Art of the Golden Age of Colonial Spain, 1492-1625* (Bloomsbury, 2014) were classics whose depth of research and authority could have earned him a teaching or research post in any Oxbridge or Ivy League city.

No amount of cash uprooted MP, who was perfectly content at Lampeter. It had no traffic lights to worry about, no roundabouts to fear crossing, no angry youths walking the streets with knives looking for trouble. His time was preoccupied with teaching, supervising a small elite group of postgrad students and always working on the next book.

A duty of care came with the honour of studying under Wolf who, it was fair to say, was a beautiful contradiction: an incomparable brain, yet a car crash of a social being. He'd never owned a mobile phone. Every day was orchestrated by a chain of walkie-talkies. Professor, time for your 11.00 am lecture on Christopher Columbus's First Voyage to the New World. A knock on the door would remind him when it was time for lunch. Since MP didn't do emails, his students ran his administration and pushed him in the direction of the next action, one foot after the other. Anything remotely sociable, beyond the academic, was a chore.

Why would I want to waste my time at a drinks reception honouring the director of some tech company who'd been given an honorary doctorate and donated a pile of cash to the university? So what if he'd made the pilgrimage all the way from Paris, he'd sincerely query. The pride of watching his students' graduation ceremony was the only cherished exception to social etiquette. The rest of the time he was a white rabbit, rushing around late with his head in the clouds.

Wolf was beloved by both students and faculty. Ever cheerful, he would bumble along arguing to himself, the bottoms of the pyjamas he forgot to take off that morning often sticking out below the ends of his favourite beige corduroy trousers. Once awake, Pasinski's brain whirred robotically, disinterested in mortal distractions. He only believed in sleeping when exhaustion knocked him out. His shock of white hair splayed out across the pages of books and manuscripts was a ritual spectacle in the hallowed Old Library. As soon as he awoke from slumber, Wolf was immediately alert with a shout of "What's that you say, brrrrr." After a vigorous shake of the head, as if a great idea had come to him in his sleep, he was back among the shadows of the past, scribbling frantically to make up for the wasted time dawdling unconscious.

Zak had befriended MP one fine summer seven years earlier, when he signed up for a summer course in Biblical Hebrew. Wolfgang Pasinski was fluent in eight dead languages: Linear B, Minoan, Akkadian, Sumerian, Canaanite, Hebrew, Greek and Latin. In his late teenage years, Zak had spent a couple of blissful summers digging ruins in Israel and figured it was time to learn the lingo.

MP and Zak had greatly enjoyed chatting and debating, the ice broken early in class after the professor asked whether anyone knew what the term *rekev* meant. Zak was the only smart alec able to smugly reply 'train', having often ridden the *rekev* from Tel Aviv to Jerusalem. After recovering from a fit of chortling, Wolf gently pointed out that you would have had a long wait for a locomotive in the era of King Solomon because it hadn't been invented. The *rekev* military chariot certainly would have been a common sight in the tenth-century BC days of the United Kingdom in Israel, the fine-humoured professor gently explained.

In the here and now it was the professor's unparalleled knowledge of the colonial New World that Zak needed to tap into. Chasing the old boy down had taken some serious investigation of its own, tracking and emailing his latest crop of postgrad students and arm-bending them to find a time slot when they could make MP magically appear on Zoom.

The lovers had emailed Wolf a translation of Juan Limbre's diary to get him up to speed and were awaiting a sign of life in limbo. Zak and Nicola spent the two days it took to hunt down Professor Pasinski and await a royal invitation in a surreal mental twilight of fleeting shadows swirling around the ancient black hole they'd been swept into. The loose threads of a shipwreck, Indians, Boca Chica, a wooden treasure box and the ramblings of Skip Raven made little sense.

*

To dull the mind, there was only so much time Nicola and Zak could spend locked up in the Pier House Spa exploring each other. Love bloomed fast and hard. Zak's public show of intimacy had taken Nicola pleasantly aback. Guarded by nature, she was proud her serious man didn't give a hoot whether bystanders thought they were misfits. His affection and pride were in direct disproportion to the eternity it had taken him to pluck up the courage to make a move. In the end he'd trusted his gut feeling. Still, Nicola fretted, even so soon, whether it was too good to be true. Could she trust their feelings or were they just part and parcel of the great adventure they shared, unreal chemical reactions?

To probe how well they might fit outside the Key West bubble, Nicola and Zak both felt the need to unload their fears, dreams and wounds of the heart. If you want to understand the adult, you have to explore the child. The pair sported sharp scars from the pains of youth, some ignored, others making mischief here and now. Could they come to terms with each other's sensitivities? Once their silly fears were let out of the box, Nic and Zak both feared their finely balanced respect would shatter into pathetic contempt.

While they impatiently awaited a sign from Pasinski, Nicola and Zak set off for a long beach walk in the hope of finding the right moment for a serious talk. Key West was in customary high spirits. The archipelago's hundreds of natural coral reefs glistened under the jagged winter sunlight. The bumbling lovers managed to dance around the real purpose of their stroll in the fear of rejection. Peering out towards the Caribbean from the town's Southernmost Point Buoy, marking the end of continental America, brought little bold inspiration. Maybe a less romantic backdrop would cut the ice. Zak steered Miss Medici inland. Of all places, he decided the historic graveyard might unlock his courage.

Down the back streets, Zak pointed out Mac Murphy's house, the cannon still guarding the fisherman's sneaky secrets on the front porch. When one of Key West's more colourful gents rode by on his bike, clad in nothing but a G-string and stovepipe hat, nobody blinked. Nancy Forrester's Secret Garden brought some light relief. For fifteen minutes Nicola played with orphaned and rescued South American macaws and forgot her worries. A particularly friendly blue parrot hopped across her shoulders and perched unceremoniously on her head. Mr Peaches cared not a jot for aristocratic titles.

The minutes passed all too quickly. It was time to confront their own ghosts. Key West's historic cemetery started life as a sanctuary for the dead when a hurricane whipped buried bodies out of older tombs dotting the foreshore near Higgs Beach. Around a hundred thousand souls were now safely buried in the higher-rise terrain. Nicola and Zak slid through the ornate wrought iron gates, kicking the feral chickens squawking around tombstones out of their way.

Wacky tombstones caught the eye. Even in death the

locals had a unique take on life. The graves made a mockery of Florida's reputation as God's waiting room, so called because of the climate's popularity with America's legions of old timers. The conches, as local residents of Key West were known, didn't sit around counting down the hours to their date with destiny. One tombstone paid its respects to Los Martires de Cuba, the fallen who died fighting to free Cuba from Spanish rule in the Ten Years War between 1868 and 1878. Another honoured two hundred and sixty casualties from the USS *Maine* battleship's sinking in Havana harbour during the Cuban War of Independence in February 1898.

The mood wasn't totally solemn. In typical Key West spirit and humour, the self-appointed General Abe Sawyer – a forty-inch-tall little person born in 1862 – made sure he was laid to rest with dignity in a full-size man's grave. By the time Nic and Zak weaved through the corridors of death, the lover's sides ached from laughter. B.P. Pearl Roberts, the local hypochondriac, had the memory 'I Told You I was Sick' engraved on his tombstone. Other notable one-liners read 'Jesus Christ, These People Are Horrible' and 'So Long and Thanks for All The Fish'.

The fate of Elena Milagro de Hoyos, a beautiful young Cuban-American woman, turned out to be the weirdest story of all. When Elena was diagnosed with tuberculosis in 1931, aged just twenty-one, a radiology technician at the US Marine Hospital fell in love with his patient. Carl Tanzler was a German immigrant who'd already abandoned his wife and two daughters hundreds of miles north in the Floridian town of Zephyrhills. Free from the burden of responsibility, the fantasist reinvented himself in Key West as Count Carl Von Cosel. He claimed to hold nine university degrees and once to have served as a submarine captain.

The count convinced Elena's family his special x-ray technology and tonics he'd concocted could cure her. Under his unhinged care the patient was showered with jewellery, clothes and an offer of marriage. No matter the inconvenience both Von Cosel and Elena were already legally wed. The inevitable came to pass and poor Elena succumbed to her disease. The count's forlorn visits to the lavish mausoleum he built her in Key West's cemetery didn't cure his broken heart. In the end the madman dug her up and rebuilt her rotting body with silk padding and mortician's wax, oils and chemicals. Finally, the count and dead bride could be together.

The insane German lived and slept with his secret wife for seven years before one breakfast morning a newspaper delivery boy spotted and lifted the lid on one of America's most grisly horror stories. The count was arrested but amazingly got away scot-free. The crime was so bizarre and the case so hard to build that the statute of limitations passed before it made it to court. Poor Elena was reburied in the cemetery in an unmarked grave to stop tampering hands from disturbing her ever again.

Suitably freaked out by Key West outweirding itself, Nicola and Zak sat down, hand in hand, on a patch of grass under a palm tree soaring into the blue sky. A light wind rustled through the leaves' spindly fingers. Lazy iguanas sunning on sun-kissed tombstones eavesdropped on the lover's confessions. It was time to come clean. After reading all about the shenanigans of Elena and the count, the unspoken felt far less troublesome. Nothing they could say could be worse than a dose of necrophilia. Both started speaking at the same time. Zak ended up holding the short straw.

Old-school manners bred in a retarded boys-only public school and a fast-firing brain stripped of a shred of arrogance, may have been exactly what attracted Nicola to Zak, but were the same qualities that pained him. The polite to a fault Oxford scholar was a contradiction. What you saw was not what you got. The outer stone-faced fortifications looked like they could withstand the mightiest attack. On the inside, insecurity was easily breached. Castle Zak was a crumbling ruin of emotional baggage.

At school just one passion got Zak's juices flowing, sport. An average rugby flanker and too small to make it in basketball, he made up for his physical limits by giving one hundred and twenty per cent. Zak could almost power lift his body weight aged fourteen. A powerful engine and high pain threshold kept him in cross-country running races when most kids flagged. On the water his rowing stroke, relentlessly powerful for a sub-six-foot boy among giants, drove him to a medal in the coxless four at Henley.

Zak passed his A Levels by the skin of his teeth, cramming at the eleventh hour under the shade of a dripping boat upturned on trestles at the national rowing championships in Nottingham. Average grades left slim pickings other than to grab with both hands an offer to study marine biology in the tiny town of Lampeter, the most rural outpost of the University of Wales. Zak didn't care. Life in the here and now was far too thrilling to worry about what lay around the bend.

A spiritual and intellectual awakening began that summer, between Zak's GCSE's and A Levels, when his mother dropped a who do you think you are bombshell on her son's lap. Over Christmas dinner, Zak innocently asked, as he annoyingly did year after year, why his family had no roots, no history, no stories of madcap great-uncles or wartime heroes.

Something hidden away for decades in Clara Fitzgrove's fiercely protective psyche snapped. Her loyal husband Freddy nodded. The time had come. Clara clattered out of the dining room to return a minute later cradling a Japanese lacquered black chest, cream painted flowers on its cover, which she ceremoniously handed over to her son with a nervous smile.

Zak stopped staring at the grass covering centuries of Key West's fallen and peered up at Nicola's kind eyes. Secrets were about to be released for the first time. From the retreat of his childhood bedroom, pealing floral purple Laura Ashley wallpaper and the ghosts of failed girlfriends rattling around his narrow window overlooking the Yorkshire Dales, from nowhere he learnt a long-buried warts-and-all family truth that day. The bolt out of the blue shocked Zak to the core.

From the recesses of the dusty Japanese chest emerged photos of Austro-Habsburg soldiers with brush moustaches and icy smiles taken before they went to some war or other. The likenesses of unknown family had been captured at the close of the nineteenth century in the Pale of deepest Poland, now annexed to southern Ukraine. Next came postcards written from a place called

Modling. Google told Zak that Modling was a small town on the outskirts of the Vienna woods. In this favoured playground, emperors kept summer lodges, screened from prying eyes, high up in the mountains ringed with crystal clear Alpine air. Ludwig van Beethoven composed the Mödlinger Tänze, the Dances of Modling, from an unspectacular house on Fisherman Street in 1820. So, this is where my people came from Zak realised for the first time in his short existence.

Wonderment was tinged with confusion. Zak had always been led to believe he came from fine old British stock. Singing Christian psalms every morning, swimming in the freezing public school pool to build character and working hard and playing hard in the waning years of Tom Brown's school days were designed to mould Zak into an English gent. Why had he been put through an education system that rewarded failure with the whack of a slipper or cane and been robbed of his genealogy he battled to understand. A red mist had risen.

From the bottom of the lacquered box, Zak next took out photos of Vienna in 1938, so smudged pencil letters on the back said. There was his gay-looking grandmother strolling in furs down the Kärntner Strasse without a care in the world. The next torn-edged black-and-white scene made his blood freeze. Zak stopped breathing and went sheet white. From every window and column of a classical looking palace or town hall in Vienna hung flags of swastikas and the demented face of Adolf Hitler.

Zak raced to the toilet and threw up his Christmas dinner. The secret was out of the box. His mother's family were paid up members of the Nazi party. Christ, what does that make me? Zak shook with baffled rage and tore down the stairs.

Clara and Freddy Fitzgrove had not expected the full barrel friendly fire from their beloved son on what they always cherished as a special family day. They let Zak empty the tank and get pent-up feelings off his chest. The gesticulating finger, hostile accusations and swearing burnt out. Clara popped on the kettle, ladled Zak a large dollop of fig pudding coated with her special brandy cream and sat him down on the sofa.

Freddy kept to himself, pouring whisky down his throat. This was his wife's mess. He'd always warned her the boy had every right to know his roots. Accusations turned to disbelief when the truth tumbled out. No, his grandparents weren't Nazis. Quite the opposite. They had been left with no option but to flee Vienna when Hitler marched into the city in January 1938. Zak's grandparents ran, leaving almost all their possessions, a shop and respected law firm, behind. The rest of the relatives were rounded up like cattle and sent to Dachau. Nobody ever saw them again. Clara pleaded she knew she'd done wrong but for the right reasons. There was nothing sinister to hide other than decades of pain. All she was desperate to do was protect Zak from the demons that chased her grandmother and herself every time they closed their eyes.

Zak instinctively knew this version of the truth was no lie. Is that why I constantly dreamt of being chased by Nazis as a kid, he asked his thunderstruck mother. Clara's own mother never spoke of Hitler or the Holocaust after fleeing to England. Instead, she worked ferociously to become a quintessential British citizen. This was the origin of Zak's own drive. No words of outlawed Yiddish would be spoken outside the new immigrants' kitchen. The family name was modernised from the too obviously Semitic Friedberg to the upstanding Fitzgrove. Clara knew no better other than to follow her mother's example. By shutting out the past she prayed Zak would be spared the emotional disconnect, constant fear of pending doom and sense of otherness that dogged her youth. Clara spent her childhood dreams hunted relentlessly by Nazis and foam-frothing attack dogs.

Mother and son had talked tenderly deep into the night, long after Freddy nodded off under a happy haze of scotch. The Fitzgroves agreed the tentacles of the past and generations of guilt can't just be outrun. What was it Carl Jung said, "history is not contained in thick books but lives in our very blood." Neither Clara nor her beloved grandmother knew how the past chases the present through silent DNA.

Zak's parents had sweated to sweep history under a happy

middle-class carpet on the British Isles to protect their only son from echoes of brutality and genocide. Why let the horrors of World War II, a relentless wrecking ball, cascade down the decades? What's done is done. By locking the genie in the bottle, the family had unintentionally created a dark heirloom of denial. And the family guilt did exactly what nobody intended. It lived on like drifting hydrogen cyanide gas, silently creeping down from the first to third generation to wreak havoc that Christmas day.

Oddly Zak felt relieved by the festive revelations, he told Nicola. His sensitive emotional compass finally made sense. This must be why he never fitted in, always felt awkward, why he'd always stood out from his pals, who called him a dark horse behind his back. The Fitzgroves forgave each other that day and buried their ghosts. The thrilling anticipation of the air ticket Freddy rustled up to send young Isak to Israel to learn about his roots before his A Level year made up for the emotional distress. A new course in life's journey was set.

At first Zak expected to hate a Holy Land full of heavy religion and the Bible. He didn't do God. Nobody had prepped him about the fun of secular Israel, a completely different land. The scorching sun caressing his back the instant he walked down the plane steps at Ben Gurion airport, the fresh Mediterranean salads, shawarma lamb kebabs and blend of wild nature and ruins were a heady sensation. The days raced by. Zak fell in love with the country and a young kibbutz girl. True happiness paid its respects for the very first time.

The next year he returned to Israel and young love. The plan was to spend his gap year before university in Wales volunteering on an excavation on the coast of Dor, where the prehistoric Carmel Mountains roll down to King Solomon's ancient port city. Thanks to a Lampeter professor, one Wolfgang Pasinski, eight delicious months lay ahead to explore biblical ruins and the girl he adored. The pressures of university next year felt a lifetime away.

By the time Zak headed up to deepest Wales, a year's living under his belt, the boy was hungry to learn. Zak approached college with the same focus he'd tackled sport at school. Dusty books replaced basketball playbooks. From marine biology he'd branched out into biblical history and dipped into underwater archaeology. Professor Pasinski turned out to be a generous mentor who fed Zak's hunger by signing off hundreds of inter-library loan books and journals. "Know yourself, young man," he'd whisper every time the pair crossed paths in the halls and lawns.

From Lampeter Zak stepped from the sublime backwater where he'd thrived on being rather big for his boots in a tiny pond to the ridiculous frontline of academia, Oxford. Peering heavenward at the dreaming spires, the old impish genies resurfaced, reminding him he was an inadequate fraud. In Oxford Zak was lost again, an ant who couldn't imagine competing with his ivory tower peers. How could he? Everyone seemed to have been educated at Eton or Roedean. Equipped with daddy's credit card, the entitled were the prime ministers, bank presidents and movers and shakers of the future. Zak wasn't cut from the same cloth.

In and out of Oxford with his doctorate in a record three years for his class, Zak was as shocked as anyone to be handed a fellowship fresh out of studies at the city's new Sea Watch Institute. The chip on his shoulder made him publish fast and furiously. Within three years his name was revered. The conference speaking offers flooded in. All the while Zak wondered where stability would come from. He was given college dining privileges and a complementary flat down the unfashionable Iffley Road. Outsiders looked on impressed.

Zak didn't feel like a winner. His research salary left just enough spare cash to cover his gym membership on the site where Sir Roger Bannister ran the first sub-four-minute mile and to see a play once every three months. That was about it. He'd inherited an old white VW Polo from his grandmother, adequate for running around town but too battered to entertain picking up a date. And so, he didn't date. All his spare time was spent plunged into the academic game of writing papers.

Privilege had not bought security, emotional or material, in any shape or form. His self-esteem dropped even lower when his uncle told him only seven people read most academic journals. And one of those was probably his mother. When Zak headed for America's East Coast and a life-changing rendezvous with Nicola Medici, he was deeply dissatisfied. His heart pulled him towards the sea, his head towards a healthier bank balance.

Down the years Nicola had witnessed every type of human existence. From social salons in Chelsea to family estates in Umbria and Hampshire, she'd learnt first-hand better than anyone: money wasn't the cause of emotional riches or fulfilment. Weren't father's gardeners, rising with the seasons, among the happiest and kindest of men she'd met?

Nicola reckoned Zak was far too serious and needed to let his hair down. She identified his problems as pretty lightweight. She'd help him stop feeling lonely, break out of his negative mind set, support his bright ideas for a sustainable future. Zak was no fraud. There was no need for him to fear rejection or be petrified of losing everything. To Nic he was the real deal who just wanted to be respected, to be loved. Before Zak had finished his chest beating, she'd already decided to flutter her angel wings, sprinkling fortune over his furrowed brow.

If the Brits from different sides of the tracks shared anything, it was a confused soul and identity crisis. Where Zak was an over-achiever, Nicola believed she was not just an underachiever but a major disappointment to parents for whom kin was the be all and end all. Sprawling under the arrowed shade of a palm tree in Key West's cemetery, Nicola was a bag of nerves. She'd never opened up her troubled heart to an outsider. The very idea was daunting. The cemetery was pretty deserted late in the afternoon. Nosy chickens grubbing around Zak's boots, begging for any morsels, brought a welcome brief distraction before the inevitable. Nic unburdened her own soul.

Nicola Medici had impossibly big boots to fill. And few families came with a more impressive price tag and big hitter reputation than the Medicis, the first family of the Italian Renaissance. The Medicis were the Rothschilds, Kardashians and

Kennedys of Europe rolled into one between the fourteenth and sixteenth centuries, trail blazing bankers and patrons of the arts with bottomless pockets. The Dukes and Duchesses of Tuscany were the front-page rock stars of the Enlightenment.

Nicola grew up breastfed on tales of her descendants' star quality. From as young as she could remember, mother dearest took every opportunity to remind her of her privilege. Our family literally sculpted the modern world, Nicola. They were the first luminaries to bring culture, fine arts and science to the great unwashed. Are you listening, dear? The Medici name is the gold standard for guiding the mob. We dragged Europe out of the Dark Ages into the light. The Medicis didn't live through the Enlightenment, we created it. Always use your wealth to help the community and State prosper. Be charitable. Nicola, wake up and take your seat at the high table of La Familia. What's wrong with you?

Lady Amelia wasn't wrong. The Medicis at first made a decent living rearing worms, weaving silk and trading with Italy's high and mighty. A pleasant life turned into mind-boggling riches in 1397 when the textile merchants opened the Banco dei Medici. This institution introduced the use of cheques to the West and invented modern banking. Within decades the venture mushroomed into Europe's biggest bank. In the hands of the family visionary, Giovanni, the Medicis became the wealthiest and most influential family on the continent, propping up a succession of kings and popes.

Nicola's kin spent its stash smartly and reaped the rewards. In thanks for sponsoring Galileo's invention of the telescope, the scientist named the first planets spotted through it the Medici stars before moving on to map the Milky Way. Under Medici patronage, Leonardo da Vinci became the world's first known vegetarian. Machiavelli dedicated *The Prince*, the model playbook for tyrants, to Lorenzo II.

Locked away in his studio in the Pitti Palace, the alchemist Francesco I found a way to fuse rock crystals and copy the translucent secrets of luxurious Chinese porcelain. When Cosimo

I, the first Grand Duke of Tuscany, hired the Florentine chef Bernardo Buontalenti to put on a banquet for Spanish VIPs in 1565, he risked his master's displeasure by trying out a sickly new dessert blending eggnog, milk and fruit. It went down a storm. Italy's and the world's love affair with *gelato*, ice cream, was born. Michelangelo, Botticelli and Benvenuto Cellini all bowed, scraped and helped forge civilisation with Medici cash.

The female Medicis were equally awesome. Catherine, the Serpent Queen, is celebrated as the mother of the modern high-heel shoe. A secret signature perfume she blended was later borrowed by Coco Chanel and re-branded as Chanel No. 5. It was the foresight and generosity of Anna Maria Luisa, the last in the direct dynastic line, that left all the Medici's property, lock, stock, barrel and billion-dollar artworks, to the State in 1734. In this inspiring age, Florence became the West's intellectual comet.

Year after year the weight of legacy weighed cripplingly on Nicola's shoulders. She hadn't asked for heavy social obligations and was still figuring out if they were a blessing or a curse. Not only did she have nothing like the spending power of the Grand Duke and Duchesses, she'd realised her mother's insistent claims to lineage were dubious, to say the least. The flashiest Medici line descended from Lorenzo the Magnificent in the far off haze of the twelfth century. Lady Amelia would never admit it, but she came from the poor side of the family, less minted stock that traced its descent from John of the Black Bands in 1498. Still, a Medici is a Medici she shrugged insistently.

Lady Amelia moved to London broke and no lady but with an impeccable name, claiming DNA with the present day's fifteenth Prince of Ottajano. Undeterred by her skewered fortunes, she started climbing the social ladder from salon to salon, sharing hilarious stories, shamelessly name dropping and enchanting audiences. Marriage to her eventual saviour and long hen-pecked husband, the Midas-blessed economist Lord Henry Cranberry, finally kept Amelia in the sparkling style to which she felt she was entitled. The technical inconvenience of marrying out and no longer bearing the Medici name was neatly hurdled by a genealogical sleight of hand. Lady Amelia did what any protector of a blue-chip brand would do. She kept her surname and grafted it to Nicola's birth certificate by deed poll. She insisted she was securing her daughter's future. Lord Henry shrugged. He wasn't immune to snobbery.

Not only did Nicola feel like a pretender to the throne, she squirmed at her family's massaged castle in the air. If only the sycophantic Hooray Henrys orbiting around her with hopes of connections, marriage proposals or financial backing knew she was fake aristocracy. Smiles would fast turn to sneers. Her mother's claim to Medicidom might have hinged on nothing more cringe-worthy than a dangerous liaison between a randy duchess and a stable boy or a duke's bored afternoon rampaging through his palace kitchen chasing a hot kitchen maid. Nobody could say for sure.

On the back of this uncertain history, Nicola told Zak that liberating day in Key West how she grew up biting her lip. Her doting parents meant the very best. The family country manor house in Beaulieu, set in the prehistoric charm of the New Forest, was padded with shelves of histories about her ancestors' antics. The more the cynical girl read, the less like her scarred ancestors she wanted to live her life. She needed to follow her own path, make her own mistakes.

The ancestral phobia included her physical well-being. The family memoirs and artistic masterpieces of her forebears hung in the world's great museums left behind a picture of refined wealth, health and privilege. Peering between the lines of centuries-old post-mortem reports and horrifying pathologies reconstructed by the University of Pisa, the University of Florence and the Superintendence for Florentine Museums unshackled a shocking alter reality. The Medici DNA was shot to pieces. Nicola desperately prayed time had bred all these defects out of her cells.

For years in her late teenage years and twenties, Nicola peered into mirrors, fearful she might grow the notoriously curved Medici chin introduced by the Habsburg side of the family. Concerned by the hint of any stray curve, she'd forcefully push her chin down to force it to behave. Please, God, spare me from the curse of Medici syndrome, she'd whisper, staring into the looking glass.

Nicola had devoured, with alarm, a scientific report showcasing six generations of suffering seen in forty-nine burials dug up in the Medici Grand Duke tombs in the icy bowels of Florence's Basilica of San Lorenzo. Francesco I de Medici, the second Grand Duke of Tuscany from 1541, was the worst of the lot. An unflattering picture of his opened tomb, painted by Giuseppe Moricci in 1857, exposed a freak show. The duke suffered from a facial droop, claw-hand and clubfoot. All this delightful anatomy was god's revenge for Francesco picking up a dose of syphilis on a jaunt to Rome at the age of twenty. A stroke, early onset baldness and cerebral palsy followed. It was hardly surprising the tormented duke was an emotional catastrophe with an evil temper who killed his stableman for accidentally bumping into him. Little wonder Francesco retreated from high society into his lab in the bowels of his sumptuous Palazzo Vecchio in Florence to immerse himself in the dark arts of alchemy.

Francesco turned out to be the edge of the horrors. The Grand Duchess Giovanna d'Austria, the first wife of Francesco I, was equally cursed from 1548. After surviving six horrendous births, she grew a hunchback. Deep religious faith did little to help. The Contessina de Bardi dei Conti di Vieri, a pillar of support for her husband Cosimo il Vecchio, went mad itching from scabies.

Starting with Piero the Gouty in 1416, Cosimo I, Ferdinand I and other relatives had to endure endless pain brought about by gout, making them immobile and obese. The disease of kings was the result of a poor diet. The Italian Renaissance aristocracy dined on wine and meat, only occasionally eggs, cheese and fish and never touched vegetables and fruit.

Things turned out so badly for Carlo, the younger son of Ferdinando I, who became a cardinal in 1615, that from the age of twenty-four he suffered years of terrible gout and eventually cervical tuberculosis of the spine from having to walk sideways from the pain. When the family's cursed hunchback started to turn up, his father called in the greatest physician of the age, Girolamo di Fabrizio d'Acquapendente from the University of Padua, to cure his son.

The *professore* committed to his diary how he used "an iron tool pushing and bringing the vertebrae in opposite position… to this purpose I have prepared a hauberk, or light body armour in iron, with particular screws pushing the vertebrae which are out of place, gradually restoring them to their original position." The cardinal's unearthed butchered skeleton showed the tell-tale painful signs of how the physician battled to fuse his left elbow, wrists, fingers, knees and metatarsal bones. The man of god ended up a Frankenstein's monster.

By the age of twenty Nicola Medici had stopped dating, couldn't bear the thought of babies, prolonging the Medici line, and ate spinach and carrots religiously. By the time she set off to escape a grey London in search of her own Vitamin D, her eyes wide open to what happiness doesn't look like, she knew wealth can't buy good health. She couldn't escape the weight of the family name, but she wanted to forge her own path and live for today, not past glory.

Nicola and Zak were sensible souls who didn't believe in destiny. Life was random. You had to create your own luck. What the lovers did know from their first kiss was that they'd lucked out. Neither would risk bursting the recently born bubble of love by airing the feeling they were soul mates. They were alike and dissimilar.

The sun set. There would be no psychological autopsy. Nicola and Isak didn't need to be on Sunset Key to grasp the scale of their luck. Somehow, thousands of miles from home, they'd found each other. On the old isle their stars would never have crossed. There would be no babbling, no judging. The afternoon's unravelled truths didn't scare either of them off. Quite the opposite. Unburdened, intimacy bound them closer. It was time to depart the place of death and start celebrating life. To start living a shared future. The shadows of personal pain were left behind among the tombstones.

25

Key West to Deepest Wales

Finally, the honour of a thirty-minute meeting with Professor Wolf Pasinski was graciously agreed to. On a chilly mid-December evening from Nic's room in the Pier House Spa, Zoom whirred to connect across the Atlantic to deepest Wales.

A girl wearing a baggy striped brown and green mohair jumper, with jet black hair streaked purple, 1970s-style NHS glasses and the scars of teenage acne, called Frederica – call me Fred, she snapped – signed into Zoom before telling the professor she'd be outside if needed and slamming the door. Wolf shuddered, sighed, ran his hand through his shock of deranged hair on seeing Nicola and, with an "Ave Isak," offered an open palm greeting and toothy sideways grin.

"Shalom Chaver," hello friend, Zak responded in Hebrew.

"Pós eísai?" how are you, MP enquired in Greek.

Fast running out of tongues, the young disciple threw his head back and laughed. "You win, not too shabby, professor, and how are you, more to the point?"

To Wolf, such a query could have nothing to do with his seventy-six-year-old mortal body or the osteoporosis, diabetes, cataract operations, double hernia and lack of appetite he'd suffered since they last spoke. It could only concern his mental well-being.

"Well now, young Zak," Wolf began, "I'm just updating the fourth edition of *Artefacts of the Spanish Colonies of Florida and Latin America*, goes down the wire to press next month. Otherwise, I'm taking a break from the New World to write up an unbelievable find in Israel's southern bible belt. You won't believe it. The Israelis have done it again. A Bedouin watering his flock deep in the Negev desert, far from the madding crowd, lit his hashish pipe and the next thing he knew his goats vanished."

"After the ill effects of some particularly strong herbs wore off – did you know Al-Qaeda were peddling drugs in the northwest Sinai peninsula? – the Bedouin scratched his stubbly chin and started roaming the hills. And there were the little goatees lying in a hole six feet down. The sand had caved in, revealing a wall painted with other-worldly human figures and clay jars propped up against it, pristine as the day they were abandoned."

"The sneaky shepherd made a fatal error, schlepping one of the jars back to Jerusalem, where he tried to sell it to the Shapira Galleries on the Via Dolorosa. So, next thing you know, I have old boy Avner on the blower asking me to run an eye over what he was certain was a forgery. Dear young Frederica got the photo inter-netted down the thingy line – it took less than a day, can you believe it? – and the likes of this treasure man has never seen."

Nicola squeezed Zak's thigh, the pair struggling to suppress their giggles. Clearly Wolfgang Pasinski didn't understand the idea of long story short. Anyway, the old boy was good value.

"The pot was a typical storage jar from the Early Iron Age IIB, if I had to guess, potted in the reign of King Jehoash II around 780 BC. But so what? More to the point, there, gloriously painted red on the side of the jar and frozen in time, was the most influential art man produced before the Enlightenment. Now you remember my paper on 'Idols of the People' delivered to the Royal Academy in 1964 – oh London, where art thou now?"

Zak indeed remembered reading the seminal paper that saw Wolf banned from Israel for five years after a front-page article in the *Jerusalem Post* entitled 'God Is Dead' quoted the professor's belief that the very roots of Judaism, monotheism, worship of the one God Yahweh in one place, Jerusalem, was fake biblical news.

Wolf had studied thousands of clay figurines of the old pagan Canaanite gods for his PhD, dug up across first-millennium BC Israel. With no political axe to grind, his only crime had been pointing out that for three centuries after King Solomon supposedly invented God in the tenth century, the archaeological proof showed that the real men and women on the street were polytheists. They worshipped a pantheon of old and new gods – El, Baal, Yahweh, Asherah. The science was crystal clear. The good folk of a tolerant Israel were more like you and me than the black hat brigade of orthodox Jews who jealously guard the young nation's religious compass today.

Zak nodded enthusiastically and tried desperately not to collapse at the sound of Nicola bent double laughing hysterically in the bathroom.

The professor went on to describe the painting on the pot of three gods standing legs akimbo side by side under Hebrew inscriptions labelling them as Baal, Yahweh and Asherah.

"You see, I hate to say it but I was right all along. There can now be no doubt. Israel was a land of divine tolerance down to at least the early sixth century BCE. You could worship whoever and whatever you wanted from the old Canaanite gods to the wind in the trees or the violent new boy in town, Yahweh the strongman. After my tipoff, the Israel Antiquities Authority marched south and excavated the Bedouin's goat hole in the ground, now known as Kuntillet Ajrud, the Hill of the Solitary Well."

"The ruin turned out to be a kind of desert motel for camel caravans carrying luxuries from the Red Sea to Gaza on the Mediterranean. The finds beggar belief – everything from pots to priests' robes, hair, human skulls and stores of pomegranates preserved in the dry air of the wilderness. A miracle to behold. The government has asked me to lead the research. All very hush hush, you know. Terribly important and all that. How could I say no after they made me a Fellow of the Israel Academy of Sciences in appreciation? Imagine that. After all those years of censorship and exile. That's the bare bones of the story, anyway. Now, back to the lands of Columbus."

The professor snapped back out of his reverie to see a refreshed Nicola beaming at him. "And who is this delightful young lady," he finally asked once his 'brief' digression ended.

Before Zak could introduce his belle, Nic dived straight in.

"Magister, salvete ex novo mundo. Nicolai Medici vocant me. Et venerit de terra Londinensi, historiae veritatem quaerere. Tu mihi spes Isak. Magister potes adiuva nos?" ("Teacher, greetings from the new world. They call me Nicola. I come from the land of London, in search of history and truth. Isak tells me you are our only hope. Can you help us teacher?").

"Ho ho," Wolf beamed. "Brains as well as beauty, I see. The gods have blessed you with abundance, the one they call Nicola. The pleasure is all mine. Now, to business. Tik tok."

With that the professor opened a dog-eared brown leather folder and carefully laid out Nicola's translation of Juan Limbre's diary alongside photos of the journal, the Indian mound of Boca Chica and the finds she'd recovered from its ruins. Wolf held a typed sheet of paper up to the screen as if the friends would be able to easily scan and read its memorized contents.

"It seems to me that your enigmatic discovery breaks down into five main questions, if I may be so bold:

1. Is the diary a forgery or real?
2. Who was Juan Limbre?
3. Did Limbre and Savarna survive?
4. What's the connection between Juan Limbre and Nicola's Indian mound hinted at by the initials JL cut into the wooden box?
5. Where do you go from here?

26

Down the Line, Lampeter to Key West

"To begin, questions one and two are intertwined," Wolfgang Pasinski opened. "This is elementary maritime history. Huguette and Pierre Chaunu's s masterpiece, *Séville et l'Atlantique, 1504-1650*, has your man Limbre commanding his own ship, originally built in Lisbon by the way, from the port of Seville to Nueva Cordoba or Venezuela to modern landlubbers. After going rogue to the Pearl Coast in search of shiny pearls, he was on his way to rendezvous with the Mainland Fleet of Tierra Firme in Havana. No doubt in my mind, your colleagues at Keys Exploration have discovered one of only two merchant ships that sank in deep seas off the Florida Keys, either the *Nuestra Señora de la Merced* or the *Nuestra Señora de la Rosario*. I see no reason to question Kurt Barracuda. Smooth-tongued he may be, but his researchers are top drawer."

"While I haven't had the chance to examine by hand the alleged diary of Juan Limbre and subject it to a WPPT analysis – the Wolf Pasinski Patina Test, otherwise known as rubbing my thumb over the leather! – the language is spot on for seventeenth-century Spain. And by the way, excellent translation, young lady. My corrections have been inter-mailed to you as file 'Wolf 1'. And with no hesitation, I declare the diary authentic. How in the world it ended up in your grasp I'd love to know. A conversation for another time, perhaps over hot chocolate with lashings of cream, dear friends."

Nic smiled appreciatively, bowed her head slightly in recognition of a greater mind and, on refreshing her gold

Macbook Air laptop, watched eight emails pop up in quick succession from an unknown address, wolfman@theshadow.co.uk. One of his students had a wacky sense of humour.

"As for questions three and four, again they interrelate, and this is where things get knotty. In fact, I'd go so far as to say your sleuthing, unbeknown, may have cracked one of ancient Florida's oldest riddles. I do not say this lightly." The professor paused, lent forward so his nose was almost touching the screen and, beaming to himself, added, "The secret to ever-lasting life."

Nicola sniggered nervously, wondering if the professor had lost the plot. There was a line to what nuttiness her classically trained mind could take. Now she felt well over the weird line. Zak, however, knew the professor never joked about ancient history and expected to have his own limited brains blown.

"Now then, we left poor Savarna, by the way a very ancient native American name meaning Daughter of the Ocean, in bad shape, seemingly beyond saving. Where was she going and why was Limbre forbidden from accompanying her? The poor man must have been beside himself with dread."

"The diary's text gives just enough morsels to reach a very grand theory. You'll like this." The professor's eyes narrowed and he began a speech at an alarming rate of fire.

"Limbre's diary refers in several places to a need to carry Savarna to the 'Lord of the Circle', while the very final sentence ends, 'Thanks be to the Great Deliver in the Fountain of our encircled mercies'. Sounds like Spanish Catholic waffle, right? Wrong, quite wrong. Now stay with me. As you've probably deduced, five hundred years ago Miami was the spiritual hometown of the Tequesta people, the same tribe the shipwrecked victims, Juan and Savarna, ran into near modern Key West in the year 1622."

"The heart of Tequesta religious life was a thirty-nine-foot-wide circle where the Miami River empties into the sea at Brickell Point. It was named after William Brickell, who founded Miami in the 1870s. There is precious little that can be called ancient in the high-rise city these days. Back in 1961, when an unlucky local property tycoon invested in a new luxury condominium development, the builders cut into a hard mass of conch shells and goodies – shark's teeth, stingray spines, barracuda and whelk bones. At this very spot the ancients used to feast hundreds of years before Brickell transformed the town's fortunes."

"Quite a lot of stuff was looted from what's known as the Miami Circle before a mysterious group called Justice For Tequesta filed an injunction against further works. The descendants won the day and the developer was found dead in his construction hut, his hair shaved as if he'd been scalped. The autopsy found he suffocated on gold dust poured down his throat. A very grisly *coup de grâce*. The police looked into the horror pretty thoroughly, only to conclude someone was stitching up Justice For Tequesta. The nature of the murder seemed to them a ridiculously staged crime. The investigation was dropped. The whole project had become a political time bomb anyway. In a matter of days, enough donations flowed in for State of Florida Preservation to force the landowner to sell the plot for $26.7 million, a fraction of its worth once developed. The power of the past when it becomes front-page news."

"And there the circle still sits or rather its meagre remains. In its twenty-four semi-rectangular holes, wooden posts once rose up between the sea and sky as early as 750 BC. If you want to understand what these holy spaces looked like in the seventeenth century, please open your e-letter Wolf 2."

Zak followed his instructions and a scene of Indians dancing wildly around posts with carved faces, arranged in a circle, popped open. Nicola recognized the painted handiwork of Theodore de Bry, a familiar friend from her own research delving into all things Tequesta.

"For these reasons, I conclude that it was to the Miami Circle that dear Savarna was carried in 1622," the professor summed up. "The precise rites the Tequesta performed there will forever remain a lost secret, but how they cured her? Well I don't expect you'll believe my reasoning. Please humour an old man."

Wolf Pasinski went on to explain how numerous myths have

survived the ages from Dracula and the Amazons to stories of werewolves, sirens, the philosopher's stone and the Holy Grail. All of these myths are rooted in a seed of truth. The question is always how big or small is that seed. Florida's greatest myth, older than literature itself, was the secret of the fountain of youth, a magical spring with youth-restoring powers.

Imagine if an explorer discovered the answer to eternal life. It would bring riches and life-affirming change beyond the wildest imagination. The world's finest minds scoured the planet for the secret. Alexander the Great sailed to India searching for the waters. Others believed it was hidden in the Persian Gulf, rising forth from paradise. Sir John Mandeville reckoned in the fourteenth century that he'd uncovered the source at the foot of a mountain in India where there stood "a fair and great well that has odour and saviour of all spices. And whoever drinks three times, fasting on the water from that well, he is healed of all manner of sickness. Some men call it the Well of Youth."

Since the earliest days of Spanish colonisation in Florida, rumours swirled about a well of eternal life in the Americas. In 1516 the historian Peter Martyr wrote to Pope Leo X in Rome, mentioning an island discovered by the explorer Juan Diaz de Solis, where old men recovered their virility and fertility after bathing.

Then in 1535 a nugget of information in the historian Gonzalo Fernandez de Oviedo's *Historia General y Natural de las Indias* reported the fable of a fountain tracked down by the Spanish conquistador turned explorer Juan Ponce de León that made old men young. Thanks to another chronicle, the *Memoria* of Hernando de Escalante Fontaneda, learned society first heard in 1575 about Ponce de León travelling to Florida to chase down rumours he picked up about a miraculous stream:

> Juan Ponce de León, giving heed to the tale of the Indians of Cuba and Santo Domingo, went to Florida in search of the River Jordan… that he might earn greater fame than he already possessed and that he may close

> his life… or if not for these objects then that he might become young from bathing in such a stream… the kings and caciques of Florida knew to the east this river which did such good work, even to the turning of aged men and women back to their youth.

By the time Luigi Cornaro wrote his classic rocking-chair anthem for the slow movement in 1560, *The Art of Living Long*, one of the most influential books of the Renaissance, he was convinced by the life-giving waters. The Venetian nobleman reported how "individuals were not destined to die at 60 or 70, but with care and good constitution, could live extremely long lives" by visiting the fountain of youth and controlling the vital energy of the body through good nutrition and exercise.

And so the last days of Ponce de León spawned a national legend. The French-born philosopher Henry Harisse was similarly persuaded in his *Discovery of North America* of 1892 that the Spanish explorer "went from his native island near the country of Florida to drink of the desired fountain, as our countrymen do from Rome or Naples to the Puteolane baths for the recovery of their health. He went and stayed and having well drunk and washed himself for many days, with the appointed remedies by those who kept the bath, he is reported to have brought home a manly strength, and to have used all manly exercises, and that he married again, and begat children." The conquistador was forty-seven years old in an age when most people met their maker aged thirty-five.

Zak immediately understood where the professor was going. His hyper-rational brain didn't buy it, though.

"Are you trying to tell us, Wolf, that in the jaws of certain death Savarna was somehow cured near the Miami Circle by being washed in or drinking from the Fountain of Youth and being magically dragged back to the land of the living by a Tequesta shaman? Sorry, but that sounds like mythical hogwash, the kind of sentimental tripe you'd find in a novel, not in serious historical records. You always told me that archaeology was about digging up facts, not theories. Where's the fact in this old wife's tale – with the greatest respect."

"Calm down, young Zak, keep your hair on. Apply brain power, not emotion, didn't I always teach you? I appreciate your concerns. Indeed, I too felt the same before I chanced upon hard physical evidence. Would you like me to continue?"

The professor pointed out that the myth of the fountain of youth was not complete pie in the sky. Even today Florida is well known for more than a thousand natural springs, the largest number on earth, which feed a thriving tourist industry. Springs formed underground in deep sinkholes run all the way from Miami to St Augustine, where cash-rich Americans have flocked since the nineteenth century to treat illnesses like tuberculosis.

Nicola interrupted. She'd never heard of a sinkhole in England as awful as the roads were, potholed by storms and ice attacks most winters. The good professor explained how they're created after limestone bedrock collapses near an underground pit or cave next to a water source. The hole in the ground becomes flooded with sulphurous spring waters. The ancients worshipped these sacred places as gateways to the afterlife and threw gifts to the gods into their murky depths. From Mexico to Florida you can find everything from fancy pottery to human skulls and gold masks dumped inside them, an archaeologist's honeypot.

Now to the facts. Recently dated wood tested from a rescue dig at St Augustine's Fountain of Youth Archaeological Park left no shadow of doubt that alongside the Spanish town's fort a spa served the locals from at least the year 1619. Elsewhere, an old pal of the prof's had made a dramatic discovery. Deep below the therapeutic surface spring waters, where an ungodly mix of sulphur and plastic surgery-enhanced faces keep the good and great afloat, pottery and tools abandoned in the seventeenth century stunned archaeologists in the 1950s at a very special spot. The spa in question was in the downtown district of Old Havana in Miami, a stone's throw from the Tequesta circle. The local tribe clearly took the waters back in the day. Suffice it to say, we are not exclusively in the realm of Mr Mickey Mouse, Wolf ended.

"I'd always believed the idea of quick-fix tonics was snake-oil quackery invented by Florida's get-rich-fast entrepreneurs," Zak replied. "But you're telling us Savarna was healed by taking the waters in the real, original Fountain of Youth? A great tale prof but this still sounds like wishful thinking to me. I'd love to buy it, I really would. We don't actually know whether Savarna survived at all. Limbre's diary ends before she's taken to the circle – the bit of the tale I can accept. How can we be sure the Tequesta didn't turn on the wreck survivors and put them in a cooking pot for dinner in the end?"

"I'm afraid Zak's deductions sound spot on, professor," Nicola added. "Surely, if the odd couple had survived, the captain would have written gushingly about it in his diary. How it ends so abruptly looks pretty damning, no?"

Pasinski smiled lopsidedly and replied, "Oh ye of little faith. Please open e-letter Number Four."

When Nicola clicked the attachment, she saw what looked like a photo of a crime scene. Two skeletons, buried upright, faced one another at the centre of an earthen mound, their arms crossed. The scene was one of death but also of disturbed intimacy.

"Now, to continue. Listen carefully. Let's time travel. Way back in February 1895 a killer freeze, the worst in living memory, struck Florida. The state's entire lemon crop was wiped out overnight. Only Miami escaped the deep frost. When the miraculous news reached James E. Ingraham, vice-president of the South Florida Railroad Company, he took a risk. He persuaded his backers to push the railroad he was building onward to Miami to invest in a resort hotel and cash in on the as yet unbuilt city's superb climate. A town that never freezes was a strong sale's pitch."

Ingraham took pity on seventy-five farmers who lost their livelihoods in the great winter of 1895. By December they were set to work clearing ground for the hotel, living in tents and huts in the weather-proof wilderness of old Miami, a place with no streets and little going for it. The engineering moved at a fast pace. Just over a year after the freeze, the first steam train would stop in Miami on 13 April 1896."

"For America's Deep South this was another chapter in the story of how the West was won. What interests us are earlier events of the first of January 1896 reported in the *St Augustine Record.* Now then, let me read you what a young reporter called Cornelius Meichel had to say about a little-known episode in old Miami in an age where archaeology was not invented and antiquarians scarce in these parts. Here we go":

> A curious episode this past week from the new settlement of Miami. Best known to these readers as a place of swamps, alligators and avoidance, a young man digging the railroad for James Ingraham, that paragon of American virtue, was last week rushed by locomotive to hospital in St Augustine with suspected heart failure. Once diagnosed with nothing less troublesome than severe shock, and restored by rum-laced coffee, Eric Maguire, an Irishman by birth, started spouting tales of dead men's bones and curses along the riverbank.
>
> When yours truly set forth to investigate within forty-eight hours, no scene of crime could be detected. Whatever had come to pass had been hushed up fast. Resigned to a wild goose chase, your humble reporter got talking at Fort Pierce railway station to a man of books, also journeying north, hiding behind a sweeping grey beard by the name of Rupert Finkelman the Second. Finkelman had been abroad these last two months researching the plight of the endangered Florida panther, *Felis concolor coryi.*
>
> Upon the first of January past, he was capturing images of wildlife along the banks of the Mayumi River in Miami when a fit of screaming led him to the edge of the railway tracks. Finkelman joined the soil-plastered diggers peering into a five-foot hole, which had broken through a low-lying mound thick with seashells. Staring up at the new dawn were two skulls sitting face to face.
>
> Finkelman helped dig out the skeletons, finally

exposed sitting upright and cross-armed, a burial tradition the likes of which no man recollected. The left hand of one of the deceased grasped a green jade bird. Ceremoniously laid out between the odd couple, Finkelman identified the bones of an intact shark and foreign works of primitive craftsmanship. The son of a New York undertaker, the scientist reckoned one of the bodies was a man of some seventy years old, seemingly Caucasian and abnormally tall at six-feet-three inches in stature. The physical likeness of the second body Finkelman had never known.

The workmen argued heatedly about the grim discovery and how to proceed. Most were for throwing the remains into the river, pulling sticks to decide who should keep the great lead box lying at the deceased man's feet and returning to schedule. Finkelman begged for a ten-minute stay of execution and added that care was essential to avoid a curse making mischief for the living. While the men lunched, he added an ambrotype of the eerie scene to his photography collection and carefully stacked the bones in an abandoned wooden shipping crate hastily emptied of Florida oranges.

Reasoning the remains were once someone's son, daughter, mother or father, when I chanced upon Finkelman he was duty-bound taking the bones on to Rollins College on Lake Virginia in northern Florida. He reckoned from the calcite wear on the bones they were hundreds of years old and had been interred in a sacred Indian burial. The ambrotype reproduced here is courtesy of the magic of a man almost as unlikely as this tale. Strange but true, dear reader.

The professor removed his half-moon glasses and grinned knowingly across the Atlantic. Night had swept down on the mountains of Dyfed. Now his thoughts were shared, the old teacher was turning groggy. It was 9.45 pm, approaching his bedtime.

“If I was a betting man, which as you know I am not, I’d guess that the lead box once housed your codex, the very diary of Juan Limbre. For a century it sat gathering dust in a Miami workman’s attic, one presumes. Decades later, perhaps a family member rediscovered the dusty manuscript and sold it to a local antique store. That’s where your friend Grant Raven entered the picture, let’s hazard picking it up for a song, unable to believe his good fortune but mystified by what it was all about. When you sauntered onto the stage, he was struggling to translate the codex without anyone’s help.”

“And as you’ve no doubt deduced, I suggest strong grounds point to the skeletons being the final resting place of your lead characters, Juan Limbre and sweet Savarna. If Rupert Finkelman II was correct in ageing the male skeleton to seventy, we may believe both lived to a ripe old age. From here the trail goes cold. If this discovery was made today, there’s a standard sequence of tests we could run to date, sex and provenance the skeletons. Alas, who knows where the lover’s mortal remains ended up.”

Zak still wasn’t buying into the shaggy dog story.

“Summing up, prof, we have a diary, a circle with miraculous waters and two skeletons nearby, right? From a hyper-realism point of view, doesn’t the pattern make it far more likely both Limbre and Savarna died soon after reaching Miami and were laid to rest in the nearest available graveyard? No disrespect, but long beard Finkelman was not a pathologist or an archaeologist. I feel the need to pour a jug of cold water over this hypothesis, professor.”

Nicola wasn’t quite so cynical. After her adventures at Boca Chica, she found herself open to strange ideas. Her time among the spirits of the Deep South had taught her to expect the unexpected. Certainly, she planned to corner Zak and at the very least check out the Miami Circle at the soonest opportunity.

Time was up. Frederica had marched in and gruffly announced it was past Wolf’s bedtime and he needed to be fresh as roses to record an episode on Did God Have a Wife? for the BBC World Service’s *Living With the Gods* the next day. MP just managed to bow and shrug before his minder pulled the plug on the cross-Atlantic wire. Zak and Nic were left bemused to pick up the pieces and make sense of an ancient crime scene.

27

5.45 am. The Antiquarium Fridge, Key West

Never prod a hornet's nest with a stick. Bad idea. Rodi had fallen asleep as usual late while cataloguing the *Merced*'s endless trail of shattered potsherds in the Fridge conservation lab, one floor above the Antiquarium museum. Hardly had he closed his eyes for the night when he was rudely brought round by a hard metal tube pressing into his chest. Unglued eyes showed a muscle-ripped hombre in a blue t-shirt, sunglasses and heavy stubble waving a gun at the innocent abroad. After a fury of red hair and frothing mouth felled the intruder with a neat punch to the nether regions, followed up by an Andalusian kiss – headbutt – it had taken three men to subdue Rodi and tie his hands behind his back with a plastic zip tie. "*Hijo de las mil putas* – son of a thousand whores," he raged.

By the time front of house security got hold of Melissa Todd, and she'd rushed to the museum in record time from her villa on the outskirts of town, the damage was done. Speeding up in her red Chevrolet Corvette Stingray, eight burly men, led by a woman in heels and a blue rain jacket, INTERPOL emblazoned on the back, were carelessly slinging the last of a stream of crates into a Securicor truck. Rodi completed a walk of shame, cursing, "*Que te folle un pez*," "I hope you get screwed by a fish", and was thrust into the back of a Florida State police car, its lights whirring in the morning haze. It was going to be a hot one.

A few minutes later, the Barracuda, Rusty and Whale skidded up to the museum entrance in a cloud of dust. Al Nassau, Alona and Mitch arrived not long after. Zak and Nic were blissfully asleep, dreaming of a golden man swimming to shore, heaving his wife and a treasure chest on his back.

Sadly, the turn of events was not unexpected to Melissa or the team. Just four days earlier the Admiralty Court of the Southern District of Florida in Miami, in the space of only a couple of hours – suspiciously fast – had found in favour of the Kingdom of Spain. Todd had pulled as many tricks as she knew from her box of legal wizardry, all falling on stony faces and deaf ears. The *Merced* was a small merchantman, obviously privately owned, sailing in the shadow of the 1622 Tierra Firme fleet, not some colossal royal warship built by Madrid and armed to the teeth with imperial cannon. In the simplest of terms, for the simplest of minds, it never was a Crown battleship. The treasures unquestionably fell under the freedom of the seas, finders keepers.

James Jorvik, resplendent in a new double-breast charcoal grey Italian suit and jaunty gold and red bowtie, had slung piles of mud at the explorers from Key West, knowing full well some would stick fast. The reptilian lawyer had banged his fist and pointed his finger. With the blazing eyes of a Crusader devoted to his divine mission, he countered that the *Merced* was not only carrying cannon typical for a warship but was under the protection of the Crown fleet. There was no doubt this noble frigate enjoyed the protection of the US Foreign Sovereign Immunities Act of 1976. In a veiled threat to the judge, Jorvik called The Kingdom of Spain versus Keys Exploration case a line in the sand. If the court found in favour of Kurt Barracuda, the very fate of America's downed warships, fighter jets and nuclear submarines now and in the future couldn't be guaranteed. They'd be abandoned, instead, at the mercy of marauding pirates.

Jorvik's murky waffle managed to mention the International Council of Cultural Heritage's Convention on the Defence of Underwater Culture and Heritage eighteen times in fifteen minutes. The very abbreviation ICOCH became a dizzying mantra of fear and intimidation for judge and jury. Keys Exploration's plans to sell the *Merced*'s booty violated Rules 2 and Article 2.11 of the Convention, the crusader spelt out. The

ICOCH Convention forbade the commercial exploitation of underwater culture and heritage for sale or speculation. Only ICOCH could save the seas from destruction by the hundreds of treasure hunters like the Barracuda queuing up to tear up the deep and violate the graves of our forefathers.

By now Todd was fighting to control her temper. Jorvik was spouting lie upon lie. From the nods in the courtroom, she was disturbed to see his arrows hitting home. Counting slow breaths to keep cool, Key West's finest corrected the court that her honourable colleague was blowing a smokescreen over reality. The jury should not be convinced by his hot air better suited to the movies. Todd read from a special report commissioned by the British think tank the Maritime Heritage Foundation, run by that paragon of good sense and fine virtue, Lord Balchin.

The thirty-page illustrated treatment painted a vivid picture for the court of how mistaking an armed merchant vessel for a frigate or a warship would be a legal stupidity. If a boat wasn't commissioned or commandeered for naval patrols or battle, it wasn't a warship. End of story. The Foundation backed up its evidence by showing how arming merchantmen with guns was normal when commanders were forced to sail in hostile waters. The English Channel had chewed up the broken backs of many seventeenth and eighteenth-century English, French and Portuguese traders littered with iron cannon. Sailing armed was an insurance policy.

If you were a Lisbon skipper negotiating your way to London in the 1640s, when the English Civil War left the coasts of the British Isles teeming with Roundheads and Cavaliers, not to mention pirates preying on both sides, eighteen guns were a common sight on traders gleaming on the high seas. Jittery Dutch East Indiamen carried even more. The *Anisterdain*, crewed in 1604 with one hundred and seventy sailors, was armed with forty cannon. Royal African Company traders heading for the Gold Coast in West Africa might travel with bad intentions and fifty shining missiles ready for trouble.

After reading from the report, to bang home its impressive

authority, Todd leaned forward and slowly articulated, "Eighteen guns doesn't make you a warship, fifty guns doesn't automatically mean you're a naval frigate. The *Merced* left Seville with just eight guns and headed home from Havana with perhaps only four. Four guns. Would you send a ship into battle with just four guns? I wouldn't," she ended exasperated.

"Even if you push the question of artillery to the side," Todd added, "the *Merced* was stocked with abundant private goods. That pattern alone meant it can't be classified as sailing on an exclusively military operation. The Foreign Sovereign Immunities Act is null and void in this case. It's not rocket science, right?"

In intimidating schoolteacher mode, Melissa Todd added to her argument the truth that America had never ratified the ICOCH Convention on the Defence of Underwater Culture and Heritage. These Gallic rules and regulations had zero legal bearing on the *Merced*. The wreck, lost outside State waters, was simply a case of finders keepers. Nothing else. Case closed.

In his own summary, Jorvik, grinning hideously, told the court that everything Melinda Todd had told them was true, true if this was the world of Disney make-believe. Her philosophy of finders keepers was the stuff of puerile fantasy without foundation among responsible grownups. Anyway, nothing she said about the *Merced*'s private trade could be backed up without the manifest for the final voyage. Could Ms Todd provide a copy of the manifest, Jorvik asked rhetorically. Keys Exploration had failed to produce the one piece of evidence that drove their entire argument. Pretty shoddy research, he advised the jury. Looking up to the skies momentarily and theatrically opening his arms wide, he ended with the killer blow: the fate of the free world's oceans was in the hands of the court.

After listening to his drivel, lacking fact or legal precedent, Melissa was quietly confident. Jorvik was risking everything on tying the *Merced* to the Foreign Sovereign Immunities Act, a wild leap of faith.

In his deliberations, Judge Prezel took particular comfort in an amicus brief filed by Edward Flanigan, the US Ambassador to

Spain, who confirmed that research in Seville left no doubt fleet voyages to the Americas always sailed under the flag of sovereign protection in the seventeenth century. The US Consulate in Madrid supported the Spanish Crown's rights to its sovereign property against the greed of Keys Exploration.

Flanigan warned that finding in favour of Kurt Barracuda and his merry men would set a dangerous precedent and mark open season on the world's three million shipwrecks. The bodies of hundreds of thousands of lost sailors seeking peace in the abyss would be at risk. A top secret presidential note put under Judge Prezel's nose, later burnt, ordered him to find in favour of the claimant.

Prezel bowed to superior minds – what did he know about rotten hulls? – and gave the Kingdom of Spain the nod. Within hours Jorvik & Silver filed for the return of Madrid's property. Down in Key West the Court's grace window of forty-eight hours for Keys Exploration to comply had been met with a wall of disdainful silence. Now the inevitable had come to pass. The team's slumped shoulders told a story of grave disappointment and loss. How could they not but feel they'd been royally screwed?

*

The lab was a mess. INTERPOL had left drawers open, papers scattered and the door to the Fridge cold storage unit gaping open. Only the Seville blue-on-white maiolica potsherds lay untouched. Clearly, Spain didn't really want anything to do with archaeology or the scientific records of the carefully excavated *Merced*, only the shiny stuff. Gone were the safes filled with gold, silver bars and silver pieces of eight. The air was pregnant with irony. Who were the real treasure hunters, Nassau asked out loud.

The Barracuda had hunted down and dusted off his emergency stash of Flor de Cana brown rum. He made the rounds, filling everyone's coffee mugs with spirit and patting his comrades on the back. All the while he was thinking about damage limitation. Whale and Rusty, muttering expletives, carefully picked up the wreck's potsherds abandoned by the court's officials, unwanted historic breadcrumbs scattered across the lab.

Slumped on the floor amidst the smashed crockery, their backs leaning against empty cupboards that once promised so much, Alona and Mitch comforted each other. The autumn adventure in Key West had certainly been a laugh but, make no bones about it, the promise of treasure had lured the surfers into the deep. Now the adventure was a bust. They'd pushed the make or break surf competition to the side to chase the end of a rainbow. Angry sponsors finally pulled the plug on the faded golden couple of surfdom. At the time Alona and Mitch hadn't cared a fig. Their cut of the *Merced* would put them into comfortable semi-retirement. Now their dreams lay shattered alongside the busted ancient crockery at their feet. Even Alona accepted at times like this there was just one remedy. Get royally sozzled.

The Barracuda's attempt to cheer up the crew's spirits with coffee mugs brimming with rum was starting to work its magic. As he poured the shiny brown spirit he sang a favourite eighteenth-century sea shanty. The team pitched in together:

Oh rum makes me pawn my clothes.
And rum gave me this red nose.
Oh rum killed my poor old dad.
And rum druv my mother mad.
Oh rum up, and rum down.
And rum all around the town.

Oh rum here and rum there.
It's I'll have rum everywhere.
Oh rum is the life of man.
It's rum in an old tin can.

The last two lines were met with an uproarious crescendo and pumping of fists as a sheepish Rodi walked in accompanied by a fresh-faced Ms Hemingway. The Spaniard made his only call from a prison cell to Maisie who, with little sweat and a few smiles, got Rodi released on bail. Sheriff Cowan's nose had been put sharply out of joint by INTERPOL invading his patch, waving warrants and warning his men out of the way on international business. If Maisie vouched for what admittedly seemed a rather deranged little Spanish dude with a violent temper and tongue to match, it was good enough for the sheriff. While Rodi caught up on a ration of rum, he re-told his tale of taking down one of INTERPOL's finest troops.

Word of the bust had raged across town like a forest fire. A small crowd of friends and shareholders worried about their savings, held back by security, had assembled on the museum's front porch. A fretful Zak and Nik turned up through the back entrance looking sheepish. Knowing looks were exchanged at the couple's ruffled hair and bedroom eyes. At least nobody had been harmed, Nicola was relieved to see.

Two bottles of rum later, the tragedy of finding and losing one of the sea's greatest treasures was starting to fade. The seriousness of events had one mixed blessing. The last of the bad feelings between the two camps of drifters – Alona, Mitch and Rodi on one side, Nicola and Zak on the other – had thawed. Life was too short. Taking to the lab's stainless steel tabletop, a swaying Barracuda waved his bottle and asked for silence.

"Ladies and gentlemen, the seas giveth and the seas taketh away. The game is not done. We'll sure fight on and challenge Jorvik & Silver to the gates of hell. All I want to tell you in the here and now folks, it's been a privilege. We may be poor, Keys Exploration may go bust tomorrow when the banks open, but fuck 'em and feed 'em fish because the real treasure are the stories we've shared and the friendships we've made for life. So, cheers and Ahoy." The brotherhood echo of Ahoy echoed across the museum.

Hugs started to replace the sorrow of witnessing the death of a beautiful adventure. Nobody would ever say a bad word about the Barracuda, whose fight for a fairer ocean for all created absolute loyalty. The boss always had everyone's backs. Down the years, without any fanfare, his team had benefited from endless small gestures. The boss quietly turned up at hospitals with cigars to celebrate a newborn. On more than one occasion, he'd handed over envelopes to help young couples pay missing rent. Without being asked, the leader even paid for the funeral of Rusty's grandmother, a cherished member of the Key West scene. Nobody could remember having paid for a single meal in the last twenty years when they went out on the town. Kurt was more than a boss, he was a confidant, a muse, a general. A sober Rodi clambered onto the same table the Barracuda had just abandoned.

"Amigos, my home is Espagne but my heart is here with you," he began. "This man Jorvik does not speak for me or my land. He is, how you say, the arse of the horse. It was us who found the *Merced* and us who, with careful respect, uncovered her historia. Nobody can take that away, whatever the law thinks it knows."

"As you wallow in the mud, like American pigs" – the friends laughed at his badly-timed humour – "I thought you should know, Rodi doesn't think the project is dead. Rodi doesn't believe we are not rich." The friends shrugged at the cheap drunk's rambling. "Remember yesterday you order me to put everything back in the crates like we found them and like they came out of the sea, Signor Whale?"

Whale wiped the tears he'd been shedding for the last hour at the loss of his carefully conserved collection and shrugged. It was certainly true Rodi was a workaholic who sweated over the tiniest detail. It was also perfectly correct that an exhausted Whale had beseeched him to clean up the dirty mess he'd left all over the lab work surfaces and put all the finds back in their place before the weekend.

"Ahora, ven conmigo, come with me," Rodi announced, jumping off the table, puffing out his chest to everyone's amusement.

The Spaniard walked into the Fridge and when everyone was crammed inside pointed to the tobacco leaves and smiled.

"Great Rodi, thank you very much," the Barracuda gently replied, putting his arm around his young European protégé, who seemed to have missed the point. "Of course, you are darned right, the Venezuelan leaves have a story to tell and, God knows, maybe we should get them turned into cigars and flog them. I fear nobody's going to pay us to carry on studying a pile of rotten baccy. Nice idea, though."

The Barracuda patted Rodi on the back, who looked confused and turned to walk away.

"So, you don't want the pearls, eh?" Rodi enquired.

"What you talking about, boy?" a confounded Barracuda replied. "While you were playing James Bond, INTERPOL impounded all our finds. Gone, the game's up."

"Pero no," said the redhead, winking at Maisie. "Mr Whale tell Rodi to fix the finds just like we found them, eh? Rodi respect Mr Whale's decision. Here."

A clammy Spanish hand started handing out tobacco leaves to everyone's confusion. The young hothead had finally lost the plot. The Barracuda was the first to grasp the lost in translation piece of luck. The dime dropped. Peeling open the leaf, he was delighted to see thirty-two pearls shining up at him in the morning light.

"You crazy bastard," the Barracuda exploded. "You put some of the *Merced*'s pearls back in the tobacco leaves?"

"No signor, I put *all* the pearls back inside the tobacco leaves, that is 28,791 shiny white gems. So, thank you very much, now we take our cut? Capitán Barracuda, I believe you owe me and my friends our half a per cent share of the *Merced*'s $76,668,595 tesoro de perlas. Rodi makes that $383,342 each. Muchas gracias."

The friends jumped on Rodi, the hero of the hour, and lifted him onto their shoulders, rum spraying over the walls and floors. Cries of 'you crazy bastard' echoed down to the Antiquarium's museum galleries below, preparing to open their doors to the public as they did, day in, day out, sharing the secrets of the deep with the wide world.

Todd and Nassau exchanged worried looks. In a low whisper the Barracuda bounded over, smiled affectionately and softly reminded them that the pearls were historic contraband and never royal property. You were never here, this never happened, he ended, pushing them out the door.

The Barracuda was not a man to sit around idle but was eternally peering out over the horizon. Calling over Rusty, he instructed him to suit up the remotely-operated vehicle Juno and fill the *Golden Margaret* with juice. Clapping his hands to get the attention of his rowdy team, he asked whether anyone was up for one last hurrah. A cunning plan had crossed his mind. All was not lost. Far from it.

28

Route 1, South Florida

The plan was a long shot, but certainly a shot. Keys Exploration was flush with the promise of contraband cash again, and the *Golden Margaret* full of juice. Perhaps for the first time, Nic and Zak wondered whether they'd made the right decision not to turn wreck hunters after all. No going back now, they decided, sticking to their guns.

The lovers were speeding north, away from Key West, towards the bright lights and grating sounds of what most of their circle called civilisation. After a couple of months immersed in mysterious ancient American Indian history and colonial greed, they weren't so sure any more where civilisation ended and barbarism began. For now they were already missing the fading view where the land of the free met the Caribbean.

Route 1 seemed to be a Bermuda Triangle of rainstorms. Zak drove gingerly. The rain bucketed down. Nic pressing him to floor the accelerator wasn't helpful. She couldn't contain her excitement at their plan to check out what, if anything, survived of the dubious Miami Circle. Was Savarna's body and soul really saved in this other-worldly space? And what other glimmers might back up Wolfgang Pasinski's madcap theory that the spot was none other than the Spanish explorer Ponce de León's Fountain of Youth? Try as they might to make sense of the nuggets of fact, the foundations felt seriously wobbly. Nic and Zak had come to a joint decision: the whole story was great fun but a dead-end lead.

The two-hour drive allowed plenty of distraction to chat over the Barracuda's latest brainstorm. The logic was simple, not necessarily rational. Mainly to screw with Spain and put one over Madrid, Marseille, Jorvik & Silver – the Keystone Kops dream team – the devilish explorer planned to risk it all by returning to the blue sea, miles from anywhere.

In the Barracuda's cunning mind, plenty of lost nights had left him convinced the shipwrecked booty recovered and seized in the name of Spain didn't tally with the amount of shiny stuff he reckoned the *Merced* carried. Not even close. The gold bars and silver coins the team had pulled up were worth a low tens of millions of dollars, drastically south of the $250 million windfall the Barracuda gambled his ship of dreams must be hiding.

The problem was once the dig went into overdrive after the threat of legal wrangling raised its ugly head, Rusty and the techies had uncovered over eighty per cent of the stern and bow ends of the sunken ship. The real estate where the treasure was expected to have been stowed turned out to be empty. The obvious conclusion, the Barracuda now imagined, was that because the vast majority of the gold and silver was private property it wouldn't have been loaded in the hold at all.

The captain surely locked it in the safety of his galley cabin to keep a very close eye on it. The *Merced* had gone from merchant vessel to floating security chest, groaning under the weight of bullion paid in return for the outward-bound cargo of iron knives and spades, leather shoes, cotton clothes and jars of quince, olives and wine sold between Venezuela and Cuba.

And the reason the team never found the bullion, the Barracuda was now one hundred per cent convinced, was because it never landed on the same stretch of seabed as the main part of the hull. The boss had explained to his team that galleys were small wooden rooms bolted onto a ship's upper deck where the captain and officers slept, the cook burnt soups and stews and where the private treasure was locked away in padlocked wooden chests. In the storm's violence it was now obvious the galley broke away, unhinged, when the *Merced* nosedived onto the seabed. How could he have overlooked an obvious rule of physics, the Barracuda had beaten himself. While the ship plummeted one way, the galley recoiled and dropped in the opposite direction. The sinking created not one but two clusters of wreckage.

The beaming Barracuda had headed offshore into his natural habitat to hunt down his missing millions. Along with the core staff, the newly minted Mitch, Alona and Rodi took little persuading to sign up for a dizzy one per cent stake as thanks for their loyalty. Zak and Nic counted themselves out. They had very different fish to fry on dry land, not in the badlands of the Straits of Florida. It might turn out to be a monumentally expensive error of judgement.

*

Caught between the old and new worlds of shifting time, Nicola and Zak didn't quite feel ready to share their new-found harmony with brash central Miami. The mean lights of the big city grated after months in genteel Key West and the old charms of the Deep South. All the sights and smells they'd craved in the summertime, high-octane bars and clubs, were now a pounding headache. Miami was a culture shock.

Nicola had rejected Uncle Les's kind offer of a room in his beachfront condominium. Instead, she booked into the oasis of the Mutiny Hotel in Coconut Grove. Nervously negotiating the city's crazy traffic left Zak's nerves frazzled. The couple decided to treat themselves to an afternoon away from sleuthing. After all, the sun had chosen to come out for a few hours. It would be rude not to honour the weather, not least because the newspapers showed freezing fog had locked down London back home.

To pass the time while she tanned, Nicola began what she considered a little light reading on her Kindle of Jedwin Smith's book *Fatal Treasure*, a tale of greed, emeralds, gold and death on the legendary *Atocha*, the lead galleon in the September 1622 Spanish fleet. From time to time she glanced up and her heart skipped watching Zak swim length after length in the hotel pool – at this time of year deserted. Zak wasn't thinking at all, just stretching his limbs, emptying his mind.

A late afternoon nap was followed by a stroll around the Coco Walk shopping district and a few English Rose cocktails – gin, strawberries, fresh lemon juice, homemade rhubarb and bitters – for old time's sake. The sun set and the day ended at the Talavera Cocina. The Mexican restaurant was pre-destined, Nicola shrewdly pointed out, being located on Ponce de León Boulevard, named after the conquistador who supposedly discovered the Fountain of Youth. Maybe the food would take years off their lives, rather than add calories of fat.

A procession of morsels filled their table, tongue-tingling mango and avocado salad, shrimp ceviche, grilled chicken prepared *a la talla* in mild chilli powder and grilled zucchini and guacamole. Large slices of key lime pie, the lovers' new favourite dessert, were picked up from a local bakery on the way home, devoured and seconds bought, despite the heavy downpour. Slipping beneath the sheets that night, Nic was finally completely relaxed, body and mind. I guess this is what the Yanks call being reborn she whispered lazily to a fast-asleep Zak.

*

Just before high noon the next day, when the pouring rain was kind enough to turn off the taps, it took half an hour to drive the couple of kilometres through city traffic up Brickell Avenue to the shore. The Miami Circle was supposed to be open to the public at an old ford opposite Berlingame Island, where the river met Biscayne Bay and streamed into the Atlantic Ocean. The sight of the city's most ancient monument transformed into a well-manicured garden hammered a nail in the romantic expectation planted in Nic and Zak's minds. The circle was wedged rudely between a highway and the high-rise monstrosity of a spanking new condominium. Modern times had bricked up any spiritual aura the circle once enjoyed. Not even the best imagination could conjure up an apparition of what the settlement looked like in the Tequesta past.

The adventurers tagged onto the back of a small tour group

and eavesdropped in on an exuberant woman rocking a rainbow sweat top with a unicorn printed on the front. The tour leader explained how this ancient place was once home to an Indian village more than two thousand years ago. Long before there were Seminole and Miccosukee Indians, white pioneers and African Americans, the Tequesta were the first citizens of south Florida. In the mouth of the Miami River, they gave birth to a thriving metropolis. Just when the heavens opened again, and the guide lost her audience, she added that the very name 'Miami' was a Tequesta word meaning 'Sweet Water'. Zak and Nic's jaws dropped.

The tourists cowered at the entrance to a nearby apartment block, much to the anger of the locals flicking them out of the way to get in and out of their homes. Darned foreigners. Nic took the chance to door-step the guide, charmingly asking in her best clipped English accent if it was true parts of a village and cemetery were dug up nearby in the late nineteenth century. The bewitching unicorn lover confirmed the site of a Tequesta town just over the river. Archaeologists had in fact discovered one of the most important ancient remains in America just last year when developers levelled the shore for a new concert hall.

Getting into her stride, Jill, as she introduced herself, described a broad flatland scraped clean by the archaeologists at the mouth of Biscayne Bay, the perfect setting for an ancient waterway linking Key West and the Everglades' interior. Where hipsters today tan, the Tequesta carved large wooden dugout canoes, built fishing weirs and stretched nets between the river's mouth and the bay to catch fish when the tide changed.

The archaeologists had carefully scooped out the black soil filling crevices in the rocks and empty sockets left behind from decomposed wooden posts once supporting thatched roofs. The ancient rocky landscape uncovered looked like the gnarled back of a dinosaur spine. Over a thousand post-holes and ten thousand finds came to light, Jill explained, mostly ceramics and animal bones the Tequesta feasted on – everything from turtle and shark to deer, racoons, squirrels, alligators and snakes. Nicola winced at the idea of squirrels, her furry friends who ran wild in the back garden of her London townhouse. The sea was so bountiful that the Tequesta didn't need to harvest crops at all.

Jill was glad to have a captive audience to pass the time while the heavens opened and the tour group cowered in misery. Nicola was far more exotic and interesting. Any signs of Spanish overlords here in Miami, the English woman asked. Try as they dared, the Spanish never managed to tame the Tequesta like they had the Timucua who lived around modern St Augustine. Pedro Menendez de Aviles did set up a church and Catholic mission on the shore of the Miami River, just behind the circle, in 1566 and his successors set up a fort in 1743. Both inexplicably burned to the ground in the space of a few weeks after opening their gates. Not a hint of a culprit was brought to justice.

Other than that, *nada*, Jill shrugged apologetically. A few Spanish bronze bells and some olive jar sherds here and there, but all early eighteenth-century from the period of the Indian holocaust when a cocktail of rum and European smallpox almost entirely wiped out the Miami Tequesta. The Spanish never got a foothold in Miami. The silver shoe buckle found in the deep pit was unexpected though. What self-respecting Tequesta Indian would wear Spanish shoes, Jill asked out loud.

Zak probed a little deeper, asking how the pit and buckle came to light.

"Same hole old boy Ingraham had cut for the railway line way back at the end of the nineteenth century," Jill clarified matter-of-factly.

"Hang on, you're telling me a Spanish silver shoe buckle was yanked up from the grave mound James Ingraham of the South Florida Railroad Company opened up in January 1896?" Zak exclaimed, overplaying his hand. "I thought the railway line ran straight through it, obliterating the past?"

"Hey fellah, you sure are well informed? Yes, that sums it up exactly with one correction. In the end the foreman moved the rail line twenty metres west after rumours started spreading about a curse on this place and the Railroad Company rep turned up dead the next day," Jill replied.

Nic decided to push even further. "Don't tell me: his mouth was choked with gold dust. I don't suppose anything else turned up last year?"

This time it was Jill whose jaw dropped. Were these Brits secret quality control assessors from Lonely Planet?

"I don't know where you guys got your intel, but I can confirm that was the word on the street – suffocated by swallowing powdered gold. How do you know, though? You're creeping me out. It's taken a year of multidisciplinary science at Miami University to figure out the crazy story and only thanks to permission from the Ingraham Foundation to go through their papers. Everyone knew Ingraham oversaw the Florida railway's extension down to Miami in 1895. Maybe his dairies up in Rollins College had more flesh to add to the meagre bones? Anyway, turns out the Dean of Rollins was more than happy to donate the Ingraham Archive to Miami University. The right home rather than gathering dust abandoned in some rat shit infested storeroom."

"Back up, please," Zac butted in. "James Ingraham's papers were housed in Rollins? How did that come about?"

"Obvious, isn't it?" Jill delighted in explaining, a step ahead of these exotic out of towners. "Rollins College was his *alma mater*. The place of learning's very survival was down to the behest Ingraham left in his will. Now everything with his name on it – files, ancient flints and potsherds – have been shipped down to Miami. The college is re-excavating his collection of oddball curios and cataloguing it as we speak. Pretty exciting stuff. Some of the antiquities are still caked in mud, never having been washed."

Now Nic and Zak were ahead of the wise Professor Pasinski. Looks like Finkelman II didn't take the uncovered bones to Rollins on a whim. No doubt a railway line foreman told the zoologist about Ingraham's college connections. Rollins must have sounded like an obvious spot to dump the Miami bones.

A genesis of hope grew in Nicola's mind. "Any chance we can get into those archives? It would mean the world to me," she slowly sighed, eyes wide and hypnotically rolling around her wrist the turquoise Indian bead bracelet Jill had been staring at for the last ten minutes.

What started out as innocent questions ended up an arm wrestle for knowledge. Nic had put her finger on Jill's weak spot – local historical knowledge – and was informed, with great satisfaction, that the guide reckoned she could pull some strings.

Jill retreated into the dry to make some calls. Zak and Nic set off through the rain to peer at what was left of the Tequesta village. Two of the hut foundations had been preserved under a glass floor in a new movie theatre, restaurant and thirty-four-story hotel complex just completed on the riverbank. The rest had been sacrificed to modern Miami's bulldozers and neon gods. A short public video about the village and Tequesta life told them nothing new. Footage showing the outlines of the huts lit up at night by green glow sticks dropped into the postholes, photographed by drones, impressed them. The aerial view gave a clear image of the village's size and layout.

The rain started to lighten. Zak and Nic darted across the bridge to stare at the overgrown mound where Rupert Finkelman II photographed two skeletons back in 1896. The couple held hands in silence. Had Juan Limbre and Savarna really ended their days in this hole in the ground? They tried to imagine smoke rising from a Tequesta village on the southern riverbank. Had the king's daughter from the Pearl Coast in Venezuela really survived disaster against all odds in the cruel depths of Florida by being reborn right here on these shores?

Back at the circle, Nic and Jill hugged. The tour guide handed over her business card with a local phone number scribbled on the back next to the name Taylor Minnehaha. What kind of name is that, Zak had enquired amused. A very ancient one, Jill explained, and then went tight lipped. Nic felt obliged to gift Jill one of her antique turquoise bracelets in thanks, which the guide made a weak attempt to refuse – "Lord, I couldn't possibly" – before eagerly grabbing the precious bauble.

Zak was no longer smiling, however. The sound of cascading

water caught his ear. He was about to state the obvious, feeling totally fed up with the pouring rain, even worse than a grey England in darkest winter, when he noticed the sun was shining. It wasn't raining at all. Along the edges of the Miami Circle water was spouting out of the ground. Nicola felt on the verge of tears at the sight but managed to hold herself together. Past and present solemnly fused. Jill shrugged. Perfectly normal, she explained, just a trick of nature. When low-lying aquifers are pressed by too much rainwater seeping into the local limestone, the spring water is pushed out. Happens every now and then. For every action, there's an equal and opposite reaction.

Zak filmed on his phone what felt like an out-of-body experience. Nicola unscrewed her water bottle and headed off to sample some of the supposedly miraculous waters. Grabbing her wrist aggressively, Jill advised her not to. Scientists from Miami University had detected unidentified heavy-metal impurities in the spring. They could be poisonous, she warned, unfit for human consumption. So far nobody had managed to source the trace elements.

"According to whom, exactly?" Nicola snapped, pulling her arm free.

Nic jogged to the centre of the circle, joined by Zak, kissed briefly and filled up her bottle from Miami's supposed fountain of eternal youth. A murmur in the background replied, "According to Taylor Minnehaha. She knows everything."

29

Golden Margaret, Straits of Florida

Somewhere below the swell, hundreds of millions in gold and silver – choked by seaweed – litter the ocean. If only it would be kind enough to show its face.

Rusty prided himself on deploying the very latest technology and robotic eyeballs to pick out anything abnormal on the sea floor. Depth didn't matter. His sophisticated toys could find a tin can in a thousand metres. The magnetometer fish, Aero, towed behind the *Golden Margaret*, sniffed out metallic anomalies and bounced readings up to the research ship's computer screens as it swam across the continental shelf. The bigger the spike, the larger the hit. He was not alone in the quest. Smith was a state-of-the-art EdgeTech 2400C Deeptow side-scan sonar, the latest version of kit invented in 1965 by the Massachusetts Institute of Technology's Professor Harold Edgerton.

Edgerton is a legend of the deep. A Nebraska man descended from a passenger on the *Mayflower*, which transported the first English pilgrims from Plymouth to the New World in 1620, made him American royalty. Down the years Edgerton worked with a who's who of marine pioneers. First off, he taught a young Jacques Cousteau how to find shipwrecks. Then he opened up his bag of tricks to pinpoint the American Civil War blockade-runner battleship the USS *Monitor*, lost in a wild storm off Cape Hatteras down by North Carolina in 1862.

Edgerton's early strobe-lit photos of the unseen deep, published in *Life Magazine*, sold out issue after issue. Amazed readers lapped up his exquisite art. Colleagues called him Papa

Flash because of the high-speed stroboscopic look he created for the 1940 film *Quicker'n a Wink*, which won him an Oscar. *National Geographic* honoured Doc Edgerton as "the man who made time stand still" thanks to his ultra-high-speed and stop-action strobe photography. The staggering results captured a bullet exploding through an apple as if frozen in time, and the 180° arcing sequence of a golfer's swing action from start to the club striking ball.

Decades later an Edgerton side-scan sonar fish built at Boca Raton in Florida, christened Smith by the heavy metal techs in the *Golden Margaret*'s ROV shack, was ploughing up and down the Straits of Florida. Its mission, 70 kilometres from shore, was to ping a signal off the back of a wooden cabin that may just have fallen off the back of the *Merced.* If the Barracuda was right, the missing galley would be stuffed with a royal ransom in gold and silver of the Americas that never made it to Seville. Not Spanish treasure, he was quick to tell everyone, but gold plundered by Spanish conquistadors from Colombia and silver stolen from Mexico and Bolivia. Rusty felt sure that if the ship's path crossed anything the size of an oil can or larger he'd ID it, no sweat. The great game was back on.

Trouble was Rusty had hardly slept for three days. Camped out in the Arc Cave, he'd kept his eyes forced open with streams of coffee. Six promising seabed targets looked like the golden ticket but were unrewarding dives. The remotely-operated vehicle Juno had been powered up and flown down, only to discover piles of modern junk. The intact car sitting on the ocean floor tens of miles from shore had everyone scratching their heads, but the blue cargo container dropped off the side of an incoming supertanker was no surprise. As for the rest: junk and mountains of plastic bags shamelessly dumped by world shipping.

Even captain exuberant, Kurt Barracuda, was starting to question his own sanity. Could a small wooden galley – the broken tip of the needle in a haystack – have survived four centuries at the back door to Key West? At least the team was busy doing what it did best, diverted from thinking about those greaseball legal eagles at Jorvik & Silver. The Barracuda would get one over them if it killed him.

Alona and Mitch were left chilling their boots. They helped out with a little eye-popping at night, staring for hours at side-scan plasma screens for the tiniest hint of wreckage spotted by Aero and Smith when Rusty nodded off here and there. The rest of the time they slept late and spent hours in the ship's bowels pounding metal in the Rocky Balboa rough and tumble gym.

Rodi hadn't been offshore before now. His role during the *Merced* misadventure had been spent sitting on the beach, so the rest of the team joked. Suggesting the honourable Andalusian was lazily tanning his pasty skin under a shock of red hair poked the sore bear into action. Rodi, chin sticking into the air, would let anyone and everyone know exactly how many hours he'd burnt scrubbing mud-encrusted pottery, cleaning metal finds and cataloguing coins. Not to mention saving their fat Western futures by fishing pearls out of rotten tobacco leaves nobody else gave a stuff about. Ungrateful sons of bitches. They could all go to *infierno*.

Rodi wasn't taking to life at sea. Not that he'd admit it. The background stench of diesel oil, constant roar of the engines and groaning of *Golden Margaret*'s bones from side to side made him queasy twenty-four hours a day and unable to sleep. In the quiet of the museum he was left to his own devices. Whale either gave him a brief pep talk or left him notes.

Working solo had suited Rodi down to the ground. He could choose his hours and slip out to take tea with Maisie Hemingway whenever it suited him. And most days it suited him plenty. The Andalusian hadn't quite finished trying to wear down poor Maisie, even if she had absolutely no intention of caving into his advances. Allowing the deluded boy to turn up unannounced and read passages of her grandfather's works to her was as close as she planned to get. Maisie was very fond of Rodi and his eccentricities but not fond enough to offer a glimmer of night-time sympathy.

Mitch, Alona and Rodi were arguing in the Nosh Pit about the meaning of the ugly ceramic cooking-pots and griddles found on the *Merced* two months ago. Alona reckoned they must have been manufactured in Seville along with the rest of the posh glazed dining sets on the ship. The Spanish skippers didn't trust Johnny Foreigner, she'd pointed out. Hadn't the dig proven the fleet stuffed its ships with enough home-grown food, bowls and plates to last a round journey without having to risk Caribbean muck and dodgy stomachs? Mitch reckoned that was why the Spanish Empire fell: it had grown weak on too much wealth, ending up soft-bellied snobs.

Springing to his feet, fists out and gesticulating wildly at the American's cheap shot, an enraged Rodi demanded respect. Espagne had been sailing the seven seas and making fine art and poetry for centuries while you damn Yankees were still swinging in the trees. Murillo, El Greco, Velazquez, Cervantes, Picasso, Dali… Rodi had only started his long list of Spanish creative geniuses when excited whooping interrupted him mid-flow, a finger hanging in the air. Even the newcomer knew what this meant. The boss had come up trumps.

The Barracuda was peering at a photo of a side-scan image just grabbed underwater by Smith. To Rodi the target looked like a turtle with a juicy leg sticking out on each side. Alona and Mitch looked equally confused and asked out loud whether the galley had finally come out to play.

"Hell no, this ain't no small box of wood and it certainly isn't pre-1800, I'd hazard," the Barracuda observed, peering at the screen. "You can make out the edges of a whopper of a ship, maybe sixty metres long, as sure as eggs is eggs. The big giveaway about this sucker are the round features on each side. I'll stake my reputation those are paddlewheels. We're looking at a mid-nineteenth-century steamship. Know what that means?"

Alona, Mitch and Rodi sadly did. It meant they'd failed yet again to find the *Merced*'s missing gold and were on a wild goose chase. Maybe they should have taken their cut of the pearls and run. God knows they deserved some fun, especially now the once eternal sun was going into hibernation. It was December, after all, a time of year when even the most committed drifter started thinking about family and home fires.

"Don't look so glum, champs," a grinning Barracuda demanded. "True, this may not be Spanish treasure, but how does California gold sound to you?"

The friends looked at one another confused. What was the wily treasure hunter up to? Rodi's knowledge of early modern US history hardly went further than Ronald McDonald.

The Barracuda stopped for a moment to gather his thoughts before explaining how "Florida was once on the hot path leading to the west coast Gold Rush fields by way of New York to New Orleans and round to San Francisco. Quite a few steamships sank under the weight of newly minted hillbillies investing west, their ears still stuffed with straw. Others went down loaded with freshly mined and hard-won shiny stuff the miners were bringing home to transform their families' lives. Between 1848 and 1855, around 300,000 prospectors harvested $2 billion of gold. In today's hard cash that's about $420 billion. Anyone interested in staking a sunken claim?"

All the arms in the room rocketed to attention, buying into the sea-battered Floridian's charms hook, line and sinker. The Barracuda was back doing what he did best, the art of selling dreams.

*

The seabed was a scene of mangled devastation. The hull had split open like a kipper, its wooden side ribs and planks eaten away by legions of shipworms, those assassins of the seas. The paddlewheels had fallen off their hinges from the pressure of flowing currents and leant drunkenly outwards. Iron anchors twice the size of a human guarded the bows and a copper-sheathed rudder the stern. Goodies were scattered far and wide.

Juno swam gracefully across the crash site. Her lights picked out piles of porcelain crucifixes and glass bottles full of what looked like gooseberries, slices of pineapple and peaches. Brass portholes, through which prospectors who had struck it rich once peered out at their futures, had popped out of the wooden walls.

The wreck mound was covered with piles of coal, white ironstone china wash basins, cups and saucers fired in the smoky kilns of Stoke-on-Trent, and thousands of ointment pots and table glass. Juno swept across a crate of the quack doctor Thomas Holloway's pure white jars. Inside, still packed tight, was the ointment he mischievously advertised in the world's press as "The universal medicine of the age. Cures all disorders of the liver, stomach, kidney and bowels, pimples, blotches, sore breasts and sore heads. A blessing in every household." In short, every ill known to man.

It was, of course, all hot air. Holloway's quack medicines had zero health benefits. That didn't stop the public from lapping it up, making the 'doctor' a multi-millionaire. The mansion he bought near leafy Sunningdale on the edge of Windsor Great Park, Tittenhurst Park, was a showstopper later bought by John Lennon. *Imagine*, one of the world's most inspiring songs, so Nicola thought, was written and recorded there. None of Keys Exploration's battled-hardened explorers had seen anything like this extraordinary snapshot of Victorian daily life.

Objects taken for granted by the passengers – combs, hairbands, clothes irons, scissors, a cleaning tube from a lady's very private douche, toothbrushes and spectacles – were abandoned across the sand. Alona, Mitch and Rodi were starstruck by the breathtaking sight. A video of the wreckage was taped before anything was touched. Time to search out anything shiny.

Juno switched direction to chase a debris field of finds trailing off the wreck into deeper water to the south. The hairs on the surfers' backs tingled. Juno landed next to a pile of rectangular plates with decayed green copper edges. The dust settled and the robot blew a spritz of air across the remains using her Sucker, its suction enabler reversed. Dozens of faces of men, women and families peered up from the six hundred and thirty metre-deep grave. Rodi made the sign of the cross over his chest.

Daguerreotype glass film plate photos, holy smokes, Rusty stuttered out loud, high emotion gripping his throat. The oldest faces seen in the deep, he reckoned. Most of the portraits belonged to the very men and women who lost their lives on this ship. The newly minted miners proudly paid hard cash in photography galleries to join the latest upper class craze. They immortalized striking it rich in photos before packing up their rags and riches and steaming out of San Francisco.

It was a once in a lifetime discovery. Rusty slid back in time to the 1850s and shared a tragic vision of hundreds of terrified passengers standing on deck, hugging their carpet bags to their chests and fighting to crowd into too few lifeboats. The captain blew his whistle for order and demanded the miners make an impossible split moment decision. Either choose to go down with their riches or leave them behind and hope to survive. The precious overweight bags would sink the lifeboats. There were no deals to be made with this devil of a tempest. It was simple. Life or death.

A respectful silence fell over the Arc Cave, only to turn into joyful hooting a few minutes later when Juno's lights settled on a pile of several dozen gold-coloured bars. Shipwreck hunting was an exhausting roller coaster ride of high and low emotions. The Barracuda slapped all the team on their shoulders and, by sleight of hand, pulled a Havana cigar out of his top pocket, especially saved for times like these. Today was going to be a mighty fine day.

Two hours later the lightly concreted bars were piled high on the *Golden Margaret*'s deck, patches of yellow metal gleaming in the midday sun. Juno stood silent and obedient, dripping water like an excited puppy fresh out of a lake after chasing a stick and about to get a treat from its master. She'd made light work of scooping up a dozen ingots. The Barracuda brushed a wet rag across a bar. The grime easily washed away. Letters started to appear: 'Waterbury Co., NRV'. Never heard of it, the boss shrugged out loud.

From the portside bridge door, a grinning Rusty carried a hard-shell black case towards the hill of ingots. He was going to enjoy this hard-won moment. Balls to Jorvik & Silver and their

Keystone Cops. On the case, stamped in red letters, Rodi read Bruker Corp., Washington, S1 Titan. Brains explained the S1 was a space age XRF machine developed with NASA. Looking none the wiser, he spelt it out for the Spaniard: X-Ray Fluorescence, a spectrometer invented to spot check the grade of metallic alloys and list their trace elements. Rusty clicked open the two heavy case fasteners and picked up what looked like a hand-held gun. Just like Q in James Bond, Mitch joked.

Rusty held the XRF's laser reader to the metal surface, cleaned by the Barracuda, for five seconds. Removing his Ray-Ban's, he peered at the digital table and cursed.

"Shit a brick. Sorry boss, it ain't the real McCoy. About sixty-five per cent copper and thirty-five per cent zinc made it shine yellow underwater. Could have been intended for melting down to make patches of brass sheathing, as and when needed, to plug the leaking hull. Close but no cigar."

On cue the Barracuda grasped the ingot and threw it and his cigar over the side of the ship.

"Back to it," he commanded. "Let's dive."

Kurt Barracuda prayed the steamer would hit pay dirt. He was damned if he was going back to port empty handed. Keys Exploration had taken a beating and he desperately needed a chunk of something with a feel-good factor to plug, change public opinion and cheer up his board of directors.

Alona and Mitch watched the JPT – Juno Pit Team – scramble to check the robot's fibre-optic cable connections, her strobe lights and change the two still photography cameras' memory cards. Each techie shouted 'Clear' and Juno was winched into the air. The *Golden Margaret* pitched violently to portside. The robot splashed down, was untethered and in an eddy of white foam plummeted into the abyss.

Rodi was keen to keep out of the way of the growling crew while Juno commuted to the wreck. He grabbed some battery acid coffee and sauntered back to the Arc Cave, where on a computer terminal he looked up Waterbury Co., NRV, the name stamped on the brass ingots. It didn't take long to work out that NRV stood for the Naugatuck River Valley in western Connecticut. Waterbury, Rodi read with respect, was known as Brass City in the mid-nineteenth century for good reason. The hub of industry once turned out a mind-boggling range of brass goods, melting down old kettles and mixing the metal with zinc to cast everything from four-fifths of the brass buttons in the United States to ships' rivets, coins, clocks, photo frames and ammunition casings.

The company hit the big time under the vision of Israel Holmes who travelled incognito to England in 1848 to spy on local brass manufacturing methods and rip them off. In those days English law banned skilled workers from emigrating. Exporting machinery brought severe fines and imprisonment. That didn't stop Holmes persuading twenty-three new disciples, handed fat contracts, to jump ship to Waterbury with their wives and children. Three new recruits had to be smuggled onto a Liverpool ship in wine barrels. By the time the Barracuda's newly discovered steamship foundered in the mid-1850s, Waterbury's motto was Quid Aere Perennius?, What Is More Lasting Than Brass? Rodi decided to sneak one of the unwanted ingots with such a cool story into his bag as a memento. It would make a great door stopper.

Juno had gently touched down, itching for fresh instructions. The techs flew her back over the southern debris trail, dropping ever deeper into murky water. More photographic daguerreotypes littered the sands, here some cufflinks, there a lady's bejewelled hat pin, all with value, but no mountain of gold. The Barracuda was still certain the wreck smelt bang on for a California Gold Rush ship. He refused to be defeated. Come on baby, I know you're down there, he grimaced.

Juno blew air from her Sucker arm at a couple of tiger sharks curious about her bright lights and slowly drifted away, reckoning she was unlikely to make a tasty meal. The remotely-operated vehicle drifted along the thinning debris trail of lost culture when Rusty pointed at the shadows. A large object loomed out of the gloom.

"Steer Juno south-southwest twenty degrees," the Barracuda commanded.

The robot followed the order and took a timeout, sitting down on the seabed while plumes of sand thrown up by her thrusters settled. The ROV team stretched their trigger-fingered hands, cramped from concentration. Rusty reckoned it would take twenty minutes for the dust to settle. Everyone downed tools and headed out for cigarettes, coffee or forty winks.

The mood was still subdued after the false alarm sparked by the golden brass when the team returned to the Arc Cave. The team huddled around a panoramic dashboard of blinking lights and plasma screens plotting the ship's location, the robot's position on the seabed, a sonar display, a multibeam image of the seabed topography and three views of Juno live on the sea bottom.

Whatever was lurking at a depth of seven hundred and ten metres was still hidden, but fast clearing up. In the space of a few agonising minutes, a blurred rectangular object gradually came into focus. The Barracuda was first to pump his fist and turn the air blue. A few minutes later the penny dropped for the rest of the crew. Bedlam broke out. Sitting untouched by human hands for a hundred and fifty years was the ship's enormous steel safe, still locked with two padlocks the size of a human fist.

"Prepare the A-frame for lift off," the Barracuda ordered. "This sucker's coming home to daddy."

30

Key West Bight Marina

The lift was a tricky operation. Rusty couldn't even guarantee the safe would make it to the surface in one piece. If it was easy, everyone would be doing it, the Barracuda reminded his young apprentices. Rusty had wiped his greasy hands on his stained shorts, ran his finger through his hair, bit his tongue and got on with it, hoping for the best. He reckoned there was a 50/50 chance of the safe busting free, dropping back into the abyss and smashing to smithereens. One way to open it, Mitch had unhelpfully advised.

The Barracuda had gone into overdrive. From a crackling satellite phone, first he called Al Nassau and told him to corral the Board, then rang through to Fox TV in Miami, offering them an exclusive. Chip Hunter didn't need asking twice and pulled some strings to arrange a network chopper to rush him down to Key West.

The *Golden Margaret*'s run to port was a far cry from the media blackout that accompanied the live *Merced* project rolled out on a strict need to know basis. This time the Barracuda wanted everyone to know. He'd make as big a splash as possible to get his company onto the front pages of the news and turn the embarrassment of the last few weeks into fish and chip wrapper. Key West was a small town. Everyone knew everyone's business. In the last two miles steaming to shore the research ship was followed by a flotilla of dive and fishing boats.

Down on the shorefront the town had turned back the clock to a summertime Mardi Gras groove. The buccaneers of Keys

Exploration were returning as local heroes. The *Golden Margaret*'s horn blasted through the air as she docked alongside Schooner Wharf. Big Dave had fired up the barbeque and was doing a roaring trade flogging grilled shrimp and ice-cold beer to the several hundred rubberneckers who had flocked to the shore. Dire Strait's old tune *Brother In Arms* played out of a colossal speaker hung out of the side window of the same room in the Schooner Wharf Bar where Alona, Mitch and Rodi spent their first night in Key West.

Peering out to land, Rodi wondered where Nicola and Zak had got to but soon lost the thought. In the same split second, he was side-tracked by Maisie nervously chatting with the directors of Keys Exploration, waiting to welcome home Poseidon's conquerors. Rodi felt as heroic as Peter O'Toole after crossing the Nefud Desert in *Lawrence of Arabia.* Surely I'll deserve a cheeky kiss out of this, Rodi hoped.

The steel safe had taken three hours to haul up from the seabed. Holes had to be dug under the box, polyester strops threaded through the muddy sediment beneath it and shackled to a hook a couple of metres above the seabed. The ship's A-frame crane took up the strain, its drum groaning under the load heaved into the light of day. The ginormous safe, two metres long and a metre and a half high, was lightly encrusted but otherwise looked in great shape. Rusty worried, nevertheless, that the corroded iron might crack at any moment. Mumbling he vanished into the chief engineer's shed, where he knocked up a flat lifting frame supported with more polyester strops.

Ten burly crew members lifted the safe, cushioned on its frame, along the wooden pier to the front of Schooner Wharf. Just then Chip Hunter's helicopter – broadcasting live across Florida at primetime early evening – landed in the Key West Bight parking lot. The presenter would pay the parking fine later. He started running to the waterline. The stars were aligning.

The Barracuda stretched, downed a beer, pulled a second Havana cigar from the top of his brown leather cowboy boot, popped it between his grinning teeth and made sure his gold piece of eight coin could be seen swaying over his newly thrown on white t-shirt, emblazoned on the front 'Keys Exploration. Deep Down We Care'.

The crowd fell silent. The Barracuda perched one foot on the top of the safe and started telling a tale as old as time, of ships sinking by their hundreds, frozen in the deep and harvested for humanity, science and knowledge. Key West's old timers, delighted day trippers and school kids crowded around in the palm of the Barracuda's hand. Chip Hunter's camerawoman zoomed in on the rugged explorer's trustful blue eyes.

Three minutes later Al Nassau circled a finger in the air in a sign for the Barracuda to wrap up. The story ended to great applause. Beer was sprayed in the air. Baptized in lager, Maisie and Rodi – their arms faintly touching, much to the Spaniard's bliss and the actress's disinterest – were far too excited to care about being soaked. This was it.

Rusty strode centre stage and, with single cracks, shattered the padlocks with a pair of pneumatic shears and signalled with a polite bow for the Barracuda to make the reveal. The experienced showman toyed with the crowd, lifting the lid a few inches and then letting it boom closed again. The crowd thronged ever closer, merrily laughing along, moths to the shining light. Chip Hunter and his camerawoman pushed to the front.

"Ladies and gentlemen, I give you the treasures of the deep blue sea," the Barracuda boomed. News cameras and mobile phones lit up the early evening night, all of Key West desperate to be part of one of the town's finest days.

The lid was thrown back, bouncing gently on its ancient hinges. A collective sigh rose. The crowd fell silent.

Hard as the Barracuda rummaged, no shiny metal could be persuaded to come out of the heavy treasure box. All that lay inside was a mass of black mush and fabric stinking of sulphur and bad eggs. The crowd gagged, the Barracuda held his head in his hands and Chip Hunter moved his hand back and forth in front of his neck, shouting 'cut' to his camerawoman. Hundreds of thousands of live television screen feeds across Florida went blank. The star reporter started composing his resignation letter.

The deep-sea explorers trudged towards Big Dave's to drown their sorrows – united they stood and united they would fall. Only Rodi stood rooted to the spot, trying to make sense of his roller-coaster emotions, supported by gentle words from Maisie Hemingway. A shock of curious red-hair squatted down in front of the safe, took one of the shattered padlocks in his hand and wondered what the letters LS stamped on its front meant. Not that any of it mattered any more, he sighed.

31

Coral Gables University, Miami

Nicola was in luck. Taylor Minnehaha was in town and replied lightning fast to her query about the James E. Ingraham behest. The assistant professor's team was about three-quarters of the way through cataloguing its contents, dry and dusty from the Florida sun and decades of neglect. She was able to confirm the archive included a hotchpotch of ancient Native American Indian finds and human bones, still coated in mud. The out-of-towners were invited to meet in two days' time. Lady luck was smiling.

Courtesy of Wolfgang Pasinski's web of contacts, Zak learnt that an old friend was on the East Coast talking at a conference in New Orleans on Bones Of Contention: Ethics and Ancient Human Remains. Dr Yellie Neplovic, Skelley to her friends, was the head expert overseeing thousands of skeletons coming to light in the long-running Crossrail project, making London transport fit for the ten million people expected to live in the capital in a few years time. The monstrosity was already £3 billion over budget, chewing up £30 million a week, and was two years behind schedule. Britain really was broken.

The forty-two kilometres of tunnels dug across the city for new stations and train lines had played havoc with commuters. The only people lapping up the chaos were the archaeologists making the most out of a boom in rescue digging. Skelley, much to her glee and everyone else's fear of catching a disease from her, started off in charge of a hundred and twenty bodies uncovered in Charterhouse Square. These poor souls were just a few of the victims of the Black Death that wiped out half the population of

London in 1348. She quickly rose up the ranks to become the top osteoarchaeologist 'bone head' for Crossrail.

Nicola agreed to risk infection and was keen to meet a formidable woman who'd clawed her way up the greasy pole to the top of her profession. Devoted to her field, it was said Skelley kept a nineteenth-century skeleton called Percy under her bed. If she awoke with a nagging research query about one of her discoveries, out came poor old Percy in the early hours for a quick check on human anatomy.

Dr Neplovic hadn't seen either Professor Pasinski or Zak for twenty years since they last chatted at Lampeter University one lunchtime, fellow students studying biblical history, about how Israel was doing bad science by refusing the study of human remains. In the Holy Land the law required all newly excavated human bones to be immediately reburied in case they turned out to be Jewish. If they weren't interred in the right place and height in the soil, they wouldn't be able to rise on the day when the Messiah rode into town. Problem was the black hat brigade couldn't tell a Jewish skeleton from a Muslim one. Even dog and pig bones ended up seized for a solemn burial in the holy city.

Archaeologists who refused to hand over their finds before they could be hastily studied on-site ended up cursed by ultra-Orthodox rabbis, entreating HaShem, God, to make their hands fall off. The famous archaeologist Aharon Kempinski had been jinxed for digging up graves in the path of a main road in Jerusalem. Within a year he died of AIDS. Six years earlier Yigal Shiloh was lost to cancer aged fifty after a curse was placed on him for excavating the City of David in Jerusalem. The current director of the Israel Antiquities Authority was under a permanent *pulsa denura*, a rabbinical curse for people who deserve to die.

Pasinski had a simple but effective solution. Keep a box of animal bones in excavated trenches and do the old switcheroo. The rabbis would scurry away to the cemetery happy with their day's haul, none the wiser about the true species in their bone box. Skelley pretended she didn't know what the mad professor was talking about. She stubbornly wouldn't confirm or deny whether such a dodgy approach was common in Israel. The walls have ears, she had whispered.

Dr Yellie Neplovic took little persuading to pop down to Miami from New Orleans for a couple of days to help hunt for the skeletons uncovered in 1896. Nic and Zak wouldn't have a clue what they were looking at without an expert to hand. The burial photo published in the *St Augustine Record* texted to her was certainly an enigma in ancient burial practices. And archaeologists live to see different discoveries that shed new light on the unknown. Ninety per cent of finds are more of the damn same.

On a cool mid-December morning, Atlantic breeze rustling the palm trees lining the approach to Coral Gables University in Miami, Nicola, Zak and Skelley sauntered past Chinatown. They nodded at Ponce de León Boulevard and turned northeast along the banks of Lake Osceola. The campus was no concrete jungle like SOAS in London – the School of Oriental and African Studies – Nicola realised, soaking in the peaceful verdant gardens and huggable trees. Zak approved of signs declaring 'Breathe Freely. Welcome to Our Smoke-Free Campus'. All Yellie was focused on was whether she'd get her hands on some exciting old bones today. The prospect made her chest heave and mouth dry up.

The Department of Anthropology was hidden at the back of a two-storey white-washed building. Neat and functional. Taylor Minnehaha was not at all what Nic expected. In her mind's eye she'd conjured up an unkempt, greasy-haired woman stuck in a time warp and decked out in a 1960s floral dress with an overbearing 'hail brethren' booming voice and roached leather sandals. Probably with awful hygiene, suffering from rank body odour. Nicola was embarrassed by her rashness. Professor Minnehaha, it turned out, was to say the least understated, so much so that the visitors had to turn their ears towards the mild-mannered woman and lean forward to hear her soft words.

From a quick online check in the hotel the night before while Nic was showering, Zak was impressed by her credentials. BA and MA degrees from Harvard with a healthy scholarship and then the carrot of teaching luring her cross-country and home to Miami. On the East Coast, Minnehaha produced a two-volume PhD on the *Material Culture of the Everglade Indians, 15,000 BC to AD 1750*, quite a swipe of time. The scholar was well published and her forthcoming *Life & Times of the Tequesta. From Tribe to Terror* looked likely to become a celebrated classic. Suffice it to say Taylor was the world expert on this elusive indigenous people. In the flesh Minnehaha was something of a surprise too. The slender, mild-mannered woman with impeccable sanitation can hardly have been in her mid-thirties.

Minnehaha welcomed the friends, her no-nonsense, long jet-black hair single braided down the back. Sporting straight-legged khaki Carhartt work trousers, a black t-shirt with 'Save the Circle. Miami' etched below a round logo made up of solid black dots and suede Redwing boots, she confidently shook Nic, Zak and Yellie's hands and asked them to call her Taylor. Explaining she was regrettably on the clock and travelling out of town on urgent business the next day, the team cut short the small talk and headed straight for the archives.

Rows of battleship grey storage carousels marched down a long, narrow room. Below a poster of an Indian pot and the mantra Archaeology is Digging Up People, Not Things, a jungle of wooden shipping crates stood on twelve trestle tables. Zak didn't expect any of the champagne stencilled on the crate sides to survive inside and, at a glance, realised this could be a long and thankless task. There were a lot of haystacks to look through if they were to luck out by plucking the smallest of pins lost a hundred years ago.

Laughing softly at Zak's concerns, Taylor Minnehaha beckoned the visitors halfway down the room, pointed at a box numbered JEIC 11/12, a coded abbreviation for the James E. Ingraham Collection, and suggested the team start there. Not only did it quickly become obvious the anthropologist had already sourced their ace, it seemed she wanted them to find the lost history at the end of the rainbow without wasting anyone's time.

Skelley peered in the box, squealed in delight and set two

skulls on an empty trestle table. Beautiful, she murmured, giving Nic and Zak the double thumbs up. Agreeing that the other living humans in the room were spare wheels, Taylor left Yellie to her pathological magic and led Zak and Nic to her office. The professor spent ten minutes doing anything to avoid talking, checking emails and taking a couple of telephone calls before she had no alternative but to engage or seem rude. And that just wasn't done in the Deep South.

Taylor folded her arms and smiled a rather forced grin.

Zak sensed he was being played and decided to tackle the gamesmanship head on. "Professor Minnehaha," he started. "Care to tell us what the Dickens is going on? I'm assuming you wanted us to find those skeletons, though I haven't got the foggiest idea why. Obviously, the history of the Tequesta is a massive deal to you. And those lost skeletons were recovered from a native Indian grave mound in downtown Miami. I'm assuming you already have a pretty good idea what's in Ingraham's old baggage? This has nothing to do with science, does it? There are less obvious agendas playing out."

Minnehaha didn't blink. Zak pressed on. "That's not it, though, is it? You're American Indian, right and, by the tattoo on your wrist, I'm guessing you've got Tequesta blood running through your veins. How am I doing?"

Minnehaha turned her wrist to show a black tattoo completely missed by Nicola. The neat artwork showed a shark imprinted with the outline of a human footprint.

No more the laidback youth, the scholar narrowed her eyes and addressed the pair. "What I am doesn't matter, Dr Fitzgrove. Sure, I have my own specific motives, though it looks like Dr Neplovic will tell us if I'm right or deluded. I have to thank you. I've been looking for a first-class osteoarchaeologist for some time, someone discrete. Out-of-towners are perfect. They aren't vested in roots."

Minnehaha opened up now that her intentions had been rumbled.

"You're right. First of all, I'm Tequesta and only a remote

second an archaeologist. Though you could say the two are related. I was brought up in the slums of Miami. Every Sunday and school holiday time my mother would drag me to the ancient burial grounds and villages between here and Key West, drilling the tales of my people deep into my bones. Year after year I'd watch the ruins of our great ancestors be erased, bulldozed in the name of what society calls progress – nightclubs, cinemas, high-rise condominiums, swimming pools and hotels. Do you have children, Dr Fitzgrove?"

Minnehaha peered closely at a blushing Nicola, trying to work out their relationship. "No children, no, no, Lordy," she babbled on Zak's behalf, turning bright red.

"Now that I have two fine sons of my own," Minnehaha continued, "I take them to those same holy places. Nothing physical survives, just the spirits. If the young can't see the past, how can they understand it? In the space of a few generations the last of the Tequesta places has been sacrificed for the sake of money-grabbing property magnates. I write books to try to keep the flames alive, but youths today don't have the bandwidth to read anything serious. I've given up trying to get my kids' faces out of their tablets, cell phones and games. I want them to live the normal American dream. At the same time, they must understand their bloodline. If you don't know where you came from, how can you understand who you are? It's a question of identity."

Zak decided to reset the sermon to the here and now. "I agree completely and sympathize with everything you say. As you Americans like to put it, the million-dollar question: why are you so keen for us to rediscover the Ingraham skeletons?"

"Let me be frank with you. There's nothing to hide. As the head of Justice For Tequesta, I have a vested interest to close a peculiar historical loop. This is going to sound strange. Bear with me. The story first. The facts second."

Minnehaha closed her eyes for an instant and centred her breathing. A secret guarded for an age by the innermost sanctum of Tequesta elders was about to be spoken among outsiders for the first time. For hundreds of years on the 5th of September, Minnehaha began, what's left of the Tequesta people gather round the fires of every city, town, village and camp between St Augustine and Key West to listen to one of our great foundation stories. They say on that day, many moons ago, a golden man and a green woman, half dead, were carried to shore on the back of a hammerhead shark."

Minnehaha paused and tapped the inside of her wrist.

"Sharks are sacred to the Tequesta. We venerate their power at the top of the food chain. In times past we ate their flesh, used their bones for tools and wore their teeth as necklaces in sacred celebrations. My tribe, it is said, saved these survivors – the golden man and the green lady – from the sea and took them in as our own, gave them medicine and shelter and taught them the ways of the Tequesta."

"In return, the golden man brought Western influences to La Florida. Around the same time, my people's way of life took a dramatic turn for the better. Towns and rectangular houses made of wood with kitchens and ovens started to appear. Spanish jars once filled with olive oil flooded Tequesta settlements. Our Casseekey king and his family added silver and glass beads to their old coral and animal bone necklaces. It's fair to say the economy of the tribe saw a seismic shift."

"Nobody knows the cause of the new wealth. My grandmother would tell a tale of the golden man from the sea. She learned it from her grandmother and so on. Every 5th September he would vanish into the outback for two weeks and return, handing out gifts to villages down south and home in Miami, sharing enough coins to keep the tribe's folk going for another year. To the Tequesta the golden man is the founding father of modern Miami."

Nicola and Zak tried to keep calm but shared electrifying looks. The shackles of the past were unlocking.

"A fun story," Zak observed, "although isn't it fair to say that native American Indian folklore is full of rich mythology? Sounds to me as though this is another epic narrative invented to allow people to make sense of who they are and where they came from. But true? Who can say?"

"In normal circumstances, I'd not disagree," Minnehaha admitted. "The 1896 discovery of two skeletons in downtown Miami may just change the landscape's logic. I'm assuming you've read Cornelius Meichel's gossipy article in the same archived edition of the *St Augustine Record* as me, all about Rupert Finkelman II? Again, why we share the same interests still intrigues me."

"If, as we both suspect, this was the burial place of the golden man and the green lady – not sure yet why she was given that name – and if Finkelman was right that one of the bodies was a man around seventy years old, seemingly Caucasian and abnormally tall at six-foot-three, then our indigenous shaggy dog story takes on a profound new twist."

"All this has come to a head in the last few months in a most distasteful way. I've always reckoned that the tale of the golden man originated among the real-world shipwrecks that littered our shores in the seventeenth and eighteenth centuries. Exactly how the golden man befriended the Tequesta who, to be honest, were rarely as hospitable as legend claims, who can say."

"Since all myths come from truths, I have followed the recent discovery of the Spanish wreck lost off Key West in 1622 with growing curiosity. And I'm afraid to say the Kingdom of Spain is about to be in for the shock of its life, its worst nightmare."

Taylor Minnehaha slid open the top drawer of her desk and pulled out a copy of what Nicola realized was an original Spanish letter, centuries old. The handwriting was identical to Grant Raven's codex in her possession. Much to Minnehaha's surprise, Nicola read out loud:

> To the grand Tequesta Casseekey of the Myaamiaki River. Warmest salutations. For thirty-five years long, we have lived as brothers in the southern lands in peace and harmony. In La Florida we found a halfway home between Las Perlas de la Margarita, the land of my lady, and Sevilla, the country of my forefathers. In our hour of need you saved my queen. In your time of strife, I opened the seas to you. Now as the evil air devours our souls I bequeath

> our secrets to the Tequesta, now and in perpetuity, both my ship and all it contains. This I swear by my God and the Lord of the Circle.

"Congrats, Ms Medici, a first-class translation. Thank you. Problem was that despite talking to numerous graphologists – including the Israeli world expert Lilach Gendel – nobody could make out the squiggly signature. So, legally the Tequesta behest didn't stand up in a court of law. We were stuck. No more avenues to research. And there was nothing to inherit, just this dried out piece of faded historical parchment handed down from generations of elders to me."

"All that changed in the last few months when those treasure hunters in Key West went fishing for a Spanish galleon and stuck a name to the discovery of a wrecked ship – the *Nuestra Señora de la Merced*. From there it was a pretty easy jump to connect the dots. Only when we learnt that the captain of the *Merced* named by Keys Exploration was one Juan Limbre of Sevilla did our signature make perfect sense. See the especially diagnostic letters Jn and Lbe?"

"Mr Kurt Barracuda and the lawyers Jorvik & Silver have done my people a mighty service. Our moment of destiny has arrived. Despite Key West and Madrid bickering about finders keepers, who owns which slice of treasure, I'm afraid this document denies both parties the captain's gold. Justice For Tequesta has filed a plea with the court of Miami for the treasure of the *Merced* to be returned to its true owner according to the last will and testament of Juan Limbre. The bounty belongs neither to the Kingdom of Spain nor to Keys Exploration. It's as simple as that."

The pin-drop silence in Taylor Minnehaha's office was broken by a panting Dr Yellie Neplovic who burst through the door without knocking, her white lab coat flying behind her. After catching her breath for a few seconds, head drooping, hands on hips, she pointed behind her and cried, "Chaps, you've got to see this, it's a beauty."

32

The Archives, Department of Anthropology,
Coral Gables University, Miami

In the peculiar twilight zone that Dr Neplovic called home – the land of the living inhabited by the dead – there was nothing duller than a natural death. Although she was an expert in finding meaning from any old bone, most of the tens of thousands of human skeletons she had fussed over in her career were unexceptional. Little pathological trauma to excite her curiosity. This was not one of those days. In fact, Neplovic was quite beside herself. Specimens she'd labelled JEICi and JEICii were truly rather splendid.

In their prayers Nicola and Zak hoped one of Ingraham's archive boxes might turn up at best a few tell-tale scattered bones. Their expectations were exceeded thanks to spectacular preservation. Out of the storage box JEIC 11/12 Yellie had pulled out teeth, toes and everything in between. The expert in human anatomy had managed to reassemble the remains quick time inside the Department of Anthropology archives room. On one trestle table the two skeletons lay reunited side by side from head to toe. Neplovic had wired up two lamps to shine a powerful light over the remains.

Nicola, Zak and Taylor Minnehaha stood to one side of the table, while Dr Skelley started reconstructing the pathology of the ancient bodies.

"Spit spot, here we go," she began, rubbing her hands down the sides of her white lab coat. "Now then, please observe that both specimens are by chance or design extremely well preserved.

Very lucky indeed, bearing in mind their round trip to Rollins College in Orlando in crude packing crates and back to Miami. Either that or someone took extraordinary care to preserve the relics. First, the collaterals. If you focus on the area between JEICi and JEICii, note there are bones from an alien species associated with the same storage crate. These are not human."

Minnehaha approached the table, bent over the bleached remains and nodded emphatically. "Shark. A cultic deposit," she declared. Three sets of eyebrows raised in unison.

"Jolly good, very well done," Skelley added. "Ok, let's move to JEICi. This is a male specimen. Six foot three inches, Caucasian, approximately seventy years old, strongly built, an abnormal right forearm radius caused by repetitive strain. Now really very queer: concreted to the upper rib section beneath the clavicle collarbone one pierced gold coin, typical of having been worn around the neck."

Neplovic passed the coin to Professor Minnehaha, who shrugged knowingly at Nicola and Zak, smiled awkwardly and confirmed, "What do you know? A golden doubloon, date stamp 1622, minted in Mexico City, rare and valuable. As for the abnormal forearm radius, Dr Neplovic could this have been caused by years of pulling on ship's ropes?" Skelley acknowledged work like that fitted the profile perfectly.

"This is where matters take a turn towards the outright confounding," Dr Neplovic claimed. "Let's now consider JEICii. This specimen is female, some five foot two inches tall, age at death forty-five to fifty, categorically not Caucasian, with severe trauma and chips to three ribs with a fourth completely missing. If I had to guess, I'd say the left bronchioles was once pierced by an angular object. Could easily have been a terminal wound, but this must have happened when JEICii was in her prime. Presumably her young age and tip-top immune system helped her heal. Otherwise, she'd have been a goner."

In the brief lull that followed, Minnehaha asked whether Skelley had picked out any markers about the woman's origins.

"Other than non-Caucasian, impossible to say really. But

these artefacts give a pretty strong clue, I'd hazard," Neplovic ended, pointing to a pile of well-polished stones at JEICii's feet. "Enough green beads for at least three ankle bracelets."

In a few swift steps, Taylor Minnehaha bore down on the finds and examined them meticulously, one by one, up close and very personal.

"No, you're wrong, Dr Neplovic. Look how thin the ulna and radius bones are. There are enough beads here for two ankle bracelets and three arm bracelets." Taylor peered at Nic and Zak before continuing.

"And this tiny greenstone, some two centimetres long and a centimetre wide, isn't a bead at all. It's a plagioclase feldspar labret."

Skelley, Nic and Zak looked at each other, none the wiser.

"Labrets cut from greenstone," Professor Minnehaha clarified, "a kind of jadeite mined in and traded out of Guatemala. Like the brand reputation of Tiffany's today, this was high-end exotica. Labrets were worn by native American chieftain families as piercings just below the lower lip. Why? The Spanish called this stuff *piedro de yjada*, stone of the loins, after watching natives grinding it into powder and mixing it with water to treat internal illnesses. Green jade was said to have the power to cure any body part it touched. Either JEICii was a medicine woman or she had been seriously ill and was in terrible need of divine protection. Ms Medici, Dr Fitzgrove, I hypothesize we've found our green lady."

In the brief discussion that followed, Nicola and Zak agreed with Professor Minnehaha's logic. Yellie Neplovic looked on bewildered. She was sufficiently well versed in the need to avoid confirmation bias in archaeology – coming up with a madcap theory and then making the evidence fit – to agree to take a sample of the woman's tooth and run a DNA profile back in the Museum of London. Hopefully it would source the skeleton's place of birth. As a personal favour to the professor, the scientist agreed to crank out a DNA sequence from one of Minnehaha's hairs, as well. She didn't have the foggiest clue why.

The weight of the world seemed to sit on Minnehaha's

shoulders after the afternoon's shattering revelations. Skelley and her friends agreed to clear up the boxes, leaving the skeletons laid out, while Taylor made her apologies and disappeared to pack and head out of town on important business. The meeting was terminated with stiff abruptness.

*

No sooner had the door shut than with hands firmly perched on hips Dr Yellie Neplovic turned and stated the obvious, "Ever have the feeling you've been lured somewhere on false pretences? Care to enlighten me, old things?"

Nicola offered to head out to the department cafeteria for a round of coffee and left the college pals to a tricky catch-up. By the time she returned, Skelley was up to speed and wearing an expression of total bewilderment. The double espresso and blueberry muffin did little to clear the fog or lift her mood.

"Let me get my head round this bonkers theory, then," she said, pacing up and down between the trestle tables and peering at the skeletons. "You chaps just happen to visit Key West, run into an old timer who weaves gold out of straw and hooks you into a shipwreck treasure hunt? Good, fine, ok. Then Nicola stumbles upon an ancient Tequesta burial mound or village and an eccentric old boy chugging around in a boat with native Indian skeleton skulls nailed to its front. I'm surprised he hasn't been lynched. Deserves to be. Then the swamp hunter sets you up to chase down some lost book that holds the diary of one Juan Limbre who skippered the *Merced*?"

"Said diary leads you to discussions with our old prof, Wolfgang Pasinski, whose uncovered archival evidence about the discovery of two peculiar skeletons in a Tequesta Indian mound rudely disturbed by the Miami railway line in 1896. Through the offices of queer fish Taylor Minnehaha, you call me and track down the two bodies, which conveniently look like the mortal remains of Captain Juan Limbre and his exotic wife Savarna. Bollocks. You're dead lucky Pasinski is involved, otherwise I'd be gone, taxi for Neplovic. Have I missed any other morsel of madness?"

"Only that we suspect Savarna was healed from her shipwrecked trauma that you identified in the sacred waters of the Miami Circle, which we're starting to think was the source of the Fountain of Youth discovered by the conquistador Ponce de León around 1575. No doubt she became known as the green lady because of the green jadeite she wore for protection in the years after her near-fatal accident," Zak added.

Skelley's reply was emphatic. "Go bugger yourselves."

To try and make the story less fantastic, Zak asked Nic to show Skelley the Limbre diary. The bone expert insisted on slipping on lab gloves to examine the centuries-old relic. Neplovic spent twenty minutes turning the diary's pages and was suitably impressed

"We are, however, stuck with the inexplicable truth that Limbre never wrote a word in his faithful diary ever again after reaching Miami. Yet we are expected to believe he and Savarna survived here for decades till the end of their days. Taylor's last will and testament to the Tequesta now leaves no shadow of a doubt this seems to have been the case," Zak admitted.

Much to Nicola's surprise, Skelley meditated for a moment, eyes closed, and started smelling the back of the diary. Surprise turned to shock when the scientist licked the corner of a page, puckered her lips and muttered, "I thought as much."

Nicola offered to go and buy Dr Neplovic a second blueberry muffin if she was that hungry, but the Londoner wasn't listening.

Skelley hooted a booming belly laugh and said, "lemon juice, a key ingredient of the sixteenth-century magus. Nicely played, Captain Limbre. In the 1570s a scholar and playwright out of Naples, Giovanni Battista della Porta, perfected a very particular art, invisible ink. I suspect the art of the master spy's been messing with your diary, chums."

Nicola crossed her arms. It was her moment to wonder what order of madness was going on.

The bone guru closely inspected the diary and explained

her thinking. "During the Spanish Inquisition many of della Porta's closest friends were imprisoned for the wrong beliefs and faith. Refused entry to visit them, and seeing any gift seized at the castle gates apart from the plainest food, he thought up a way to send them secret messages written on eggshell using a blend of plant pigments and alum. The ink seeped through the porous shell. When it was dry, the magus boiled the eggshell in hot water and the ink on the outside vanished. All della Porta's imprisoned friends had to do was peel the egg and read a short message imprinted on the inside of the shell. Really quite simple, yet ingenious, one must admit."

"The magician published his *Magia Naturalis* in 1579, outing the secrets of the spy's art. It's there you can read all about a dark art that directly concerns us. A variant in early invisible ink was cooked up by powdering lead in an earthenware pot, filling it with water and vinegar, then boiling and straining the concoction. At that stage, lemon juice was added – though sometimes oranges, cherry juice, onions or milk, depending on what was available – and you wrote your letter. To read the invisible you just needed to heat up the page in front of a fire. Voila. By the smell and taste, I imagine someone wrote with lemon juice in Limbre's diary."

Yellie certainly knew her beans, mightily impressing Nic and Zak.

"Crude it may sound," Skelly ended, "but it was damned effective. Lemon juice stayed the standard invisible ink for spies in the American Revolution, the Civil War and throughout World Wars I and II. The most famous case was when German spies used lemon juice to feed top-secret information to the Fatherland. British counterespionage caught them in the act in 1915."

"I'm not especially big on the idea of putting a flame near this prized book," Nicola replied. "Any modern way to detect our missing link?"

"Worry not my pretty," Skelley replied. "This archive ought to have something up to date to replicate the same effect. Now then."

Dr Neplovic disappeared into the back of the room and, after crashes, banging and swearing, returned with a fluorescent lighting tube. A standard tool for examining faded letters and inscriptions, she explained, heading to the light switch and plunging the room into semi-darkness.

The drama was not matched by a revelation. Page after page of the Juan Limbre's diary failed to turn up anything significant, not even a coffee cup stain. Come on, come on, I can smell you're in there, Skelley pleaded through gritted teeth.

The friends were forced to agree that the truth actually was not out there. Limbre's words really did end in Miami, with Savarna being carried to the Lord of the Circle.

Skelley collapsed into a leather chair in defeat and exclaimed, "balls." Nicola followed her lead and patted her on the back with a consoling "Don't worry, nice try. The smell was probably Zak's breath from the double portion of artichoke and vinaigrette sauce he scoffed last night."

Silence enveloped the dark room. For no reason, Zak switched the thirty-centimetre-long fluorescent lighting tube back on, thought of re-enacting the death fight scene of Luke Skywalker and Darth Vader from *Return of the Jedi* to cut the mood but decided perhaps this wasn't the right moment. Instead, he opened the diary's leather cover and scanned the inside page. To his shock a series of lines and words peered back at him, the contours of some land mass. Juan Limbre's last words committed to his diary weren't entries making sense of how he and Savarna survived among the Tequesta, but a series of X's marking spots on a map.

"Folks, check this out," Zak cried.

33

Route 1, Key West to Miami

Christmas was almost at the door. Another year was over. The Truthmobile was rolling north up Route 1 through deep puddles dumped by last night's rain. The drizzle matched the friends' mood. The weeping mangroves still sighed amidst the prehistoric landscape. Some things never change. The seascape, where America met the Caribbean, was no longer foreign. Its people and places had become a cherished home away from home. Down by the shore, brown pelicans with binocular vision peered into the deep for their next meal. Ospreys glided overhead, waving the melancholy friends back to civilisation.

In the space of three short months the drifters' lives had turned upside down and inside out. Each one had come in search of change, diversion, and ended up reborn. The great highs and crushing lows felt chasing Spanish gold had brought Alona and Mitch together beyond any expectation. The more Mitch went cold turkey, laying off hard booze, the less he was distracted by partying and female guile.

His bad boy reputation may have been shattered, but he didn't give a fig. He was head over heels in love. Alona had achieved the impossible, taming the surfer who now appreciated he'd lucked out in her blend of beauty, humour and common sense. Mitch was punching well above his weight. In the great arc of shipwreck discovery, recovery and loss, set against an almost overpowering thin-slice of colonial Florida's history, the happy-go-lucky hedonists had been forced to grow up. Our time on planet Earth is fleeting. When you see a good thing, grab it and don't let go. Both looked forward to sharing a Christmas stuff up with Alona's parents in Ocean City and beyond then – the rest of their lives. The ex-surfers planned to go to the bank, look into a loan and open up a surf shop fitted out with a coffee bar on the West Coast. Chilled San Francisco was calling.

The Volkswagen Camper's grating windscreen wipers matched Nicola's mood. Her adventure south was not at all what she'd expected and far from a smooth ride. She'd gone looking for identity, for purpose, a life-affirming space to calm her frayed soul. Nic smiled mischievously when the Truthmobile zipped past the turn-off for the Boca Chica nudist beach. Not under scorching blue skies, but deep in the secret undergrowth she'd found her personal El Dorado. Home at the centre of the world in London, she'd never heard of the Tequesta and would probably have switched channels if a feature about them popped up on National Geographic. Now their spirits dwelt in the shadow of her very soul, day and night.

The new oddballs she'd run into – the Barracuda, Rusty, Taylor Minnehaha and particularly the tragically coma-ridden Grant Raven – in many ways touched her heart more deeply than her own family. None cared to judge her. Beyond an initial good-humoured raised eyebrow, the Medici reputation didn't precede her. It was meaningless in the Deep South, where she was taken not for who she was but for what she was.

Outsiders who took the time to look beneath her plummy voice and privileged education found a sensitive soul. Key West had opened its doors to her with a sincerity rare in England. It was true, the Americans were warm, the Brits cold as ice. Most of her crowd were busy being busy and never stopped to look at the cosmic forces outside their blessed isle. Nicola was done keeping up appearances.

Not that she'd admit it – the idea was far too new age – but the Londoner was born again. She now knew who she didn't want to be, even if she wasn't sure exactly what the Dickens she'd do back in the Big Smoke. For sure, drift no more. Maybe start a charity. Nicola grasped Zak's hand a little tighter. This one I won't be letting go of, she promised. Energy gushed through her body.

I found home, Nicola reminisced, in the middle of nowhere. The drunken cheap joke stencilled onto the side of the VW Camper last September, Truthmobile World Tour, added when the friends celebrated drifting south together from New York and Miami, had started to peel off. It was barely legible. Answers had arrived. Nicola, healthy and curious in everyone and everything, wasn't like her ancestors. The Medici curse had skipped a generation, thank the Lord. Nicola would not live a good or pleasant life. She'd aim for a meaningful life.

*

Zak was lost in bittersweet memories too, playing back the endgame of the last few days while he drove gingerly. Nothing had worked out, but everything was exactly as it should be. The night before leaving Kew West the adventure came to an end in the Schooner Wharf Bar, where the friends first landed in Key West and were bewitched by a golden-tongued Kurt Barracuda. Nic, Zak, Mitch, Alona and Rodi had shared their highs and lows and put all their cards on the table. Friends who'd turned drifters and then frenemies ended up snorting at their pointless bickering. Adventure would bond them forever, thick as thieving pirates.

Big Dave plied the exotic gang, for whom he would always have a soft spot, with bottomless beer on the house. The bar was unchanged. Just a few more uncashed bounced cheques pinned to the wooden rafters. Snowden, the green parrot with a red beak named after a certain National Security Agency whistleblower, continued hopping between Johnny Walker and Southern Comfort bottles, squawking to anyone who'd listen.

Rodi was mesmerized when Nicola showed him Limbre's diary and explained how the captain of the *Merced* ended up cast away on the key of Matecumbe. Savarna's plight was shared in public for the first time. After reading the diary, there and then in one sitting, Rodi had offered to buy it from Nicola for $15,000 dollars.

First off, she explained, it didn't belong to her. Second, it was worth a hell of a lot more than that. And thirdly, where did Rodi think he could get his paws on cash like that? This was the penniless red-headed madman Zak had stumbled across sleeping rough on the summer shore of Miami after hitchhiking all the way to the USA. The hothead could hardly afford a round of beers. Everyone knew. Nobody cared.

The Andalusian sheepishly asked if the friends remembered the iron safe the Barracuda yanked up from the mid-nineteenth century steamship, expecting it to be stuffed with California Gold Rush gold. Nic and Zak were brought up to date about the calamity. Alona played a video of the chest's shoreside reveal she'd taken on her iPhone. The friends laughed good naturedly at the embarrassing failure. Only Rodi looked serious.

After the *Golden Margaret*'s crew headed off to drown their sorrows, he'd dragged the box back to the Antiquarium Museum lab. The following morning the Barracuda had lost his temper confronted by the physical memory of his failure. Rodi had stepped in and offered the Barracuda $500 for the box and its contents. The treasure hunter waved Rodi away with a flick of the wrist and one dismissive word, "deal". The crafty Andalusian hothead forced the Barracuda to sign a scrap of paper authenticating the agreement. 'You're now the formal owner of a pile of crap," the Barracuda had sworn. "Congratulations and good riddance. Get it out of my sight."

Rodi didn't sleep the night after the safe landed and the PR nightmare played out across America. For no good reason other than his new discipline in marine conservation, and the memory of Whale pressing him that anything brought up from the deep has to be recorded, he'd decided to catalogue the box's repulsive innards. It was archaeology, after all, and would kill some time. Protocol needed to be respected. When he started rinsing the stinking mush, to his delight pair after pair of denim trousers appeared. The reality dropped like a hammer blow. The initials LS engraved on the front of the chest's padlocks stood for Levi Strauss & Co.

Overnight Rodi left the sixty pairs of brand new Levi jeans and overalls to dry and spent most of the next hours studying online. A German industrialist called Loeb Strauss emigrated from Bavaria in 1829 to work in the wholesale cloth and linen industry in New York, he learnt, before sailing west in 1853 to seek a fortune in San Francisco. Strauss was just twenty-three years old. A new start deserved a new name. Loeb became Levi. It didn't take long for the entrepreneur with a big vision to notice how the gold miners out West always looked like tramps, their worn-out clothes not fit for punishing labour in the mines.

Levi started importing denim from New Hampshire and, inspired by his friend Jacob Davis, who'd been making clothes for miners with copper rivets down in Reno, joined forces to found Levi Strauss & Co. The rest is legendary, Rodi knew. The Barracuda's pants were America's oldest surviving Levis. A stamp on the inside base of the chest was marked 1875, pre-dating the earliest known pair by eighteen years. Rodi had grinned in shocked delight. Maybe he wasn't a natural-born loser after all.

The night after the Barracuda sold the decrepit strongbox to the cunning Andalusian, Rodi emailed several Japanese dealers with photos of his denim bonanza. Rising late his mood went sky high when a dealer from Kyoto offered him $2.3 million, sight unseen, for the collection.

The friends didn't know whether to cry with rage at having been upstaged, ring his neck, mug or hug him. The tramp ended up the only drifter to come out of Key West with serious cash in his pocket. He'd never have to work again. If only his mother had lived to see this day. Key West taught Rodi a life-long lesson. Nobody there thought he was a basket case. Rodi had learned he was no different to most people on earth. Just another colourful oddball and misfit, which made him a perfect fit in Key Weird.

Rodi wasn't going anywhere. He planned to stay in town, buy a townhouse on Front Street, treat himself to first editions of Ernest Hemingway's life works and keep chipping away at Maisie. Otherwise, Rodi reasoned, he was quite happy to carry on the Plato relationship. Platonic, Nicola had corrected him. The friends fell apart in good-natured laughter and happiness at their dear amigo's good fortune.

Zak had arrived in town obsessed with exposing the dangers of canyon buster fishing trawlers bulldozing the world's fragile marine ecosystems. Most uncharacteristically, for the first time in his life it was the sober academic with the backwards emotional antennae who let his plans drift.

While Alona, Mitch and Rodi had bought into the swashbuckling dream of a chunk of Spanish gold, Zak had kept his healthy scepticism. Something that looks too good to be true generally is, he'd learned donkey's years ago. To the Barracuda the treasure of the *Nuestra Señora de la Merced* still lay out there, somewhere amid the swirling sands of the Straits of Florida, achingly just beyond the horizon. One day he'd land it, he just knew.

What did the Barracuda really have to show for his spit and toil? He'd dropped a king's ransom on a new deep-sea diving robot. Juno had done her job with frightening efficiency. Was the age of the diver coming to an end, Zak wondered, and the rise of the robots taking over? Keys Exploration had spent over $10 million exploring the *Merced*. The scientific archaeology Keys Exploration promised and delivered was probably twice as expensive as just ripping the wreck apart to grab the gold. There was no doubting the Barracuda's love of history, which forced him to do the right thing by those rotten hulls. Many salvors wouldn't have bothered. And yet he still had to put up with appalling stick from the legal profession, sneering university profs and iron-fisted governments. Was it all worth the pain?

From his critical distance, Zak had worked out that the Barracuda allowed his thinking and business to be clouded by romance and wishful thinking. The man was born with rose-tinted dive goggles. Sure, the *Merced* was a treasure ship but thanks to a chain of sorry coincidences, by the time the ship sank, the bounty was long gone, spirited ashore by Juan Limbre and Savarna.

What the captain hadn't landed on a barren beach in La Florida had been largely scattered to the four winds. None of the olive jars and fine crockery made in Seville actually lay where the *Merced* collided with the seabed in September 1622. Generations of fishing trawlers blitzing the deep had scrambled the sorry wreckage.

Zak had nailed his newspaper scoop in *The Times* alright, only it was more horrifying than expected. Marine ecosystems – coral reefs and kelp fields – at least have a chance of recovering over months, years and decades. Once a wooden shipwreck is hit by stark contract, the damage is permanent. Game over. The heavy chains and nets that trawlers drag across rolling seabeds smash delicate remains and tear up timbers. Currents and tides then wash away the broken remains to the devil and the deep blue sea, never to be seen again.

A vast slice of the sunken past no longer lies innocently frozen in the abyss. Zak had seen the casualties of this catastrophe with his own eyes in the maritime garbage hidden under Mac Murphy's house, landed by the *Lazy Jane* and sold to pay for his luxurious villa on Front Street and keep Jen happy. The old galleon had made many of Key West's fishermen rich as thieves.

To Zak the *Merced* wasn't a golden opportunity, it was a nightmare canary in a coal mine sending a message to the present day. Greed, technology and the stripping of the sea's resources were nothing, the tip of the iceberg. The overfishing of the Keys to the end of the line was a deadly wake-up call. Mankind pushes nature over the edge at its peril. A more appalling environmental catastrophe was heading this way.

Global warming meant that Florida would change beyond recognition within Zak and Nic's lifetime. In the next few decades, six million people were expected to be forced to flee rising seas and killer hurricanes. Forty per cent of the most at-risk lands in America are found in Florida. Soon, the wrecks would get deeper and the old Tequesta villages and tombs slip underwater. They'd become underwater archaeology, too. Key West would party no more. This was the warning Zak planned to shout from Oxford's ivory towers when he got home.

From the start Zak had been convinced Captain Limbre

must have buried his fortune from preying eyes as soon as he was cast away on the shores of Matecumbe. The man hadn't crossed the ferocious Atlantic and survived one of its worst hurricanes to give up his legacy. Where it was hidden was anybody's guess. Nic's discovery at Boca Chica, thanks to the call of nature, got Zak's alarm bells ringing. Their finest hour – digging up ebony rosary beads, lead musket balls and a wooden box engraved JL, stuffed full of Spanish pieces of eight – proved Juan Limbre squirrelled away his riches in the sacred burial mounds of the Tequesta inshore of Boca Chica. Whatever Nic and Zak had unearthed was pocket change compared to the motherlode, if anyone could ever get to it.

Had Limbre bought sanctuary from the Tequesta chief of Matecumbe with his treasure or had the chief just taken pity on the couple? If the green lady was native Indian that might explain the Tequesta's sympathy and how the Spaniard escaped being boiled alive. Whatever the truth, Limbre and Savarna enjoyed a long life in the shadow of Miami's Indians. The captain kept the peace and showed his gratitude by sprinkling wealth over the tribe every 5th of September.

The celebration of the golden man's survival – brought to shore on the back of a hammerhead shark in Tequesta tradition – lived on in unwritten memory. One turn of events was a step too far to believe: the idea that Savarna was resurrected by the healing power of the Miami Circle. The Fountain of Youth was mythical cobblers. She just got lucky in the skilled hands of a Myaamiaki shaman's wisdom and medicine.

The day after Skelley Neplovic weaved her own magic over the invisible lemon ink in Juan Limbre's diary before flying home with a tooth from the female skeleton to sample, Nic and Zak had sped back to Key West. Late into the night they'd pored over Limbre's treasure map, peering at it from every angle. Overlaying the map with Google Earth, the contours of a headland and river looked strikingly similar to what had been known since Spanish colonial times as Boca Chica, the Small Mouth, where a narrow stream ran into the ocean. This was the only kidney bean-shaped island along the lower coast. Limbre's map showed a cross inscribed next to two mounds, one close to shore, another half a mile inland where the coastal plain gave way to low hills.

The lovers agreed Nic's burial mound was the site of the first 'X' in Limbre's diary map and reasoned the captain must have pretty much exhausted its riches. What was left at the second site, deeper inland, was anyone's guess. The London rose and once emotionally detached Oxford academic lost no time hurtling back into the dripping mangroves the day after leaving Miami. Thanks to Zak's former GPS fix they trekked to the Tequesta mound in twenty minutes. Reasoning water always determined where the Tequesta built their villages and camps, they hiked northeast through the dense undergrowth for over an hour until they reached an open plain. There the stream emptied into a small pond.

Low bumps and the odd piece of crude pottery covered the promising spot, surely an ancient settlement or tombs deeply choked in river mud. Juan Limbre's treasure would have been safe under metres of silt if it were not for an alarming sign announcing 'Boca Chica Casino and Hotel. Change Your Destiny in Ultimate Luxury'. No ground had been broken in a short stay of developer execution. The resort was scheduled to open in eighteen months. Zak took some photos of the sign, mounds and pottery scatters and, as soon as internet coverage reappeared, sent Professor Taylor Minnehaha the bad news along with a short account of what brought them to Boca Chica. "We need to talk," Zak ended cryptically.

*

Guilt-tripping Mitch, Alona and Rodi into accepting Nic and Zak's plan had been a hard sell. In the end the friends accepted there was just one honourable endgame. Nicola pleaded that Limbre's will to the Tequesta people meant any finds taken out of the *Merced* and loot scooped up in court by Spain belonged neither to the Barracuda nor Madrid. The friends agreed with little argument until Nic added the unwelcome bombshell that the Tequesta windfall included the pearls. In the friends' hands they were no better than blood diamonds. In any case, Nic pleaded, Justice For Tequesta would need a war chest to see off the Boca Chica casino and hotel developers. They'd probably have to buy up the land.

The bounty of the *Merced* was nobody's truth other than the Tequesta's. Rodi, Mitch and Alona would each need to hand over their stash of $383,342, doled out by the Barracuda not in cash but in the form of raw pearls. The highly principled Rodi was the first to agree, while the surfers felt as if they were being asked to give up their first born. The pearls were their nest egg to open a surf shop, the keys to a new life. Only after Nicola promised to sign a personal financial guarantee for a business loan towards their future did the surfers' reasoning run out of rope.

Alona and Mitch had arrived with nothing and would leave with nothing, just grand stories and the best of memories. They were spiritual millionaires. And they had each other for keeps. Nothing for it but to get royally sozzled and bounce a cheque with Big Dave. The lost evening in the Schooner Wharf Bar ended up messy after Rusty, Brains, Whale, Al Nassau and Maisie Hemingway dropped in for one last hurrah. The Barracuda made a point of stopping by. No grand speeches. He quietly nodded to the out-of-towners and gave each one a shell. The friends knew their meaning and were deeply touched. Key West, the self-styled Conch Republic, had appointed this motley crew the ultimate honour of being what they called freshwater conches, cherished citizens.

Tucked away in the corner of the bar, writing up his scoop for *The Times*, 'Finders Keepers on the High Seas', Zak learned three pieces of news that last evening in Key West. The friends had awful voices. Their rendition of *Monty Python and the Holy Grail*'s Always Look On The Bright Side of Life made his ears bleed, he joked. Secondly, Dr Neplovic had pulled in a favour to fast-track the tests on the tooth from JEICii, the female skeleton buried at the Miami Circle site, in the Museum of London's state-of-the-art

Ancient DNA Laboratory.

Skelley had come up trumps. Zak had scanned through her heavy report describing the scientific method of her study, which set out how "The samples collected *ex situ* were cleaned as precautions against contamination with a sterile surgical blade in a sterile hood, washed with diluted bleach and irradiated for 15 minutes with ultraviolet light to eliminate potential surface contamination. Each sample was ground, and the resultant powder was incubated overnight at 55°C with agitation in a lysis solution (0.5 M EDTA, NaOH, 1–2 mg ml^{-1} Proteinase K and 0.5% N-lauryl sarcosyl). For some samples, DNA was extracted using a phenol chloroform-based protocol."

Now the interesting stuff. Zak read on how Skelley managed to identify a mitochondrial haplogroup pointing to a distinct Amerindian lineage. A T195C polymorphism showed specifically that sample JEICii originated among the Carib tribe. By way of simple conclusion, Dr Neplovic explained in simpler English for mere mortals that "Since the *Merced* sailed solo to Nueva Cordoba, the Pearl Coast on the northwest coast of Venezuela, it's a fair bet this brave traveller, this Savarna, once lived among the Cumanagoto tribal people. Her green jade identifies her as what the West would call a princess. Little doubt she was given special treatment by the Tequesta for this reason. Lineage explains how Limbre escaped the cooking pot."

The curse of Europe eventually caught up with the survivors, Skelley added. Scrutinising her photos of skeletons JEICi and JEICii, she'd noticed the tell-tale symptoms of *osteomyelitis variolosa*, lesions symmetrical and localized to the distal parts of the *radii*, *ulnae*, metacarpals, *fibulae* and metatarsals. The other bones were perfectly normal. There was no doubt of the final cause of Juan Limbre and Savarna's death: smallpox. "One last thing. JECii's DNA sequence is a precise match with Minnehaha's hair if that helps. Toodle pip," Yellie had signed off.

Sadly, this made all too much sense. Thanks to Nicola's research Zak knew how sailors and conquistadors brought smallpox to Florida from Andalusia in the early 1650s. The furious plague wiped out anywhere from fifty to seventy-five per cent of Americas' Native Indians. The Tequesta thought the disease was a Bad Spirit, a curse on them for dealing with white devils. It was the beginning of the end. A mortally crippled Florida was easy prey for British soldiers. When the Spanish fled to Havana at the tip of King George III of England's bayonets, most of the South Florida Indians were forced out with them. The fear of Nickaleer – Englishmen – and the horrors they could inflict, according to Spanish scaremongering, spread a fatal terror.

Nicola and Zak embraced, weeping happy tears, when the final piece of the puzzle slotted into place. Savarna didn't end up a victim of shipwrecked tragedy in 1622 after the admiral of Spain's Tierra Firme fleet made the awful mistake of risking untrustworthy autumnal weather. Savarna was blessed with decades of joy and good health with the rogue she loved. Bit like someone else Nic knew close by.

The third piece of curious news Zak learnt that last evening in the Schooner Wharf Bar, scrolling through ancient names, was that Minnehaha was ancient Tequestan. It meant Laughing Water. Why would you christen a kid with a name bound to attract school bullies?

*

The bright lights of Miami intruded on Zak's reminiscing. Before the friends for life took their emotional goodbyes, the Americans driving up to New Jersey for Christmas and the Brits expected in Beaulieu at Lady Amelia Medici's Hampshire country retreat for the festivities, the four dropped off a sealed package containing Juan Limbre's diary and around $1.1 million worth of pearls at the Department of Anthropology in Coral Gables University. Zak's scribbled letter explained that Dr Neplovic's DNA analysis of Savarna's bones and Taylor's hair matched. History hadn't recorded the name of their child but Minnehaha was a descendant of the shipwrecked lovers, Savarna and Juan Limbre. Exactly as the wily professor no doubt had imagined all her life.

Alona insisted the weary college office manager, keen to start her holidays, safely lock the package in Minnehaha's office. The poker-faced professor was in for the shock of her life but, now equipped with a big war chest, could start fighting the Boca Chica casino development and buy back her ancestral land. Who knows, perhaps Justice for Tequesta might speculate on digging up a vast landlocked shipwrecked treasure. Zak reckoned a geophysical survey could pinpoint any buried sea chest stuffed with gold and silver if it truly existed.

Job done, yet much to Alona and Mitch's annoyance – forcing them to break open the vodka packed for the holidays in early desperation – Nicola insisted on one final uncomfortable stop.

Grant Raven's room in Mount Sinai Medical Center was sterile, warm and lonely. Skip was bedridden in the middle of the unit, connected to an invasion of electronic monitoring equipment. Christmas cheer was on hold. He breathed unaided and appeared at peace. Nic had called Lauren Hoffman for permission to visit and learnt gramps didn't have much time left. She should hurry. No doubt he was dreaming about chugging up and down the backwater streams of La Florida in search of the Vanished People, the *Gollum*'s ghoulish skulls pointing the way. Zak touched Nicola's arm and reminded her that thanks to the last few months' adventures, the Tequesta were no longer invisible and were now coming out of the shadows.

Skip was lost in a deep coma. There was little point in delaying the inevitable. Respects had been paid. Nic found it hard to hold back her tears. The last time she'd visited him he'd been so full of passion, energy and a love for past and present. A final ritual remained before she'd give up the ghosts of La Florida.

Nic rummaged around her rucksack and pulled out her reusable bottle, still full of water drained off the Miami Circle when it started spouting into the air. Like Zak she was beyond sceptical whether the legend of the Fountain of Youth was true or complete nonsense, let alone could be tied to a real-world city block in Miami. Somehow she sensed that Skip, deeply connected to the memory of the Tequesta, who he'd spent a lifetime chasing, would have appreciated the gesture. Holding up Grant Raven's head, she poured a little of the precious liquid down his throat.

A few slow minutes ticked by. Skip showed no signs of choking or any other reaction at all. Nic sighed, kissed the old man on the forehead and left with Zak's arm wrapped round her shoulders. The door slowly closed behind her. Time to head to the airport and the end of the best of times.

If only she'd hung on just a few seconds more, she would have had the fright of her life.

"Hello, little missy, sonny jim? Anyone there?" a hoarse voice croaked.

34

Dover Street, London

Friday the 20th of December started majestically for Jorvik & Silver and their merry band of henchmen. 'London Lawyers Save Spanish Treasure', the bold front page of the Thursday issue of *The Telegraph* exclaimed next to a photo of Eva Clermont-Ganneau, Director of the International Council of Cultural Heritage, Spain's Minister of Culture, César Solano, and yours truly, James Jorvik.

Even Mrs Jorvik had shown a glimpse of interest in her husband when he mentioned he had it on good authority Spain was looking to honour him with a knighthood. Would being gonged with the Commander's Cross of the Order of Merit for saving Madrid's heritage make her a Dame? If so, maybe worth putting up with the arrogant trollop for another year.

Once he'd stopped salivating at the photo of himself, *gloria in excelsis*, Jorvik had turned to the paper's world news section and wallowed in the double satisfaction of seeing the final piece of his cunning scheme slotted into place. A photo of Camille Pissarro's 1897 oil on canvas, Rue Saint-Honoré in the Afternoon, accompanied a single-column piece. The Museum of Fine Arts in Seville had agreed terms with the Cassirer family to return the painting. The family had long fought to have its ancestral rights, looted by the Third Reich from their Berlin home in 1939, come home. The canvas had already gone on display at the Museum of Latin Art in Los Angeles.

What wasn't published was the wheeling dealing behind Spain's dubious act of good grace, the *Merced* for Pissarro's finest. Jorvik's nasty brand of politricks guaranteed America's support for Spain's claim to the treasure of the *Merced* in exchange for Pissarro's masterpiece heading in the opposite direction. It was a genius piece of cultural diplomacy if he dared say so himself. Nobody would ever connect the dots.

The offices of Jorvik & Silver were in party mood. The weekend and then the long winter break were upon them. The partners had booked a large table at the Dover Street Wine Bar tucked two streets away from their Old Bond Street office. A treat in thanks for the office's moral crusade with Spain offered the chance to save a few thousand pounds, doubling up as a Christmas party. Even Bob Brooker had donned a black suit jacket for the occasion, a relic bequeathed by his father. Noting its stench of dust and mothballs, Jorvik made a mental note to position himself at the opposite end of the dining table that evening.

The party proceeded with dull precedent. Before dinner Jorvik took centre stage, rehashing for his sycophantic paralegals and eager-to-please interns how the letter of the International Council of Cultural Heritage's Convention had shaken Kurt Barracuda to his Yankee cowboy boots. Dominic Silver's eyes rarely looked up from monitoring his stocks and shares online, other than to wonder when the alcoholic fog would let him discretely slip away and head home without being missed.

Rather put out that the jazz bar didn't stock Magners cider, Brooker had been forced to share the poncey champagne doing the rounds and was a bottle and a half deep before his main course arrived. At least the all-female jazz band, Razz & the Tazzers, were a colourful distraction. By their smiles and whooping, Brooker reckoned they were right up for it. Maybe he'd get lucky tonight.

After dinner – all a bit fishy and Frenchy for Brooker – as tradition dictated Silver took to the floor to thank his staff for the year's work. Duty awaited. Then he'd make his silent escape to a glass of vintage Scotch and a quiet evening by the fire watching the Graham Norton Show with Mrs S. Perfect.

Barely had be begun speaking in a lazy drawl when all the lawyers' phones started tweeting in unison like a demented bird song dawn chorus. And then nobody was listening any more.

A deathly silence swept the table. The ground opened up and swallowed their smug smiles. One by one the team felt the wind knocked out of them, absorbing the press release just put out across the wire from Miami. The notification, 'Justice For Tequesta Claims Spanish Shipwreck Treasure', was crushing news. James Jorvik slipped out his phone and read the impossible:

> Following recent events in the Straits of Florida that saw Keys Exploration discover the long-lost wreck of the *Merced* from the 1622 Spanish Americas fleet, and its treasures declared the sovereign property of Madrid, Justice For Tequesta has filed proceedings for return of its property.
>
> The United States District Court of Florida in Admiralty, Miami, has allowed a plea to be entered by the ancestral descendants of the Tequesta tribe. Newly found historical documentation bears the hand and signature of Juan Limbre, captain of the 1622 merchantman the *Nuestra Señora de la Merced.* The letter bequeaths in perpetuity the ship and its contents to the Tequesta.
>
> Taylor Minnehaha, professor of anthropology at Coral Gables University in Miami, announced that 'Graphoanlysis of a 390-year-old letter by the renowned expert Professor Wolfgang Pasinski authenticates the precious document and ties its authorship to the captain of the *Merced.* In return for the Tequesta's compassion to Limbre and his wife, Limbre left them by last will and testament all his personal belongings. Ancient colonial greed is only matched by modern Spanish arrogance, patronizing the indigenous peoples of the Americas for the sake of long-faded imperial glory. Madrid must understand the despicable days of empire are gone. Justice For Tequesta hereby demands a formal apology from the King of Spain for the atrocities rained down on its people by La Florida's colonial forebears.'

> Ownership of the shipwrecked treasure is supported by an *amicus curiae* brief submitted by Keys Exploration. Justice For Tequesta has retained Mr Kurt Barracuda and his outstanding team, recognizing them as salvor-in-possession, to recommence scientific excavation of the *Merced* with immediate effect.
>
> Justice For Tequesta does not recognize the Crown of Spain's claims of sovereign ownership over the abandoned vessel. The shipwreck lies outside US territorial waters, a country that has not signed the ICOCH Convention on the Defence of Underwater Culture and Heritage, which is thus null and void.

James Jorvik's order that everyone get back to work pronto to counter the ridiculous claim was met with sideways looks. Undervalued and unpaid, the interns decided to head for the Goat Tavern on Stafford Street to wash down the champagne with some cool beer. The paralegals pointed out it was already gone 10 pm and they had family commitments. In the melee Dominic Silver slipped out into the night. He grimaced, as he always did, but this time it wasn't just his face. It was the shocking news. Silver's bowels gave up, soiling his finest Savile Row suit.

At least James Jorvik knew he could rely on his number one trooper, Bob Brooker. By now Brooker had vanished too, thrown out of the back of the club after pinching the well-appointed derrière of the Razz & the Tazzers' saxophonist. While an infuriated Jorvik marched back to the office to try and awaken his brothers in arms in Madrid and Marseille, Brooker sat among the trash cans and discarded fish scales in the alley behind the Dover Street Wine Bar nursing a black eye. All in all, he reckoned it had been a good evening. The musician had been well worth the unfriendly fire. The night was still young.

The campaigner zig-zagged across the road and peered briefly in the window of Peter Harrington's antique book shop, pride of place given to odd bedfellows. Dr Seuss's *There's a Wocket in my Pocket* was on show next to George Soros's timely *The Crisis of Global Capitalism* and the evergreen favourite, a pricey first edition of *Treasure Island.* Noticing the Aston Martin shop at number eight Dover Street, the great campaigner threw an arm in the air as if waving down a taxi and shouted, "I'll take two, my good man" at nobody in particular.

Into the urine-stenched Dover Yard, barely wide enough for one person, Brooker slumped. He weaved his way onto Piccadilly, past the Wolseley. On the façade of the Ritz Hotel, Roman stone statues glared above pine wreaths studded with shiny red and silver Christmas balls and golden festive lights. Brooker wasn't impressed by the sewer of humanity passing by, foreigners of every hue – yellow, brown, black. His back supported by the walls of Santander, another non-British bank, he scowled, a beggar holding an 'I'm Hungry. God Bless' sign struggled to keep warm in a crusty tracksuit. This posh shopping street boasted more beggars than there were Starbucks and Pret à Manger shops, and that was a feat.

After negotiating the pavement opposite the In and Out Club, the old Naval and Military founded in 1862, a navy Rolls Royce hit its furious horn, swerving in a bid to save Brooker's skin. You're welcome, he replied blurry-eyed, thinking that maybe the third bottle of champers hadn't been a first-rate idea after all. Cool Chinese girls swanned by in cosy white faux fur jackets and white leather boots. In the opposite direction, strangers shouted Arabic into diamond-cased mobile phones. One dandy sported a ridiculously waxed handlebar moustache. What ever happened to the London town Private Brooker remembered before going to war? The temperature dropped to minus two degrees centigrade.

At least White Horse Street was nice and quiet beyond the well-heeled bankers poncing down Bond Street, no longer giving him a splitting headache. Hatchett's of Mayfair may have closed its doors for good, a faded sign the only memory of glorious 'Great Eats'. The jazz and blues it uproariously championed were no more, but London was still spoilt for choice.

Brooker wondered what he should do first, turning his gaze away from the invasion of Lebanese restaurants, old England taken over by the Middle East. The stench of perfumed shisha smoke made him gag. A lamb kebab with extra chilli sauce, pay his respects to one of the ladies of the night burning their red lamps on first and second-floor houses or a few more jars of the good stuff?

The proper sequence seemed to be a drink in Shepherd's Market, a treat for the ladies and then an extra-large Turkish Doner kebab to jump onto the number 476 bus with back to Tottenham. The Ye Grapes pub, an oasis for the parched since 1882, was heaving with more annoying yuppies. Just my luck. Brooker pushed through the navy blue doors and waded to the bar. The silly little girl and effeminate boy behind the counter wearing tight white jeans repeatedly ignored the swaying war hero. Or maybe it was a girl? There was no telling these days.

Banging on the sticky wooden tabletop did little to win any sympathy, only the attention of a grouchy bouncer. Just when it looked like the great campaigner was about to be thrown out on his backside, a dark-skinned foreigner calmed Brooker down and offered to buy him a round of Doom beer. Don't mind if I do, the ex-soldier kindly agreed.

Bob Brooker had little memory what the new friends discussed or how much they drank. Busy boasting about his important government work, all very hush-hush you know, he didn't notice the swarthy looking woman empty the contents of a small leather pouch into his beer glass. It all ended in rather a daze.

When the cleaning lady called the authorities at six o'clock the next morning to the small first-floor room with peeling red paint tucked two lanes away from the pub in Shepherd Market, the police found Brooker tied to a wooden chair. He was dressed in a pink tutu and matching lipstick in a hooker's first-floor boudoir. His hands were bound at the back with palm fibre rope. An eagle feather had been inserted behind his ear below newly scalped hair. Yellow dust coating Brooker's throat, mouth and white shirt front made the cause of death no secret. The bloated man appeared to have choked. An autopsy identified the powder as Colombian gold dust.

*

Dawn approached. The musclebound executioner confidently made her way, fleet of foot, down the Queen's Walk. Green Park was still covered with crisp leaves. Her step made no sound. No shadow was cast by the rows of black iron Victorian streetlamps across the brick walls facing Clarence House. The grey squirrels ferreting for acorns and fried chicken bones – they'd learnt not to be fussy – didn't notice the phantom gliding south.

A semblance of a hopeful future reigned down The Mall where the flags of South Africa, Germany and Albania mingled and fluttered in front of Buckingham Palace. The woman's long braded pigtail swung from side to side as she darted into St James's Park, stopping to bend down briefly next to a homeless pensioner. The beggar curled up on a wooden bench, his eight plastic bags of worldly goods for bedding, thanked the heavens for the £50 miracle note that magically appeared in his back pocket the next morning. A Canada goose hissed.

The Princess of Wales Memorial Walk gave way to Birdcage Walk, in late December still carpeted with a dazzling celebration of golden brown pine leaves. White blossom glistened in confused trees. Frozen London was lifeless, other than a dozen black ravens hopping around oak branches, struggling to keep the party going. At Storey's Gate the Houses of Parliament's roofs came into view.

A yellow banner signed by Extinction Rebellion announced its members were on day fifteen of a hunger strike. Passers-by were asked in another sign to support its three emergency demands to save the world from climate change: Tell the Truth, Act Now and appoint a citizens assembly to go Beyond Politics. Next door, the Royal Institution of Chartered Surveyors at 12 Great George Street wasn't having its fun spoilt. A trellis of crimson purple lights showered down its façade. These were confusing times.

The phantom glided past Big Ben, the mighty heart of the faded British Empire on which the sun never set once upon a time. On Westminster Bridge – soulless yet breathtaking – she stopped to drink in the pained beauty of a perfect winter's day before the world awoke. The assassin ripped open her shirt.

On the far bank a lone jogger suffering from insomnia would later swear that peering through the London mist hanging above the River Thames, enchanted by the sleeping silhouette of Parliament, the world's most powerful political machine, he had made out the silhouette of a naked woman. The Indian had thrown back her head and howled into the morning sky.

Afterword

In the three decades I've lived with the sea, exploring its sunken mysteries, I've found the old cliché fact is stranger than fiction to be all too true. The lure of knowledge, and to some riches, attracts larger than life personalities to extraordinary adventures, as well as colossal greed and jealousy. Treasure brings out the best and worst in humanity, a world in which those who believe create and those who are suffocated by their own limits destroy.

Suffice it to say that whereas the characters in *Finders Keepers* are all invented, and any resemblance to individuals alive or dead is purely coincidental, the whacky discoveries and wreck hunts are rooted in reality. Only artistic licence has been taken about how, when and why to merge various real-world sagas for the fun of the reader.

That said, the family curse Nicola fears she'll inherit is a real condition. Skeletons dug up from the family chapel of San Lorenzo in Florence revealed more than six generations of gout, rickets, malaria, smallpox, typhus, tuberculosis, pneumonia, syphilis and the plague, today classified as Medici Syndrome. For this colourful horror I'm grateful to the detailed work of the University of Pisa, the University of Florence and the Superintendence for Florentine Museums' Medici Project.

The Florida Keys really are shipwreck central for treasure hunters. By 1966 forty-seven treasure companies were pressing the State of Florida for search permits. In 1988 the pioneering underwater archaeologist and former journalist Peter Throckmorton flew over the east coast of Florida in a light plane and spotted seven different salvage vessels blowing sand off the seabed at Vera Beach, where the 1715 Spanish fleet sank.

Most shipwreck ventures fail spectacularly and founder fast, tail between legs, with lost cash but fond tall stories to share about the one that got away. To Throckmorton these dreams of discovery were an "assault on antiquity" because they lacked scientific rigour. The projects' destructive salvage boats, installed with massive propeller blowers known in the salvage business as Mail Boxes, can blast away five hundred tons of sand in fifteen minutes, threatening anything delicate that might come to light. Even worse, fleets of ancient wooden hulls were supposedly ripped apart in the chase for glitter across the Caribbean in the bad old days. Throckmorton believed shipwreck treasure hunting was "the world's worst investment."

Love it or loathe it, the discovery of the Spanish galleons that sunk off the Florida Keys in the hurricane of the 5th of September 1622 made this tip of Florida world famous. The larger than life Mel Fisher, the once Indiana chicken farmer, pulled up legendary treasures from the *Nuestra Señora de Atocha* in 1985 and the *Santa Margarita* that paid sweet dividends for investors. To his great credit he created an enduring legacy by founding a wonderful museum in Key West stuffed full of incredible finds, shiny and plain, that the public enjoys to this day (now relocated to Sebastian, Florida). Like the characters in my book, Mel Fisher went to court 112 times over sixteen years to decide who owns the sunken past. In the end he won. And the value of Florida Keys' sunken hulls? Anywhere from $75 to $600 million, depending on who you talk to.

What was wrecked far offshore in 1622, not close to Key West, is the inspiration behind *Finders Keepers.* In 1989 Greg Stemm and John Morris side-stepped out of real estate investment into buying a ship and a grubby map with an 'X' marking a supposed lucky strike. They went fishing. Not only did they find one of the missing iconic merchantmen from the fabled 1622 Spanish fleet in 405 metres of water in the Straits of Florida, they splashed a large chunk of cash to build a wizard of a remotely-operated vehicle (ROV) called Merlin to scientifically dig up the treasures and everything else in 1990 and 1991. The science of deep-sea robotic shipwreck exploration was born south of the Dry Tortugas islands, not by academics but by forward-thinking entrepreneurs.

Many years later I had the good fortune to work with Greg Stemm and his team and identified that lost ship as the *Buen Jesús y Nuestra Señora del Rosario* (see G. Stemm and S. Kingsley, eds., *Oceans Odyssey 3. The Deep-Sea Tortugas Shipwreck, Straits of Florida: a Merchant Vessel from Spain's 1622 Tierra Firme Fleet*, Oxford). Yes, the wreck cocooned gold bars, silver coins and 6,639 pearls, but to the explorers' immense credit the positions and meaning of every one of 16,903 artefacts were precisely recorded on the seabed using cutting-edge robotic technology.

It's not the shiny stuff that is especially remembered today, but the collections of olive jars, Andalusian glazed ceramics and the slithers of the unexpected. To me the most superb discovery is the Tom and Jerry image of the ship's cat salivating over a cage of blue-headed parrots while rats infested the hold, reconstructed thanks to the careful recovery and study of the wreck's animal bones.

Clouded memory attached a *Nuestra Señora de la Merced* to the 1622 Tierra Firme Spanish fleet, but a trader by this name never actually travelled to the Americas that sorry year. The *Merced* was added to the 1622 fleet list by mistake. It was an imaginary ghost ship and, being fictional, the candidate I adopted for this book.

A far greater scandal than surrounds the make-believe *Merced* in *Finders Keepers* played out on the world's stage when the Floridian experts in deep-sea search, Odyssey Marine Exploration, found the wreck of the *Nuestra Señora de las Mercedes* in 1,100 metres off Portugal in 2007. An armed Spanish frigate blown up by the British in 1804, its discovery is one of marine exploration's greatest coups. Odyssey flew seventeen tons of gold and silver coins out of Gibraltar to Florida on two chartered passenger planes, buckets of treasure seated and belted where people normally enjoyed films and peanuts.

What became famous as the Black Swan case, and the battle

for almost 594,000 silver coins, rumbled on all the way to the US Supreme Court. Odyssey claimed the vast majority of the coins belonged to private merchants and were never the sovereign property of the Kingdom of Spain. Madrid begged to differ and even seized at sea the American's research ship and computers. Despite the *Mercedes* transporting women and children, and its captain ripping out some cannon to free up space for more cargo and passengers' accommodation, and although the ship's manifest proves that seventy-four per cent of the coins were private property and not the State's, the courts found in favour of Spain in 2011.

The Black Swan controversy marked a great shift in millennia-old salvage law. Only in 2015 did the coins fly back to Spain after Odyssey appealed to the Supreme Court and lost. Odyssey was fined $1 million. The Black Swan saga captivated the press and public, spawned a Discovery Channel documentary and a best-selling Spanish graphic novel. Stanley Tucci signed up to play a treasure hunter in Oscar award winning director Alejandro Amenábar's take on the *Mercedes* treasure, *La Fortuna.* Rumour has it, meanwhile, that Madrid can't afford the treasure's preservation. A large part lies buried in the ground for safekeeping.

The idea of James Jorvik negotiating a back-channel deal between Madrid and America – return of the *Merced*'s treasure in exchange for Camille Pissarro's 1897 painting Rue Saint-Honoré in the Afternoon – may sound ludicrous but really happened. In 2010 Julian Assange's Wikileaks outed discussions between Spain's culture minister and the US ambassador in Madrid about *quid pro quo* diplomatic back scratching. A leaked embassy cable said that "while the Odyssey and Cassirer claim were on separate legal tracks, it was in both governments' interest to avail themselves of whatever margin for manoeuvre they had, consistent with their legal obligations, to resolve both matters in a way that favoured the bilateral relationship."

Nobody can say for sure how this deal ultimately influenced the case's outcome. Rumour again has it that orders for the return of the *Mercedes'* treasure to Spain went all the way up to the US president's office. I set Pissarro's painting in Seville's Museum of Fine Arts, but today it is still on show in the Museo Nacional Thyssen-Bornemisza in Madrid. Spain refuses to give back the Nazi loot. A court in Pasadena, California, also ruled in Spain's favour in 2024.

The early twenty-first century is witnessing the most extreme tipping point in the history of marine exploration. Who owns the sunken past is playing out in a vicious political game between old-time wreck hunters and heritage groups supporting UNESCO's Underwater Convention on the Protection of the Underwater Cultural Heritage. Explorers want to carry on doing what nations have always encouraged, recovering lost property from the seas since the fifth century BC. It's a birthright, in man's blood, they argue. Modern heritage crusaders not unjustly point out that too much of the underwater realm has been ravaged. The bad old days of rummaging through destroyed hulls for treasure, recording little, are dead and buried. The innocent age of finders keepers is no more.

Whether the elder fathers of the oceans are right to order mankind to stop digging up the sunken past and leave it alone for the sake of future generations – take photos and leave bubbles – is questionable. Ripping currents, pounding waves, fishing trawling and creeping industrial fallout – oil and gas pipelines, wind farms, internet infrastructure and gravel and sand dredging – may make this hope an irresponsible Utopia. Certainly, fishing trawlers, the bulldozers of the deep that play a major role in this book, are a massive threat to the world's three million wrecks. Balance and sanity are badly needed but in short supply.

The diary of Juan Limbre, describing being wrecked with Savarna on the keys of Matacumbe, and coming face to face with the Tequesta Indians, is inspired by two works. The first is the short pamphlet *A True Relation of That Which Lately Hapned to the Great Spanish Fleet and Galleons of Terra Firma in America* published in English by Nathaniel Butter of London in 1623. The second is a far longer and more detailed work: the beautifully romantic journal of Jonathan Dickinson published in Philadelphia in 1699. In September 1696 Dickinson really was wrecked off Florida, but he wasn't Spanish. This Quaker from Jamaica was cast away off Jupiter Island and got up very close and personal with the local native Indian Vanished People, who he called the Furies.

In a foreword to the most recent publication of the Dickinson diary by Yale University Press in 1961, Ernest Lyons, editor of the *Stuart News* of Florida and an expert in local history, reminisced how he was first introduced to the story by a certain Captain Charles H. Coe. It was Coe who in real life, between his seventies and the age of eighty-nine, re-traced Dickinson's route from nearly sinking to salvation, mapping the old American Indian villages where the shipwrecked victims found rest. Coe owned a launch called the *Buccaneer I* whose sides were lined with grinning human skulls he dug up along the way. I should have loved to meet the incurable romantic and eccentric. I agree with Ernest Lyons that Dickinson's journal should qualify as the first American classic.

The life and times of the Tequesta Indians remain extremely poorly known, even inside the USA. The publicity around how the Miami Circle was saved from destruction by urban construction sheds welcome light on the earliest human footsteps in eastern America.

Finally, historic records show that Ponce de León did go hunting for the Fountain of Youth and fame and fortune in 1513, but had to make do with discovering a new land mass he called Pasqua Florida, Easter of the Flowers – modern Florida. A Ponce de León Fountain of Youth Archaeological Park can be visited today in St Augustine.

As for the rest, take it or leave it.

Acknowledgements

Finders Keepers isn't a true book. But it is based largely on my real experiences on deep-sea shipwreck hunts, court cases and travels. I wrote this novel under the radar, but sincerely thank everyone at Odyssey Marine Exploration in Tampa. For many years, Greg Stemm led the organisation in the greatest show on Earth, searching for old ships at the bottom of the seas with futuristic robots. It was then that I learned all about the secrets of the 1622 Spanish fleet when I was invited to study the Tortugas wreck in 400 metres, found by Greg in the Straits of Florida years before, and with whom I published the results – the gold bars, silver coins, pearls, crockery and so much more that feature in this book.

Key West, where *Finders Keepers* is set, is an amazing town. It does things strictly its way and I salute the good folk of the Conch Republic for their unique individuality and love of life.

Big thanks to my agent, Joelle Delbourgo, for all her time and belief in representing this book. After flagging when I was advised that only women write and buy novels these days – seriously? – I am very grateful to Dayna Cussler for her encouragement, a timely tonic. I have stuck at it! Marine archaeologist and bestselling author David Gibbins very generously shared his experiences and ideas from the publishing world and, again, kindly encouraged me to publish *Finders Keepers*. Fred Van de Walle offered very welcome feedback on the manuscript. I am incredibly humbled by the kind support of Dirk Cussler, Sir Tim Smit and Mensun Bound and the energy boost it brought.

At Spiffing Publishing, a deep tip of the hat to James Willis and Stefan Proudfoot for guiding me wisely in setting up Deep

Down Press; and to them and Joseph Hewes, Chris Hancock and Philip May for making publishing this book fun.

This book is dedicated to my three-year-old son, Felix Sky, who has inherited the love of a fine story, as long as it starts "One time" and has a "then suddenly" change of pace swiftly after. Felix, as long as you listen to good stories and learn how to tell them, you'll never be bored and will always have beautiful dreams.

Growing up I had two dreams: to write something for *National Geographic* and publish a novel. These were inspired by my parents, Madeleine and Andrew, and the creative environment where we were brought up. Sawdust and paint from my father's art and pipe making, and the tap, tap, tap of my mother's typewriter as she burned the candle at night to file copy as a journalist. As the wind whistled through the willow tree outside my window, her world of words felt mysterious and romantic. The most heart-felt thanks Madeleine, too, for pouring over *Finders Keepers* for superbly welcome advice, all the while sharing the warmest encouragement. This book really is for you.

Special thanks, then, to my wife Lexia Deng, Madeleine and Andrew Kingsley and Sally Kingsley.

As I write, another team I have the pleasure to work with, Allen Exploration, is hunting for sunken history off the northern Bahamas where another vast treasure galleon, the *Maravillas*, sank and shattered in January 1656. AllenX's divers are working in very tough conditions, following a sprawling scatter of wreckage, and filling a museum with gold chains, Spanish artworks, silver coins, swords and pottery. I salute all the hardy crew, and especially Carl Allen and Gigi Allen for bringing their own dreams and wonderful long-forgotten history to life.

I'm yet to discover the Fountain of Youth that features in *Finders Keepers*. But with my dreams fulfilled, I'll start chasing new ones where the past meets the present, wherever they may be. See you along the way.

Printed in Great Britain
by Amazon